FORTRESS MANHATTAN

FORTRESS MANHATTAN

David Callinan

VICTOR GOLLANCZ

LONDON

First published in Great Britain 1995
by Victor Gollancz
An imprint of the Cassell Group
Wellington House, 125 Strand, London WC2R 0BB

A catalogue record for this book is
available from the British Library.

ISBN 0 575 06058 1

Typeset in Great Britain by
CentraCet Ltd, Cambridge
Printed in Great Britain by
St Edmundsbury Press Ltd, Bury St Edmunds, Suffolk

There are people to thank.
Firstly, my screenwriting partner
and friend David Chitty, who worked
with me on the original screenplay
version of this story.
Also, Jon Thurley, my agent, for
all his hard work and support;
Richard Evans, my editor, for
having faith and patience
and, finally,
my wife Rosie – for everything.

Chapter One

Some dreams can infect the blood.

And some dreams were never dreams but currents of existences beyond the web-matrix of time and space.

Johnny Raine awoke alone. A trickle of saliva washed his locked larynx. The dream had returned. With all the pain of an ice-pick being removed from his heart, he surfaced from a half-waking lucid nightmare. Shit, he thought incoherently. He had lived the dream on several occasions since Angelica's death, but this had been by far the worst experience. Even now his mind recoiled from the horrific images.

It's been two years, he reminded himself.

It had been two years since that creature from hell appeared out of nowhere and ripped his young wife to pieces before she could draw a second breath or he could move to rescue her.

His own life had been saved only by a passing Zone Police patrol. In the flash of the laser explosion the creature had been illuminated momentarily. The blast had ripped its body to shreds from the waist down, turning its legs into a bloody soup. It had garrotted Angelica with a thin metal flail and ripped her body, using serrated blades attached to its metal-spiked fingers.

Johnny had screamed, but his own legs had been shocked into immobility. He noticed with painful clarity the eyes of the assailant. Intelligent eyes set within a dark Hispanic face. The creature had once been a man. Now it was a patchwork quilt of flesh and silicon carbide bio-parts. But the eyes spoke of a razor-sharp brain buried within the mutant body.

Then everything had happened so quickly that Johnny's mind had partly erased the events. He could only remember when immersed in the dream. His subconscious had clearly registered events too painful to recollect in his waking state. Angelica, his beautiful, blue-eyed, blonde goddess, was slithering down

beneath the pavement, dragged bodily and incapable of screaming, into an open sewer. She was dead. He knew it with a
certainty that had virtually unhinged his mind. The assailant, a
Badland mutant, and Angelica were bonded together in a death-
like embrace by an adhesive of blood, bone and muscle.

The blast had knocked him unconscious. When he awoke, his
wife was dead and his life went into deep freeze. Oh, he went
through the motions, but for two years his spirit had atrophied.

Then, in a twist of events that had left him breathless, his
emotional floodgates had opened. He met Jordan. Although his
pain still vibrated inside him like a lurking rattlesnake, Jordan
had simply captivated him. They were now both treading the
delicate path towards something real and special. She had given
him back his sanity. If only she could wave her magic wand over
his subconscious and banish this nightmare.

He got up and dressed, feeling the emptiness of the apartment
wrap around him like a shroud. Enough! he said to himself.
Come on, let's get it together! Bottle the angst, Johnny boy,
you've got a meeting with Maurice Freiberg. That's enough angst
for anybody to handle.

Johnny Raine stepped into Madison Avenue and took a deep
lungful of fragrant air. It was a bright Manhattan morning, clear
and fresh. Spring daffodils lined up like a regimented yellow
army all the way to East 34th Street. As usual traffic was light,
mostly high-powered electro-coupés and sedans. Some were
privately owned and elaborately customized, but many were
communal and owned by the Free State of Manhattan. A few
delivery trucks were pulling into the unloading bays behind the
stores, ferrying goods from the central heliport at Washington
Heights.

Johnny strolled along Madison, acknowledging the frequent
glances of recognition. He glanced at his watch. He had an hour
before his meeting with Freiberg, programme chief at Media
City.

He thought about Jordan. He recalled the smell and taste of
her skin; that warm, sensual, deeply personal scent. Johnny
could have had many women. He still had the boyish, innocent
air of youth although he was in his mid-thirties and he had one

of the best-known faces in America as a result of his hit TV show. Jordan had been aloof, elegant, almost shy when they first met at the Brewster's cocktail party six months ago. For Johnny it had been like lightning striking. She had been cool, as though she didn't know or didn't care who he was. He had liked that. It meant they could start at the same point with no preconceptions.

Just time for coffee and a doughnut before my meeting with Maurice, he thought and he sat at a sidewalk table outside Felice's. He placed his order and looked around. He had lived through the worst years of the Isolation when Manhattan, from the tip of Battery Park to the border with the Bronx, had been cleared of mobsters, drug dealers, prostitutes, cyberfreaks and low life of every kind. It had been one of the most savage and intensive cultural cleansing operations ever seen – a blitzkrieg on a scale that had shocked the world. The chief target had been victims of the AIDS virus that had decimated huge tracts of the globe. Anyone HIV positive had been shipped out with the other rejects as Manhattan put up the shutters.

Now, Manhattan was an enclave. If you didn't earn enough credits to stay solvent you stood the risk of being banished to the Badlands, the nightmare world that surrounded the island of Manhattan on all sides. You still had the rigorous medical and HIV tests to go through. They were mandatory. Since the disastrous, and some believed scandalous, trial of Axis Three, the drug that had promised a near normal life to AIDS sufferers, and the subsequent discovery of its horrific side-effects, border security had been stepped up to unprecedented levels.

The Badlands of the Bronx, Queens and Brooklyn were now alien territories, a nightmare world of mutated freaks and vicious gangs with their own laws and perverted culture. Manhattan was protected from the Badlands by the Zone Police, or ZeePees – paid for by the citizens of Manhattan and growing in power and influence.

Johnny sighed and looked up at the blue sky. He signalled for a refill and glanced at his watch. Felice himself served the coffee.

'A lovely morning, Mr Raine,' he said.

'Certainly is.'

'Anything special on the show this week?'

'You'll have to wait and see, Felice. I can definitely promise you something special.'

'I love your show, Mr Raine, don't you?' Felice wiped the table clear of crumbs and cleared away.

'Course I love it, Felice. It's the highest-rating show on the media-web.'

'You're too clever for me, Mr Raine,' Felice smiled.

Johnny looked at Felice's broad, almost innocent face, dark skin and large eyes and he saw his audience. Millions of Felices and Brads and Wilmas all over America glued to their seats every Saturday night watching 'All the Way' – the show in which the American public confessed its sins and took its punishment.

He looked at his watch again, waved at Felice and carried on up Madison. The Media City building was a tribute to the age of the image. Acres of dark reflective glass and chrome stretched towards the sky.

Johnny swallowed his periodic bout of cynicism and fixed his TV presenter expression to his face; the slightly lopsided grin and creased eye smile that beguiled millions every week.

He entered the building and crossed the cavernous lobby, smiling and waving, dodging a guided tour group from out-of-state. There was a split second of blank stares before the dawning realization that a celebrity was on the loose. But it was enough time for Johnny to leap into an elevator and be on his way to the atrium office suite.

Maurice Freiberg had his back to the door as Johnny entered his office. He was gazing out over a spectacular view of the Manhattan skyline. His short but powerful figure cast an elongated shadow across the thick pile Arab carpet. 'Sit down, Johnny,' he wheezed without turning around. 'Help yourself to some coffee.'

'Just had some, Maurice. How's the asthma?'

'Under control, under control.' Maurice Freiberg turned and walked slowly to his desk. 'The show's doing well Johnny. Has been for three years.'

'What's on your mind, Maurice?'

'We're coming under attack from CyberTel.' Freiberg selected a cigar from a wooden box on his desk, looked at it lovingly and put it back.

'What's new?' Johnny replied. 'We've been under attack from all the major networks for years. We're always under attack. It's the nature of the business. We've still got five of the best-rating shows on the web. The shareholders should be very happy. The shareholders should be fucking ecstatic.'

'Don't get all defensive on me. This business always needs something new. "All the Way" has hit a seam of gold. People taking their punishment on prime time, it hits the psychic button right on the head.'

Johnny had to smile. Freiberg wouldn't know a psychic button if it grew out of his navel. So, what was coming next?

'Our best intelligence tells us that CyberTel is planning something big to compete with "All the Way". We don't know what but we hear their new chief, Jack Silverman, is going all the way to knock us off the top of the perch.'

'They've tried before.'

'They've got no scruples,' Freiberg growled.

Johnny could hardly contain his mirth.

Freiberg continued.

'The thing is, Johnny, the board feels that Channel Boom Boom needs to combat this attack by going on the offensive. We need to keep ahead, keep fresh. I was talking to Commissioner Halloran only yesterday. Things are getting worse over there.' He nodded in the direction of the river. 'We're holding back a tidal wave of shit, sick fucks and mutants. And it's getting worse. And we know that TV is like therapy to them just like it is everywhere else. It keeps the lid on.'

'We screw their minds and they love it.' Johnny shook his head.

'The ZeePees think some kind of monster mutations are evolving – but no one knows. That, plus the fact that we want to keep our own show, your show, as fresh as possible means we need to come up with some new twist, some new angle, something to keep the lid on tighter, and screw Jack Silverman into the ground,' said Freiberg.

'As long as we don't mess with a winning formula,' Johnny

said with a slight edge to his voice. 'Live TV has made a come-back. People either freaked out or just got bored with Cybernet. Do you have anything in mind?'

Maurice Freiberg shrugged, took a cigar, lit it, and stood and walked around the room.

'You remember that party given by Senator Bradley? Remember there were about half a dozen of us talking informally after. Most of the board was there, Newman, Princetti, Barolo, Riley, the whole bunch. The ones who kick my ass if ratings drop. Remember?''

'Sure I remember, we were all pretty drunk.'

'Maybe, but you came up with something then that stuck in their minds.'

'I did?'

'You sure did. I happen to think, Johnny, that it's a great idea for the show.'

'I don't remember.'

'Well, now that Silverman is making waves, the board would like to endorse your idea.'

Freiberg turned and smiled his vacant smile at his star performer.

'Care to remind me what it is?' asked Johnny.

When Johnny Raine walked back around the circular atrium balcony towards his office, his face was grey. He entered the room slowly and sank into his chair. He was thinking deeply as his PA, Veronica, came in.

'Morning,' she burbled brightly as she flicked through his diary. 'You've got a production meeting at eleven thirty and you're seeing Dan Wilson at three. He's the guy from Oklahoma who's confessed to having six wives. He's a history freak by all accounts. You know I sometimes think a lot of these people just want a day out in Manhattan to do their shopping. It must be . . .'

'Postpone production,' Johnny snapped. 'I'll take that meeting after lunch. And get Carey to see the cowboy bigamist.' He turned to her. 'Sorry, I need to think for a while.'

Veronica glanced at him curiously. 'Sure! Anything wrong? You look a little frayed.'

'I'm fine. Thanks, Veronica, that'll be all.'

Veronica pouted and shrugged, then left the office, closing the door softly behind her. Johnny punched Jordan's number on the vidi-phone. After a short pause Jordan's voice answered.

'Who is it?'

'It's me, I need to see you.'

Jordan's face shimmered into electronic life on the vidi-screen. For a second Johnny contemplated the calm and beautiful oval face and wide-set eyes. She smiled.

'Hi! You sound upset. What's wrong?'

'Nothing, nothing.' He smiled back at her. 'Just felt like talking to you. What are you doing for lunch?'

'I was going to work through. I've got some files I need to get finished.'

'Can I tempt you to lunch at Grey's?'

'You can always tempt me, you know that. OK, one o'clock?'

'It's a date, love you.'

'I know.' Jordan's image smiled back at him before flickering into oblivion.

Johnny parked his low-slung electro-turbo sedan in the parking area behind the restaurant in the Village. An attendant took his keys and Johnny walked to the entrance and inserted his ID credit card into the receptor. A door swished open and he entered the soft, grey interior. Grey's was busy as always. It had the hushed reverential atmosphere of a temple. The head waiter smiled a welcome just as Johnny saw Jordan at the bar. He marvelled again at her beauty as she turned and saw him. She was wearing a simple green dress, low cut at the back. The colour accentuated the slight tan of her skin and her long slim legs. Her dark hair was shoulder length and sculpted to frame her face. He went to her and she came into his arms to be kissed. The experience was like being absorbed by warm, scented cream. Johnny felt a familiar hardening in his crotch. He ordered two tequila golds.

'You look fantastic,' he breathed.

'Flatterer,' she laughed. Johnny loved the sound of her laugh. It slipped straight through his defences, intimate yet with a hint of a sexual challenge.

When they were seated at the table, Johnny ordered a bottle of Chardonnay, a Roquefort salad for her and grilled salmon for himself.

'So,' she said, 'what's so important it couldn't wait till tonight?'

'I just wanted to see you, that's all,' he replied.

'Come on, you've always got an ulterior motive. It's part of your charm.'

'I'm not as hard-nosed as that, am I?'

'Not when you find your soft centre.'

'What do you think of the show?' he asked her quickly.

'I thought we agreed never to discuss business. You don't ask about my work and I don't bring up your superstardom.' She smiled at him as the food was served.

Johnny poured wine for them both.

'I'd like to know,' he said.

'Well,' she replied slowly, chewing a mouthful of salad, 'it's a highly successful, highly commercial show which catches the mood of our times.'

'But do you like it?' Johnny persisted.

'It's not my glass of Chardonnay,' said Jordan. 'Frankly, I find it cynical, and soulless. But it works. And you are very good. But when I look at you I don't see a media star, I see a man I like and care about, maybe even love. That's why we shouldn't talk about work. It's another part of our lives. I don't want your career to be a barrier to my feelings about you.'

'You think I'm cynical and soulless?'

'No, of course not. If you were I'd walk away from this conversation, and this relationship. No, I think you're playing a part. I only hope you don't start to believe your own public image. Don't let that happen, Johnny.' She paused. 'Why all the questions? It's too nice a day to get serious.'

'Look, I've got to make a decision,' he replied gravely.

'A decision?' She raised her eyebrows.

'Have you ever been to the Badlands?' he asked.

'Are you crazy? No one in their right mind goes there.'

'There are some who do. There are some who go for the danger.'

'What's this got to do with your show, or with us?' she looked at him seriously.

'The pot's boiling over,' he told her. 'Don't kid yourself that things are going to stay the way they are for ever. People in Manhattan pay ten per cent of their income for protection. And even so the freaks get through. We're sitting on a time bomb, honey. Shows like mine help keep stability. Only now it might not be enough. They really want me to go all the way.'

'What do you mean?'

'They want me to put the freaks and shurmheads from the Badlands on prime-time TV.'

Johnny poured more wine and Jordan regarded him coolly.

'They must be insane,' she said.

'We're in a ratings war. If I want to survive, I have to go all the way or take a one-way ticket out of here. Look, death means nothing to those freaks. You've heard about the Feeks and Farooks? Well, they worship death.'

'But who goes to the Badlands voluntarily?' Jordan asked urgently, worried now.

'Apart from the die-hard brigade, there's Frank Brady.'

'Frank Brady? What's he got to do with it?'

'He might have everything to do with it,' Johnny explained. 'Apart from being the greatest photographer of women in America, he is also the one person who has documented the Badlands. He gets in and he gets out. His photographs, his images, have given us our picture of the Badlands. He's got an exhibition at the Lepri Gallery coming up.'

'I know,' said Jordan. 'I'm a fan of his like everyone else. I think he's a genius. But what has he got to do with your show? What exactly does Channel Boom Boom want you to do?'

Johnny paused. He swallowed the last morsel of salmon and drained his wine glass before answering.

'They want live suicide on prime-time TV. They want me to get the denizens of the dark side on to the show to confess their sins and really go all the way. And Frank Brady might be the way to reach them.'

Chapter Two

Jordan looked at Johnny for a long moment. Then she glanced out of the window quickly. He was watching her, gauging her reaction. She decided to keep her immediate thoughts to herself.

Since Angelica's death he had been something of a recluse. Strange really, given his public profile. But maybe not so strange. He had loved her, Jordan knew that. And she and Angelica had been schoolfriends. Like most kids whose parents could meet the credit qualifications, they had seen out the horrors of the Isolation cocooned inside an elite, authoritarian finishing school in Midtown. Their friendship had blossomed but they lost touch when Angelica's modelling career took off and Jordan developed her talent with neural network computers.

Johnny seldom mentioned the connection. Maybe he just didn't think it was important. Something had snapped inside him after the brutal murder took place. His therapy had helped. He was convinced that Marek Grohmann, the eminent parapsychologist, had been instrumental in preventing him from going completely over the edge. Grohmann had developed unique but experimental regression techniques to explore areas of the subconscious which had hitherto lain hidden, clouded by pain and trauma.

The Johnny Raine of two years ago would have been shocked at the hideous idea of live suicide on TV. What the hell was the place coming to? And just how would they handle the virtuality version? Maybe it was just a desire to wreak revenge.

'Suicide?' she said. 'Are you crazy?'

'I now it sounds grotesque. I've got to admit it threw me at first, especially when I was reminded that it was my idea to begin with. I mean, it was a party, I was drunk. It was just one of those off-the-cuff remarks. Now it's a question of do it or maybe we'll be looking for a new face next season.'

'Would that be so bad?'

'Hey, come on, look at the alternatives?'

'I bet you could do any number of things if you really tried.'
She smiled at him.

'Maybe. Well, what do you think?'

'One half of me is horrified because it's so totally dehumaniz-
ing. It's ground zero in terms of taste. But the other half of me is
intrigued.'

'Let's keep taste out of this. We're talking about mass culture.
Don't give me any post-millennium angst. I don't make the rules.
It takes millicredits to get out of this city. It's a trap. You earn to
get the right to stay here. LA is the same, so is Washington. The
Midwest is being overrun. Tell you what I think?'

'Go on,' said Jordan.

'I think the idea is vile. But I think it's great television. Those
shurmheads in the Badlands are on a short fuse. They want to go
out with a bang. In a crazy way it may even give them some
kind of dignity.'

'You don't have to make excuses or convince me. I know
you're worth much more than some lousy TV show. I know you
do what you do to survive. So do I. So do we all. So, what's the
Frank Brady angle?'

'Brady has connections on the other side of the river and he
also loves beautiful women.'

Jordan stood up. 'I've got to get back.'

Johnny stood and took her hand. 'I want you to be my good
luck charm.'

'Aren't you worried I might fall under his spell?' she smiled at
him, half serious.

'Look, it's just a question of being with me. How would you
like to go to the Badlands?'

Jordan backed away. 'Now I know you're crazy.'

'If we take precautions, we'll be OK,' Johnny insisted. 'I
happen to know that Brady is hoping to set up a fashion shoot
there very soon. They're looking for a touch of so-called reality.
He'll have an army going in with him; reinforced sloop jets, a
crack ZeePee squad, public order nukes, the works. If it comes
off I'm going to try and join the entourage. How about it? See
the Badlands and weep.'

Jordan laughed at his boyish exuberance. He made it sound like a children's birthday party.

'All right,' she said hesitantly. 'But let's get one thing straight right now. If I go it'll be because I'm curious. Scared but curious. And I will only go if it's absolutely one hundred per cent safe. I will not, however, be used as bait.'

She turned on her heel and walked to the door, only pausing when Johnny caught up with her and kissed her ear.

'My place or yours tonight?' he whispered.

'Call me. I might have a headache.' She patted him on the cheek as the waiter opened the door with a barely perceptible bow.

Later, as the evening sun spread a silky red and gold web over the city, Jordan stood on the balcony of her apartment and thought about Johnny, trying to make sense of her feelings for him. She had never been that promiscuous. The AIDS epidemic had seen to that. It was a little easier now with the advances made in medi-care in the last decade. But even so, she was still a private kind of person and didn't cast her emotional net too widely or too often. Johnny was a native New Yorker with a lineage that stretched back to the early immigrant days. She was first generation. Her Turkish father and American mother had settled in New York. He was a fashionable carpet dealer and she was an airline stewardess.

She had loved her father and, if she was honest, had found very few men to match up to him. But Johnny had simply bowled her over. She told herself he was everything she didn't like in a man. Just that bit too good looking. Just that bit too charming. And he had fallen for her the moment he set eyes on her. She had known that instantly. The trouble was, she was falling in love with him. She sighed, poured herself another glass of wine and watched the sunset spreading its glow through the trees.

Then she thought about Frank Brady, the errant, erratic English photographer who had settled in New York just before the Isolation. Now, there was a womanizer. He had a fascinating, well-used face and that interesting English accent made famous by that rock group that had enjoyed a nostalgic revival a few years back, the Beatles. How strange that stuff sounded. Not like music at all. Liverpool, that was the place. She had to admit, she would like to meet him. He was the most exciting visual artist in New York. No one photographed real life like Frank Brady. No one photographed real life period. Yes, she mused, it would be interesting to meet him.

His Liverpool roots were the last things on Frank Brady's mind at that moment. He was running, his breath rasping, his sweat clouding his eyes. His lightweight body armour was slowing him down although it had just saved his life. He could still feel the impact of the home-made bullet in his back.

The dying rays of the sun washed the heartbroken landscape with a lurid glow, bestowing a strange kind of beauty. Still Brady ran, sprinting through the rubble-strewn street. Behind him he could hear his pursuer. Instinct made him slew to the left as a shell exploded by his ankles. This wasn't the way it was supposed to be. He would have to have a serious word with Bobby Bolero, the hybrid gang leader he paid for protection.

He held his motorized, gun-handled Mitsuki camera tightly in his right hand. It was his own fault, he thought grimly. At a time when still photography was an arcane science, he held true to the static image, rooted in a time frame. It had power. It had power after decades of sophisticated video and virtuality image production to capture the imagination and shock the psyche.

He skittered around a bend and gasped with thanks at the sight of his armoured sloop jet. He aimed his remote at the heavily reinforced, armour-plated shell and the door slid open. The sloop jet was a hybrid, just like almost everything else in the Badlands. Powered by miniature reactors using quadruple aero-jets it was the fastest thing on wheels or on tracks.

Brady dived into the vehicle and rammed his fist on to the security control. The last thing he heard before the door slid shut was a gurgling scream followed by an explosion. In the background came the familiar sound of the Badlands – the insistent throb of a mechanistic rock track, elusive, vaguely familiar, yet alienating.

Brady glanced through the twin-skinned, slatted windscreen

and punched some controls. He took the Mitsuki and carefully slotted it into a housing close to his right eye. The housing contained a lens arrangement which allowed Brady to photograph anything outside from the protection of the sloop jet.

He stared out into the bleak urban landscape, a hideous parody of its former self. This used to be Astoria, a place famous for its Greek immigrant population and its film studios. Now it was a cesspit of burnt-out buildings, ruptured sewers and an encyclopedia of graffiti. Brady saw his pursuer, a hybrid with a life-termination complex. Brady knew the Badlands could be insanely violent, a place where life expectancy could be measured in the blink of an eye but where a strange, hierarchical society survived. Some had left the towns, cities and even rural areas voluntarily and made their way here, but the majority had been forced out, deported – this was no-hope city.

The hybrid that shuffled towards the sloop jet was a Plater – a semi-human construction built from metal bio-parts. It was impossible to tell what sex it was. The head was huge and misshapen, riveted with metal plates. The eyes were blank and the mouth a savage gash. Metal teeth flashed as the dying rays of the sun caught them. The creature had no arms to speak of, just two obscene machine guns sewn on to its shoulders. Various metal instruments served as hands along the length of the gun barrels. It was virtually brain dead. That's why Platers were so useful to people like Bobby Bolero. He might look like one, but he was far from brain dead.

The Plater was panting and raising its gun arms at the sloop jet.

'You ought to get fit, matey,' whispered Brady as he focused the Mitsuki and, with his other hand, slipped the vehicle into low gear and eased it towards the crippled figure. Slowly, Brady manoeuvred the sloop jet and started to circle the Plater.

With a scream the creature fired both guns. They spat flame and home-made shells which burst harmlessly on the exterior of the sloop jet. Brady rapid-fired the Mitsuki, catching the Plater in full frontal assault mode. Screaming, the creature ran at the sloop jet, hammering its gun hands on the bodywork, its face rammed against the windscreen protectors. The Plater started to eat the metal strips that ran across the windscreen. With a cracking noise a piece of protective metal shattered. The Plater chewed with obvious pleasure.

Suddenly, with a deafening explosion, the Plater's head disintegrated, spewing blood, gristle and shrapnel all over the front protector shields. Brady slammed the vehicle into reverse and stared into the darkening night. Shapes were moving towards him and they might not be human.

'Got it,' breathed Brady. 'Now, time for a word with Mr Bolero.'

He gunned the sloop jet and it whined with power. He squinted through the windscreen. The shapes were still there. Whoever, or whatever, had sent the Plater's last rites wrapped in a miniature guided missile was somewhere out there.

Within nearby buildings he could see fires springing into life and everywhere, in eyeless windows, down alleys and on roofs, the glow of countless media-web terminals. He switched on his two-way microphone and listened. Floating in the air came the usual cacophony of noises overlaid with the sound of disembodied broadcast voices, courtesy of Media City.

Brady headed down towards Riker's Island, a former prison and now the stronghold of Bobby Bolero. The Badlands were coming alive now, crowds were moving, fights already breaking out. Here and there streetlights flickered as the unpredictable power system shuddered into life. Street hawkers sold a vast array of drugs, exchanged for dollars, still the currency here. In the Badlands there was a crazy kind of social structure which remained stable for a time, then collapsed as another gang war flared. Essential services were maintained, again for a time, depending upon who was in the ascendancy. Anarchy remained the only true vital force in the Badlands but now, after a decade or more, even the anarchy had atrophied into a kind of weary stability.

Frank Brady cruised through a wasteland of broken buildings. He had spotted the one he wanted to use for his imminent fashion shoot. The advertising agency had been nervous, to say the least, about photographing the world's most expensive lingerie in the world's most dangerous city. But Brady had convinced them, and the French client, that it would be safe. There would be a small army with them, and, hopefully, Bolero's protection.

'There it is,' Brady muttered to himself.

He had entered a square surrounded by a semi-circle of tall, gaping ruins. In the half-light they resembled a forgotten Roman amphitheatre. He slowed the sloop jet to a crawl, disturbing a group of mutant children masturbating around a fire. Bolero would protect him here. Brady had his payment in the back of the sloop jet, the most precious commodity in the Badlands.

'Perfect,' he breathed, 'absolutely bloody perfect.'

He revved the powerful engine and started the long descent towards the waterfront and Bobby Bolero.

In doorways and in shadows, disembodied eyes gleamed, watchful and ruthless. Brady's sloop jet was well known here. He was tolerated. And not just because he supplied the most powerful drug ever produced but because Frank Brady was the voice of the Badlands in Manhattan. He alone had portrayed the faces and the conditions in this God-forsaken graveyard of humanity. He had given them some dignity. His photographs were lauded in the galleries and penthouses of Fifth Avenue but they also hung on the blood-stained walls of Bobby Bolero's factory-like headquarters. And, most important of all, they had appeared on the media-web.

Brady rolled to a halt not far from the waterfront. His sensitive two-way intercom picked up the sound of footfalls, the scrape of a match striking and the river lapping against the old wooden quay. He glanced to his left, opening his protective windscreen grid a fraction to take in the reflected lights of the Big Apple. From here, in the comparative darkness, the city took on the appearance of a mighty, glowing starship; a city of dreams from another universe. Which of course, thought Brady wryly, is exactly what it was.

He waited. Then a searchlight pierced the darkness, almost blinding him. The sound of a rusty loudspeaker grated wheezily then a cool but metallic voice snapped an instruction.

'OK, Frank, you can come out now.'

Brady reached back into the interior of the vehicle and picked up a small phial. For a moment he gazed at it, sighed heavily and slipped it into his pocket. He switched the sloop jet into voice-operate mode and opened the door.

He stepped out and the door slid shut behind him. Now it would only open at his command. He was standing in front of an imposing building of dark stone with heavy-duty wrought-iron gates set into solid concrete pillars. The gates opened. At the same moment Brady knew he was surrounded. He glanced around. Half a dozen of Bolero's guerrillas stood watching him languidly. They carried a variety of weapons. All were uniformly ugly, heavily scarred and disfigured. Many were patched up with steel plates and bars. Some were almost leprous in appearance.

He walked inside. Flickering lights sputtered. Somewhere a generator was humming. Brady walked into a large, cavernous area crammed with rusted, long-dead machines whose purpose was unknown. There were about fifty people inside. Most were street warrior types, many were badly mutated and scarred. There were quite a few women and some children. The women were cooking at open braziers fuelled by some kind of animal fat. The smell was obnoxious. They stared at Brady vacantly. At the far end of the building, seated on a throne-like construction made of iron and leather, was Bobby Bolero.

He was about fifty years old and of Hispanic stock. In contrast to the rabble he commanded he was a good-looking man with a quizzical, intelligent face and luminous dark eyes. He was clad in light body armour which did little to disguise the power in the arms and torso. Brady noticed with a shudder the withered legs encased in a form of metal frame. He smiled at Brady with his mouth, which was a red slit. His tongue flicked out to moisten his lips.

'Welcome, Frank. Come, take a seat. Have a drink.'

Brady walked to a table near the dais. Bolero rose and walked towards him stiffly, the metal joints of his artificial legs clanking a little. They sat at a table made from a couple of upturned boxes. An old woman limped forward, spread a thick cloth over them and placed a bottle and two glasses on the makeshift bar. Bolero poured two shots of something unnameable. Brady took a deep breath, and swallowed his shot in one. He coughed slightly although his stomach was on fire. Bolero watched him with amusement, selected a cheroot from his jerkin and clenched his left fist. Instantly, five metal caps on his knuckles flipped open and five, needle-sharp gunmetal spikes flicked out. Bolero smiled broadly, moved his little finger and a flame appeared at the tip of a spike. He lit his cheroot and unclenched his fist, retracting the fearsome spikes.

'Sorry about that, Frank. It's my party piece. You've seen it before.'

'It still frightens the shit out of me,' said Brady.

Bolero smiled humourlessly. 'So, what do you have for me?'

Brady placed the phial on the table. 'Two hundred proof pure shurm, straight from the mortuary.'

Bolero picked up the phial delicately, unscrewed the lid and brought it to his nose. He sniffed and his features softened like melted butter.

'Shit! This stuff is enough to make the angels jerk off,' he murmured appreciatively.

'There's enough joy juice there to turn the whole population of Manhattan into zombies for a year. Treat it carefully. It's a rare commodity.'

'Around here it's the only commodity,' Bolero said. 'What do you want from me? The usual?'

'That's right. But I've got a special favour,' Brady replied.

'Let's have it.'

'I want to bring a party in. About thirty or so, mostly advertising types with weak hearts and big wallets. I also want to bring in three of the most beautiful women in the world to pose almost naked in a building near here. I'll have the usual trigger-happy security set-up to protect them. But we both know that means zip here.'

'It's done. You'll be left alone, except for sightseers come to take a look at the freaks from the Rotten Apple.' He chuckled hoarsely. 'But remember this, Frank. My protection is only skin-deep. One minute you're up, then you're down. You've got to take a philosophic approach to life here, you know that.'

'Still waiting for the second coming are you, Bobby?' Brady smiled.

Bolero's face tightened. Brady was reminded just how dangerous this man could be. He had a reputation for unbridled, sadistic violence. What made him doubly dangerous was his innate intelligence.

'You know the word according to Guru Lennon,' muttered the gang leader. 'There will be one coming who will take us all out of this shit and lead us back to the promised land. Remember that, Frank. You think I'm crazy, like all the other freakos and blubber brains. I'm tellin' you, if only you look deeply into the words left behind by Guru Lennon you will know for yourself. Sure, I'm a shurm-shit brain like the rest. This stuff blows your fuckin' brain cells away like popcorn in a hurricane. But I see the signs. I see the visions. There is a power approaching. It will destroy the present world order and set us all free. And I will be here to lead us. That is my destiny.'

Brady rose. He felt suddenly tired. His stomach was rebelling against the vile spirit he had drunk. And the stench and smoke and sense of fear were beginning to make him sweat.

'Let's hope I'm around to take the picture. Look, I have to go. Somehow I'll let you know when I'm bringing this party through.'

'No need, Frank, I'll know before your wheels leave the bridge.'

Bolero stood and extended his hand. Brady hesitated then clasped the iron skeleton with a firm grip. He withdrew his hand quickly.

'Remember,' said Bobby Bolero, 'the power is coming. And it's comin' for you too, I can tell.'

Brady turned and walked slowly away through the semi-darkness. Minutes later he was screaming at top speed through the now pulsating landscape. Dark lights, half-lit bars, huddled groups and parading parodies of sexual deviance were out on the town. Brady just wanted to get back home. His forays into this world always left him feeling bleak and empty.

He roared towards the Queensboro Bridge and the brightly lit boundary with Manhattan. An army of Zone Police kept constant vigil all along the Manhattan shoreline and occupied the bridges. His sloop jet hurtled towards the bridge then screeched to a halt inside a pool of laser light. He watched as laser beams locked on to the sloop jet. A loud, harsh, metallic voice screamed a command.

'Move into zone two,' said the voice. 'You have three seconds.'

Brady edged the sloop jet into the shadow of the bridge and a wall of light dropped like a curtain behind him.

'Halt!' commanded the voice. 'You have one second.'

The sloop jet stopped dead. A guard emerged from the darkness, pulse rifle aimed at the windscreen. Brady opened the automatic windows. The guard stood menacingly, staring at Brady for a moment before removing his helmet visor. He smiled.

'Don't you ever get enough, Mr Brady? One of these days . . .'

'I'll be back next week, Sergeant,' Brady told the ZeePee as he handed him his permit, 'with a party. It's all arranged, armed escort, the works. And some of the most beautiful women in the world.'

'It's your funeral,' said the guard, 'now get out of here.'

Brady needed no second bidding.

Later, he was relaxing in a warm bath. His Japanese servant, Satoko, massaged his neck. He sighed languorously. After his bath he wandered through the apartment sipping a nightcap. The apartment was salubrious, decorated in mock Byzantine style, spacious and elegant. With a final glance at the Manhattan nightscape, Brady slipped into his circular bed between black silk sheets. He was drowsy, heavy with sleep. He smiled as he felt the weight and warmth of soft skin slipping in beside him. Tender fingers traced their way along his spine, down over his thigh until they reached their destination.

Chapter Three

The audience in the 'All the Way' studio had been queuing for hours. Now they sat riveted to their seats. Subtle fragrances wafted through the studio undetected. Mood-altering aromatherapy was a standard part of live entertainment in Manhattan. From experimental beginnings the show had grown into a monster with a life of its own. The format was simple. People came on stage and confessed their sins. A mock judge and jury which included friends, relatives, enemies of the accused, as well as actors tore into their victim with a ferocity never seen before on TV. The underlying theme had its origins in the confrontational shows of the past and was based loosely on a similar show running in Japan. The big difference was that the audience of millions got to see the accused take the punishment which was sometimes severe, often just funny.

Live TV had enjoyed a resurgence in recent years after decades of the virtuality revolution. Among the population sectors identified for deportation during the Isolation were the cybercrazies, hooked on the excesses of virtuality and overdosing on alternative reality. Indeed, there were many going through the motions of existence in the Badlands, high on the hormone-altering shurm, whose neuro-structures had been permanently altered. State governments worldwide still refused to recognize the existence of a human sub-species which was unable to communicate on a normal human level. Virtuality versions of successful TV shows were produced by the big networks. Most people had full cyberspace media-web sets in their homes which were true multimedia terminals. Some of the more sophisticated ran on trained neural networks which could do everything from run the house, order food, simulate soft or hard porn full sensory experiences and even invent non-existent partners or friends for the lonely. But, increasingly, the full service, wraparound cocoon provided by the hugely successful companies which devised and distributed such programs was losing its appeal. The mood was swinging from techno-life to real life.

This was one of the reasons why 'All the Way' had become such a huge hit. It was a re-hash of shows from a dead era. And it worked. On occasions it was the accused who volunteered to appear on the show and confess. Sometimes the victim was simply invited as a member of the audience and 'selected' as the jury came on.

Johnny Raine played the role of judge. Sometimes he was warm, compassionate, even sympathetic. Other times he was vitriolic, insulting, almost out of control. But Johnny Raine was never really out of control. Punishment on the show could be severe. Physical violence was not uncommon. Psychological tricks were played to the hilt. And the crowd loved it. There was nothing else like it on the web.

Tonight, Dan Wilson, the Oklahoma bigamist, stood naked in the centre of the stage. His hands were tied behind his back. His ankles were bound. Multi-coloured lights played over his body. In the jury box sat six women, none of whom had met before the show. They sat rigidly in their seats. Some gripped the rail in obvious distress. Wilson had married each of the women over a fifteen-year period. Although the marital state had been through a decline before the AIDS virus really caught hold of the world population, monogamy and various forms of marriage and partnership had enjoyed a resurgence in the last twenty years. Johnny Raine was walking around Wilson, looking him up and down. There was a tense silence in the auditorium.

'Can't see what they saw in you Dan,' he smiled into the raw-boned farm-boy face. 'Six women for Chrissake, six lives you set out deliberately to ruin. You're just a shit, you know that?'

'I know that. I want to be punished. Do anything to me. Torture me, beat me, burn me, I deserve it.'

'You deserve it!' Johnny turned to the audience. 'Does he deserve to be punished?'

The audience responded to the catch-phrase with predictable enthusiasm. Johnny looked out over the audience. This was no representative selection of the downtrodden masses. There were few of those left in Manhattan. There were some well-known faces staring back at the stage and into the four cameras positioned to catch every expression, every mood and live action incident that took place.

Johnny turned back to the trussed figure, looking smaller and more insignificant as the minutes ticked by.

'Naw!' he said. 'You're too pathetic. You're not worth it. Let the State take care of you. We'll buy you a one-way ticket to the shurm-town riviera. How about that? You're a waste of fucking time.' Johnny yelled these last words directly into Wilson's face. The man flinched, his expression betraying his growing uncertainty. He wanted something to happen. He wanted action. He started to struggle.

'Please, I came here to confess. But I swear, I loved each one of them. I still do.'

'You know what I think, Mr Wilson, Mr Big Shot bigamist. I think you're not worth punishing because no one cares. No one cares a ZeePee's ass whether you live or die. What are you doing here? Look at you.' Johnny poured scorn on his victim. 'I've talked to all of your wives, yes, those good women sitting over there. You know what, they could hardly remember your fucking name. You loved them did you? Well you must have made some big impression. You could leave this studio tonight and it would be as if you had never been born. Premature ejaculation was your big problem. I can see why. Wilson, you are a nonentity; a useless piece of waste material; a handful of dust. When you die even the worms won't remember you.'

'That's not true,' screamed Wilson, 'I am somebody. I'm a human being.'

Johnny turned to the wives in the jury. 'Want to come down and tell Danny boy what you think of him, while I ask the audience if we should really go – all the way?'

Music blared and lights flashed as the audience pressed a series of buttons. Various punishment options appeared on a screen above the stage. Meanwhile, Dan Wilson's incensed harem confronted him. They flung a barrage of insults at the cowboy, who, either because he had lost a few brain cells on the long flight from the Midwest and simply didn't understand character assassination when he heard it, or had discovered a taste for abuse, seemed to grow in stature.

Careful research in advance of the show yielded a mass of information on contestants, including their pet phobias, pleasures, finances, debts, mistresses, lovers; anything that could be used to humiliate, embarrass or even damage them. Privately, and unknown to millions of viewers, a comprehensive counselling service was offered by the TV station to offset the worst effects of their media mauling. This had been at Johnny's insistence. Maurice Freiberg was not one of nature's philanthropists. Few in Manhattan knew the meaning of the word.

Johnny gazed at the punishment screen as lights raced around to find the audience's random selection. No one really believed the choice was made by the audience but, still, belief was suspended week after week.

Johnny strode to centre stage. He screamed at Wilson. He screamed at the audience. He pointed to the punishment board. Wilson's eyes followed. His expression was part fear, part anticipation. When he saw the choice of punishment the anticipation drained from his features.

'You're going to drown, Dan,' yelled Johnny. 'How do you like that, eh?'

The wives cheered. The audience took up the chant, 'Drown, drown, drown.'

Behind Johnny and Wilson, curtains opened. They revealed a large tank filled almost to the brim with water. At the side, steps led to a small platform above which a hoist had been erected. A digital clock stood at the side and the tank was ringed with cameras so that every movement and expression could be recorded.

Wilson stared at the tank. One of his jilted wives cried with joy.

'He's terrified of water. He almost drowned as a child.'

Johnny slapped Wilson on his naked shoulder. The bigamist was shivering, his eyes were dilated, he could hardly talk. Johnny whispered to him out of the side of his mouth. 'Don't worry, you'll be all right.' Then he called for the stagehands to escort Wilson to the steps. The man was terrified. He fought and struggled but could not escape the iron grip of the muscle-bound assistants.

They dragged Wilson up the steps to the platform as the music matched the drama. The secret aromas changed. Purple and red lights flashed. Johnny was working the audience, asking them how long, how long should he have?

From the wings, Jordan watched without expression.

Wilson was attached to the hoist and swung out head downwards, facing the audience. His body struggled pathetically as the top of his head was positioned just above the water. He was screaming. He was begging for mercy, for anything but this. But this was just what the audience and the TV viewing millions had been waiting for. The audience had rushed to the stage, engulfing the six wives of Dan Wilson, pushing against a line of stewards.

Wilson was immersed, screaming and struggling. The count began. After thirty seconds Wilson was hoisted out. He was gasping and gagging. His six wives had a ringside view of their errant husband and they were screaming abuse till their voices were hoarse. One of them, a dark-haired, dumpy, Jewish-looking woman, just stared at Wilson with empty eyes. Johnny was in full swing, conducting the baying audience, castigating Wilson. Down he went into the water for a second time. Thirty seconds passed, then forty. Then he was hauled out. He coughed briefly. Johnny had his eyes on him. He glanced over to where the medi-team was positioned. Wilson was hardly moving now. His eyes looked glazed.

'OK, that's enough,' he called, 'take him out.'

The crowd screamed. Johnny hesitated, then signalled for another immersion. Wilson just hung there, suspended like a white side of beef, pale and insipid. The clock moved on. The crowd chanted. In the tank Wilson hung immobile. Bubbles had ceased to issue from his nose and mouth. Johnny felt a cold, clammy hand grasp his heart. He felt sudden fear. There had never been a fatality on the show. There had been plenty of near misses and many times viewers had fully believed that one of the victims had been killed. But it had always been all right afterwards.

Johnny signalled and Wilson was brought out, then lowered carefully to the studio floor. The medi-team rushed to his side, stewards cleared the area, Johnny hustled and fussed around his victim then ran to centre stage for the finale.

Johnny wrapped the show up to camera while behind him the live action of resuscitation provided a real-life feel to the finale.

Millions of viewers saw it happen. Johnny was smiling at camera making his familiar eye contact with his viewers when a figure holding a long-bladed knife moved into frame behind him. Johnny was momentarily thrown when the producer switched cameras. Then everything happened quickly. The figure holding the knife screamed at the comatose body of Wilson. Before anybody could move, the Jewish-looking wife was running and falling on to him. She plunged the knife into his chest. Wilson was lucky. The blade missed his heart and his carotid artery. The wife raised the knife again but was instantly overpowered.

The show closed with the nation and the live audience on the edge of their seats.

Panic set in, a mixture of shock and exhilaration. Within seconds, Wilson had been lifted on to a stretcher and removed. The wife had been hustled away. Johnny was surrounded by clamouring voices. The producer arrived and put his arms around Johnny's shoulders.

'Magnificent,' he whimpered, 'that'll bust the ratings wide open.'

'Is he going to be all right?' asked Johnny.

'Who? Oh, I'm sure he'll be OK. He'll have the best medical help credits can buy. Just wait till we get the live stuff on camera. That'll take the ratings into the stratosphere.'

Johnny looked at him, opened his mouth to speak, then thought better of it. He paused, then said, 'I've got to go, Lloyd. OK!'

'Sure you don't want to come to Trixie's party tonight? It will be amazing, I just know it.'

'No, no thanks, see you at the Monday conference.'

Johnny turned on his heel and headed for the wings. Jordan

was waiting for him. Without a word she took him in her arms. Then for a long moment she stared at him.

'My place,' she whispered.

That night there was a full and heavy moon pinned to the sky over Manhattan. The balcony blinds were open and a patchwork mesh of moonlight bathed the room in patterns of light and shade. The patterns rippled along Jordan's body as she straddled Johnny, moving her hips slowly and rhythmically. Her hands stroked his chest and her breasts hung tantalizingly close to his hungry mouth. And he was hungry for her tonight. He had ripped her clothes from her body in a frenzy of passion the second they had got back to the apartment.

But, slowly, she had assumed control until his body melted with hers. She held back, then she increased the circular movements of her groin on his. He could barely breathe. She muttered soft whisperings and sounds as they came into her mind. He reached out his arms as she brought him to a gut-bursting orgasm, riding him like a stallion in the moonlight. He tried to scream but nothing came. His eyes were wide and dilated. Jordan was bucking now in a fluid movement. She threw her head back and flicked her tongue in and out of her mouth like a reptile searching for sunlight.

Then she came, timing her orgasm with his. The white beams of dusty light flickered and reflected from the beads of sweat bathing both their bodies.

Morning came. Johnny pressed his mouth into her neck, savouring the musky morning smell of her. She stirred and turned to him, slipping her thigh over his waist. He was as hard as an iron bar in seconds. She toyed with it, her fingers drifting along its stem almost indifferently. Johnny loved this kind of foreplay. It could go on for ever as far as he was concerned.

'Do you want to talk about the show?' she asked him.

'Not this second,' he said huskily.

'Are you really going ahead with this Badlands suicide business?'

'Guess I'll have to. One half of me hates the idea, the other thinks it'll decimate every other TV network in the country.'

'Why don't we just get away from all this,' she asked him suddenly. 'Get out of Manhattan, get out of America. Go to England maybe, or somewhere in Europe. Lots of people are doing it.'

'Mmm, sounds a good idea. Sounds wonderful. Maybe, I don't know. You need a lot of credits to do that. It takes time to salt away foreign currency. If I deliver this show to Channel Boom Boom, I'm into a big hunk of credit. Give it a little longer then get out. What's wrong with that?'

'Do you really mean it,' she said, 'would you really get out of this madness?'

'Like a bullet from a gun,' he said with a catch in his voice.

Her hand was warming to its task. Johnny began to feel disembodied, totally under Jordan's control.

She sighed.

Before she could speak he had rolled on top of her and spread her thighs, slipping his arms under her knees. Then he slipped inside her like an oiled piston. She gave a small scream, then relaxed and let him make love to her.

Marek Grohmann was experiencing his own death. At least that is what he believed. For many years the socialite psychoanalyst had practised another art. With a carefully controlled cocktail of hallucinogens and a homeopathic quantity of shurm, he had travelled the universe. He had pushed his psyche into areas explored only by a few great occultists, whose grimoires lined the walls of his private den.

In the last few years he had discovered the existence of a dimension where the regimented order of the supposedly solid material world dissolved into the chaos of the creative forces which manipulated the human experiment. Only a few others had unwittingly travelled this path. The photographer, Frank Brady, had been one. He had exhibited a natural cosmic talent. The only other had been the media star, Johnny Raine. He had experienced the awesome truth of the illusory nature of human life and of the powers that encircled and ensnared it.

There was another, he had heard, who could be found deep in the Badlands, who had awesome powers of cosmic clairvoyance and who had gone beyond even Grohmann in the exploration of the mysteries.

Right now, in his discreet private room in a secret part of his palatial offices near the New World Trade Centre, he was experiencing the pain and trauma of his own murder. The images inserted into his consciousness by the entity which nurtured him were incomplete. He could sense the entity and its power but could not discern whether it meant him good or ill; or even if those definitions were relevant. The entity could be an angel or a demon, he could not tell. He knew that the clairvoyant visions he experienced had been transmitted by the entity. He also knew this entity wanted more life energy than he could provide. He could not see the face or discern the identity of his murderer. He felt no physical pain as his body was ritually mutilated. Instead, a strange kind of exhilaration swept through him; he was captivated by the pain of release. As we are born so we die and re-form.

His analytical ability remained detached and observing, noting his demise. His initial terror had been replaced by grateful release.

A tower loomed before him, hovering within a gloomy land-scape. Within the glimmering edifice was the gateway. Grohmann had learned of the stellar currents and influences which were now seeking even greater control of the material world. In the depths of his being, as his physical body was carved and reshaped by his nemesis, he experienced a rare lucidity; a crystal-clear awareness of the dark abyss into which the soul of man must enter in order to survive.

He sat up, bathed in sweat. The vision ceased abruptly. Grohmann glanced at an old stained photograph sitting at an angle on a nearby coffee table. His wife, Imelda, cruelly killed during the Isolation war, had been life and death to him. All his life he had feared death to the point where he had been driven to experience it in advance. He should have felt calm and prepared. Instead he shook with post-hypnotic tremors. Back in the rational world, he knew he had been experiencing a delusion. He did not want to die. Life was comfortable, if unexciting.

Marek Grohmann ran a highly successful but discreetly low-

key psychiatric practice. He catered for and prospered from the
neuroses and traumas of the rich and the super-rich. As a result
he enjoyed a level-two standard of living and relaxed at week-
ends at his adobe-style residence out in the Hamptons. The
nightmarish Badlands stretched out as far as the wilder parts of
Long Island until they reached the massive barrier that stretched
from Bay Shore to Stony Brook. The urban deathworld was
concentrated in the former outer boroughs of New York. Further
out, on Long Island, marauding bands of nomadic desperadoes
roamed, laws to themselves but trading with each other and
with their urban brothers with whom they joined forces to pillage
and hijack supplies. It was a case of survival economics holding
utter anarchy at bay. Flying over the wasteland on his way to his
weekend retreat with fellow Manhattanites, he could barely
conceal a shiver of fear and alarm at the prospect of crash-
landing in that wilderness.

Grohmann had interests in many aspects of Manhattan life. He
was a regular contributor to the more heavyweight periodicals
and video nets as well as the popular science end of the weekend
leisure media market. He dabbled in politics and was an adviser
to the State legislature on many matters; in particular, the nature
of psychosis and socio-economic breakdown. He sat on numerous committees and advisory boards, particularly those dealing
with population control and communications.

He was also a key adviser to Media City.

He was an old-fashioned man; in appearance a kind of
throwback to the middle period of the twentieth century. His
consulting room was heavily masculine with its dark, somewhat
oppressive, furniture, thick drapes, enormous mahogany desk
and antique leather couch. He always dressed formally, usually
in light tweed suits which covered his portly figure. Nature and
good fortune had blessed him with the perfect face for his
profession. It was the face of everybody's favourite uncle. Leading political and financial figures had been known to divulge
their most intimate secrets after only half an hour in his professional company. He was that kind of man, with that kind of
face.

His cosmic journeys added a distinct and arcane spice to an

otherwise ordered and bland existence. His persistent longing was that some of the molecule-bursting excitement he experienced in the astral voids of light could somehow be transferred to his everyday life. Oh for the joy of a real adventure.

The contemplation of death added a distinct frisson to his daily routine. There had been no indication of the time or precise moment the event might occur. He still largely dismissed the notion, rationalizing his illusion as one created by absorbing too many of his patients' traumas. On the other hand, the exhilaration of communicating, even in a crude sense, with a genuinely extraterrestrial being was something he desperately wanted to continue. Maybe it was simply playing with his psyche, using him as a kind of human video.

Chapter Four

The next day Johnny called for Jordan at her apartment on Lexington. The roar of the sloop jet air-turbos could be heard half a mile away. Jordan had dressed in a one-piece outfit of black leather. Over this she wore a short red leather jacket. She stood waiting for Johnny on the sidewalk. From any angle she was one hell of a woman. Passers-by let their eyes linger. Men's eyes did more than linger. They devoured her as she fed their instant fantasies.

The arrival of the sloop jet in a squeal of rubberized composite almost stopped the sedate Manhattan traffic. Sloop jets were not that common. They were used mainly by the Zone Police on patrol around the perimeter. Johnny had had to use a lot of influence and Media City money to get his hands on one. The armoured shields were withdrawn as he declutched to a halt.

The sloop jet was a hybrid version of a saloon car and armoured deployment vehicle. It seated two comfortably with room in the back for equipment or luggage. It was fitted with laser-guided, rapid-fire Lexus mini-rocket launchers. These were not so much rockets as high-calibre bullets with small detonators in the nose. The guns could be fired in any direction. With its shields up the sloop jet had a single, moulded, twin-skinned, bullet-proof window that wrapped itself around the body. A small sliding door was the only way in, operated by remote or from the inside. The power of the sloop jet was legendary as was its remarkable alloy body and protector shields.

The door slid open and Johnny beamed out from the driver's seat. Jordan gazed around her. Between them they were stopping traffic. There was a touch of Spring in the air, a feeling of contentedness and plenty. Jordan took a deep breath. In less than half an hour she would be entering no man's land, the nightside of hell as it was often called.

'You look incredible. Get in before I forget myself and take you on the sidewalk.' Johnny smiled up at her.

Jordan slid in through the narrow door and allowed Johnny to clip her into the crossover safety straps.

He looked at her. 'Nervous?' he asked.

'Terrified.'

'Don't worry. Everything will be OK.' He glanced at his watch. 'Shit, we're late.'

He gunned the sloop jet and they roared away in the direction of the Queensboro Bridge.

'You've gone to a lot of trouble,' said Jordan.

'It'll be worth it.'

'Did you mean what you said yesterday?' she asked.

'What, about getting out of this shit-hole? Sure I did. It's only a matter of time before they,' he nodded in the direction they were driving, 'come after us. It'll take more than the ZeePees to keep 'em out.'

'How is that man, Wilson?'

'OK. We had the City Security investigators over. Wilson is fine. It's a bad stab wound but he'll live. We pulled him out just in time.'

'And you want to put live suicide on the TV screen?' Jordan was shaking her head.

'You think I like it? Look, Manhattan security and everyone connected with the running of the city has been canvassed. This is not just a TV show any more. It's a political statement. They see the freaks as expendable. As long as there's a way to get some of them over here, under tight security, willing to die in public, they'll give it their full support. They've got the idea that by putting them on screen, letting them take their own lives in any way they like, they will turn them into martyrs, you know. They'll become symbols, and that will act as an escape valve for their alienation.'

'And you believe that?' Jordan was staring at Johnny.

'All I know is, honey, I'm just as expendable as they are. I've negotiated a two-million credit deal, guaranteed if I can pull this off. That's enough to get us both out of here and over to Europe or even Japan. I know someone who can launder that kind of money. But, to answer your question. Will it work? Maybe. For a time. But then, who knows?' He shrugged as they came in sight of Queensboro Bridge, encased in its protective flexiglass tube.

The area in front of the bridge was a military encampment. Observation towers lined the waterfront as far as the eye could see. Sloop jets and other quasi-military vehicles, including fast attack jet foils, were lined up ready for instant despatch. Blue-suited Zone Police were everywhere, many in the lightweight body armour developed in the last few years. A barricaded area lay in front of the bridge. There was only one entrance. This was through a channel of vehicle width lined with sonic detectors and laser equipment.

Johnny could see, high up on the ramparts of the bridge, the sophisticated laserjet beams that could destroy anything, even sloop jets, within a mile radius. There was no sign of the Frank Brady party.

'We've missed them,' snapped Johnny. 'We were supposed to tag on the end.'

'What now?' muttered Jordan.

'We'll see. Here comes a ZeePee guard.'

A hugely muscular figure was approaching. Johnny could see out of the corner of his eye other weapons trained on the vehicle. The guard carried a high-powered shell rifle. He carried it loosely but with the muzzle pointed directly at Johnny.

He pulled his visor up and his grim expression softened as he recognized Johnny.

'You're Johnny Raine, aren't you?' said the guard, lounging casually against the body of the sloop jet and eyeing Jordan at the same time.

'Sure am,' Johnny replied.

The guard nodded at Jordan. 'You're carrying a passenger.'

'Jordan Semiramis, a friend.'

The guard grunted and took a small flip-top electronic messenger from his pocket. He examined it carefully.

'You're going on the Frank Brady trip,' he said.

'Yes, we seem to have missed them.'

''Bout five minutes. You sure you want to go in there? You know you're on your own if you get attacked.'

'Frank Brady's got protection,' said Johnny.

'Sure has. Looks like the whole goddamn army's gone through. Can I see your permit please, Mr Raine?'

Johnny took some papers from his jacket pocket and handed them to the guard who scrutinized them briefly.

'You know the agreed route?' he asked.

'It's printed on my brain cells,' said Johnny.

'OK. You know the rules, Mr Raine. Put your shields down.'

The guard stepped back, raising his rifle. From both sides came others, all with their rifles trained on the sloop jet. The first guard grinned at his companions. 'First time through,' he said and he winked knowingly at the others. They grinned back. This was a favourite game.

Johnny punched the controls that lowered the protective armour and caused the sloop jet to resemble a jungle-grey armadillo.

'What's happening?' Jordan looked worried.

'They've got to put the sloop jet to the test. It'll be OK, don't worry. I've got a guarantee.'

'What do you mean, put it to the test?'

At that instant, Jordan's words were drowned in a sudden explosion of sound. She screamed but she screamed in silence. Johnny held her as the Zone Police raked the sloop jet with a hail of fire. Smoke billowed, and the whine of high-impact bullets shattered the strange stillness of the bridge.

Then it stopped. Jordan threw herself into Johnny's arms, trembling.

'See, it was all right, we're fine.' Johnny comforted her but his face was ashen. 'It's because it's our first time through.'

'I'm getting out of here now,' screamed Jordan but Johnny held her back.

'Trust me. We're unharmed aren't we? Besides, there's no time.'

Before Jordan could protest, Johnny had received the go signal from the guard. He revved the engine and rammed the sloop jet into gear. The sound was muffled inside. Jordan sat tense and white-lipped, staring through the slatted windscreen as they hit the ramp at speed and raced over the bridge cocooned inside the tube. Ahead lay the Badlands. They could see the Zone Police high-security encampment at the other end of the bridge, a replica of the other. A disembodied voice suddenly crackled, picked up through the microphone link on the sloop jet, 'Don't stop . . . proceed at speed . . . don't stop . . . proceed at speed.'

With Jordan clinging to his arm, Johnny accelerated and hurtled from the safety of the sterile and artificial world over the river to the seething, tribal world of the Badlands.

Facing the bridge were the only high buildings left intact. Daubed in phosphorescent colours over every inch of the facades were acres of graffiti. In huge letters the chilling messages were daubed, gaudy but with an animal power.

'Nightmare City', 'Fragmentation No Stagnation', 'Reality Sucks', 'No Love', screamed the messages, the slogans of the Badlands. A band of wild-looking dogs appeared from the depths of a broken building. Groups of figures, hard to make out in the shadows, could be seen moving. Despite the Spring sunshine, there was a dark and menacing feel to the wasted landscape. Johnny gunned the sloop jet, fascinated despite his fear, and roared over the rubble-strewn streets. They entered a long boulevard, lined by long-dead shops and stores. Some were clearly occupied, feeble lights burning inside.

Johnny suddenly swerved to avoid a two-wheeled vehicle which shot out from a side alley. It was a grotesque parody of a motorcycle. It resembled a modernistic sculpture on wheels. But it was the rider that sent chills through Johnny. Jordan clung to his arm as they stared at the powerfully built man whose legs formed part of the motorcycle. He was built into the machine. He was bald with a wildly painted skull into which were embedded several steel spikes. His face was deformed and vacant. He stared at the sloop jet for a second and Jordan recoiled at the gaze of sheer malevolence.

Johnny didn't wait around to ask directions. He sped off down the boulevard, eyes flicking left and right. Now they could see people moving, walking, talking on street corners. Instinctively, they started to relax. There was an air of normality about the scene, rather like the history CDs in the Manhattan Library, decadent and savage but with the feeling that life in some form of structured society was trying to survive.

The figures were drab, with hunted, watchful expressions. Many were clearly dying. Many were deformed, scabrous, infected. Where they could see young men, they were always in groups, heavy with weapons, mostly home-made or improvised. They were decorated with ferocious tribal symbols and many proudly highlighted their deformities with glittering jewellery and bright colours.

There were vehicles here too. All were customized and fabricated from wrecks and most were personalized with the language of graffiti, the art form of the Badlands. Johnny noticed a number of vehicles pulling out to fall in behind the sloop jet. He looked over at Jordan and noticed with some surprise that, instead of exhibiting repulsion and fear, she seemed strangely excited and stimulated.

Raw sewage overflowed between buildings and poured into open drains. There were street lights and there was food in what looked like central markets. Johnny wondered how they obtained food here. It was something he had simply taken for granted in Manhattan. Over the skies of the city, a constant stream of helijet transporters ferried goods from distant ports and cities. Trade in that sense was normal. But here, they must be organized, he thought. He had heard that they sent regular organized raiding parties far out into New York State. They also did business in the normal way, obtaining goods from way outside the city limits.

Johnny realized with a start that what he called the Badlands were, in fact, just another part of the United States. It had been Manhattan that had severed its ties and become an enclave. This had set a trend within the US and in other parts of the world. The alienation of the proletariat, the poor, the subversive, the cybercrazy and the infectious had finally erupted during the Isolation War. Large tracts of the United States had been overrun. Urban sprawls had grown up. Most of them were diseased shanty towns like the Badlands. It was a boom time for private armies, hired to protect the established cities, many of which were now exclusive fortresses.

Jordan tugged at his sleeve and pointed. 'Look,' she said.

Johnny looked, keeping an eye on the growing convoy behind. Moving across the road in front of them and turning to travel along the other side was the most bizarre sight he had ever seen. He almost laughed aloud at the incongruity of it. Here, in the centre of the Badlands, was a small circus parade. Brightly painted caravans were being pulled by resigned-looking horses, moving at a slow but regular plod. There were cages housing a few skulking animals and a small troupe of performers posed on an open trailer shouting at the crowds. Bringing up the rear was a caravan pulled by a near-dead horse whose nose almost touched the ground. Painted on the side was the name: 'Madame Speranza – Fortune Teller, Clairvoyant, Palmist, Cyberpsyche'.

'I don't believe it,' breathed Johnny, suppressing a laugh.

'It's wonderful,' said Jordan. 'I love the circus.'

Johnny roused himself with a start and accelerated past the retinue and was pleased to see the convoy of home-made cars falling away behind. He swung right into a large square surrounded by crumbling apartment buildings. Only the facades were still standing. Behind was a mountain of rubble and twisted metal.

A hundred or so spectators were milling around watching silently; immobile, expressionless. They stood outside a protective barrier of nervous ZeePees. As Johnny and Jordan arrived, they noticed again the uniformly ugly, twisted and ravaged faces, filled with a kind of animal pride, staring vacantly from outside the barrier as if waiting for a signal which would kindle activity within their empty minds. Their number was growing.

He felt a sudden backwash of sadness and echoes of feelings he hadn't experienced since he was a child. Drifting among the downtrodden grey masses were gangs of warrior types. Clearly, these gangs ran the city. Johnny had heard that, although open warfare was common here, some kind of uneasy agreement existed so that at least the bare essentials of life could be provided.

In the centre of the square was a ring of armoured personnel carriers and sloop jets. A small army of Zone Police faced out towards the crowd. Johnny drove over to the cordon. Within the cordon stood a crane, reaching up to the top of the buildings. Suspended from the crane was a cradle, idly swinging from side to side like a metronome.

Johnny showed his permit to a nervous ZeePee sergeant who let them through. Johnny parked near a cluster of vehicles which included Frank Brady's own sloop jet. The base of the crane resembled a film set. A clutch of sweaty advertising executives stood huddled around a small, foreign-looking man. They all seemed agitated and the small man kept looking around anxiously. Elsewhere, groups of Manhattanite voyeurs were laughing and swigging champagne, and assistants were scurrying around adjusting cables, lights and music. One young man was crouched over what looked like a rocket launcher. Johnny realized it was a distress flare gun.

Jordan looked up at the crane and squinted.

'Is that Frank Brady?' she asked.

Johnny followed her gaze and saw a figure in the cradle. He seemed to be talking into a neck mike and his head was encased by some kind of equipment.

Music suddenly blared from loudspeakers. Only Frank Brady knew it was the opening bars of Scriabin's *Mysterium*. Somehow, the music fitted the environment and seemed to cast a spell on everyone around.

High up in the cradle, Frank Brady was adjusting his cameras. They were attached to his head by a simple frame which, like a movie camera, had several lenses that rotated into position automatically. Brady was unshaven. He wore a black silk anorak with the words 'Overt Divergence' emblazoned on the back.

'OK,' he snapped into his microphone, 'let's tango.'

The cradle began to swing gently from left to right. Brady stared at the top of the building in front of him. Many of the windows were in place but the walls were encrusted with vegetation. Behind, parts of the walls and floors were still standing.

Brady adjusted a control on a hand-gun remote he held in his right hand and suddenly his nasal, English accent boomed all over the square.

'All right, ladies, as soon as the flare explodes, you're on.'

Brady paused, then snapped another instruction. 'OK, Mike, let 'em go.'

From the base of the crane, flares shot up between the cradle and the building, bursting in puffs of red and blue smoke which hung in the air and drifted over the buildings. At that precise moment, at the top of the building, three beautiful models emerged from behind the rotting walls to pose in front of three empty windows. They stretched like athletes going for gold. One of the models was black, another white and the other Eurasian. They were wearing the skimpiest and most erotic lingerie in the world, Erotique.

Brady rapid-fired his Mitsuki, using the camera like a third eye. The three models moved through a smooth routine with Brady firing instructions at them.

'Marcia, hands like claws. Suki, squat like you're giving birth. Roxy, show me those tits, darling. Come on, give me some fucking action. A million blokes out there want to screw you so give 'em something back. Mike, more flares, now. Yellow, yellow, come on, the light's going. Tell Dubois he's gonna make another couple of million.'

In shadows, deep inside the dark and dank interior of the building, watching with red-eyed intensity, were the real denizens of the Badlands. The ones that only came out at night; the secret ones that lived in the sewers and the unknown places. At this moment they couldn't be seen, but their eyes were watching.

Johnny recognized two of the advertising executives from the Have A Nice Day agency. Mike Fearnley and Paul Wilson were refilling the client's champagne glass. The client gazed impassively at the figure of Brady high above.

'He's the best there is, Louis, believe me. If Frank Brady can't deliver the goods, no one can.' Fearnley was reassuring Louis Dubois, the boss of Erotique, the world's most expensive lingerie.

'Mike's right, Louis. Every credit you spend here will pay you back a million,' smarmed Wilson.

Jordan looked at Johnny. 'What's the master plan?'

'I'll get to talk to Brady after the shoot's over. You just be there. He'll be fascinated by you.'

'You make me sound like a present you're about to unwrap. I've told you, that kind of thing is out of the question.'

'What do you think I am? Look, let's just enjoy the experience.'

Brady was winding up the shoot.

'OK girls, I want a quick change. Put something warm on and get those knickers off. Watch your step. Don't move around too much.'

The models smiled at Brady and he smiled back. Carefully, they adjusted their weight, slipped on warm wraps hidden behind the wall and started to change into another set of sexy silk.

Brady saw her first. The crowd was only seconds behind. Jordan grabbed Johnny's arm and dug her nails into his flesh.

It took place in slow motion. Marcia had bent to pick up a pair of panties when the heel of her shoe caught in a fissure. It was stuck. She tried to pull her shoe clear but it had jammed fast. Roxy and Suki laughed but then their smiles froze on their faces. Marcia had stood up and was intelligently slipping her foot out of the shoe when she happened to glance backwards into the dark recesses of the building. She froze, her body rigid, and the blood drained from her face. She began to shake. From her position she could see something the others could not.

'Oh my God, 'cried Marcia. 'No, no.' Her eyes were wide and her jaw was locked solid with fear. She began to sway uncontrollably, all the time staring fixedly at something down in the building.

'Marcia, what is it? What's wrong? Wait, I'm coming,' shouted Suki. It was too late. Brady screamed at Marcia to hold on and yelled into his mike to bring the cradle up to the building's edge.

But Marcia was slipping, losing her balance and tottering from the narrow ledge at the top of the building.

Jordan screamed as Marcia fell. At the same time she felt a charge of adrenalin run through her. She also noticed with the high-intensity awareness experienced during sudden drama that Brady was photographing the model as she plummeted to the ground.

Brady kept shooting, freezing Marcia's fall as it happened. Behind the lens, tears were running down his face. But he could not stop himself. He was shooting rapid-fire until and beyond the point of impact.

At the base of the building, yards from the onlookers and the guards, stood some old, rusted and rotting machinery. A six-foot iron girder jutted up from the ground like a rusted tooth.

Marcia hit the girder at speed. Her legs were open. The girder speared her through her vagina and up through her body, shattering her head and emerging through her skull, impaling her like a bloody marionette.

The silence was tangible. The throb of the Badlands music backdrop, merging with the strains of the *Mysterium* were the only sounds to be heard. Then a searing sob rent the air, followed by a collective wail which burst into uncontrolled weeping. Mike vomited at the base of the crane. The Manhattanites dropped their champagne bottles and stared like startled rabbits. The crane operator had the presence of mind to respond to Brady's instruction. Brady had taken Roxy and Suki into the cradle and was hugging them as they descended.

The small group of onlookers began to walk slowly towards the bloody mess spiked like a kebab on the girder. Marcia's blood dripped into the dust and rust. Jordan and Johnny were transfixed as they joined the group. As they came closer, Marcia's body spasmed in a dying kick. This brought screams from the group and two women and one man fainted. The paramedic group attached to the Zone Police was running across from the ambulance, yelling at the crowd to get out of the way. The ambulance turned and followed.

The paramedics and a ZeePee guard began to remove Marcia's body from the girder. 'We'll have to cut her off,' one shouted.

Fearnley and Wilson were shaking their heads in disbelief as the cradle with Brady and the two models on board reached the ground.

'What a fuck-up,' snarled Fearnley.

'How's Dubois taking it?' Wilson asked.

'He's asking serious questions about our competence. This could blow the account for Chrissake. Stupid bitch!'

'This is the Badlands, Mike, it comes with the territory.'

Brady passed the two tearful models over to one of his assistants as the cradle reached the ground. He leaped out, ripped his camera assembly from his head and flung it to another assistant.

'Check security,' he instructed, 'we've got to get out of here in one piece.'

'That's more than you can say for Marcia,' the assistant replied. Brady glared at him.

He strode towards the dead model, ignoring every call. As he reached her, two paramedics had heaved her body halfway off the spike. Nearby Johnny and Jordan watched. Johnny took her arm.

'Come on, I'll take you home. My business will have to wait.'

'No,' she said strangely, 'I want to stay.'

Johnny looked at her and saw the almost morbid fascination written across her face. She began to walk towards the dead body. Johnny walked with her.

Brady meanwhile was gazing at the torn and ripped body with compassion as the paramedics lifted Marcia on to a stretcher. Fearnley came over to Brady and put his arm around his shoulder.

'Frank, it was going so well. This is awful.'

'She was the best,' replied the photographer.

'Look, Frank.' Fearnley was nervous. 'Dubois is getting edgy. This place, now this. I don't know what he's going to do. Security says we should get back to Manhattan fast.'

Slowly, Brady turned away, his face still drawn with shock. He looked up and saw Johnny and Jordan. For a moment all three stood perfectly still. Johnny was uncertain about approaching Brady in this state. Brady was staring at Jordan as though he recognized her. Johnny walked up to him.

'Frank, I'm Johnny Raine.'

'I know who you are,' Brady replied.

'I'd like to talk to you,' said Johnny, 'but obviously not here.'

Jordan was watching Brady with an odd expression. Then her attention shifted to the body of Marcia on the stretcher. She seemed to stagger then regain control of herself. Blood was still glistening on the rusty girder.

'Not now!' snapped Brady. He turned on his heel and walked quickly to his sloop jet. All around, the shoot was wrapping up fast. The armed convoy was on the move. Johnny half dragged Jordan away from her contemplation of Marcia's body.

'This is sick,' he said urgently. 'Come on, we're getting out of here.'

He took Jordan's arm and hustled her to their sloop jet. Around the neighbouring streets, the small crowd had grown to the proportions of a mob. An atmosphere was brewing within the silent watching faces, a malevolence and hatred which could be felt in the thick Spring sunshine.

Suddenly, the convoy started to move. Johnny positioned himself within the protective ring of Zone Police vehicles and they all roared off. Behind, in the darkness of the building, something was slithering towards the girder, something attracted to the tangy smell of fresh blood. Within an hour every trace of blood and flesh would have disappeared.

The journey back to Manhattan was tense. The convoy came under attack from home-made petrol bombs and rocket launchers along the boulevard that led to the bridge. Johnny's sloop jet took a direct hit. It rocked the vehicle several feet sideways but otherwise did no damage. Jordan looked flushed and disoriented.

'You all right?'' Johnny asked.

'Yes, yes, I'm fine,' she said.

'You seemed, I don't know, excited by what happened back there.'

'There was something about it. I don't know. I feel confused. It's very strange.'

Johnny looked at her curiously as they followed the convoy over the bridge, halting to go through the obligatory laser checks.

Back in Manhattan the convoy split up but Johnny kept Brady in his sights, turning west towards the park. Brady eventually drove slowly into a select group of apartments near Central Park West. Johnny rolled the sloop jet to a halt across the street and watched as Brady parked his own vehicle in front of a well-concealed garage door. Johnny got out and signalled for Jordan to follow. She did so at a distance, as if reluctant to approach too closely.

Brady was clearly preoccupied and had forgotten their quick meeting earlier. He opened the garage doors and was about to get back into the driving seat when Johnny called to him.

'Hi, Frank, Frank Brady. It's Johnny Raine.'

Brady turned and looked at Johnny, his impassive face never changing expression.

'Are you going all the way or just too far?' he said.

Johnny didn't know whether he was serious or not. It was hard to tell. The model's violent death had clearly stunned him.

'I'd like to talk to you, seriously. I've got a proposition to put to you. If it's a bad time I'll understand.'

'Aren't you going to introduce me?' said Brady.

Johnny introduced Jordan. They shook hands briefly, the merest touch. Johnny experienced a twinge of jealousy, yet something told him the reaction between Jordan and Brady was not really sexual. It was something else, something different. Brady looked at Johnny. His face was weatherbeaten; the face of a merchant seaman, which, of course, is exactly what Brady had been before he jumped ship in New York and created a career for himself within five years.

'What do you want?' he asked.

'I'll get straight to the point,' Johnny said. 'I want you to take me to the Badlands, the real Badlands. I want to put some of those freaks on the show. I'll pay. Channel Boom Boom has its own credit bank.'

'What's your connection with all this?' Brady asked Jordan.

'I'm just an interested bystander,' she replied, touching Johnny's arm, 'but I'm a great admirer of your work. I loved your last exhibition, "The Warrior Within". It was wonderful.'

'You must come to my next show, "The Savage Eye". It'll be in a few weeks.'

'I'd love to,' said Jordan.

Brady turned to Johnny and the younger man felt a dark

power-surge prickle his skin as though he was being dissected and analysed. He sensed a chilling depth to the man and decided that it would be unwise to get on the wrong side of him.

'If you're serious, I'll think about it. It could be interesting.'

'You got it, Frank,' said Johnny brightly. Brady turned and climbed back into the sloop jet which he rolled into the garage. The doors came down behind the car and he was gone.

On the way back across the street Jordan asked Johnny, 'Well, was that a yes or a no?'

'It was a maybe.' he smiled. 'But he'll do it, I know he will. And not for the money.' He paused, took Jordan in his arms and kissed her tenderly. 'My place I think,' he said.

Brady watched from his balcony. He saw Johnny Raine's sloop jet disappear into the distance. 'Well, well,' he whispered, 'how the wheel turns.'

He strolled into the apartment and went to a large, dark bureau. He ran his index finger along a row of folders and selected one. Opening it, he took a deep breath.

The album contained a collection of reportage-like photographs, many grainy and taken at long distance. The subject was clearly unaware of the camera's presence and of the searching, secret eye behind the lens.

The beautiful blonde had been caught, talking, dancing, running, embracing. They were paparazzi snapshots but taken with the artistry of a Cartier-Bresson.

'Angelica,' Brady breathed through clenched teeth. 'Our lady of obsession has come to haunt me again. You were so beautiful. But you married Mr Media. And now he has another. She excites me, just as you did, my darling Angelica. I could never tell you . . . I could never . . .' He broke off, slamming the album shut and replacing it on the bureau shelf.

So Johnny Raine wanted to visit the Badlands, did he? A television tourist with the intellect of a cashier, that's all he was. And yet, Brady knew, he was more than that. He could remember the dream. He could recall Grohmann's words as he held the photographer down on his couch and prevented him from swallowing his tongue.

'Repeat the mantra, Frank . . . repeat the mantra . . .' Grohmann had been terrified after that session and had refused point blank to carry out any more.

Brady could still almost taste the dream. He fought hard to prevent the shakes overwhelming him as he remembered the purple chaos.

Brady knew that his own personal demon lay waiting; slumbering patiently until awakened. Then, he knew, he would have to summon up all his power, all his magical experience to defeat it. And it would be, he knew with certainty, a battle to the death.

Chapter Five

The centrepiece of the circular room was a recess containing a vibra-spring bed covered in thin silk sheets. The furniture was abstract and spare, and so not a distraction from the main purpose of the room. A small Japanese water garden burbled happily in one corner near a low-slung couch. Around the walls were colourful paintings, some abstract, some vaguely erotic, and set into the walls at intervals were small grilles behind which were tiny fans. The grilles could be opened and various essences, oils, spices and erotic herbs mixed and placed into small high-pressure vessels. The aromas, sometimes strong and vibrant, sometimes undetectable, permeated the room with a deeply sensual effect.

It was a hedonistic bedroom and had been Johnny and Angelica's private love-nest. Jordan was the first woman in two years to share it with him.

Right now Johnny lay spreadeagled on the bed, naked. Around the perimeter of the bed lay discarded wine bottles, a small pipe, and jars of pills. He was just nicely high. Jordan emerged from the kitchen with a tray containing two salads. She was also naked. She curled up beside Johnny who raised himself on his elbow. Wordlessly they ate, watching each other. Johnny poured more wine for both of them and they drank thirstily. Jordan lay back and Johnny poured a little of the classy Californian vintage over her nipples and into her navel. He began to lap the wine with his tongue. She moaned quietly as he worked his tongue towards her inner thighs. She threw the dishes away and rolled over. The combination of wine, erotic essences drifting through the room and the little blue and white orgasm pills they had popped shortly before was now driving them into a state of sensual overdose.

Johnny shivered as he felt sparks of static jumping from Jordan's skin as he caressed her intimately. Every movement of a finger, every touch of skin upon skin sent exquisite tremors through them both.

Johnny felt supercharged, scarcely able to hold back the onrush of power. Jordan moaned and the sound vibrated within Johnny, echoing deep inside the pit of his stomach.

Then they made love and it felt to them both as though their very molecules, their very essences, were harmonizing and exploding with bliss.

At that moment a sudden Spring storm hit the city. Lightning streaked across the rapidly darkening afternoon. The first crack of thunder coincided with their first orgasm.

It was much later, while Johnny was sleeping, curled up in the darkness, smiling and relaxed, that Jordan's eyes opened suddenly, although she was still sound asleep. She grated her teeth and writhed in a sudden outburst of sweat as the dream within her took hold.

The corridors were bare and white. Here and there a closed door was set flush with the wall. Jordan was young and her long hair was flowing over her shoulders. She saw herself clearly in her dream. She was smiling because she knew her father was close by. She even heard his voice calling her from somewhere in the building.

She passed a mirror and gazed at her reflection. Her young, smiling face looked back. But there was something else. There was something behind her. She perceived it like something hovering at the corner of her field of vision.

She continued to walk and a feeling of uncertainty came over her. What if her father were not here? Where was he? Then she heard his voice again. It sounded anxious. Looking around she was now in a large, empty, white room. Sunlight streamed through two large windows so brightly that she was dazzled. There were three doors in the room. Her father's voice was louder here and more urgent. It seemed to be pleading with her. She couldn't quite make out the words. She suddenly felt very young, yet very old. It was a strange feeling and she approached the first door nervously. She pushed it open and saw a room. It was bare just like the one she was in. At first it appeared empty. Then she heard the slow, rhythmic sound of breathing.

A naked woman with skin the colour of alabaster lay still on the bare floorboards. She was breathing slowly, very slowly, in the midst of her death trance. Her skin was pure and unblemished. Around her, issuing from the tiniest of cracks in the floorboards, were puffs of purple smoke which slowly gathered into a gauze-like web. As the tendrils of smoke wriggled and reached around the woman's contours her veins began to appear through her pale skin until they covered her body in a network of blood like the rapid incisions of a surgeon's scalpel.

The veins grew darker, thicker and more pronounced. The woman was now imprisoned in a purple shroud, her veins bulging through the diaphanous web. The tips of the purple tendrils attached to the web pierced the veins at a hundred or more points around her body. They began to suckle the woman's life-blood. The web grew in profusion as it took sustenance until it was bloated and swollen to excess.

The woman's face suddenly lolled sideways, her mouth agape, her dazzling blue eyes the only colour left in her body. Jordan gasped.

Angelica!

Ribbons of pain were now pulsating between Jordan's temples like an electric current sizzling between opposing terminals. As Jordan watched in horror and with mounting terror Angelica's face began to split apart. Inside her skull another, and much larger, head was emerging. Coarse hair sprouted from the animal skull which cracked the beautiful face of its host like an eggshell.

A dog-like beast gazed at Jordan. The mouth drooled, exposing the fangs. Jordan recoiled from the metamorphosis. She was unable to scream.

A trickle of blood fell from the beast's mouth and began to writhe and wriggle its way across the dusty floor. Jordan backed away.

Her father's voice was calling her, protecting her. Terrified she ran from the room and, without thinking, opened the second door. Within, it was dark but soon the light-show began. Migraine-inducing pulses of purple luminescence shifted and merged in a crazy cosmic dance. The purple veil increased in size. Behind it lay chaos. Jordan knew this instinctively. Behind her the trickle of blood was still seeking her out.

Jordan backed away again and ran to the third and final door. Behind this door might be her only means of escape. But something was going to bar her way. She was gripped with an icy-cold fear as she touched the handle. She had to get away from the blood and the purple mist. She must not allow herself to be swallowed by the mist or infected by the blood. But she knew with absolute certainty that there was something behind this door that would destroy her soul for ever. Her hand was stuck to the door handle. Whatever was inside the room was somehow inside her too. She felt dwarfed by the psychic finger-prints as she fell to the floor.

She could not leave the room or enter the one behind her. But she could still hear her father's voice calling, reassuring her, protecting her.

Jordan awoke with a start. She took a few moments to recover. Her skin was clammy and she was shivering despite the warmth of the room. Her arms ached and she realized that she was holding Johnny with a fierce bear-hug. He was still sleeping soundly. Slowly, she relaxed her muscles, released him and turned on to her back, breathing deeply, trying to find her focus. The dream was still with her, vivid and alarming. She had never had a nightmare like this before and it had completely dis-oriented her. The overwhelming sense of foreboding and fear was so tangible, so real. She tried to rationalize the experience but found that the power of the nightmare had frozen the faculty for rational thought. She could still see Angelica's face, before it had changed so horrifically.

Then she started to cry softly. It had been years since she had wept. Her soul felt as though it was about to break out and escape through the front of her head. Suddenly she feared sleep with a terror she had never before experienced.

Dreams were rife in Manhattan that night. Frank Brady prowled his apartment, gazing at, but not seeing, his surreal sculptures, his Bacon and Fuchs originals. Brady was distracted and he couldn't understand the reason. He had replayed Marcia's terrible death over and over in his mind. But something else nagged at him, something he could not place. Try as he might he could not erase the image of Jordan's face. He had felt a closeness to her the moment he had seen her that morning.

He was a man capable of the most powerful obsessions. He knew that. It was one of the elements that made his work so perceptive and disturbing. He had always lived close to the edge, he liked it there. He liked to stare into the face of the unknown and thumb his nose at it.

The sweet irony of this situation was that Johnny Raine, a man he had not met before, except casually at the occasional media event, was involved with two women who had captured his soul in a way no other women ever had. Angelica had been a successful model in Manhattan, some time before she met Raine. Brady had photographed her like so many others had done when he worked almost exclusively in advertising. She had ignored him, or at least treated him with the same disdain as she did all the others. Brady could not take too much rejection. So, he had channelled his obsession into his work. He could snap his fingers and most young up-and-coming models would have been over within the hour. They would have even brought their own bed for the chance of sleeping with the *enfant terrible* of Manhattan. But not Angelica. She had been immune to his hormonal attraction.

He then began the most exciting and covert experiment. He photographed Angelica in secret. He created a temple within his apartment and had bestowed love upon her images through erotic, magic ceremonies.

Then she had married Johnny Raine. Brady had been devastated. Raine, a man he regarded as an intellectual lightweight, had won her. Strangely he felt little animosity towards the media star. But he had wished Angelica dead.

When it happened however, it had shocked him to the core. It was the manner of her death which shattered him.

And now, he smiled thinly, Raine was at it again. He had found another totem of obsession. And he had come to him, right in his face. Did Raine somehow know that he would be incapable of refusing his request just to stay close to Jordan? Like

Angelica, Brady knew she would reject his advances. But she represented more than sexual power. She exuded a cosmic energy that was electrifying. Brady needed an infusion of that power. He shrugged. Whatever Raine had, he should bottle it.

Where Johnny's place was hedonistic, Brady's apartment had a heavy, brooding atmosphere and was crammed with books and *objets d'art*. There was a chaotic feel to the jumble of sculptures and paintings. At the centre of the room was a low, black dining-room table with gold edges and gold and black chairs. At that moment, Satoko was arranging flowers, her pale oriental face calm and tranquil. Elsewhere, the apartment contained a studio and darkroom, bedrooms and a large empty gallery where Brady sometimes arranged impromptu viewings of his work. Many of the photographs destined for his forthcoming exhibition at the Lepri Gallery were stored there, awaiting collection.

Brady gazed at his Japanese housekeeper fondly.

'Take the night off Satoko,' he told her, 'go and see your mother.'

She returned his gaze unblinkingly, then bowed imperceptibly and left the room.

Brady poured himself a drink, downed it in one and took a shower. When he had finished he returned, poured himself a nightcap and went to his bedroom. The enormous bed was dominated by a massive, ornate headboard in the form of a bas-relief sculpture of Dante's *Inferno* painted black and gold.

Brady examined his lean frame in a full-length mirror. He was well-built with good muscle tone. It was worth the hours of work he put in at the gym, he thought. Then his thoughts strayed to Jordan again and his hand slid to his crotch. There was something wrong, he thought. His attraction to her was not just sexual. In fact, there was something even more powerful taking place, another kind of chemistry; the meaning of which lay just outside the range of his subconscious.

On a large table by the window lay an array of photographs. Brady contemplated them intensely. His eyes roved over the images of the three models. The shots were good. They were sensational, even if he said so himself. Then there were the other shots. Marcia, mouth open, terrified, falling from the building. There were still shots of her descent and then the chilling stills of her spiked and unrecognizable body speared on the girder. Brady was engrossed.

The phone rang, jarring his nerves. He picked up the receiver.

'Brady,' he said tersely.

It was Mike Fearnley.

'Frank, you OK?'

'Never better. You're going to love the pictures.'

'We can't use them, Frank,' Fearnley said.

'What do you mean? I broke my bollocks getting these shots. And Marcia's dead as a result. There's blood on these pictures, Mike.'

Fearnley was comforting. 'Dubois has insisted you reshoot in Paris. The whole thing. A different feel. He just thinks the contrast, the setting, is too ... You know what clients are like. Besides, this Marcia business has put a kind of jinx on the project. I must say I have to agree, Frank. I'm afraid it's Paris or nothing.'

There was a silence as Brady looked at the photographs spread out before him. Then he sighed with resignation.

'Sure,' he said, 'he's paying the bills.'

'He wants to talk to you about it, Frank,' said Fearnley. 'He feels he's messed you about but he's adamant about reshooting. He wants to buy you dinner tomorrow night at Shabam's.'

'Shabam's! OK, I'll be there.'

Brady replaced the receiver. Shabam's club was the latest hot spot in Manhattan, a town where clubs and restaurants came and went like the tide.

Brady felt tired and drained. He snapped off the lights, opened the balcony windows a fraction and climbed into bed. Within seconds he was asleep.

Frank Brady could not see himself in his dream. He was witnessing scenes as they happened on the opaque screen of his sleeping mind.

He was in the Badlands, inside a partially demolished building. A group of winos and addicts lay around a crackling fire, their faces glowing in its flickering reflections. A slatternly woman of indeterminate age, face caked with dirt and excreta was sitting with her legs apart and her filthy skirts hoisted up over her thighs. She was screaming at the men or at anyone within shouting distance.

'Want some then?' she shrieked, pointing to her stinking groin. 'Want some, you dogs? If you want it, come and get it.'

She cackled insanely. Two men began to fight like animals after a bone. Their faces were a parody of lustful desire. They struggled like ancient stags, lurching and gouging, slavering at the mouth. Another man picked up a rusty knife.

'Who's she calling a dog? I'll tear her liver out.'

He suddenly reverted to the Ivy League accent of his former life.

'I will sacrifice the bitch on the altar of unrequited love,' he shouted.

While the two old winos were rolling around in the dust to the amusement of the other derelicts, the man with the rusty knife leaped at the woman and stabbed her repeatedly. She clawed at him, scratching his face and collapsing in the dust, sobbing. He fell on her, grabbing at his thin penis and trying to feel between her legs. With blood dribbling from her mouth, the woman scrabbled around the ground until she found a loose brick. She heaved it high and rammed it on to the man's head until he fell unconscious in a shower of bloody gristle.

At that moment, Marcia entered the glow of the fire. She was beautiful and statuesque. The derelicts watched her for a moment and then, like a pack of wild dogs, they were upon her. She did nothing to resist but tears rolled down her face as they ripped her clothes off and dug their black and encrusted nails into her perfect flesh. As she was being torn and raped another face appeared fleetingly, superimposed on Marcia's. Angelica stared blindly out at the world, a dead skull, empty and lifeless. The eyes were black sockets and the mouth a slash of red. As Brady watched, helpless in his dream, maggots began to wriggle and squirm inside the eyes.

In a swirling change of image, Brady was now fighting a female demon as she leaped on his prostrate body. Brady felt his resistance ebbing as the woman's body rapidly grew a coat of green and blue scales, her reptilian tongue licking out towards his face.

Swirling around the demon was a wondrous mist of purple light. The demon was trying to break through. The demon was aware.

Brady jumped from the bed, shivering. His eyes shot open. He looked around the bedroom frantically, seeing nothing except shadows. At that moment he knew he was being haunted.

'My God,' he muttered to himself, 'Jesus fucking Christ!'

Chapter Six

The atrium floor of the Media City office was buzzing with activity. Harassed executives ran from office to office. The babble of business conversations ebbed and flowed in a constant flux of deals, contracts, lunch dates and ratings arguments. Maurice Freiberg was happy. He was about to bestow his greatest gift upon his executive team. Maurice Freiberg was going to smile.

This was such a rare occurrence that it could stop producers in their tracks and cause secretaries to pause while sipping coffee. Freiberg was leaning on the balcony rail surveying his empire, gazing down below at the floor of the building where even more executives, producers and, of course, members of the viewing public, scurried like ants beneath his feet.

Johnny watched him from his adjacent office. It was not yet midday and Freiberg was unwrapping a cigar. In a non-smoking world this was tantamount to sacrilege; this was a symbol of power. No one would dare to tell Maurice Freiberg where to stuff his cigar.

A silence descended. Freiberg puffed like a contented elephant. Then he took a deep breath and yelled, 'Last week's show was a world record. We've sold the rights to ten more countries in four days. We've increased our viewing population by six per cent, I said six per cent. The virtuality version is ready for the cybernet. Jack Silverman eat your heart out.'

There was a burst of applause. Freiberg held up his hands.

'And it's down to our man of the moment, a man whose latest fifty-megaton creative idea for the show is guaranteed to make "All the Way" quite simply the most watched television show in the history of the world: Johnny Raine.'

The cheering lasted for a full minute. Johnny stood by his office door in shirtsleeves and black slacks and smiled his crooked smile. Shit, he would have to go through with it now, he thought, Maurice had gone public.

Veronica brought him his mail and coffee.

'Production wants to know about this Badlands deal. I mean, is this real? They want to meet at ten.'

'Fine,' said Johnny, 'I can give them an update.'

'And Mr Freiberg wants to see you right away, I almost forgot.' She teased him with her eyes. 'Oh, and Frank Brady returned your call. Would you like to meet him at Shabam's this evening? He'll be with a client but you could still talk.'

Johnny smiled back and walked across to Maurice Freiberg's office.

'Hey Johnny, come in.' Freiberg was wreathed in cigar smoke. Johnny sat down and waited.

'The city fathers are right behind this Badlands idea,' Freiberg began. 'How's it going?'

'I'm meeting Frank Brady tonight. He's the key. I think he'll play ball.'

'Good, good.' He paused. 'The powers really believe this might do something to prevent Armageddon. It's a long-shot in my opinion, but it's still good television. Production has dreamed up a kind of execution machine, for the ones who don't have their own crazy ideas of how to end it all. It's a bit freaky. I know the show's called "All the Way" but how far do you think we can really go?'

'It's hard to say,' Johnny answered. 'It's difficult to get your mind around the sight of freaks ending it all on TV. Could be a lot of blood and stuff. It's got to be stage-managed. We don't *have* to have a public execution every week and there might be practical problems, like ensuring a supply of willing victims. But an execution machine? Shit! I don't know, Maurice. What about the moral issues? We don't want to become State executioners. There's a press backlash already.'

'I'll handle the press,' said Freiberg. 'It's only a whisper at the moment. Keep 'em guessing, that's the secret. I'll issue a denial, off the record of course. Frankly,' he blew a cloud of cigar smoke into the air, 'it's all a bit sick, don't you think?'

'I thought you were all in favour,' said Johnny.

'Oh I am. Don't get me wrong. But I don't like it, do you?'

'I'm ashamed to say it was my idea.'

'You've got big bucks riding on this one, Johnny. Just close your eyes and your conscience and take the credits.'

'So what's this machine like?' asked Johnny.

'Got an outline drawing here. It's a kind of electronic crucifix. What do you think?'

Freiberg pushed some sheets of cartridge paper across the table. Johnny picked them up and stared at them incredulously.

'I don't believe it,' he said. 'We're really going to kill people on TV with this? And what about the virtuality version? Maybe the whole idea's got out of hand, Maurice. We're in the entertainment business. We're not murderers.'

The line drawing depicted a metal crucifix with a central boom from which a cable with a metal skullcap dangling at the end was suspended.

On one side of the support stanchion was what looked like a clasp-knife blade. Johnny could see the principle. Electric currents would light up the crucifix like a fairground ride, pushing megawatts into the victim's brain. Then they would be beheaded by the giant flick-knife, leaving the head dangling from the central suspension boom.

'We're not dealing with real people, Johnny. These are sick deviants, mutants, killers. Where are their morals? Anyway, morals went out in the last century. Besides,' he leaned forward puffing his cigar and pinned Johnny with his small, colourless and vacant eyes, 'whether it's morally right or not, some people, some very important people, think it might just serve as a warning. And those very important people control your credit rating and, what's even more important, mine. Now, I don't know about you, Johnny, but I like living here. I like the peace and tranquillity. If you don't want to go through with it, kid, you might just find yourself with a one-way ticket to the Bronx.'

Johnny stared at Freiberg in silence. In all the years he had known him, the programme controller had never come even remotely close to making any kind of personal statement or disclosing anything other than superficial information about himself. Johnny now saw him for what he was. Just the same as ninety-nine per cent of Manhattanites – scared. The gloss and style of Manhattan was just skin deep. How far away was total dissolution and destruction? So how did he feel? He thought of Jordan. He thought of heading into the sun on a stratocruiser and never returning. He thought of the photo shoot. The images of the Badlands had stayed with him. It was true what they said about the place. Life was cheap there. But then wasn't life cheap here, but more comfortable.

'Don't worry, Maurice,' he smiled back, 'this is the Johnny Raine show after all.'

The big man visibly relaxed and closed his eyes.

'I'm glad to hear you say that, Johnny. Thanks for stopping by. Good luck with Brady. I guess a lot depends on your persuasive talents, eh?'

Johnny said nothing. He just smiled humourlessly and left, his footfall hushed, almost secret.

A little later he found himself taking a detour through a neighbourhood which used to be known as the Lower East Side. This had been one of the poorest areas of New York, especially the area known as Alphabet City. Now it was sleek and well-heeled. Johnny had been brought up here, his had been one of the few Irish families in the area. He hadn't been back for years. Memories suddenly washed over him; the faces of his mother and father, and the noisy and dangerous days of childhood.

Funny the things you remember, he thought, as he pulled over on an impulse. The sound of his father's voice singing those old songs about days gone by. There was something about those songs, something old and magical. His father's lilting voice sang of love and innocence and horses and Dublin City. And Johnny remembered with pleasure his father's hand ruffling his hair and the smell of him after he had shaved and dried his face with a hot towel.

His mother retained a quiet dignity. She worshipped the two men in her life and the very ground they walked on. She had no particular ambition to do anything other than keep her little family together. It was odd, Johnny thought, seeing that both his parents had been born in an era of female emancipation and independence, that she had preferred the old values. His family had been part of an Irish enclave in the northern part of the neighbourhood, away from the Puerto Rican ghetto. The Irish community had settled in New York over generations and retained a fierce pride in their history and culture. They were more Irish than the Irish themselves.

Johnny had been fifteen when his mother and father were murdered in the riots that preceded the Isolation programme. They had been caught up in the incident known as the siege of Houston Street when over five hundred people had died in a drug-crazed bloodbath.

Luckily, Johnny's father had done fairly well for himself and he was bequeathed enough money to qualify for resident status in the newly formed Free State of Manhattan. He went to live for a time with a friend of the family before striking out on his own as a young journalist on the *Manhattan Monitor*, where his style and wit brought him a degree of success as a columnist.

He sighed deeply and thought about Media City. He had come a long way. His credit rating was healthy but not healthy enough to pay the extortionate rates charged by the foreign-exchange dealers. This was one of the ways stability was enforced within Manhattan. You feared a drop in income because that meant banishment. It was hard to get out because the exchange rate from credits to dollars was artificially controlled. But, then again, people were travelling all over the world on business and pleasure. However, their finances were always controlled by the State. They had to return or face bankruptcy and disgrace in another part of the world when their assets were frozen.

His eyes were moist as he thought again of his parents. He was an only child and it wasn't until he had met and fallen in love with Angelica that he found some kind of emotional self-confidence. He blotted out the memory of her death with well practised mental dexterity. He despised his weakness; the ease with which the inevitable rhythms of self-pity, love and loss rose to a crescendo and swamped him.

But now he had Jordan. And maybe, if he could blot out his deep-seated revulsion at the depths to which he was sinking in the name of entertainment, he would find a way out. The image of the two of them lifting off from Staten Island and heading out into the blue horizon was so tantalizing, so seductive that he forced himself to face what was to come.

First things first however. Tonight he must perform and sell the oddball Frank Brady on the idea, the crazy idea, of persuading the Badland deviants to kill themselves for the masses. Tonight at Shabam's he would only have one chance.

There was a small group of early evening revellers posturing outside Shabam's. The club was situated on the edge of Chinatown and Little Italy in a side street which, pre-Isolation, would have been more than a little dangerous. From the outside it looked nondescript with its mock-Arabian portico and dull green-and-gold canopied entrance. Johnny led Jordan inside, through the waiting group, and they found themselves in a heaving mass of bodies hoping to be admitted. Part of Shabam's attraction was its exclusivity. Johnny shouldered his way through, pulling Jordan in his wake. A few of the unlucky ones who had to wait their turn stared at them spitefully. The huge Arab club manager barred the entrance to the club impassively.

Johnny sidestepped his way to the front and pulled Jordan into his arms. The manager smiled broadly.

'Good evening, Mr Raine,' his voice rumbled like a Cairo drain.

'Good evening, Hadj. May I introduce Jordan Semiramis.'

Hadj regarded Jordan with the eyes of a harem scout. She was, Johnny thought, quite stunning in a simple red dress and black stockings. The dress was cut low to reveal the round swell of her breasts. Her hair had a burnished glow in the half-light. Her oval face was lightly made up and she had chosen a darker shade of lipstick than usual. Tonight she wore her favourite perfume, Sensual by Sammy Chan, and it clearly had the right effect on Hadj. With a gracious bow he moved to one side and opened the door to the warm, dark interior in one movement.

'You grace my humble abode with your presence,' he purred.

Shabam's was designed as a replica of a Babylonian bordello. Dim but warmly lit alcoves lay partly hidden around the perimeter. On a floor above, similar discreet tables offered a view of the dance floor. Scattered around the ground floor were enormous cushions and low tables. Burning brands cast flames and shadows across the club. Guests were sprawled on cushions or crammed around the small bar at the back.

On a small stage a tall Nubian dancer writhed erotically. Behind her a band beat out a hypnotic Middle Eastern rhythm.

It took a few moments for Johnny to locate Brady. The photographer was sitting with Fearnley, Wilson and Dubois. He was wearing a black silk loose-fitting suit with ornate motifs decorating the lapels. The others were near drunk and groping a gaggle of girls hired for the night. Brady looked around, spotted Johnny and Jordan, let his gaze remain for a moment then turned his attention back to the others. A waiter led Johnny and Jordan to a table nearby. Johnny ordered champagne and smiled at Jordan who was gazing around, drinking in the atmosphere.

Fearnley had his hand on Brady's arm.

'Glad you could make it, Frank,' he chuckled. The three girls were starting to earn their fee. Their hands began tracing patterns along the men's thighs. Wilson was breathing heavily. Dubois watched him, then gently removed a soft hand from his groin and whispered something to the girl before turning his attention to Frank Brady.

'I am sorry we have not had a chance to meet properly, Mr Brady. May I say your work is quite wonderful, quite wonderful. As you know, I have taken the decision to reshoot. The death of that poor girl. It was tragic. I am afraid that whenever I looked at those photographs in the press it would bring it all back. I am sorry. I think a trip to Paris is a little compensation, yes?'

'It was an accident, Louis,' said Brady, 'and yes, Paris would be great. It's been a long time.'

'Some people say accidents never happen, Mr Brady,' smiled the Frenchman.

'Maybe if we weren't so three dimensional,' Brady replied.

'For Chrissake, Frank,' slurred Fearnley, 'we're here to have a good time, not listen to all your paranormal mumbo-jumbo.'

'Existence,' shouted Wilson suddenly.

'Oh Jesus, we've set him off,' said Fearnley.

'What is existence?' repeated Wilson. One of the girls had wriggled her fingers inside his fly.

'I dunno,' she said seriously, pausing briefly, 'but it's fun while it lasts.'

'Existence is about perfection,' said Brady as more drinks arrived.

'Talking about perfection, get a load of that,' gasped Fearnley.

Johnny and Jordan were dancing in the flickering light of the flames. Brady followed Fearnley's gaze and his eyes were held fast by Jordan. She glanced over at him and an invisible electrical charge sizzled between them. The music stopped and Johnny led Jordan back to their table. He smiled at Brady on the way and raised his shoulders questioningly. At that moment, the band struck up a powerful raga. Jordan let go of Johnny's hand and walked backwards on to the dance floor.

Jordan began to dance. Other dancers on the floor stopped to watch, then withdrew, leaving the space to her. Johnny was gazing at her in astonished admiration. Brady was transfixed. Jordan's eyes were glazed as she let her body move and ripple with barely controlled abandon. A hush descended upon the club. Waiters paused and were staring.

At that moment, with Jordan dancing sinuously in front of him, Johnny fell into the grip of an illusion.

He was standing alone within an arid, barren landscape. Drifting towards him, merging with puffs of wind-blown sand, shimmered a deep-purple curtain.

He heard Marek Grohmann's voice then, replaying the words he had spoken when Johnny had gone under during his final session with the benign therapist.

'Mr Raine,' came Grohmann's softly modulated baritone. 'There are places rarely visited by any of us. They are, however, only an eye-blink away from our waking state. They are the gateways to spiritual adventure, and great psychic danger. No one can predict the outcome of venturing through the window of chaos. A warning. The highway is a two-way lane. Entities lurking beyond the abyss may sense a human presence. Be careful . . . be careful!'

Johnny's temperature plummeted as he became enveloped in the purple astral gauze. Fears from countless previous existences swept through him. Swirling visions, avatars of the spirit, perceived him. He saw the eyes of indescribable beasts, heard the buzzing, insect-like rasp of vampyric creatures from beyond the void. His spirit was dwarfed by the confrontations. His individuality could be assimilated at any moment.

Then he saw the demon. That was the only word to describe the phantom which appeared before him out of the fabric of the void. It had an arachnid appearance but an almost human demeanour. It had seen him, sensed him, explored his soul with the speed of a laser. The demon, he knew, desired sentience, true human awareness. He knew, as Grohmann had told him, that some entities were inextricably linked to human life; bound by a psychic chain.

Grohmann's voice was calling him urgently, insistently. He was held by the eyes of the demon. The creature exuded a hypnotic fascination. Johnny knew the demon would never leave him. It was searching for a way through but had not yet reached a fraction of its potential power.

With the snap of an elastic band breaking, he was back in the nightclub. His blood tingled from the impact of the experience. Jordan was approaching amid thunderous applause. He glanced over and saw Brady watching him. The photographer was tight-lipped, seemingly carved out of the very atmosphere. Had he also experienced the vision?

'They would like us to join them,' Jordan said to him. She touched him on the shoulder. 'Are you all right? You look as if you've seen a ghost.'

'What? Yes, I'm OK,' he managed to garble as he stood up. his clothes clung to his body, glued by perspiration. He took Jordan's arm and they made their way across to join Dubois.

Brady looked up and saw that Johnny and Jordan had joined the group. Dubois kissed Jordan's hand.

'Your dancing would set all Paris alight my dear,' he crooned, then turned to Johnny. 'You're a lucky man, monsieur.'

'Love your show, Raine,' slurred Wilson.

Fearnley then refilled everyone's glass and raised his in a wordless toast. Everyone drank. Wilson belched and farted noisily.

Johnny turned to Brady who had paled under his slight tan. He looked unwell.

'You OK, Frank?' he enquired.

'Don't worry about me, mate,' said Brady. 'You want to worry about yourself if you intend to go over the river.'

Johnny had recovered sufficiently to force himself to remember why he was there.

'Will you take me? Will you help me find the ones we want? Will they go all the way? This could be the ultimate show – live suicide with ceremony.'

'Some of them die for death style,' said Brady. 'The more style and grace they exhibit when they croak, the bigger their legend.'

'That's it,' said Johnny excitedly, 'that's what I want. I have to get some of them on the show. What do you think? Is it possible?'

'Can you go all the way, Raine? If this goes wrong you could end up on a spit. They say roast TV star is a rare delicacy.'

'Then you'll do it. When do we go?'

'Leave it to me. But, I warn you, if anything goes wrong you're on your own. I'll save my hairy ass before yours any day of the week. Do you understand that, matey?'

'I understand perfectly,' said Johnny. But there was a chill in his voice.

Brady and Jordan locked eyes again. Johnny had the sudden and empty feeling of being excluded from a higher form of communication. His sharp jealousy produced an immediate and startling erection. His stomach felt weak and his mouth tasted of dry ash. Finally he forced himself to speak. 'When do we go?' he asked Brady.

Without taking his eyes from Jordan, Brady replied languidly, 'Soon. Things have to be arranged. By the way, you better make sure you bring plenty of dollar bills and get yourself some body armour and a weapon. I can't make any promises but I'll get the word out before we go in. If there are any takers, they'll find us.'

Fearnley and Wilson had sunk deep into the sumptuous cushions with two of the girls. Dubois still held his free gift at arm's length as she tried to stimulate his interest. He cleared his throat and addressed Brady.

'It will take a little time to arrange the next shoot, Mr Brady.'

'Frank, call me Frank,' said Brady.

'OK, Frank. I will instruct the agency in due course. Maybe not the same agency, you understand. Meanwhile, do you wish to partake?' Dubois indicated the girl. Brady shook his head. Johnny chose this moment to take Jordan's arm.

'We'd better be going. Wouldn't mind an early night,' Johnny smiled at Brady. Jordan looked at Johnny oddly as if about to object but then complied, allowing herself to be escorted from the table.

'Have a good night,' he laughed.

Johnny felt as though he had been treated like a naughty schoolboy but could not figure out how Brady had done it. He put his arm around Jordan and kissed her ear lobe as they walked across the floor. Soon they were outside in the cool evening and heading for the sleek electro-turbo.

As soon as they had gone, Brady stood up and patted Dubois on the shoulder.

'Thanks for a great evening, Louis. Let's have a civilized evening together soon, eh mate?'

Brady looked pale. He dabbed his forehead with a handkerchief and hurried from the floor. Just as he reached the lobby a drunken couple lurched into him. The woman snarled instinctively.

'Hey, watch where you're ... Frank! Frank baby! It's me. Dolores. Just say the word and I'll dump the sap.'

'Hello, Dolores. Not tonight, all right? I've got a headache.'

'I just love the way you talk, Frank.'

Brady patted the front of her dress between her legs.

'Keep it warm for me, Dolly. A man can't live on memories alone.'

The heavy-set guy hanging on to her arm shoved his face into Brady's.

'OK, Romeo, keep your stinkin' hands to yourself or I'll squeeze your lemon till the juice runs,' he rasped.

'Relax, Lucky,' said Dolores, 'this is an old friend of mine.'

Lucky grabbed Brady by the lapels.

'Take your hands off the tailoring, pasta brain,' snarled Brady.

Lucky snorted. 'I'm gonna twist your fucking balls off.'

'Hey, Lucky,' said Brady, 'have you ever heard of a Liverpool kiss?'

'A what?' slurred Lucky.

'Pucker up!' ordered Brady as he slammed his forehead into the drunk's nose. Lucky shot backwards straight into the powerful arms of Hadj. Brady shrugged, kissed Dolores on the cheek and ran out of the club.

Outside, Brady looked around. Then he saw them emerge at the end of the block. He ran to his own coupé, panting now, fumbling with his remote. In seconds he was following Johnny's rear lights along Broadway.

Brady had no idea why he was following them. He was acting on a impulse which he was powerless to resist. As he drove, he sang quietly under his breath, an old Liverpool folksong.

The big ship sails on the alley, alley-o,
The alley, alley-o, the alley, alley-o.
The big ship sails on the alley, alley-o,
On the fifth day of November.

Brady followed them to a wide, half-full parking area. Johnny had parked near a clump of trees at the edge of the lot. Brady rolled forward reaching into his glove compartment and picking up his mini-Mitsuki with light-enhancing lens. Brady was excited. He was sweating and nervous as he checked the camera and slipped quietly out of the car. The air felt cool against his skin as the professional photographer in him took over and he crept silently between the parked-up vehicles and Johnny's electro-turbo. There was a hint of a moon passing through night clouds and, on a ridge above the car park, a string of street-lights enabled Brady to make out the two figures in the car. He could see Jordan clearly now. Johnny had taken her dress off and was caressing her breasts. They were almost in silhouette. Brady was breathing deeply and, with a shock, noticed his hands were trembling. He moved slowly forward, training the lens on the rear window.

They were making love. Brady felt a wash of emotion, part jealousy, part fascination, as he reeled off a series of pictures. He thought of Jordan.

'Who are you?' he whispered hoarsely to himself. 'Who the hell are you?'

Chapter Seven

Johnny heard nothing from Frank Brady for nearly a week. He had resisted the impulse to call him, even though he was under pressure from the network to get things moving on the new show quickly.

Johnny felt he was being put under a little too much pressure and was privately startled at the speed with which the idea had caught hold of the production team. The prospect of real death and rivers of blood on the studio floor did not appear to bother them in the slightest. Lloyd, the producer who had been with the show for the last two years, was even discussing ways in which the freaks could rehearse their final departure from this life so as to extract the maximum drama from the spectacular event. Johnny's brief trip to the Badlands had taught him one thing. The network had no idea what it was letting itself in for. It might prove impossible even to communicate with the Badland freaks. Mind you, he thought to himself, it was hard to have sympathy for some of the broken human beings he had seen there. If they wanted to take their own lives voluntarily, then why shouldn't they? It sounded fine put like that. But still something nagged at Johnny's conscience. He kept asking himself why he didn't feel more strongly about the whole thing and refuse to do it. He could just walk out now. But the lure of the big credit bonanza and the shadow of powers behind the scenes pulling Maurice Freiberg's strings focused his mind. He would go through with it just one time.

He was growing more certain day by day that Jordan was right. It was time to get out before he ended up believing his own public image. Johnny was smart enough to know that if the media-web could make you it could also break you. There was a whole world out there, even though large tracts of it had followed the Manhattan example and enforced a policy of isolation. However, only Los Angeles could now compare with the Big Apple in the extent of the separation of rich and poor. Other cities he had heard about, like London, Rome, Madrid, Berlin and Moscow, had enforced a kind of half-baked isolation based on economic exclusion, harassment and massive private police forces. But the belief was that they too would go all the way to complete isolation of the wealthy.

If Frank Brady had kept Johnny waiting it was not because the presenter was not on his mind. He had already made contact with Bolero and the word was spreading through the tentacle-like communications network on the other side of the river. But he had something else to dwell on. His fascination with Jordan Semiramis was growing. It was not just that he wanted to go to bed with her. In fact, that was not the basis of the attraction. True, he felt a healthy lust for her body, but who wouldn't? He felt mildly jealous of Johnny Raine and was deeply interested in the ironic synchronicity of the situation. That was not it either. Since the moment he had met Raine and Jordan beneath the crane he had found himself compelled, almost directed, to think about the past. It was unlike him to be nostalgic. Living for the moment was good enough for Frank Brady. But, despite his best endeavours, images of life in Liverpool came flooding back.

His family had been poor and young Frank had grown up with a healthy respect for his father's right hook. He was the middle one of five children and went hungry more often than he could remember. England had lost everything, all its world status, and had spiralled down to become a Third World nation, living on its heritage. The rich had deserted the country in droves. Even the monarchy had decamped to Switzerland. The only bright spot in Frank's life had been Liverpool Football Club. After seasons in the doldrums they had made a comeback. The Reds had inspired and sustained him.

When he was seventeen he joined the merchant navy and this proved to be the pivotal and liberating event of his life. He suddenly realized that the world as seen on the media was just a pallid imitation of the real thing. His rakish good looks got him into a lot of trouble, especially with irate husbands. If there was one thing certain in Frank Brady's life it was that trouble, in various shapes and guises, was never far away.

Brady loaded two compact Mitsukis and prowled around his apartment, letting the images of the past flood into his mind unimpeded. In the merchant navy he had travelled the world for many years. Several times he left the sea and tried his hand at various jobs but he always returned to the ocean and the tides. Only the permanently distant horizon was able to capture the promise and magic of his deepest desires.

Alternative quasi-religious movements had abounded at that time. Brady became fascinated by many of them but began to take a serious interest in Buddhism. This led indirectly to an interest in magic and the occult. He became involved with a number of magical societies and was initiated into several, coming under the influence of a number of practising magicians. But something about these practices and the powers that could be obtained as a result unnerved him. He was too wild a spirit to conform to any kind of rigid religious or magical discipline. One of his gurus had told him that his time would come. He had to work out of his life the powerful impulses that drove him but that he would, eventually, reveal within himself true magical powers.

Brady didn't know if he believed all that. When he first came to New York the Isolation was just beginning to gather momentum. He had always been interested in photography and had kept a folio of work from his days at sea. He showed this to one of the city's leading advertising agencies and they saw him as a breath of fresh air. His work was exciting and different. The first assignments were modest but his work was unusual. It proved to be just the kind of approach the advertising business needed. Everything had become predictable. Within a short space of time Brady had become one of the most sought-after photographers in the city. He had found it all incredibly easy. In Manhattan then, as now, imagination and flair had all but disappeared. He was a hit. Brady loved it all, the parties, the women, mingling with the rich and famous. And they loved this wild Englishman with the funny accent and the disturbing habit of showing little respect for anything or anyone.

Brady shook his head as if to erase the memories. He was smart enough to know when something unusual or karmic was taking place. He knew his mounting obsession with Jordan was significant in some way. He also knew he had no choice but to obey the demands the obsession was making of him.

He had done his homework meticulously. He had studied the location of Jordan's sixth-floor apartment carefully and rented a room directly opposite, with a view straight in through her balcony windows. He had checked out her career and discovered she was a sought-after programmer, particularly in the financial markets. She worked from home, had one sister who lived in Canada with her mother. Her father had died several years before. She jogged every day in the park and took dance and aerobics classes. She had many acquaintances, some influential clients in the financial sector, but few real friends. She had met Johnny Raine six months ago and it looked like something serious was developing. Raine attracted women, no question, but since his wife's death he had become something of a sexual recluse. Brady knew all about Angelica, of course; she was one woman who had been oblivious to his own dangerous charm. Jordan was the first woman Raine had been with in the last two years, despite the Media City hype. Brady had checked Jordan's HIV record and it was clean. He had a special relationship with the Manhattan medical records department, and especially the mortuary division, ever since he had photographed an anti-AIDS commercial in the midst of a hundred corpses. He had developed a little business enterprise with one of the attendants, a man named Fredericks. Shurm was one of the chemical cocktails used in the embalming process. Doctored with formaldehyde, it had become the favourite drug of the new generation when mixed with cocaine. When mixed with rage, the more powerful crack derivative, it took the mind to universes totally unknown to mankind. What it did to the body could be seen all over the Badlands.

Brady left his apartment and crossed towards Central Park close to the Metropolitan Museum. He knew that this was where Jordan began her daily jogging circuit. He checked his watch. It was just before 10 a.m. Hurrying into the park he kept to the shaded tree-lined path that started by the gate. The Spring weather had brought Manhattanites out in droves. Brady smiled as he checked his cameras and began to jog slowly across the grass. In his light-maroon jogging suit he was one of hundreds of figures crisscrossing the park at that moment. He paused by an oak, leaned against it and trained his lens on the gate. He didn't have to wait long before he saw her. For a second his heart stopped. She wore a pair of yellow shorts, a green T-shirt, and deluxe iso-trainers worn without socks. Even from here her legs looked long, slim and nicely muscled. Brady appreciated her beauty like a professional wine taster appreciates an exceptional vintage. Shit, Brady swore to himself, she's not alone.

Jordan and a friend chatted for a while as they ran along the path. Then, with a wave, the friend veered off to the right, leaving Jordan alone. Head up into the sunshine, she kept an even pace, going straight across the grass towards the centre of the park. She had no idea that a pair of hungry eyes was watching or that her face and body were being committed to high-performance silicon laser cells.

Brady tracked Jordan through the park, dodging other joggers, horses and screaming children chasing long-legged dogs. He picked his spot ahead and lay in wait.

When she was halfway round her circuit, Brady left her and jogged back to Fifth Avenue and headed towards Lexington. Sweating with exertion and an excitement he had not felt in years, he ran to the room he had rented, ripped off his clothes and threw himself under an icily cold shower. Shivering, he dressed in a shirt and slacks, swept his wet hair back with his fingers and crossed to the camera and tripod by the window.

There she was, panting, sweat-stained, pausing to buy a newsvid and a doughnut. Brady caught her in mid-pose. She disappeared into the building and Brady focused on the apartment. The 1.7 light-enhancing Fuji lens he was using cut through the dimness of the interior. Lucky the windows are wide, he thought, I can cover most of the apartment.

Through the viewfinder Brady saw her enter, chewing her doughnut and yanking off her clothes. She was naked in seconds. For a while she just stood there finishing her doughnut. Her body glistened with sweat and so did Brady's trigger finger as he exposed her repeatedly. He got some excellent close-shots here and, as she turned, he recorded every aspect of her body.

When she went to take a shower, Brady called it a day. There would be other times. He had not finished with Jordan Semiramis yet.

For days, Brady followed Jordan to her dance class, photographing her through the windows, drinking coffee with friends, meeting Johnny, shopping in a nearby mall.

After each expedition Brady would spend hours in his darkroom. He worked feverishly, with a passion that surprised him. He prepared a number of giant enlargements and a host of life-size blow-ups of particular shots. His darkroom was littered with photographs of Jordan. He made montages from many of them, carefully tidying up the snipped-off pieces.

He was preparing his sanctum. Soon it would be ready. The room he used for viewing had been cleared. This was his magical room. Sometimes he carried out certain necromantic rites here. All of his occult paraphernalia was stored in a locked room at the end. The viewing gallery itself was the largest room in the apartment. It was simple, painted white and unfurnished, except for one padded swivel chair placed in the centre.

Brady was now ready. He meditated for an hour, naked, facing east. Then he massaged his body with aromatic oils, slipped a mildly hallucinogenic tablet into his mouth and washed it down with a glass of vintage Krug. Carrying the champagne and glass he entered the sanctum.

He walked slowly and reverently to the centre of the room and sat in the chair. From here he could see his creation. Every inch of wall and ceiling space had been plastered with photographs of Jordan. Her face, her body, her multitude of expressions, her poses, all had been caught and transformed into a photographic altar of worship. Brady gazed at the images until his head began to swim. Slowly, he spun around in his chair, sipping champagne, sometimes muttering seemingly unrelated phrases, sometimes singing a snatch of a song.

He moved on to a higher plane and he felt himself to be actually inside this woman. This was infinitely more satisfying than sex, he thought as he kept himself turning and turning in a slow dervish spin. Images flickered into his mind like tongues of flame, often before his observing mind could catch hold of them. Perhaps they were glimpses of other lives, he remembered thinking, yes, perhaps they were. The woman known as Jordan and he had a kind of spiritual bond. He was sure of that now. More than that he could not deduce. He was not in a state where rational thought was possible. He believed that he truly possessed her in a much more intimate way than mere physical bonding. He was in touch with her and he knew it would only be a matter of time before she would sense that. What would happen then, he did not know.

Grohmann's words came to him again and a shiver shimmied down to base of his spine. 'The Purple Zone, Mr Brady, few ever enter the Purple Zone. It is the place of mind-sleep which slips past your consciousness before you are aware of its existence. And so it has no existence, for most people. It is the wellspring of your obsession and of all your obsessions. You have been touched by the tentacle of an entity reaching out from the abyss and the vale of sleep. It imbues you with creative power and heightened instincts. It could also claim you for its own. It must not breach your defences, Mr Brady. It must not.'

He stopped spinning and allowed himself to come back into the world. He poured more champagne and sipped it contemplatively.

What was happening? Some kind of force was present, working in the subterranean world of thought and perception. It was useless to try and guess what it was or what its intentions were. He just knew it was connected with Jordan.

One thing was certain. Whatever was happening, it was not by chance. And it would not stop. Like a leaf in the wind he was being swept along some cosmic highway. And so was the woman, and so also was the other actor in this play, Johnny Raine.

Brady shook his head. He was trembling very slightly. He was cold now and tired. He poured the last of the champagne and stood up, swaying. As he left the room he thought he could feel a presence behind him. Perhaps it's just a residue of my heightened state, he said to himself. Then he started to sing under his breath.

The big ship sails on the alley, alley-o,
The alley, alley-o, the alley, alley-o.

Then, very slowly, he punched Johnny Raine's number into the vidi-phone dial.

Chapter Eight

From street level, the top two floors of the Media City building resembled a spectacular Christmas cake. Chains of coloured lights had been festooned around the building. The roof was ablaze with splendour and the shifting silhouettes of giant shadows cast by the heaving, dancing guests could be seen reflected on the facade of the building opposite.

Two off-duty Zone Police guards were settling down to their second beer of the evening at Felice's. Madison Avenue was quiet except for the stimulation bars and bistros that littered the area.

'Must be having quite a party,' one of the guards remarked, wiping foam from his lips.

'Yeah,' muttered his buddy. 'How the other half live, eh Mike?'

'I like that Johnny Raine show, I've got to admit,' said Mike, draining his beer and signalling to Felice for a couple more.

'He comes in here, you know,' said Felice as he brought over the beers. 'In fact he was in here just the other day.'

'He's all right I guess,' admitted Jack.

'You're just old-fashioned, eh Jack?' Mike smiled up at Felice and winked. 'He likes reading books and stuff like that.'

'And what's wrong with that?' Jack retorted. 'It would do you good to read a few books. Might improve your vocabulary.'

Mike laughed. 'There's nothing wrong with my vocabulary that a good woman wouldn't cure, eh Felice?'

'I tried reading once,' said the Spaniard, 'but it took so long I gave up. My kids read though. They love books. They used to be hooked on virtuality, but since they started to grow up they've had their heads buried in books.'

Jack gazed up at the glowing building two blocks up the road. Music was drifting down from the roof, blending with the early evening voices on the street and the laughter from the stimu-bar nearby.

'I was just saying that in spite of everything there are still the haves and the have-nots. And we, my friends, are in the latter category.'

'We don't do so bad. Count yourself lucky you can afford to live here. You know the alternatives,' Mike reminded his friend.

'Is it really as bad as they say over there?' enquired Felice.

'Worse,' said Mike, 'don't ask.'

'We're too close to it all, see,' said Jack, 'and there's no way out for us. We're just like slaves, do you know that? Think about it. We can't afford to get out of here because we don't get paid in hard currency and we certainly won't get a better paid job, so we're stuck here.'

'Come on, we could leave any time we wanted. All you do is pack your grip and head for the heliport, then out to Staten Island airport and off into the sunset. OK, so you'd be as good as broke unless you knew how to salt away some currency but you could survive.'

'They tell me hard currency will soon be history,' said Felice, bringing over a plate of olives for the two guards.

'Could be,' said Jack, 'that's why we should be getting out fast. If only we could. Oh, you can get hard currency all right but only if you're going on a trip or a vacation, and they still call the shots. The State of Manhattan needs us, that's what they keep saying. So, as I said, it's all right for them dancing on the roof. What troubles do they have? They're all worth millicredits. They probably crap diamonds.'

He gazed up at the Media City party just as the fireworks went up. In an instant the sky was transformed into a rainbow of fiery lights as rockets burst one upon the other in a fabulous display of pyrotechnics.

The two guards could hear the laughter drifting down on the back of the soft music. Jack shook his head and signalled Felice to line up two more beers.

The party was in full swing. About two hundred guests had crammed into the atrium and roof of Media City. Channel Boom

Boom hosted the best parties in Manhattan. The party was in honour of the company's newest star, whose new series had recently broken viewing records for romantic drama. Like many of the actors and actresses, stars and hopefuls who worked on the three major channels, Sapphire O'Hara rarely left the confines of Manhattan, except to holiday in Bermuda or on the privately owned island of Cuba.

She was a stunning beauty, there was no doubt about that, Johnny thought as he mingled with the glittering crowd. Her black curls cascaded over her pure white shoulders, and she was tall and elegant with the kind of voice that insinuated its way into your subconscious. She was the centre of attention tonight. The usual Manhattan mix of media operators, financial whiz-kids and just plain rich were clamouring to get close to her. Fame had come suddenly to Sapphire and reputedly she had broken records for the number of beds she had graced to get her big break. Her little-girl charm was so convincing you could almost believe every word she uttered. Johnny rescued a glass of champagne from a passing waiter and waved across the room at Jordan. She ran Sapphire a close second and, for him, no other woman in the room really existed.

Jordan was locked into a bunch of financial types, mostly clients of hers. Johnny accepted that at a function like this she had her own social milieu to massage and charm. They had agreed they would not make a big deal out of their relationship. Only a few close friends here tonight knew about them. They were happy to keep it that way. Still, he could not prevent a shiver of jealousy at the sight of her dancing with a tall, blond, good-looking man whose hands could not resist wandering over her body. Jordan coolly managed to avoid any extremes of groping. He was clearly getting drunk and horny.

Maurice Freiberg presided over the affair like a media sheik, always making sure that Media City big shots like Frank Barolo and Mike Riley were introduced to the prettiest women in the room.

Most of the women, and the men come to that, were ambitious social robots, devoid of any real understanding of life. They were the products of the money machine and were dedicated to only one thing, their own survival in as much opulence as could be won, stolen, earned or screwed for.

Johnny was leaning on the roof balcony, looking pensively over Manhattan but finding his gaze drawn repeatedly to the darkness across the river where pinpoints of light were the only evidence of habitation. He had prised himself away from the usual clutch of admirers to grab a few moments alone.

'Penny for them?' said a deep husky voice.

Johnny turned and found himself looking into the limpid eyes of Pandora Yamani, one of Manhattan's highest-paid women executives, head of the Praxis Corporation, a global pharmaceutical conglomerate. She was in her mid-thirties, not too tall but attractive. Johnny knew she was on her fourth husband. None of them had lasted long. When her last spouse was found in bed with a young ZeePee guard he had been despatched without ceremony. Liking a bit of rough was one thing, but getting caught was unforgivable.

'What's going on in that mind of yours, Johnny?' she laughed. 'Thinking about your next victim?'

'Pandora, how lovely to see you.' Johnny kissed her cheek and was slightly surprised when she turned her head and brushed his lips with hers. 'No, nothing like that. Just dreaming.''

'Shame on you. A man like you should never have time to dream.' She breathed champagne fumes softly into his face. 'Unless it's about me. This town is getting so boring and predictable, don't you think? That's why your show is so successful. Everything else is so false and so artificial.'

'Don't kid yourself. It's just mind seduction.' Johnny smiled at her, then glanced over her shoulder to find Jordan. He suddenly felt Pandora's warm palm on his bulge. Against his will it started to swell.

'Pandora, I don't think this is a good idea,' he said.

'Darling, it's a wonderful idea. I've always thought you must have a lovely dick. And let me tell you, darling, I've seen a few.'

Johnny felt a wave of relief as Pandora's husband emerged from the crowd. He was a tight-suited banker with iron-grey hair and an embezzler's smile. He looked at Johnny coldly, then said to his wife, 'There you are, darling. I've been looking all over for you and here you are. Having a good time?'

'Oh yes, it's not so hard,' she replied, stepping back.

Johnny made an excuse then slipped away. Pandora watched him go with amused regret.

For the next hour Johnny made small talk with a sea of faces. He managed to dance with Jordan once. He stepped on her toe and she laughed. Then she was whisked away by a short, dark, currency dealer.

One of the board, Doug Newman, slapped him on the back.

'Johnny,' he said lowering his voice, 'I hear you're making progress on our special project.'

'Could be, Doug,' Johnny told him, 'I had a call tonight. Looks like tomorrow night's the night. I'm going in. It's pretty scary you know.'

'I can imagine,' said Newman sagely, 'but you'll take adequate precautions I trust?'

'You bet, I want to get back in one piece.'

Newman was shepherded away by Freiberg and then Johnny was buttonholed by Alex Hamlisch of the *Manhattan Times*. In the centre of the room, Sapphire O'Hara was dancing with Freiberg, shimmying up against him sexily. That bitch will go far, Johnny mused to himself, then paid attention to Hamlisch. The journalist was slightly unkempt with a prominent nose and thin, sandy hair.

'Quite a turnout.' He smiled up at Johnny.

'The usual. You've been to most Manhattan functions, Alex, you know what they're like.'

'Listen, Johnny, there's a whisper going round. I was at Trixie Levy's party recently and someone, not very far from here, was dropping some very big hints about a new twist to the show. Care to comment?'

'Alex, shame on you. You should know better than to believe the drunken ravings of someone not very far from here. Let's just say we're always looking for ways to keep the show fresh or else it dies. But why change a winning formula?'

'The word suicide was mentioned, Johnny.' Hamlisch licked his lips and sipped his martini with obvious relish.

'You'll have to speak to Maurice about that, Alex. What do you think the great viewing public would think about seeing people taking their lives on television?'

'I think your ratings would go right off the scale. You'd have the church, the government and every freak from here to the West Coast fighting to praise you or damn you. If it's true, let's hope you're big enough to cope with the ructions.'

'Look, Alex, if you'll excuse me there's someone I must see.'

Hamlisch watched him cross the room with a look of wry amusement on his face.

Johnny rescued Jordan from the clutches of the blond guy who, by now, was having difficulty standing. She looked relieved, but her escort began to shape up. His friends held his arms as he swayed in front of Johnny. Almost unnoticed two very large men appeared by the blond man's side and took hold of him. His feet were lifted off the ground by a fraction, enough to make his passage to the door that much easier.

'Thanks,' said Jordan, 'that was getting a little fraught.'

'You OK?'

'I think so. Listen, I've been talking to Bob Stein, he's over at Lazarus's. He says a lot of people are thinking about getting out. It's all hush-hush. No one knows a thing till you're gone.'

'And?' said Johnny.

'Well, it seems the best deal around is four to one, credits to currency, in London.'

'London!'

'Ssh! Four to one is not bad. It just shows that, if there is a market for something, someone, somewhere, will provide it.'

'Last I heard, the exchange deals were running at more like twenty or thirty to one,' Johnny said.

'Well, things are changing.'

'I'll still have to go through with the show. I can't back out now. My deal says I get two million. The truth is, I don't know if we can get even one show together. By the way, I'm going in tomorrow night with Brady.'

Jordan clutched his arm and swayed slightly. She stared at Johnny with unusual intensity.

'Don't go, darling, please. Look, I know what I said but let's get away now. I've had a premonition. I don't know. I feel strange.'

'You look terrible. It's the heat and the drink.'

'No, I've only had a couple of drinks.' She paused. 'Why you? Why do you have to go? Can't they send someone else?'

Johnny looked at her fondly. 'You really do care, don't you?'

'Isn't that obvious?' She leaned against him.

'I have to go because I'm the face they'll recognize,' he told her.

'Aren't you scared? Once was enough for me.' The colour was draining from her face as she spoke.

'I'm terrified. All my instincts tell me not to go. But . . .'

'He's challenging you, isn't he?' Jordan murmured weakly.

'That's got nothing to do with it. Hey, come on, I'm getting you out of here.'

Jordan's eyes rolled upwards and she fell into Johnny's arms. A few people nearby smiled. He put his arm around her waist and began to dance her towards the door. As they reached it she began to recover. Her pallor glistened with beads of sweat. Johnny helped her to a nearby office and got her into a swivel chair. He opened the window and let the cool night air flow in. A breeze rustled papers on the desk. Jordan was only half conscious. Johnny patted her cheeks and called her name softly but urgently. He had never seen her like this before. She had never been even the slightest bit ill since he had known her. Gradually she began to come round. She looked washed-out.

'I'm going to take you home, all right?' He was stroking her hand, trying to coax her back to normal. He picked up the vidiphone and tapped in the number of the company's cab service, giving his name to the operator. Then he tried to get Jordan to stand. She managed to get to her feet but swayed into his arms.

'Sorry,' she said weakly, 'I don't know what came over me. I felt suddenly drained. It was like something had pulled the plug on me. Take me home.'

'Of course,' said Johnny, 'that's just where we're going.'

A thin voice spoke from the doorway.

'Early night, eh Johnny? Is there a story here for the social page?'

Hamlisch was leaning against the office door arrogantly. Johnny glared at him.

'Fuck you, Alex. I'm taking Ms Semiramis home, that's all.'

'You don't have to explain anything to me. You don't have a reputation to keep up. Thing is, Johnny, no one knows who you've been screwing these last few years. You know you can't believe the Media City press vids. No one believes you've been celibate, they couldn't even spell it. The social page would love to know.'

Johnny took a step towards the reporter but Jordan restrained him.

'I'm feeling a little better now, thank you.'

Johnny put his arm around her while Hamlisch retreated back to the party, winking at Johnny as he went.

'Sweet dreams,' he chuckled.

'You can stay if you want,' Jordan said. 'I don't mind. I'll be OK on my own. In fact, I'd rather not see you until you get back. You will come back, won't you Johnny?'

'Nothing will stop me, believe me.' He held her close to him for a moment. 'Now, that's enough talk about premonitions. I'll be OK.'

Jordan was tempted then to tell him about her nightmare. Its imagery had left an indelible mark. She was terrified she was going to re-visit that room and experience the feeling of unmitigated terror that the locked door evoked in her.

They emerged at street level near Madison Square Park. The evening was cool and the street-lights cast a warm glow along the sidewalk and the rows of flowerbeds that lined the avenue for miles. There was the usual Manhattan crowd, quite sparse in the early evening, promenading in style or emerging from electro-cabs. Music from the Media City party gave the scene an almost poetic atmosphere. If Lautrec could have painted the future this is what he would have painted.

Johnny noticed a tight group of men wearing tuxedos standing on the corner of East 26th Street. Among them he recognized the blond financier who had been ejected from the party earlier. Presumably his friends were attempting to sober him up.

An electro-cab stood waiting. Johnny began to lead Jordan to the door but she held back.

'Let's walk home. It's not far and it'll do me good.'

'Sure.' Johnny smiled and dismissed the cab.

He took her arm and began to cross towards the small, envelope-sized park with a tiny waterfall in the centre.

Down the avenue, about a block away, the two off-duty ZeePees had left Felice's after quite a few beers and several helpings of pasta. Neither was drunk but they'd had enough to see rainbows above the Media City building. They were looking for an electro-cab to take them back to their wives waiting in the new precinct conurbation of Harlem, known in the city as the ZeePeedrome.

They were approaching the corner of East 26th Street when they noticed a tall blond man arguing with three or four others. He was clearly drunk and looking for trouble. All the guys were smartly dressed and had probably been at the Media City hoolee. Mike noticed a couple walking on the other side of the street by the park. The man also was smartly dressed in a tuxedo. He had his arm around the woman's shoulders. They were obviously lovers.

The occasional electro-cab or turbo cruised by, otherwise traffic was light. A few people were strolling down the avenue. East 26th Street itself was almost deserted but well lit all the way to the river.

Mike nudged Jack as they reached the corner and smiled. The blond drunk had shrugged off the protestations of his friends and staggered into the centre of the street. His tie was askew and his clothes were stained. He looked wild and angry.

'Think we'd better call the State cops. This is not our jurisdiction,' Mike remarked.

'Maybe, let's just see what happens,' replied his partner.

The blond man stood swaying in the middle of the street, staring and pointing at the couple across the avenue.

'Hey, Raine,' the blond screamed, 'hey, bigshot media man. Get your ass over here before I come over after you. I'll take you all the way, Raine. She's nothing but a whore, Raine. What do you know about her, eh? She does it for credits, boy. Didn't you know that? Her whole business is a front. If you won't come to me, Raine, I'm coming over to you. Guess you just really haven't got the guts.'

Johnny had stopped and was staring white-lipped at the swaying drunk. Jordan was rigid with fear and anger.

'Who is that bastard?' Johnny choked out the words.

'It's Bruce, Bruce Willard. He's drunk, Johnny. Ignore him.'

Johnny looked at Jordan hard. 'Is what he says true? Tell me.'

'No,' Jordan hissed, 'of course it's not true. He tried to buy me once, a long time ago. He's had a thing about me for years. Look, he's drunk. Don't get involved.'

'And have the world know Johnny Raine walked away from a fight? You wait here.'

Johnny pushed Jordan gently against the park railings. By now a small and interested crowd had gathered in anticipation of some excitement. Fights were seldom seen in Manhattan these days. Johnny stepped into the street and started to cross towards Willard who had put up his fists in a parody of a boxing stance.

It was Johnny who saw it first and it sent a paroxysm of fear through him. It was racing up East 26th Street from the direction of the river. With everyone's eyes focused on the two men it was seconds before anyone else saw it. A gasp of fear and terror issued from the crowd.

Bruce Willard never saw it at all. His life was seconds away from being ripped from him. The beast that hurtled towards him could hardly be called a dog. It was far larger, with a mane of fur flowing behind its back. There was something unusual about its large head and gaping teeth. Johnny realized with a shock that they were almost human. The beast's body was black and scaly and its huge paws ended in claws which were ripping up pieces of the road surface, scattering dust as it powered its way towards its victim. Johnny could not take his eyes from the face of the beast. Its eyes were like nothing he had ever seen before. They were alien, ferocious, red-hot.

As the beast reached Bruce Willard, the sound of its rasping breath was turning into a growling howl of blood lust. Willard started to turn but it was too late. The beast-dog had opened its enormous jaws and was leaping at him, sinking its fangs into his neck and ripping muscle, sinew and bone from his body in one bite. Before anyone could move, the beast had ripped open Willard's stomach, spewing entrails and bone across the street. Willard was screaming but his screams were short-lived. His body ruptured from the inside as the weight of the creature landed on his prone form. His head had lolled to one side, connected to his neck muscles by a single tendon. The beast now had his left leg in its mouth. With a mighty crunching sound, its teeth shattered his knee-cap like powder. Blood and viscera hung from its mouth. The animal shook its head in triumph, spraying pieces of flesh and Willard's organs across the street.

The nearest bystanders were drenched in blood and gore. Before the beast could sink its teeth once more into the torn carcass of Bruce Willard, Mike and Jack had reacted instinctively, dropping to their knees and pulling their automatic pulse revolvers from their holsters. Their training called for the protection of their customers' lives as top priority.

'Get down!' Mike bellowed at the crowd.

'Down, down, down,' screamed Jack as he took aim.

For a moment the beast paused. Johnny watched it. It was less than ten feet away from him. He was frozen into immobility. He could hear Jordan collapsing in hysterics behind him but something, some force, kept him rooted to the spot.

The beast saw him and for a moment Johnny saw a look of sadness flicker across its hybrid face. Before anyone else could move, there were two explosions and the beast burst into a shower of bone and tissue. In slow motion Johnny watched as the dog's head spun towards him. Still he could not move.

The head hit Johnny in the chest and knocked him to the ground. Instinctively, he had stretched out his hands to protect himself. He held the dog's head for a second and felt its final, fetid breath enveloping him. He started to vomit and scream at the feel of the matted, coarse hair and warm blood.

Lying prone on the ground, with the sound of human voices merging into a cacophonous whole, he turned his head and stared directly into the face of the dog-beast. The head was enormous, about the size of a lion's. Johnny convulsed, then stared again in compulsive horror at the expression in the eyes.

The red light of wanton fear was ebbing. Behind it, the eyes seemed human. The beast looked as if it was about to cry. For a brief moment the beast's orbs turned an impossible shade of blue, reminiscent of a summer's day in childhood. Johnny thought, Angelica's eyes were just as blue, exactly the same shade and intensity.

Angelica's eyes.

It couldn't be. It was not possible. He was going insane with fear, that was certain. But they were so blue and expressive and haunting, as though memories lay just beyond. Then the eyes closed and strong hands were pulling Johnny to his feet.

Johnny stayed with Jordan that night. Neither of them had spoken much. There was little to say. They had both been taken for compulsory medical check-ups and would be called in due course to attend the official investigation of the incident. Jordan took a powerful sedative and fell sound asleep, although she was disturbed and restless.

Johnny could not sleep. He lay awake on an improvised bed of cushions, reliving the events of the evening. Something was happening to him, and to Jordan. Whatever it was filled him with fear. Try as he might, he could not forget the sight of Willard's ruined body or the face of that creature. The press would be crawling all over the place by now. Luckily they had both managed to get away before the real police and media presence arrived.

The whole thing was insane, he told himself. This whole sacrificial suicide business on TV, Frank Brady and the Badlands, the death of that model and now this. Suddenly the prospect of going into the Badlands tomorrow night with Brady shifted from being a kind of crazy adventure where what you were getting into wasn't truly real, to the shattering revelation that it was only too real. In fact, it brought reality into focus.

So, why go? Why not quit the whole crazy show while you've got your sanity and your youth? As soon as the thought entered his mind he knew that, whatever happened, he would have to go. It wasn't about credits any more. If he was that desperate to escape the insane world he lived in, Jordan was right, he could get out now and live poor but maybe happy in a part of the world untainted by the psychoses of the modern age – if such a place existed.

No, something was compelling him to see this thing through. He could not analyse the nature of the compulsion but that made it no less real. Something, call it fate if you like, was dealing out the hands. He had no alternative but to play for whatever stakes had been decreed.

Chapter Nine

Jordan said little at breakfast next morning. Neither of them had been the least interested in sex during the night. She watched Johnny for a time until he glanced at his watch and prepared to leave for the office.

'So you're going then?' she asked him.

'Yes.' It was all he could find to say.

Silently, Jordan cleared away the breakfast things, tied her hair in a bun and went to her office. As the door closed quietly behind her, he saw her settling down in front of her VDU and switching on. With a sigh, he turned and left the apartment.

It was eight o'clock when Frank Brady pulled up in front of Johnny's apartment building. His iron-grey sloop jet throbbed with latent power. Johnny had spent the previous two hours getting used to his body armour and practising with his newly acquired pulse revolver. His earlier bladder-weakening fear had given way to an icy calm he never knew he possessed.

The body armour was really a high-density suit clipped together at the shoulders, waist and ankles. It felt cumbersome at first but, after a time, Johnny began to feel at home in it. The weapon was another matter. Johnny had never used a gun in his life although he had been brought up with them. The snub nose, automatic-reload pulser worked on a laser principle except that, instead of a laser beam, it pulsed a light jet from an optic fibre so powerful it could blow a hole the size of a car wheel through an electro-coupé. Johnny wore a one-piece black jump suit over the armour and clipped the pistol to its hook on his belt. Behind his back, also clipped to the belt, was a spare.

When the bell rang, his nerves jangled, then he calmed himself and prepared to enter the unknown.

Frank Brady was also dressed in dark clothes. He was waiting for Johnny on the street. As Johnny stood by the sloop jet, Brady photographed him quickly with his wrist camera.

'That's enough of that,' snapped Johnny. 'You ready?'

'Question is, are you?' smiled Brady. 'Come on, let's go and see what fate awaits us.'

For a time they drove slowly through the streets of Manhattan. They passed the junction of East 26th Street. Johnny shivered at the memory. The roadway was clean. There was no trace of last night's bloodbath. Johnny regarded the stony-faced photographer with interest.

'Tell me,' he asked him, 'how come you are able to come and go as you please? What kind of guardian angel looks after you over there?'

Brady did not reply at first and Johnny was about to repeat the question. When he did answer, his voice had lost its sharp edge, almost as though Johnny had passed some kind of initiation test.

'You really want to know?' He smiled.

'Yes, I do.'

'OK, there are two reasons. The first is economic. The second is, shall we say, spiritual.'

'OK, I'm hooked. Let's hear it.'

Johnny felt himself warming a little to this saturnine individual.

'I have a protector. He is probably the most vicious creature the Badlands have ever spewed up. He rules large areas of the territory but, of course, is constantly at war with other tribes. They all have their particular customs and ceremonies and, let's call them philosophies. This doesn't give me complete protection. At any time I might find he has been deposed or even killed. It might happen tonight. So, I supply him with something which is prized beyond belief and this gives him a certain amount of economic muscle. Don't forget, most people pay protection anyway. They trade and steal among themselves as they trade with other cultures on the mainland. Remember, Manhattan is isolated in more ways than one.'

'Go on,' said Johnny, 'what is this Holy Grail?'

'I supply him with shurm,' said Brady.

Johnny was stunned. 'Did I hear you right? Did you say shurm?'

'You heard me right,' said Brady. 'I have a connection here

that produces the real thing. I'm not the only supplier. There are many others, and some of the names would surprise you. Let's just say that this buys me a certain amount of protection. And many of the tribal bosses like the way I take pictures. My last exhibition put them on a pedestal. My pictures, their names and faces, appeared on prime-time TV. They were famous overnight. There are TV and virtuality shows produced by your own channel in which these characters are exploited. They love that. Badland tribal kings sell everything from tourist crap to perfume. Your smart-assed admen on Madison have used the images of the Badlands to sell a whole culture.'

'So, we have created the Badlands myth ourselves?' Johnny asked.

'To some extent, yes.'

'So, what's the second reason? You said there were two. What's the spiritual angle?'

'Yes,' answered Brady, 'that is the most interesting angle of all. The reason is, Liverpool.'

'Liverpool?' Johnny was amused and surprised.

'My protector is a man called Bobby Bolero. You may have heard of him.'

'Bolero, but he's . . .' At the sound of the name his heart almost stopped. He had heard about him, heard about the crude surgery which had saved his legs, and he had long incubated a dark suspicion about him. Both his legs had been blown off in an incident within Manhattan. A chill had begun to grip Johnny's insides.

'Yes,' Brady said, 'he's everything that has ever been written about him and more. Bobby Bolero believes John Lennon is some kind of messiah. So the words and songs of John Lennon, whom Bolero calls Guru Lennon, inspire him. His followers believe anything he says. They believe a force is coming to liberate them from the shit state they live in. Now, because I'm from Liverpool and so was John Lennon, Bobby Bolero thinks I'm some kind of catalyst, a sort of John the Baptist figure.'

'What do you think of all that?' Johnny stared at Brady who looked at him sharply with a quick smile.

'I think he's stone fucking mad, that's what I think. But I'm happy to let him go on believing it as long as it gets me in and out.'

'You're fascinated by the place, aren't you?'

'Whatever you say about it, it's bloody real. Not like the champagne sham of this place. Mind you, I'm not stupid. I couldn't live there. Like you and everybody else, I've opted out. Fuck 'em, that's what we say. And now we continue the glorification of a subculture we have created by inviting them to appear on your show and top themselves.'

'Do you think they'll do it?' asked Johnny.

'I think they'll be queuing up,' laughed Brady wildly.

For a moment Johnny wondered who was the craziest, Brady or himself. As they reached the Queensboro Bridge he decided they both were equally wired.

Just before they went through the security ritual Brady said quietly, 'And how's the girlfriend? Jordan isn't it?'

'She's fine. But she's not happy about tonight.'

'That's understandable, isn't it? You might not come back.'

Johnny looked at Brady and felt suddenly very alone and very scared. But there was no way he was going to show it.

'You must tell me all about her sometime. She's a fascinating woman,' Brady remarked almost too casually.

'Sure, sometime. You must come to dinner.'

Brady almost snorted with derision. 'I'm not the dinner party type. Sorry.' He paused again, then glanced slyly at his passenger. 'You seem to attract fascinating women. I remember Angelica.'

'You knew her?' Johnny turned to him sharply.

'Sure I knew her. I'm a photographer. I knew plenty of models. Don't worry, Raine, I didn't know her that well.'

Johnny remained silent, keeping his thoughts to himself. Brady gritted his teeth.

'OK, get ready, here we go.'

Brady gunned the sloop jet and they were in.

The Badlands at night were a different proposition from the last time. Johnny squinted through the slatted armoured shields and saw nothing but total darkness alleviated only by glimmers of light from numerous fires. There were people out there. He could see shapes moving and lights from unseen vehicles blinking. He could hear the throb of the Badlands music and he could hear echoes of hoarse laughter and screams. There were many screams.

Slowly, they moved into a brighter thoroughfare and Johnny had to take a deep breath. It was crowded, alive, vibrant. Makeshift shops were open. The misshapen masses hobbled and slithered in their rags, many just wandering aimlessly. Hideous street warriors were everywhere, smoking, painting themselves, draped over a motley collection of rustmobiles – anything that had wheels moved, it was as simple as that. On one street corner a mutant preacher was perched on a railing, screaming abuse at God. He was cheered by the multitude. The sloop jet was stared at and shot at with anything that came to hand.

'I thought you said we had protection,' complained Johnny.

'I said, up to a point,' replied Brady. 'They're just using us as target practice. It's not serious. If it was we'd know about it.'

'It's a long way from Manhattan,' Johnny said with a touch of regret.

'It bloody well is,' said Brady. 'It's a long way from Paris too.'

'When are you going?'

'Day after tomorrow. I might be tempted never to come back. Springtime in Paris, now there's a civilized thought.'

'Will you come back?'

'Yeah, I'll come back. I've got the exhibition to finalize. After that maybe I will piss off for good. You can have too much of a good thing, you know.'

It took Johnny a few moments to realize that Brady was being humorous. He shook his head and smiled.

'We're approaching the Latin Quarter,' Brady remarked. 'We'll be getting out soon. Make sure you're prepared for anything. By the way, give me the money.'

'What!'

'I'm the one they know here. I'll do the paying.'

Johnny sighed and handed a fat bundle of dollar bills to Brady who glanced quickly at it and stuffed it into an inside pocket.

'That ought to be enough for a few drinks, he said.

'Where are we going?'

'A little place I know where the Feeks and Farooks hang out. If you're lucky you'll see some action. It'll make your show look like summer camp.'

Brady steered the sloop jet along a narrow, almost deserted alley. Up ahead Johnny could just make out a blinking neon sign.

Brady looked for a suitable place to park. Cautiously he reversed the sloop jet into the darkness of a side alley.

'We'll be as safe here as anywhere,' he muttered and checked his equipment before turning to Johnny. 'Ready?'

'Ready,' Johnny replied with more confidence than he felt. This was it. A lump formed in his throat and slipped like a ball of ice into his stomach. He had an intense desire to take a crap but fought against it as the side doors of the sloop jet slid open and he stepped out into the night.

Instinctively, Johnny let his hand fall on the comforting shape of the pulse-gun handle as if expecting an immediate attack. Outside, in the open, the atmosphere was thick, heavy, almost tangible. And there was the stench. It filled Johnny's nostrils and forced him to gulp air. Brady seemed unaffected by it as he stood by the side of the vehicle keying in a security code. The doors slid shut and Johnny realized with a jolt that he was now completely in the hands of this unpredictable photographer. Across the street and a little way along he could see the sign flickering in patchy violet neon. The sign announced the Ancestor Club. Brady saw him watching.

'Come on, let's go. It's not safe to stand still for too long.'

Johnny had not taken two steps when he heard a noise behind him. He swivelled round to face two, well-armed street soldiers, heavily scarred and badly mutilated. Their bare chests displayed a solid mass of tattoos. They were both bald. One had only a single pin-sized eye. And they both stank; a foul, fetid odour that made Johnny want to throw up. Instead he drew his gun. Brady took a step back and drew his camera.

'Well,' said the uglier of the two, 'which one shall we eat first, Marvin?'

'You choose, Kirk, I'm not fussy,' replied the other.

Brady was busy photographing the confrontation, but glancing around between shots in a practised movement. His wrist camera left his gun hand free.

The two creatures selected some vicious-looking blades from their armoury and started to move in on Johnny.

'What the fuck are you waiting for?' snarled Brady. 'Shoot, shoot now, come on.'

Johnny hesitated for a split second. A circular blade hissed past his neck. He felt it miss his jugular by a hair's breadth. That's when he killed for the first time. He aimed and pressed the trigger, twice. Both assailants were blasted three feet into the air and their burning, screaming bodies landed with a thump. Almost immediately a number of small squat creatures, covered in slime, appeared from the labyrinthine network of alleys that led off from the shadowed street of dark, threatening buildings and, like vultures, hauled the two dead bodies into the darkness. It took Johnny a couple of seconds to realize they were children.

'Nice to see you've got a practical side to you,' smiled Brady. 'Come on, time for drink.'

Johnny was still shaking as they approached the entrance to the club. The killings had found a weak nerve. He assumed a bravado he did not feel.

'So what's this place,' he said nervously, 'the hub of their social life?'

'If you want specimens and maybe volunteers then this is where they'll be. It's a club with a theme.'

'Oh yes,' said Johnny, 'what sort of theme?'

Brady glanced at him as he knocked on the graffiti-covered door.

'Why, suicide of course. That's why we're here, isn't it?'

Chapter Ten

A bulging red eye glared at them through a spy-hole. There was a pause before the door creaked open. A large man blocked their path. At least, Johnny assumed he was a man. His bright-orange hair was frizzled into a wild electric storm and his deformed face was heavily made-up to disguise the ravages of the disfigurement. In parts his skin was peeling like a snake's.

He was powerfully built and dressed in a tight, pink leotard with a furry codpiece. Around his waist he wore a heavy, studded belt and a holstered, laser-converted Colt 45. He showed no sign of moving until Brady whispered something to him and he moved back a few paces to allow them to enter. He glared suspiciously at Johnny.

'Who's the flooz?' he asked of Brady.

'He's a friend of Bobby's too, Samson. You ever watch the web? Well, this is Mr Johnny Raine in person.'

Samson's expression started to change. He smiled, displaying a huge set of multi-coloured teeth.

'You're kiddin' me,' he breathed. 'Wait till they hear this.'

'Hey no, Samson. We're here kind of incognito, mate, you understand?' smiled Brady.

'Oh sure, go on in. Enter.' Samson stretched out a huge paw and stroked Johnny's arm.

'He likes you,' Brady said. 'That's good.'

As they moved inside the club, all Johnny's senses were assaulted simultaneously. The blistering music came at him like a sledgehammer. Shuddering strobes illuminated a steaming, dancing, primping collection of the most fantastically dressed freaks Johnny had ever seen. Nothing he had heard had prepared him for this. He almost choked in the thick atmosphere, heavy with smoke and narcotics. Before him was a kaleidoscope of colour and noise. He had the impression of a vast room but such was the atmosphere that he could not see more than ten feet in front of his face. He felt Brady tugging at his arm and pulling him through the crowd, which gaped at both of them as though they had just arrived from Mars. Johnny had been recognized. He could hear his name repeated in whispered falsetto around the club. He resisted lashing out as he followed Brady to the bar. Hands stroked him as he pushed through the heavily perfumed *habitués* of the Ancestor Club. There were hands on his backside, running up and along his thighs, exploring his crotch. Someone breathed in his ear.

'Don't react,' Brady shouted at him over his shoulder, 'they're just being polite.'

Johnny steeled himself and pushed harder till finally they found space at a long bar that ran the length of the room. Johnny squeezed in next to Brady.

'I feel like I've been gang-raped,' he gasped.

'Ssh! Don't give them any ideas.'

Johnny stared at him just as a hulking dwarf arrived, primping and pirouetting along the top of the bar.

Brady placed a thick bundle of notes on the counter. Carefully, the dwarf picked up the bills and counted them. Johnny noticed that the dwarf bartender was covered in thick, matted hair. Even the palms of his hands sprouted black, wiry tufts. He shuddered. Satisfied, the dwarf blew them a kiss, jumped behind the bar and reappeared with a bottle and two glasses.

Brady noticed Johnny looking aghast at the amount of money he had just handed over.

'Protection,' he explained. 'Now we drink all night. But you'd better warn your stomach this stuff is coming down.'

He poured two shots and Johnny examined the pale, green liquid.

'What is it?' He sniffed and recoiled.

'Don't ask,' retorted Brady. 'It gets worse after the first.'

Johnny was acutely conscious that eyes were boring their way into his back from all corners of the club. He glanced at Brady out of the corner of his eye as the Englishman prepared to down his shot. Taking a deep breath, Johnny joined him. At first he felt nothing. Then his legs almost gave way as a lead weight dropped from his stomach, through his bowels and down to his knees.

The taste was indescribable but the effect was instantaneous. He suddenly saw everything around him with a new clarity. He watched stone-faced as Brady poured another two shots and realized with a shock that he was expected to repeat the experience. The second belt was an improvement on the first and Johnny suddenly felt warm. He knew he was smiling. He couldn't stop himself.

'Which are the Feeks and which are the Farooks?' he whispered loudly to Brady. Even so, Brady had to put his mouth close to Johnny's ear to be heard.

'Feeks and Farooks are extreme, and I mean extreme, transvestites. They believe that if you die in style you go to Edendeath and from there to Dreamheaven. The Feeks are the males who think they're females and the Farooks, well, they're the opposite. To them, style in death is everything. It's what they live for. When they die, they hold their death pose as long as possible. It's an extreme form of bushido.'

'Jesus.' Johnny shook his head.

'Some of this lot try to emulate the crucifixion. We might see one tonight. They're all on shurm or hermdoom – drugs that can change their sexual orientation. They're like highly refined steroids. But they have to kill after they've had sex.'

Johnny could not take his eyes off the parade of deviant life-forms that danced and strutted and waddled and screamed all around him. He and Brady had picked a dark corner to avoid appearing conspicuous.

The Farooks paraded on one side of the club. Many wore giant, luminous codpieces decorated with flashing lights. Touching each other's codpieces triggered off a light storm.

From the other side the Feeks watched the Farooks with barely disguised malice. They nearly all wore giant, brightly coloured, elaborate and erotic vaginas embellished with names or phrases. Johnny picked out a couple. One was 'Gina's Diner'. Another proclaimed, 'The Last Supper'.

Johnny scanned the freak-filled room, wondering how the hell he was going to get any of these creatures to appear on the show. The studio might as well be on another planet for all the relevance it had here. Freiberg just had no idea. This was like a

scene from Dante's *Inferno*. The noise, the music, the screams
and the arguments filled the air with an ocean of noise. Johnny
noticed Brady refilling their glasses and raising his hand to his
face. With a start he realized he was using his tiny wrist camera.
Johnny looked away for a moment, straight into the face of a
creature who held his gaze like a cobra. He stared at the creature,
unable to tear his eyes away. She was small and horribly
deformed, yet recognizably female. She was covered in scales
and tumours. Some of the boils looked as though they had
recently burst. Puss oozed from them. Her small hands ended in
hooked talons. But it was her face that fascinated Johnny. It was
part metal mask, part doll-face complete with a single pigtail.
The eyes that gazed so steadily at Johnny were bright and the
half-metal mouth was touched by an ironic smile.

In spite of his revulsion, Johnny found himself entranced by
the child-monster, almost attracted to her. She exuded something
hormonal. He could feel it reaching out and touching him. He
shook his head and forced himself to look away.

Brady's rasping voice cut in, 'Well, Raine, what do you think?
Insanity is a great crowd pleaser. I think your suicide idea might
just work. Come on, the real action takes place out back. This is
where they psych themselves out.'

Brady grabbed Johnny's arm and they sidled around the edge
of the room. Then they stopped. Just in front of them a space
was clearing. Two sets of Feeks and Farooks were facing up to
each other. A sort of hush descended in anticipation of the main
event of the evening – confrontation. One of the Feeks, who
sported an enormous black and red vagina covered in baubles,
sneered loudly in a husky gravel voice.

'Fuckin' slag, Farook. Satan's asshole! Run on, drool mouth.'

One of the Farooks took a mincing step forward, spitting at
the Feek while stroking her three-foot long black rubber phallus.

'Shurm head! Shit brain! Aluma weh! Mongor corpse angel.
Piss yourself to death.'

A cheer arose from the ranks of the Farooks behind, urging
their champion on.

'Psychon! All over you, dildo head,' snarled the Feek.

'Bitch phantom!' retorted the Farook. 'No need for your death style. Your crackout is dead right now!'

The Farook retreated, never taking her eyes from the Feek. Surrounded by her Farook group she backed into the darkness. Slowly, and with menace, the Feek followed, incited by his followers.

Brady slipped away like a ghost and Johnny followed, suddenly panicking. Briefly he looked around and saw the child-monster close behind. He also noticed a number of Feeks and Farooks grimacing at him, indicating they wanted to talk.

Outside the rear of the club was a large paved area lit by burning braziers hanging from the crumbling walls. Johnny was reminded of Shabam's. He made sure he stuck close to Brady. His earlier concerns about the ease with which Brady could just leave him still nagged at him.

The Feeks and Farooks gathered around the combatants, whispering advice. Then, before Johnny could really see what was happening the two were on each other, kicking, biting and gouging. After a few seconds the Feek reeled back minus an ear. The Farook stared at him, chewing it with obvious pleasure. The Feek suddenly froze, posing dramatically. The crowd cheered. Then the Feek dropped the pose and pulled a pulse pistol, blowing the Farook's arm to smithereens. Instantly the Farook held her pose, bottling her pain despite the blood gushing from the wound. The Farooks cheered ecstatically.

The Feek primped triumphantly ignoring the missing ear. The posing Farook reached behind her back and drew out a thin, metal whiplash like a cat-o'-nine-tails, except that each strand was barbed with stranded blades. Without hesitating the Farook began to flail the Feek, who shrank and screamed in pain as his skin was ripped from his body in bleeding strips. But still he posed, hand on brow, curtseying unsteadily as he was transformed rapidly into a sea of bloody blubber. Finally, to the accompaniment of howls of disappointment from the Feeks and screams of victory from the Farooks, he collapsed in a bloody heap. A couple of deformed dogs appeared from nowhere and started to devour the remains.

Johnny turned away and Brady noticed.

'You all right? This is nothing compared to the mess your studio's going to be in. Come on, let's get a drink. We're among friends.'

As they hunched their way back inside, trying to remain unnoticed, a scented hand appeared out of the gloom and touched Johnny's arm. He froze. Brady turned to watch as a Feek detached himself from a sea of decadent life-forms and smiled into Johnny's face. Like many of the others, the Feek wore an ornate mask. This one just covered the top of his face, which was heavily whitened. His mouth was a red slash. His costume was liquid gold, shimmering in the strobes, and he had pink breasts and his blue pubic hair had been manicured into the shape of a swastika. One hand was sheathed in a leather-and-iron spiked glove. The whole outfit was sequinned and completed by a loose, torn chain vest and see-through silk panties. He put his arm around Johnny's shoulders. His breath was heavily scented and he spoke with a deep, silky lisp.

'Hi Lone Ranger! Psychon from another world. I will guard you. You come from Lusherland to seek a new star.'

The Feek's other hand slid down Johnny's chest and settled between his legs. He was about to react when he noticed Brady shaking his head imperceptibly.

'You like metal, love?' continued the Feek, leading Johnny back to the bar. 'I will mongor corpse anyone for you. You want I give hermdoom to an amigo for you?'

Johnny was in a quandary. He didn't know how to react. He tried bravado. He glanced at Brady for help. The photographer smiled.

'He means he'll kill for you,' he muttered.

'Hey man, I can do my own killing.' And he regretted it the moment he uttered the words.

'You think so?' hissed the Feek, stroking Johnny's neck with two fingers.

They reached the bar. The Feek drew his knuckles along the counter, leaving a trail of splintered wood. Brady watched the encounter with a curious lopsided smile and sipped his drink. He was clearly known here and treated with a degree of respect.

Johnny nervously cleared his throat, his spittle had dried and he experienced a warm watery feeling deep in his guts. He managed to avoid wetting himself by an effort of will.

At that moment a tall blonde Farook, the leader of a giggling group of younger transvestites, squeezed up close to Johnny's other side. He was now sandwiched between the two who gazed at each other with undisguised venom. The Farook grinned hideously at Johnny and stuck her painted tongue out at the Feek. The Farook was obscenely macho, covered in glistening tattoos in silver and gold. Knives and blades jangled from her leather one-piece suit. The Farook simpered at Johnny.

'You're going all the way tonight, Johnny boy.' She touched Johnny's face with a claw-like hand. The skin on her hand was pale and peeling from her bones in small clumps.

'Satino skin,' she continued. 'I'd like to peel you like a banana.'

With the speed of a snake striking, the Feek pushed Johnny out of the way roughly and swiped the Farook across her neck with a small blade palmed in his hand. The Farook's head lolled, partly decapitated. Johnny almost passed out. Fear clawed at his intestines and he felt himself breaking out in an icy sweat. The Feek turned to Johnny.

'I mongor for you, now you lick-flick for me.'

Johnny summoned up as much courage as he could muster. He glanced at Brady who was still watching sardonically.

'Only on TV,' he croaked. 'I'll pay you. I'll pay you all.'

Brady suddenly moved, shoving Johnny back into the crowd. In that instant they were both forgotten. Violence on a savage scale suddenly erupted as the incensed followers of the dead Farook drew their metal whips. They whirled them around their heads and they whistled melodically. The Feek prepared himself, posing dramatically as the flails descended. Within seconds he had been reduced to bloody ribbons, unrecognizable as a human being. The Farooks stared, wild-eyed, at Johnny and began to chant.

'Raine, Raine, Johnny Raine, take away the death and pain.'

Even Brady now looked fearful, slipping his hand on to the comforting shape of his pulse gun. Johnny was shaking so much he could hardly think. Then, as one, the Farooks stopped, replacing their metal flails and backing away. A couple of infested, semi-human shapes scuttled through the legs of the crowd and began scraping the dead Feek into a dirty, blood-stained sack.

The hush that had descended on the club was broken by the approaching sound of clanking footsteps. A passage was made by a suddenly respectful crowd as Bobby Bolero emerged, flanked by two hugely muscled and well-armed Platers.

For a long moment, he stared at Brady and Johnny. His mouth widened a fraction, the nearest he could get to a smile. Then he turned to the massed ranks of Feeks, Farooks and other *habitués* of the club and roared, 'Who wants to be a media-web star?'

Almost immediately there was a cheering, screaming response.

'Yes, yes, yes!' yelled the voices.

'Well you've gotta join actor's equity first,' shouted Bolero.

This was greeted with raucous, contrived laughter.

'Johnny Raine and my friend, Frank Brady, who is from the holy city of Liverpool, birthplace of Guru Lennon, are under my protection.'

Bolero glared around him. No one dared make eye contact. He lumbered over to the two Manhattanites and shouted for a table. In seconds, two dwarves had placed a table and chairs in a space near the bar. The two Platers turned to face the crowd. Bolero indicated that Johnny and Brady should sit down. For another long moment his small eyes appraised Johnny.

'It is a sign,' he said. 'You being here is part of the revelation of Guru Lennon.'

'I didn't realize . . .' Johnny began, but Brady kicked his ankle under the table.

'You will have more volunteers than you can handle,' Bolero continued, 'so you will need someone to help you.'

After the insanity of the last few hours Johnny was surprised by Bolero. He appeared almost civilized. But he reminded himself of Brady's description of him as wantonly violent.

Johnny felt bile rising as he saw Bolero's reconstructed legs; a fabrication of hydraulic aerojet shafts, pumps and ball joints. He glanced at the face. Give it a few years, illuminate it with the blinding flash from a laser strobe and it could be. Yes it could be. And if it was? Johnny had no idea what he would do. He would bide his time and find a way to take revenge. He choked back the onset of emotion. This was not the time or the place. But, somehow, somewhere, sometime, the chance would present itself.

'I've brought you here, Raine,' Brady smiled, 'now it's up to you, media man.'

Bolero signalled to someone in the darkness. With a start, Johnny saw it was the child-monster who had been watching him. She joined them, still looking at Johnny.

'This is Shell,' explained Bolero. 'She is a very special person. She will help you in your search. They will be killing each other to kill themselves on your show. Now, I recommend the cabaret.'

Abruptly, he stood up, clasped Brady's hand briefly then moved away into the crowd.

'Hello, Shell,' said Brady.

'Aloyo weh, Frank.' She kept her eyes fixed on Johnny. 'That means nice to see you again,' said Shell. Her voice was distorted as though it was forcing its way through an artificial larynx. She continued, 'Johnny Raine in person. This is a privilege. Let me introduce you to your first volunteers.'

Johnny was getting used to the way people suddenly seemed to appear out of nowhere. For the first time since he had arrived in the Badlands he allowed himself to relax. But he stiffened again when three hideous deformities joined them, throwing themselves into the chairs and posturing defiantly.

'Johnny, meet Spelo Bey-Root, Ix-Tab and Deep Cut. Friends, meet Mr Johnny Raine. They'll speak so you understand.'

Spelo Bey-Root regarded Johnny with cold, fish eyes.

'Well,' he lisped, 'he's no thunderfuck, I can tell. But he'd pass for a touch in the nightshade with a cold scalpel.'

'Sew your crotch up, shurm brain,' snapped Ix-Tab. 'Dreamo mongoring and corpsing in front of twenty million people.'

The enormity of the proposition seemed suddenly all too real. Johnny was thinking of Maurice Freiberg and the production team. He was also wondering how the hell he was going to pull this off. For a moment too he thought of Jordan and something made him glance at Brady. The photographer was watching him curiously. Three more freaks arrived. Johnny couldn't tell

whether they were Feeks or Farooks or even human. Again, Shell
made the introductions.

'Johnny Raine, meet Marshmallow Heart, Mister Sister and
Lady Flame.' He stared at the three Farooks. Now that they were
all gathered around regarding him like a laboratory specimen,
he could see the differences. Spelo Bey-Root was covered in
hieroglyphics. Ix-Tab wore a costume of ropes, strings and
snares. Deep Cut was a mass of cuts and scars. These were the
Feeks. Marshmallow Heart was covered in a kind of glutinous
substance with heart-shaped sweets covering her body. Mister
Sister was hermaphrodite with one metal breast and a solid
metal penis. Lady Flame was a mass of burns in patterns. Her
hair was a piled mountain of red curls from which smoke was
slowly rising.

The Feeks lined up on one side of the table, the Farooks on the
other. Brady remained detached and observant, occasionally
raising his wrist to his eye. Shell exerted a strange fascination
over Johnny who was now feeling the effects of the strange,
absinthe-like spirit he had been drinking. He felt light-headed,
almost carefree. He had to force himself to remain cool. A silence
had descended. They were clearly waiting for him to speak. He
didn't think their patience would hold out too long.

'You're all just, perfect,' he managed.

'This was clearly the right thing to say. They began to preen
themselves. Despite his initial aversion to this onslaught of
anarchic decadence, the Feeks and Farooks had a strange kind of
beauty, despite their deformities. They were living life on the
edge and for the moment. They had no future except death, so
the very act of death itself had become elevated to the level of an
apocalyptic art form.

Johnny decided there was little point in discussion. Bolero had
said he would have volunteers clamouring to die on his show.
This fact alone altered his attitude. If they saw their deaths as
beautiful works of art why should he suffer the moral uncertain-
ties he had been feeling? Nothing now would change his plans
to get out while he could but, in a strange way, the act of suicide
on TV was exactly the kind of television Channel Boom Boom's
audience deserved.

'Who wants to be first?' he asked.

The hunted, lonely and terrifying faces regarded him stonily. At last Ix-Tab replied.

'I will mongor my corpse first. My death will live in the firmament of Eden. I will hold my corpse raga till my final breath.'

The others did not agree. Violence was about to break out.

'You will all be beautiful,' Brady suddenly interjected. 'There are no firsts or seconds. You are all first because you are all totally unique.'

Johnny released his pent-up breath and made a mental note to thank the Englishman. His remark defused the situation.

'We've just got to fix up how to get you across,' he yelled over the noise.

'I will arrange it,' said Shell. 'There are ways.'

Johnny had a vision of the mutant dog as it pounded mercilessly up from the river. So there was a way into Manhattan the ZeePees didn't know about.

'Great,' he said. 'What about payment? Channel Boom Boom can be very generous.'

By way of an answer, Mister Sister stroked her large metal penis, which appeared to have a foreskin or sleeve. Johnny watched with fascination.

'Don't move,' hissed Brady.

There was a small burst of flame from the end of the iron phallus. Johnny felt the bullet whistle past his left ear and could smell the cordite burning through the air. A hole appeared in the wooden partition behind him. Mister Sister replaced her smoking member and grimaced at Johnny, hissing at him.

'We mongor for beauty. Beauty is nothing but the beginning of terror.'

Johnny had no reply. He swallowed his dry spittle. He coughed to try and clear his head. He managed to croak, 'How soon?'

'I will arrange everything.' Shell appeared to be smiling. 'I will show you how to reach me or I may get a message to you. It'll be a couple of weeks.' Her strange metallic voice clearly fascinated Johnny. Behind the barrier of the mask lurked an unbridled sexual power.

That seemed to be the end of the conversation because a high-pitched growl of anticipation rippled through the club. Brady stood to watch. Shell climbed on to the table. The Feeks and Farooks stood and one by one bent over to kiss Johnny. Each one kissed him on the lips. Each kiss was more passionate. Marshmallow Heart was last. She thrust her tongue deep into Johnny's mouth. He was fighting an erection and losing.

They dispersed into the sea of freaks. Johnny stood up, panting heavily, totally disoriented. With a shudder he realized that Shell was standing on the table and had placed her hand around his shoulders. Her talons began to trace shivering patterns on his neck.

His attention was suddenly directed towards a stage he had not seen before. Spotlights blazed and the house-lights dimmed. The babble of voices subsided as a tall Feek stepped under the yellow glow. He was dressed only in black, thigh-length crocodile boots with crocodile heads as toe-caps. From his crotch sprouted a vermilion, fibrillated orchid whose tendrils wrapped themselves sinuously around his waist. His pubic hair was tufted and dyed bright green. His erect member protruded through the orchid like a stamen and was heavily decorated with glittering gold dust.

As Johnny gazed around the room, the hideous faces and costumes of the clientele seemed to waver and then freeze into a surreal tableau. For a moment he thought he was dreaming. The leering, pouting, dazzling mob had blended into the blue haze that permeated the club to form into a still life. For an instant everything froze. Johnny felt light-headed and dizzy. The insistent probing of Shell's sharp nails was having an effect. He was terrified to move in case those same nails sank into his flesh, ripping and gouging. He glanced at Brady quickly. The photographer looked tired and drained but fascinated. Manhattan seemed light-years away.

The Feek on stage was pulling on a silver chain, hauling something or someone out from behind the stage curtains. A bleeding, half-naked man tumbled into the spotlight. He wore a pair of pants and nothing else. He was neither Feek nor Farook nor Plater nor any other kind of Badlands creature. He was just an ordinary guy. Johnny wondered how he had got here. With a shiver he wondered how many others were here, maybe kidnapped from the city across the river. Another Feek leaped on to the stage and placed a fur coat over the performer's shoulders. Raunchy music started up. The fur-coated Feek began to dance seductively. Then, in an incredibly deep voice, he started to intone:

'A taxi driver from the Bronx
A fur coat from Alaska
A belly dancer from Baghdad
No mother please don't ask her
A lighter on the table
A train that's running late
A driver in a hurry
Who's just smashed up a crate
Of bottles lying broken
By a body from the Bronx
Of a taxi driver dying
To the sound of honky tonk.'

The Feek hauled on the chain. The half-conscious prisoner fell. He had dozens of Manhattan taxi IDs pinned to his chest in a network of bloody gashes. The audience was cheering and screaming. The cheers and screams rose to a crescendo as the Feek drew a long, thin knife from his waistband and plunged it to the hilt into each of the man's eyes, twisting until his eyeballs popped out of their sockets and rolled across the stage. The Feek bowed and hauled his victim off stage.

The music changed. Brady pricked up his ears. The riff sounded familiar, like an old love song that drifted tantalizingly through the memory banks.

Then Bobby Bolero entered, stamping and screaming, leaping on to the stage. The audience went wild, in a paroxysm of drug-crazed frenzy. Against his will Johnny was sucked into the atmosphere. He let his mind drift and found himself clapping along and shouting with the rest. Bolero began to sing. It was clearly an anthem of some kind because it triggered an ecstatic, almost religious, reaction from the audience.

Bolero sang in a hoarse shout. He screamed with messianic passion, pounding his metal legs like pistons until the dust from the floorboards pumped in time to the music.

'Psychon, sigophon, psychon, sigophon,' chanted the audience.

Bolero worked the crowd into a stomping chorus. Flails were whistling through the air, Feeks sank their teeth into the necks of Farooks, drawing bubbles of blood. A powerful electric charge had started a chain reaction. Johnny felt a hand on his arm. It was Brady. Shell had not moved.

'Time to go, Raine,' he said.

'Take me with you,' whispered Shell. 'I will show you where I live. If you want to fill your show with corpses you will have to do it through me.'

Johnny nodded vacantly and allowed himself to be hustled through the dense, packed crowd. He was gasping now, straining for breath and sweating profusely. He felt ill and wanted to vomit. With images whirling around inside his head he found himself pushed suddenly out into the night. He gulped lungfuls of air and closed his eyes for a moment. He coughed harshly and looked around. Brady and Shell had crossed the street.

Blocking Johnny's path was a huge, squat, gruesome hunch-back. The head was enormous and had been crudely sewn on to its shoulders in a back-street operation. The head had a lopsided look to it as though it had belonged originally to a different owner. What made Johnny take a step back was the crude iron crossbow in the hunchback's hands. A barbarous-looking metal bolt, tipped with angled blades, was aimed directly at his stomach. He tried to move his hand slowly towards his pulse revolver but the hunchback shook his head.

'Uh-oh, sweet prince,' he blubbered through oversized lips which had been drawn back over long yellow teeth. 'Well, what have we here? A little leather freak all ready to have her hide flayed.'

Johnny's heart was racing. Where the hell was Brady? He glanced over the street. There was no sign of him. Bastard, thought Johnny, the bastard has dumped me here. His bladder froze inside. So this was it. This is what it felt like to face death. It didn't feel like anything. It just felt like it could not really be happening. Johnny remembered his spare pulse pistol jammed into the back of his belt. He wondered if his body armour could withstand the vicious-looking bolt. His mind was racing and his eyes were glued to the creature's stubby finger hooked around the trigger. If it moved a fraction he would leap to one side and pray he could get to his gun before the hunchback attacked.

There didn't appear to be anyone else around. He could hear a rising crescendo from inside the club but no one was entering or leaving. Where the hell was Brady? Johnny's mind moved into hyper-gear. Everything seemed to slow down. He decided to try to reason with the mutant hobgoblin.

'Look, do you know who I am? I can get you whatever you want. Let's talk about this. You look like a reasonable man.'

'Cut the shit,' he snarled and his finger tightened on the crossbow trigger. 'I want to eat your heart. If that's all right with you, that is.'

'As a matter of fact, it's not. You want to be mongored?' whispered Johnny.

'Oh, as a matter of fact is it? Mongored is it? Say goodbye, Flooz. Too bad I'm not a vegetarian.'

Before Johnny could draw his next, and maybe final, breath the hunchback screamed in agony, dropped the crossbow and staggered across the street. Now a few more shadowy figures had appeared on the street and were watching and waiting. Something had attached itself to the creature's back and was systematically ripping his neck with powerful claws. With a start, Johnny realized it was Shell. The hunchback threw her off with a shrug of his powerful shoulders. At that moment Johnny saw Brady burst out from the darkness. Simultaneously, Johnny drew his pulse pistol and took aim.

The door of the Ancestor Club burst open and Bobby Bolero emerged, laughing and smoking a cheroot. Behind him lumbered his coterie of protectors and sycophants. His smile faded. He stopped near Johnny and appraised the situation. The hunchback was rising to his feet, snarling and spitting blood. Bolero moved with incredible speed. His knuckle spikes were extended and his other hand formed into a semi-circular blade. Before the hunch-back could blink, Bolero had rammed his spiked fist into his head, splintering his skull and emptying his brains on to the street. Bolero raised one of his metal legs and hammered it like a piston into his ribcage. It went all the way through his obese body. Some kind of kinetic power mechanism operated the leg because it withdrew with enormous power and a sucking, bilious sound. Laughing, Bolero stepped back. The hunchback kicked once, then lay still in a rapidly expanding pool of blood. Bolero stood, macho and proud, like a matador after a kill and smiled at each one of them in turn. He raised an arm in Frank Brady's direction and moved off.

Johnny ran across the street to where Brady was standing with Shell by the sloop jet. Before he could say anything he heard a noise behind him. He turned and saw Bobby Bolero stamping on a black metal manhole cover. As Johnny watched, the cover slowly started to move. The body of the hunchback lay near the hole and trickles of blood had started to run in rivulets towards the drainage point. Bolero and his entourage walked away and the street appeared empty again.

Something was emerging from the sewer. In the half-light it was impossible to see clearly. The shape that appeared was black as night. A black tentacle snaked out and wrapped itself around the hunchback's neck and began dragging the body towards the manhole. The black shape rose from the sewer and something white glinted within. Johnny realized they were teeth. There came a sudden slurping sound as the dense black sewer-creature dipped into the stomach of the hunchback. Then came the sound of the hobgoblin's intestines and stomach being sucked and chewed as the carcass started to tip over and disappear below. Within seconds the hunchback had vanished and the manhole cover had been pushed back into position.

Johnny turned to Brady and opened his mouth to bawl him out. Instead he closed it again. There was nothing to say. He was aching with tiredness and, glancing at his watch, he saw that it was three a.m. Shell touched his arm and they followed Brady into the protective womb of the sloop jet.

Minutes later they were racing through the streets. The Badlands were really alive now. Turning a corner they were blinded by sudden glaring lights and assailed by the sound of a fairground organ. The incongruous sight of the circus and crowds of people, music, lights and even laughter made Johnny shake his head in wonderment. He felt as though he had aged a couple of lifetimes in one night.

They drove past the glittering circus and into the darkness again. The sloop jet's powerful headlights finally illuminated the base of a tall crumbling building, the tallest building Johnny had seen this side of the river. It was rotting and covered in vegetation. It looked uninhabited.

Shell's metallic voice ordered them to stop. 'I live here,' she told them, 'in the penthouse suite.'

They all got out and looked around nervously. Shell touched Johnny's arm and pulled him towards her. He bent down and she kissed him. The feel of her part-metal mouth on his sent an unexpected shiver running through him. Brady was silent and had been for some time.

'This is where you must come when you want to pick up your victims. But I will get a message to you. Then you will come. It will be soon, I promise.'

The strange half-woman, half-machine walked with unusual grace towards the base of the building. She turned to look at both of them and then was gone, vanishing into the shadows. Brady was watching Johnny who was now so tired he could hardly stand.

After they got back into the sloop jet and headed towards the bridge and the security check, Brady spoke.

'Well, Raine, you've done well. You've done better than I expected. If anyone can get those shurm freaks on to your show then Shell can.'

'What happened to her?' Johnny asked.

'I don't know. I've only met her a couple of times. You'll see her again at the exhibition, but hanging on a wall. By the way, I'm throwing a party before the opening. You're invited and so is Jordan.'

'Thanks,' said Johnny, 'and thanks for saving my life tonight.

I've seen more death, blood and destruction in the last couple of weeks than I've seen since the Isolation. You must attract it.'

'Funny,' Brady said, 'I was thinking the same thing about you.'

They drove in silence for a while, through the ZeePee security checks. As they rumbled into Manhattan Johnny felt as though he had been away from the lights and the comfort for a lifetime. All he wanted now was a hot bath and bed.

'We haven't talked about your fee,' he said to Brady.

'I don't want your money,' the photographer said. 'Let's just say you owe me one. I'll think of something.'

'I'm not sure I like that idea.'

'Not much you can do about that now, is there?' Brady smiled. After a short pause he looked over at his passenger. 'Ever think about the past, Raine?'

'The past?' Johnny remembered how he had found himself in the Lower East Side dredging up memories. 'Why do you ask?' he said.

'Oh, no reason,' replied Brady casually, 'it's just that I have. I think there are some cosmic connections falling into place.'

Johnny choked back his laughter. 'Cosmic connections, what the hell are they?'

'Everything is connected, Mr TV star. Time and space wait for no man.'

Johnny did not reply. He was thinking about the hunchback and the unseen creature that had emerged from the sewer to feed on the cadaver. Maybe these were the creatures which had been lurking at the edge of his nightmare, unseen but potent with horrifying danger.

'How do they get over here?' he asked Brady. 'Is there some way over we don't know about?'

'They say some of the tunnels are still passable. But, who knows? Don't worry about getting them across. Your people will make sure it's all organized. You can bet your pension that State Security will be involved. They'll probably want to send an armed escort. If they do, refuse. The people you want will come only if you are there on your own. If they see a small army around you they'll vanish like ghosts, believe me.'

'And the sewers,' Johnny persisted, 'what kind of monsters are down there?'

'They say there are some really serious mutants living in the sewers. I've never seen any.'

'What about dogs? Ever seen any giant dogs that don't look like dogs?'

Brady looked at Johnny strangely. 'No, no dogs,' he said.

They drove in silence for a while till they were close to Johnny's apartment. He coughed and looked at Brady.

'By the way, I meant to say it before, but I'm sorry about the model. That was just horrific.'

Brady said nothing for a moment but he was struggling with something.

'We were close once. We were friends,' he muttered.

Dawn was breaking over Manhattan as Johnny hauled himself out of his steaming bath. He called Jordan and left a message on her screen mail, then collapsed into bed. He was asleep instantly.

His dreams were violent and brutally real. Now, instead of fractured images riddled with unspeakable horror, the dream was more cohesive. There was an almost nursery-rhyme quality about the opening sequences. Bright, sparkling lights and soft, whimpering cries were followed by a searing close-up of bright blue eyes filling with blood.

He saw the demon then and knew instantly that it was more than a fiction conjured up from the darkest recesses of his mind; or a composite ghoul created from something he'd seen or read. No, this creature was aware of him as if they were both wide awake. He quaked in the vibration of the creature's power. But he sighed in his dream because the creature was almost blind. It knew he was there. It had his psychic fingerprints.

Brady spent some time in his sanctum immersing himself in images of Jordan. Then he went to his bedroom and discovered Satoko lying awake. She did not speak as Brady slipped in between the sheets.

Chapter Eleven

Maurice Freiberg was happy. He had been happy now for a couple of weeks. This unusual state of affairs had resulted in a condition of near euphoria within the station. Freiberg had dealt with the press, especially that little shit Alex Hamlisch. He was happy that rumours were spreading. He would confirm or deny nothing. But the word was out that something big was about to happen at Channel Boom Boom. Maurice believed there was only one area of concern. If Johnny Raine did not deliver the goods, his own credibility and position could be seriously threatened. Freiberg had been careful to distance himself from the idea. He maintained to his executives and his board that it was taking shape but it was all in the hands of Johnny Raine.

If America's top media host did not deliver, then he might as well stay in Shurmtown because he would disappear from the public eye quicker than a crocodile tear. Freiberg had a contingency plan. If the suicide show did not come off, or could not come off for any reason, he was going to switch the story to the arrival of a new presenter for 'All the Way'. That would be the big news. Commissioner Halloran and the city fathers would just have to bite the bullet on that one. Freiberg wasn't convinced about this psychological shit the Free State of Manhattan analysts had hoodwinked the administration with. Suicide on TV keeping the lid on that tinder box across the river? No way. The programme controller had another contingency plan. A personal one. On the roof of his mansion overlooking Battery Park he had stashed away his own personal heli-jet. And he and Mrs Freiberg had bought a little hideaway in Cuba.

Right now he was on his way across the office, treading heavily on sound-muffling carpets, preparing to ingratiate himself with the board. He had kept the existence of the crucifix machine strictly under wraps. Only a few people knew about it. They had all been sworn to secrecy under pain of immediate dismissal. Now he was taking Princetti, Newman, Riley and Barolo to see the prototype. He knew it would be a couple of weeks before everything was ready for the show. Sure, it was a risk but what the hell, he wouldn't be risking *his* neck, would he? It would take Raine time to organize things at the other end, assuming he could and also assuming he ever came back. Either way the crucifix machine could still be used, maybe as a symbol of Manhattan's power, to enforce stability and compliance. The idea amused Freiberg. Instead of the sword of Damocles, they'd have the crucifix of Halloran.

In a deserted warehouse behind the building the four most powerful media moguls in Manhattan were watching a demonstration. Their faces were wooden as they stood in their creaseless suits and let Maurice Freiberg talk them through the concept.

The crucifix machine had the sort of awesome power that was able to unnerve the strongest mind. It contained within it all the inherent majesty of ceremonial death. The highly polished metal frame had been constructed to resemble a gibbet. Lights pulsed in sequential madness like a fairground ride. The designers moved smoothly through their well-rehearsed routine, explaining about power surges and decapitation techniques. The boom that extended like a broken finger in front of the machine held the metal skullcap in suspension. The cap was swaying slightly like a pendulum. The board of Channel Boom Boom stared fixedly at the cap.

At that moment, Commissioner Halloran arrived with a party from the State legislature. Their voices dropped when they set eyes on the machine. Slowly, they joined the small group already watching and became silent.

In the background shadows a portly figure stood watching. The special guest of Commissioner Halloran had been asked to present his private opinion personally. Marek Grohmann watched the demonstration impassively. The board of Media City has also requested his advice, but for different reasons. Mike Halloran was concerned about escalating violence. Reports had been coming for some time now which showed a small but marked increase or shift in the level of violent crime on the island. Crime could never be totally eradicated but Halloran was a realist. When his senior police officers pooled their statistics and their experience and came to the conclusion that Manhattan was going through a mini-surge, then it could be time to get worried. So, would this suicide business inflame the situation or serve as a demonstration of municipal power? Grohmann was not at all sure he had an answer.

The Media City moguls had other things on their minds. How would this show effect the ratings? Someone's head would roll all the way down Madison if this experiment in the macabre backfired. Freiberg would blame his presenter, Johnny Raine. Grohmann was concerned how the whole extravaganza would affect a young man whom he liked and admired. When the demonstration was over he had his first meeting with Halloran.

'Marek,' muttered the Commissioner grimly, 'I don't know about you but this whole charade leaves me with a nasty taste. Now come on, we go back a long way. So, let me have it. Do I sanction televised slaughter or not?'

'I can't advise you either way, Mike,' said Grohmann, 'but I believe it could have the opposite effect to the one you expect. The disenfranchised mobs over the river have, for several years, been forming alliances with other groups outside the State. For the first time since the Isolation, they have a truly charismatic leader – Bobby Bolero. So far their minds have been seduced by the huge doses of media tranquillizers we beam at them but, if some of their own kind are turned into martyrs, it is my belief that at first it would have the effect of glorifying them. But then, I think things could turn nasty. They would see the show for what it really is, the soft underbelly of corporate fear. It could be the final straw, the final humiliation. And, with a leader like Bolero to motivate them, we could have a new war on our hands.'

Halloran was silent for a time. Then he spoke quietly.

'I thought that's what you would say. Unfortunately, I think we have already lost the argument. Ratings will be the final judge. Trouble is, Marek, people in this city think it's impregnable. Well, I can tell you it's not fucking impregnable. How about you? What would you do if the balloon went up again?'

'I'm too old to worry about it, Mike.' Grohmann laughed. 'You know, since Imelda passed away, I've been going through the motions. My emotions were partly cauterized some time ago. I'd probably hole up out in the Hamptons if the truth be told. When the chips are down, I'll try and save my old Austrian ass.'

'So, what will you tell the Media City boys?'

'First I'll tell them exactly what I've told you. I'll watch their reactions and then I will tell them their ratings will shoot to the stratosphere. They'll probably get fruitcakes from all over the country volunteering, but . . . Any one of those guys could be off this island in ten minutes. They would just leave the city to its fate.'

'You're lucky you don't have any kids,' Halloran remarked, 'although I know you won't agree with that. There's no future for the young folks, unless they were born with a silver spoon or a fat wallet up their asses.'

'I learned one thing a long time ago, Mike. It's a piece of advice I keep giving myself. A holy man once said that the whole material world is an illusion, created by ourselves; maybe by some kind of collective mental madness. So, I keep telling myself this. For most of my life I could either not understand it or didn't want to accept it. At my age, after a fairly conventional life, you know, school, university, doctorate, wife, no family, career, I realize that it all means nothing. It is all totally meaningless. So I devote my life now to massaging the delicate temperaments of the rich and to contemplating the reason for existence. Self-knowledge is the only pursuit of any value. You should try it.'

'What time do I have for self-knowledge? I've got a city to run, a schedule to keep. Maybe when I retire . . .'

Halloran walked with Grohmann to the shadowy entrance where they both turned as one to take a final look at the crucifix machine, isolated like some metal mantis in a pool of light.

'May God forgive us,' Halloran lamented.

'God doesn't live in Manhattan,' Grohmann remarked heavily then turned to leave.

The doorbell rang and shattered Johnny's restless sleep. He got up and went to answer it, still drowsy and disturbed. It was Jordan. She looked drawn and worried. For a moment she stood watching him. He smiled that little crooked smile of his and she was in his arms.

She undressed quickly and pulled him into the warm bed. Then they just held each other close, both lost in their own private dreams. There was no need for anything else at that moment. They had each other and that was enough. There was no need even for sex. That would come later.

Two days after his trip to the Badlands, Frank Brady was sitting in luxury aboard an Air Manhattan super jumbo taxiing along the five-mile runway at Staten Island airport. As he circled over the islands and headed out over Jamaica Bay towards Long Island he experienced a flush of freedom the like of which he thought he had forgotten. He was suddenly transported back to his days as a seaman when travel to, and more especially, arrival at some exotic destination held a magic for him which had since been doused by success and fame.

He gazed down over the Badlands as he sipped pink champagne. How small and insignificant it all looked from this distance. He saw then the huge barrier wall that cut off Long Island from the former outer boroughs of New York. Long Island formed part of the State of Manhattan and was the ultimate in luxury locations. If you lived in Long Island now you had arrived. It was for the super-rich only. And the only way in was by air. There were no roads. The old highways had been destroyed, then mines had been laid. Brady sighed and looked over at the eager profiles of the three advertising executives assigned to the Erotique account.

What did they know? thought Brady. They had been born and raised in isolation. The outside world, even the rest of America, was like another planet to them. Louis Dubois had sacked the Have A Nice Day agency. To Brady these three were simply clones of Fearnley and Wilson, just younger. They smiled at Brady and one of them called for more champagne. Keep the unpredictable English photographer sweet and happy and preferably inebriated until it's time for him to go to work. Their instructions had been clear. Brady looked out of the window and thought about Jordan. He thought about her all the way to Paris.

Brady had booked the Paris Opera House for the shoot which had been planned to take three days. He wanted some time to himself in the city to wander and reminisce. He needed to charge his spiritual batteries before returning to Manhattan to set up 'The Savage Eye', the exhibition which he truly believed would finally establish him as a major artist.

The second day found him strolling through Paris. The feeling of freedom and freshness revived him like an aphrodisiac. Brady knew that Paris too was moving towards a policy of isolationism, but for now it still retained some of its old magic. Brady gravitated towards the Pompidou Centre, that old dinosaur of traditional architecture. Before going in he enjoyed a light lunch at a pavement restaurant just watching the crowd and sipping calvados. He gazed lovingly at the girls as they flounced by and suddenly felt old and forgotten. He sighed, finished his drink, then joined the moving throng of tourists flooding in and out of the building.

He bought a guide and consulted it briefly, then decided to drift as his instincts prompted him. Half an hour later he found himself away from the crowds, walking towards a small gallery. The display above the door said simply 'Hans Bellmer 1902–1975'. Brady's skin began to erupt into goose bumps at the sight of the name and at the prospect of seeing a collection from one of the greatest artists of the erotic who had ever lived.

He entered the gallery and immediately lost track of time. Around the large white room Bellmer's work had been carefully arranged to display the artist's development from his original line drawings and sketches to the detailed anatomical sexual and surreal drawings of his middle years. But the exhibition was dominated by the creations that had made Bellmer famous – his dolls.

Photographs, drawings and the dolls themselves were frozen in time. Brady stared at the array of life-size dolls constructed from a variety of materials but particularly wood. The torsos and limbs were detachable as were parts of the head. Bellmer used to arrange his dolls in the most unusual and erotic configurations and poses then draw or photograph them. The pelvis was reversible and could be arranged to represent buttocks, thighs, breasts or shoulders. The photographs stopped Brady dead. Partly dressed dolls with limbs missing; dolls heavily made-up like prostitutes with swollen limbs and three breasts; dolls posing on staircases or in fields, their erotic beauty stirred dark desires within him. The images were sadistic, erotic, disturbing.

A soft voice spoke behind Brady, causing him to jump.

'Bellmer said that imagination has its roots exclusively in an awareness of the body. Language has few ways of describing bodily awareness.'

Brady turned to see a small brown-skinned man standing a few feet away. The man wore a guide's uniform which hung from his spare frame and flapped gently as he moved. His eyes were sharp and his command of English was excellent.

'You are American?' he asked Brady.

'English,' replied the photographer, 'but I live in America.'

'Hmm!' The little man did not seem impressed. 'And you are interested in Bellmer?'

'Yes, but I've never seen the dolls in the flesh, so to speak.'

'Bellmer constructed his first doll in 1933,' explained the guide. 'He wanted to make an artificial girl with anatomical possibilities capable of re-creating the heights of passion, even inventing new desires. Bellmer explored the hidden depths of erotic and sexual fantasy. The dolls represent a liberation of eroticism. He was regarded as a degenerate in Hitler's Germany but he broke away to come and live in Paris at the time of the post-Dada Surrealist movement.' The little man paused for breath. 'I'm not boring you?'

Brady shook his head and waited for him to continue.

'He developed and flourished here in Paris,' the guide carried on, 'and his doll developed into the cult of excess or convulsive beauty. Eroticism, you see, is related to knowledge of evil and the inevitability of death, rather than a simple expression of joyful passion. Gradually, however, the doll became a physical expression of Bellmer's own sexual fantasies – a plaything with the potential of continual manipulation. His dolls, and there were many, were photographed and exhibited all over the world, mainly in Surrealist galleries.'

The guide stopped. He gazed peacefully into space, allowing

Brady to immerse himself in the power of the dolls. One held a particular fascination for him. It was a large colour photograph of a doll without a head but with legs at both ends, tied and bound to a dead tree.

The mannequins had uncovered a lust for the satisfaction of desires he had either buried or ignored. He imagined decorating the dolls, painting them with love bites or worshipping them on a altar of passion.

As he stared at the exhibits, he caught sight of his reflection in several glass cases. It was fragmented and distorted. His face was unrecognizable. He experienced a powerful shock which shifted his perception of time. He was no longer Frank Brady. He knew that he was one of the ancients and had experienced many lives. Something outside himself was kindling his desire. A voice whispered something in his inner ear. He listened intently without understanding.

He knew, with spiritual clarity, that the dolls had opened a pathway in his mind, a disturbing and ultimately destructive highway along which he must travel.

He turned, shaking himself free from his reverie. The little guide had gone. Brady stood, allowing conflicting emotions and memories to wash through him. And now another image had forced its way on to his mental screen processor. He saw Jordan's face superimposed on the faces of the dolls. And then he knew what he had to do.

As he left the Pompidou Centre that day and walked off into the afternoon sun, he knew he was about to begin something which would almost inevitably lead to destruction and pain. But he knew also that the wheel was turning. What was to be had been set in motion long in the past.

Chapter Twelve

Johnny poured orange juice into a long tumbler and filled it with cracked ice. He passed it to Jordan who was toying with a slice of melon. Without make-up she still looked beautiful, but she was pale and drawn. She smiled at him and sipped her juice.

'You look terrible,' he told her with a smile.

She sighed. 'I didn't think I'd miss you so much.'

'Look, I'm OK. Not a scratch on me. You should know, you checked every inch.'

She responded with a weak chuckle. 'So, was it awful?'

'Pretty awful. It's like nothing on earth.'

'And were you able to find your victims?'

'I think so.' He paused. 'I don't know if I can pull this off. You just can't trust those freaks.'

'The whole thing sounds totally and utterly bizarre.'

They watched the dawn sun rising over the misty cityscape and ate their breakfast in silence for a time.

'Tell me about these nightmares,' coaxed Johnny.

A shadow of fear fell over Jordan's face and for a second her eyes clouded with pain. 'What can I tell you?' she whispered. 'I started having this recurring dream. Each time it's the same. And each time it fills me with such fear. There's a woman and blood and a purple curtain I'm terrified to touch and a door I'm too terrified to open. I know if I ever open it I might not wake up.'

Johnny sat up straight. She decided to tell him something she had promised herself she never would.

'Johnny, look, I . . .wasn't going to tell you this,' she said, 'but the woman in the dream, it's Angelica. I'm so sorry.'

Johnny said nothing for a moment. He couldn't speak. Then he found his breath.

'I've been having dreams too,' he told her. 'They started soon after I began my course of therapy. Angelica was in them at first.

Then something else took her place. Something from what Grohmann calls the Purple Zone.'

They said nothing for a short time until Jordan spoke.

'The police were here. They wanted to talk to you.'

'What did they want?' he asked a little too sharply. She looked up at him.

'They were checking out Bruce Willard's death. They were asking about that . . . that thing that killed him.'

'Did they say what it was?'

'No, they didn't say. They looked frightened, Johnny. Something is happening. I can feel it.'

'Nothing's going to happen.'

'I didn't imagine that creature. There were witnesses. The police are just doing their job. You were there too, remember.'

'How could I forget? Look, I've told you. We will get out. Just as soon as I get this show over with and get my hands on those credits. Then they can screw their contract. London sounds fine to me, by the way.'

There were those who knew precisely where the mutant dog had come from and exactly how it came to be created. At that moment, within a vast subterranean pump house, where a network of sewers conjoined, the dank walls resounded to the echoing sound of metal legs marching.

Bobby Bolero, accompanied by two silent Plater hybrids, was inspecting his creations. As he approached the hundred or so metal grilles that formed the aeration ducts on the floor of the station, he grunted and cracked his teeth.

In the bowels of the system, the inhabitants of sewer city heard the distinctive sound of his iron footsteps and they became excited and began to scream, with hunger. Although they feasted on the carrion bodies of the dead, the dying and the diseased, they had long ago mutated their internal organs. They had grown large and powerful. They had interbred. And they had mated with fresh blood and tissue to form a new breed.

Bolero had cultivated his alternative army by providing them with a cocktail of shurm-based drugs mixed with as much waste food and fresh flesh as could be found or newly slaughtered. It had taken only a few years for the mutations to evolve. Now they were dependent upon their supply. In their hundreds, in their thousands, they slavered and slobbered in the pits beneath the city. And the pace with which they mutated was now terrifying. A human being could fall into the sewer and become infected. The breath, the blood, the semen, even the kiss of such creatures could begin the process of cell destruction and regeneration. And they were not stupid. Many were smart, real smart. Bolero had no idea just how smart some of them had become. They gathered at the mighty sluice gates that shut off the Badlands sewers from the conduits beneath Manhattan. And they remembered. They remembered the good life in the opulence of the city. And they hungered, they thirsted for their share. And they knew that their only hope of reclaiming what was theirs by right lay with Bolero. He was their father now, and their mother. They listened to the voice of Bobby Bolero and through him to the words of Guru Lennon. They knew liberation was at hand. Bolero would lead them when the time was right.

They loved him. It was as simple as that. But, more importantly, they needed him.

'Now my beauties,' called Bolero, 'you all know who I am. Feeding time is here. So far, you've been my own little secret. Oh, you prowl the city but those who see you have not lived to speak of you. You are feared. You are legends. You are the shadows in the night.' Bolero paused amid a cacophony of distorted, larynx-bursting screams. 'One of you has escaped to the other side and has been seen. She was one of my favourites but her desire to escape proved too great. I am here to tell you that it won't be long. The day I promised you is almost here. The Guru Lennon has confided in me. I am his prince on earth. Now, eat!'

Bolero stomped to a bank of levers and one by one pulled them to half mast. Beneath the slippery rancid grilles, conduits opened and a mush of poisonous slime, excreta laced with shurm gushed into the sewers and into the hungry mouths of those who waited for liberation. Satisfied, Bolero lit a cheroot, clapped his spiked hands together and strolled on stiff legs to the exit ramp. He felt good. He was still alive. That was always a reason to feel good. He was somebody, unlike his old man who had been a bum from birth. They had walked all over him till he could have passed for the sidewalk. But not me, thought Bolero. Not this time. We are at the dawn of a new age, he thought, and his thin mouth slid open a little wider. He liked the thought. It was poetic. But then, he was a poet, just like Guru Lennon. He inhaled deeply and second-hand smoke issued from several orifices embedded in his leathery skin.

On an impulse, Bolero began to dance. A series of hoarse barks made do as an impromptu bossa nova rhythm section as he huffed and puffed in a parody of a Latin tune. His metal feet began to shuffle in time to his tune and he clicked his metal fingers. Sparks flew from the tips of his fingers and his heels, and the noise rebounded and echoed from the vast labyrinth of tunnels.

His two Plater compatriots stared impassively as their leader appeared to go into a paroxysm of shudders and shuffles, his metal and flesh pelvis gyrating in time to his snapping metal digits. A shudder went through their bodies as the rhythm got to them. With no sense of timing, they too began to dance; a jerk here, a stomp there. What passed for a smile briefly flickered across their hybrid faces and they remembered. Somewhere in the recesses of the remnants of their brains, they remembered music and light and laughter. And they remembered being in love. Their tear ducts still operated, though they had almost atrophied. Now, however, with the snarling sounds of the subterranean beasts throbbing beneath their feet and their leader executing a robotic cha-cha in front of them, they were happy. And, for the first time in years, they cried.

Johnny's mind was filled with the images of the Badlands. Looking across the table at Jordan and down at the streets where people strolled and laughed and traffic flowed at a uniform speed along Fifth Avenue it was hard to believe that the other world really existed.

'Brady's invited us to a party to launch his new exhibition. It'll be soon. Want to come?'

'Maybe,' she murmured. 'I haven't been feeling so good lately.

It's not just the nightmares. It's something else.' She paused. 'What's he like? Is he anything like his image?'

'He's a little bit crazy. But then you'd have to be doing what he does. He's self-centred, arrogant and clever.'

Jordan gazed quietly into the bottom of her tumbler.

'So, what's next? When are you bringing these creatures over?'

'There's a mutant there. She's going to help. She'll be in touch. The network will handle the logistics.'

'You said she,' said Jordan. 'What's she like?'

'Like?' mused Johnny. 'She's like a cross between Godzilla and Little Red Riding Hood. She's totally deformed, patched up with metal parts. You're not jealous, are you?' he laughed.

'No, of course not,' she said airily.

Johnny cleared his throat. 'I just want to say, I love you.'

She watched him for a moment. 'And I love you,' she said. 'You know, that's the first time I've ever said that to anyone.'

He looked at her. He wanted to speak but could not find the words.

She gazed over towards the East River and a small frown compressed her forehead.

'What's the matter?' said Johnny.

'I was just wondering. Why aren't these freaks pouring over here in their thousands?'

'I don't know,' he replied thoughtfully. 'The fact is some do come over. They say violent crime is on the up again. There are places they could cross without being seen. You never hear about the ones they don't catch.'

'How big a problem is it?' she asked.

'The ZeePees say it's under control. I've talked to a couple of guys on the newsvid desk. It's the critical mass factor. If a horde of screaming shurm freaks breached the river defences in some kind of mass attack then we could be in deep shit. But singly or in small groups they have no chance. They'd have to be sharp and alert *and* not be smashed out of their skulls to pose a real threat.' Johnny glanced at his watch and then gulped down the remainder of his orange juice. He got up from the table, leaned over and kissed her gently.

'I've got to go,' he said. 'I've got to put Maurice out of his misery. Why don't you try to get some rest. Get yourself a sauna and massage. You'll feel much better.'

She watched him cross the apartment until he turned and blew her a kiss as he left.

While Johnny was preparing to brief Freiberg and the senior production team on 'All the Way', Frank Brady had driven over to Morningside, a rambling middle-income residential area. He hadn't been there for years. He cruised around the quiet streets searching for a house he used to know well. When he first started in the business, one of his few real friends had been an old man named Otto Hahn, a German émigré who had started working as a sculptor before the Isolation and who had built a reputation amongst the avant-garde for his severe and anarchic figures and figurines. During the last decade the market for truly innovative art had all but disappeared, so Hahn had turned to the television and film industry, working as a model-maker and special-effects designer.

He had been Brady's mentor for a time, introducing him to the buyers and art dealers in the city and encouraging him to resist corrupting his true work. Hahn still sculpted for pleasure but showed his work only rarely. He had always been a reclusive and private person whose sheer genius and skill kept him in enough credits to reside in Manhattan.

Brady pulled up outside an old ramshackle corner brownstone and rang the bell, making sure he was seen by the hidden security system built into the reinforced door. A voice crackled a welcome and the door opened. Inside Brady walked softly along a dark corridor.

'Otto, it's me, Frank.'

A door at the end opened, flooding the hallway with light. Slivers of illumination etched the contours of a staircase which led from the gloomy interior to gathering shadows above. A small, dark figure emerged from a room along the corridor. Otto Hahn was thin with hollowed-out cheeks and piercing eyes that belied his age.

'For Frank Brady I will break open my last bottle of genuine malt.' His voice was soft with a slight accent. He opened his arms and the two men embraced with genuine fondness.

'How long has it been, Frank?' Hahn asked him with mock severity. 'Has fame corrupted you so much you have forgotten your old friends?'

'You taught me too well, Otto. I should have come before. It's just that . . .'

'You've been so busy,' Hahn chuckled, 'and now of course you are here because you want something, yes?'

'You could always see right through me couldn't you, Otto?' said Brady.

'Come in, come in. Let's drink together. It's been a long time.'

Otto Hahn lived, worked and slept in one enormous room. At the far end was a door which led to a small kitchen and from there to a patch of garden which could also be reached by a path at the side of the house. Apart from a bed and some chairs, a bookcase full to overflowing and a wardrobe, the room was crammed with a bizarre mixture of objects. Pieces of sculpture, prosthetic models from various film and TV projects, drawing boards, workbenches and tools, computers and design aids were scattered everywhere.

Hahn indicated Brady should take a seat while he fetched a bottle of Scotch and two glasses. Slowly and ceremoniously he opened the whisky and poured two large shots. The men raised their glasses. No toast was necessary. They drank in silence and sighed with appreciation. Hahn refilled their glasses, settled back in his chair and regarded Brady with an amused smile.

'Now, Frank, what brings you to see your old friend after all this time?'

Brady took a piece of paper from his inside pocket, unfolded it carefully and placed it on the table. Hahn retrieved a pair of thin gold spectacles from the top pocket of his tattered overalls and regarded the drawing in silence. Finally he looked up.

'Well, well. The spirit of Hans Bellmer lives,' he sighed with obvious pleasure.

Before Johnny joined the routine production meeting with Lloyd and other senior members of the team, he stopped off at the third-floor office of Stan Michaels, the Channel's financial controller.

Michaels was a bright-eyed, owl-like individual dressed casually in a silk shirt and tan slacks. His office was a model of efficiency. Not one credit passed in or out of the Channel's accounts without his knowing about it. He was one of the select breed in Manhattan who understood how its complex financial structure operated. When Johnny entered the office, Michaels smiled a welcome.

'Well, well, the star descends from the heavens. What brings you down from the dizzy heights of the top floor?'

'You're the most important person in the building, Stan,' Johnny grinned. 'I've just come to see how you are.'

Michaels laughed and poured two coffees from a nearby percolator.

'You've come to check on your credit rating no doubt,' said the accountant, leaning back in his comfortable chair.

'You must be psychic. I just dropped in for some civilized conversation and a cup of coffee when I found that thought just popping into my mind.'

Stan Michaels swivelled around and faced his multimedia terminal. He spoke to a screen, issued a series of coded commands and a spreadsheet of figures scrolled up. He was tapping his teeth with a pencil when he suddenly leaned forward and held up his hand. The screen locked instantly. Then he appraised the mass of figures like he was reading a map. He squinted over at Johnny and shrugged.

'So what's your problem, superstar? Your credit bank is healthy, you're at level three credit rating, and that's as high as you or I can ever get unless we run this place or run the city and live out in Long Island.'

'Has Freiberg mentioned our deal?' Johnny tried to keep any anxiety out of his voice.

'Deal?' murmured Michaels vaguely. 'What deal?'

Johnny's top lip was suddenly damp. He leaned forward and rested his elbows on Michael's desk.

'I'm working on a new idea for the show. I discussed with Freiberg a two million credit deposit. It's a kind of bonus.'

Michaels feigned innocence for a moment then couldn't keep from breaking into a grin.

'Hey, your face, you should take a look in the mirror. Relax, it's all noted. But it hasn't been finally authorized yet. Guess you're going to have to deliver whatever it is everyone's talking about before I get the sanction.' Michaels shook his head and whistled softly. 'I'll tell you something: two million credits puts you in the super-income bracket. You might just be able to afford a place over on Long Island. Congratulations, whatever it is you're working on must be pretty big potatoes.'

Johnny let his muscles relax and he smiled warmly. 'Do me a favour Stan, when it gets the sanction, let me know, will you?'

'Sure thing. I'll even let you buy me dinner.'

Johnny laughed and left the office feeling calm and buoyant. Minutes later he was lounging comfortably in the atrium-floor production meeting-room. Lloyd was there looking a little fragile. The usual bunch were sitting around: Jack Carey, Wilma Rubenstein and Phil Razzman. Two others were also at the meeting. Clark Taylor was head of the Channel's PR department and Johnny came into contact with him fairly regularly. It was unusual for anyone from PR to attend a routine production meeting, however. But the figure causing Lloyd to sweat nervously was a tall, mean-looking stranger who sat rigidly stiff-backed and looked uncomfortable as though unused to this kind of informality. Taylor had introduced him as Mr Solo, from State Security.

Johnny sat up when it was Taylor and not Lloyd who opened the meeting.

'Ladies and gentlemen, I'm sure you won't mind this departure from your usual format but there are one or two things which need to be discussed and explained. I'll come straight to the point. Channel Boom Boom, for reasons better known to the board, has decided to go on a ratings attack against CyberTel by putting some of the inhabitants of the other side on the show in the hope they will be prepared to, well, kill themselves on live television. Johnny, I understand this was your idea and that you have made some contacts in the Badlands and may be able to bring them over here. I'll come back to that point later. Personally, and I don't mind being personal here, I find the whole idea distasteful and degrading but I, like all of you, have a job to do.

There is however growing evidence of unrest across the river and that's why Mr Solo here is going to be in sole charge of security on this project. He will explain his role in a moment.' Taylor paused and mopped his forehead with a napkin, then sipped some water before continuing. 'Now, there is another dimension to this situation. Rumours of live suicide on TV have been spreading. In an organization like this leaks occur. From a PR point of view, we don't mind the rumours. It means we don't have to spend so much on promotion. So there is an audience out there waiting in anticipation of these rumours being true. The press is calling from all over the country and from all over the world. Our story is wait and see, something is going to happen but we will not confirm or deny what that something might be. It might not be live`suicide because no one, except Johnny, has any idea whether this whole thing can be pulled off.'

'Do you want me to bring you up to date?' Johnny asked.

'In a moment Johnny,' said Taylor firmly. 'OK, now, apart from the board of Channel Boom Boom, certain individuals at State level, programme director Maurice Freiberg and a number of designers, we in this room are the only ones who know about the other, and may I say, most bizarre dimension of this whole business. The crucifix machine. The existence of this machine must remain totally, and I repeat, totally secret. We don't know yet if it will be used but it seems likely. The fact is, ladies and gentlemen, that we have not got so much a show here as a piece of political theatre. The PR ramifications of this are staggering. I have advised the board against its use and they have elected to ignore my advice. What matters now is timing. We need to know precisely what is happening, when it will happen, how many shows can we put on, how do we handle these freaks when and if they ever get here. The production details I will leave to the experts. Whether suicide on live TV will keep a lid on growing unrest no one knows. It might even inflame the situation. Thank you for listening so patiently. I just wanted to put things into context. So, Lloyd, Johnny, where do we stand?'

The producer sighed and looked over at Johnny.

'Thank you, Clark. Can I just say that I too have reservations about turning a piece of entertainment into something much more sinister. In my defence I've got to tell you that although the idea was mine originally, it was actually meant as a joke. I had no idea until a couple of weeks back that certain people would take it seriously. However, we now have no option but to proceed. I can tell you, having been to the Badlands, that it's like nowhere on earth. I was lucky. I had protection. And I managed to make contact with a group of Feeks and Farooks who regard stylized death as their life's work. If it doesn't sound too crazy, they live for death. They want to die on public display. That's a fact. Whatever we think about it won't change that. I have a contact who has promised to arrange everything on their side. I've still got to go back in. I'm not looking forward to it. I want to get back in one piece with or without them. Let me make that clear right from the start. They won't play ball if I've got half the ZeePee force with me. But, and this is the big but, I don't know when, if at all, we will have lift-off. We're not dealing with rational people here. I'm waiting for a message. That's all I can tell you. I don't know about rehearsals, Lloyd, we may really have to do this one live.'

'You're developing your sense of humour, Johnny,' chuckled Phil Razzman with heavy irony.

'You make it sound like a weekend break.' Wilma Rubenstein was clearly upset and disturbed.

Solo spoke for the first time and his voice was thin and humourless.

'OK, let me say one or two things and then you can get on with whatever it is you do here.'

The production team looked at each other and then back at the hard, sallow face of the security chief.

'Mr Raine, you will bring them in over the bridge,' Solo continued in his flat, toneless voice. 'You will collect the individuals concerned because yours is the face they recognize and trust. If the slightest thing goes wrong I have orders to destroy these weirdo scum without question. Have no doubt about that. Mr Raine, you will cease to be under our protection the moment you cross the bridge. We cannot guarantee your safety in shitsville if we cannot send a protection squad with you. You must understand that the risk is yours and yours alone. The

Zone Police on Queensboro will be fully briefed. Mr Raine, you will transport your guests in a secure vehicle which we will provide and we will make certain structural arrangements inside the studio to ensure the security of the building and the safety of your audience until it is time for these freaks to perform.'

'You mean they'll be locked up,' said Johnny.

'I'm afraid I must insist they be allowed a certain freedom,' said Lloyd, breathing heavily. 'They are human beings after all. They need to move around, take direction. We have to work with these people.'

Solo snorted. He regarded Lloyd bleakly, as if the producer was just another equally deviant life-form. But it was clear he was under instructions to be cooperative with these creative people. It didn't come naturally. He chose his words carefully.

'We will construct a safe environment and have enough discreet manpower to cope with any breach of security. Your guests will be permitted a certain amount of freedom of move-ment. Is that all right with you?'

Lloyd looked around at his production team with an air of triumph.

'Good, now, time is marching on and we have a meeting to get through.'

Without changing expression Solo stood up and addressed himself to Johnny.

'You will keep me informed, Mr Raine. I need to know when and where. Is that clear?'

'Perfectly.' Johnny replied.

'And Johnny,' said Taylor, 'the same goes for me. As soon as you know it's going to come off, definitely, we're going public. So I need to know the second you know. OK?'

Johnny nodded in agreement.

Clark Taylor smiled weakly at the production team, then left with Solo. As soon as the door had closed there was a collective sigh of relief. Then everyone started to talk at once.

That afternoon Frank Brady arrived at the Lepri Gallery. He had left Otto Hahn in a state of rare excitement. The old model-maker would work non-stop to breathe prosthetic life into Frank

Brady's vision. Hahn's creation would be a futuristic Bellmer using all the skills and materials unavailable back in the 1930s. A network of electronic arteries would honeycomb the creature but the overall creation would remain true to Bellmer's own obsessive design principles.

Brady looked good. He stood outside the discreet portico of Manhattan's leading art gallery and permitted a tingle of excitement to run through him. He enjoyed the feeling. Something was driving him forward to a date with destiny. Far from being fearful he was excited, filled with the anticipation of a schoolboy. The woman Jordan, the man Raine, Hans Bellmer, Otto Hahn and now the most important exhibition of his career, all were coming together and joining forces in a synchronous whole. And the TV suicide business, that too was connected. Everything was connected. Brady took a strange form of comfort from this thought as he entered the gallery and experienced the familiar hushed reverence it engendered. He walked across the entrance hall, acknowledging various members of staff. He was heading for the main gallery, on the east side. As he approached the entrance he noted with satisfaction that it had been roped off and guarded by two attendants. He was recognized as he approached.

'Is Antonio inside?' he asked one of the guards.

'Sure is, Mr Brady,' answered the guard as he unclipped a rope barrier to let him through.

Brady went in and stood gazing around the spacious, semi-circular gallery. There were windows in the roof area and around the perimeter allowing natural light to flood in. Discreet spotlights were positioned around the room to provide additional lighting for particular exhibits.

There were about ten people in the room assembling the exhibition. Photographs of various sizes had been stacked around the walls and partitions had been erected to separate aspects of Brady's work. Supervising every detail of the show was a large man with a strong, leonine head crowned with flowing grey curls. He was lightly tanned and wore a flourishing grey moustache. He was dressed in a simple but elegant, dark-blue suit that emphasized his powerful shoulders. He turned and beamed at Brady as the photographer entered.

'Frank, how kind of you to show up at your own exhibition,' he said playfully.

'Antonio, I could never beat you at this game, mate,' smiled Brady.

The two men embraced briefly and Antonio Lepri, the gallery owner and one of the most influential personalities in the world art business, indicated the work with a graceful gesture.

'This is going to be, quite simply, one of the most staggering exhibitions we have put on in Manhattan in the last twenty years.'

Brady looked across to where an assistant was placing a series of photographs diagonally down one wall. He couldn't avoid an involuntary gasp as he gazed at the images of Marcia's death dive. The final photograph of the model impaled on the girder was simply terrifying when viewed in the civilized surroundings of this elegant white room. Lepri noticed his reaction.

'I think that one is going to cause a few heart attacks,' he remarked.

The two men regarded some of the photographs in silence. At the far end of the gallery was a huge enlargement, some ten feet by six feet, grainy as hell but just as powerful. It depicted a mutant strapped to a makeshift crucifix. Around his neck an old tyre was burning fiercely. The mutant's expression had been caught to perfection. A frozen, immobile scream of terror from a tortured soul. Around the base of the cross a gang of Badland warriors were cheering.

'So, what are you calling that one, Frank?' asked Lepri.

'Hmm! I thought, "For Christ's sake", said Brady. 'It has a certain ring to it, don't you think.'

A shiver of displeasure crossed Lepri's face.

'It might upset our one and only Christian,' said the gallery owner.

'What do you want, Toni? Shots of rich women dribbling over their diamonds? This might just provoke a single moment of compassion.'

'It's terrible,' said Lepri quietly as they looked at the image.

'Old habits die hard, mate, don't forget that. Now, Toni, I want to make a late addition to the show.'

'What!' Lepri turned to him. 'Everything has been planned in meticulous detail, the space requirement, the balance, the essence of your work. How can we add more photographs?'

'This is not a photograph, Toni,' Brady explained. 'Call it a sculpture. I will arrange for it to be delivered and supervise its positioning personally. It will be in a glass case covered with black drapes. No one, and that includes you, me darlin' boy, will be allowed to see it until the opening night. I want to unveil it myself.'

'A sculpture?' Lepri was fascinated. 'I didn't know you sculpted, Frank?'

'It's a kind of sculpture. Call it a photo-sculpture if you like.'

'It's your show, Frank. Just let me know where you want this object to be positioned.'

Brady slapped Lepri on the shoulders. 'It's looking fantastic Toni. "The Savage Eye" is going to frighten the fuck out of some of the rich, complacent bastards who live in this town. And you know what? It's just what they need. A spiritual kick in the groin. How are we doing on numbers?'

'We're going to break records with this one. We've had interest from all over the world. It's incredible how you can work in a tightly controlled cauldron like Manhattan yet become world famous.'

Brady shook hands with Antonio Lepri and walked slowly across the polished wooden floor towards the door.

That night Johnny Raine returned to his apartment on Fifth Avenue. His own private entrance was situated at the side of the building through a secluded archway. He was about to reach for his compu-key when the sky fell in. A stinking black hood was rammed over his head almost choking him. Someone or some-thing grabbed him from behind, pinning his arms to his sides. Whatever it was it possessed enormous strength. Johnny could feel his bones creaking. A dampness began to seep through his lightweight suit on to his back as he was held in a vice-like embrace. Whatever was holding him so tightly he could hardly breathe was covered in slime, a stinking, fetid, death-sweat. Through the thin hood he could hear the creature's hoarse breath and could feel its animal-like warmth filtering through the fabric of the hood and almost suffocating him. He gasped with pain and fear, sucking the hood into his mouth and tasting its foul stench on his tongue. Bile rose from his stomach and he started to retch.

He felt himself lifted bodily off the ground as though he was weightless. He was carried a short distance. Then he was aware that there were two of them. Something small was making sounds. Johnny could hear little except the grunting breath of his captor and strange muttering sounds from the other.

Now he was lifted into the air and spun around. He was totally disoriented. When the impact came it knocked the breath out of his body. He was lying face down on the ground. A blackness was approaching and he passed out.

How long he lay there he did not know. He came to and thought immediately that he was blind. Trickles of vomit issued from his mouth as he lay, too terrified to move. Every part of his body ached. His mind was racing. He was alive. That much he was sure of. He listened hard. Nothing except a pounding in his ears. With a shock he realized it was his own heart beating. Thank God, he cried to himself, tears bursting from his eyes uncontrollably. For an age he lay there, fighting nausea, straining his ears for the slightest sound.

At last he moved. He was covered in a slimy, glutinous substance which made it difficult. Desperately, he ripped the hood from his head and gulped in mouthfuls of air. Gasping with relief, he rolled on to his back and stared up at the night sky. The stars were particularly bright, he thought to himself for no apparent reason. Slowly he raised his head and focused. He was alone in the small patch of garden at the back of the apartment. He sat up with difficulty. His ribs were aching and sore. Then he became aware of the stench. With a shock he realized it was coming from him. He swore with fear and revulsion. The glutinous mess he was covered in stank like excreta mixed with other bodily fluids. He was almost sick again.

He got to his feet, then noticed that something was pinned to the front of his jacket. It was a note of some description. Breathing heavily, he trudged across the grass, leaving a trail of slime. Whoever or whatever had attacked him had vanished. Johnny could see slimy trails and footprints leading out into the street. He fumbled in his jacket pocket for his compu-key and opened the door to his apartment.

As soon as he got inside he ripped off his clothes and stuffed them into the disposal macerator. Now naked, he still stank to high heaven and there were bruises on his ribcage where his attacker had gripped him. He put the note down and ran to the shower.

He gasped with pleasure and pain as the needle spray hit him. He soaked for a long time, slumped against the shower wall, water streaming over his body. Finally he towelled dry, slipped into his dressing gown and poured himself a drink before picking up the note. Carefully he washed it free of slime, then opened the soggy envelope. Inside was a single torn sheet of paper with the words: 'It will be soon, don't forget me, Shell', written in some kind of crayon. He frowned. She said she would be in touch but he hadn't expected a courier service. Maybe the creatures who delivered the message were her only choice.

Johnny thought about Shell. Could he trust that strange, mutant creature? She had a weird power, that much was certain, despite her horrific appearance. The prospect of going into the Badlands again, this time on his own, filled him with a fear he could almost taste. This time there would be no Frank Brady. He would have to find that building again. He would need to organize a sloop jet and weapons again.

But the thought that gripped his heart with icy fear was the prospect of not returning and of never seeing Jordan again. He poured another drink to steady his nerves. He knew with certainty he would not sleep that night.

Chapter Thirteen

Frank Brady knew that Otto Hahn would not take long to complete the task he had set him. The old man had long been an admirer of Hans Bellmer, so to be asked to emulate his work would be a pleasure. He waited for three days before calling Hahn and checking on progress. With his excitement mounting, Brady learned it was ready.

That evening, he parked near the old brownstone and rang the bell. This time there was no hiss of recognition from the vidcom. He tried again and got no response. Puzzled, he retreated a few steps, then slowly walked down the side of the house towards the little garden and the kitchen. By now he was a little nervous. He looked around him, checking for intruder alarms and, seeing no obvious signs that one of the tiny peephole scanners was installed, he tried the back door. He knew that undetectable and virtually infallible security systems were widespread, but he knew Otto Hahn as an old-fashioned man who would probably not bother with the more sophisticated protection systems. No alarm sounded. The door was locked. Otto wouldn't have gone out, not with Frank Brady coming over.

He noticed a window near the kitchen door. Standing on tiptoe he pushed his face close to the glass and stared through. For a moment he could see nothing. Then he noticed the flickering images on a media-web screen. He was looking directly into Hahn's studio. It was dark, except for the terminal in the corner. Brady couldn't resist a smile when he saw Johnny Raine gesticulating wildly and soundlessly on screen.

Then he spotted something that wiped the smile of anticipation from his face and froze his blood. In the patchy light from the TV something was lying on the floor, jutting out from behind an easy chair. It was an arm. And it was lifeless.

Resisting the impulse to panic, Brady pulled his sleeve over his fist and punched in the window. He found an old brick lying on the ground and he used it to knock away the jagged edges. With a final swift glance around he heaved himself up on to the window sill and then squeezed through the window. He snagged his trousers on the way in, then pushed hard and fell with a heavy thud on to the floor.

He stood up and looked around the dark room.

'Otto!' he called out. There was no reply. In the dim light, the room took on a strange tomb-like appearance. Shapes appeared in menacing poses, especially the prosthetic models. The very air was oppressive and there were patches of denser air within the room which were so compressed they appeared like columns or figures. Brady called Otto's name again, feeling his way towards the chair. In the corner, Johnny Raine was grinning at him on screen. The sound had been switched off and, as Brady watched the young man's image, he seemed to be talking directly to Brady, almost warning him, mouthing the words 'no, no no!'

Brady walked very softly across the room. On his left he could see more workshop materials and something tall covered with a dust sheet. With his eyes on the chair he moved forward and knelt down. He sniffed. A strong smell of charred flesh filled the room. Behind Brady, the reflected image of Johnny Raine flickered on the sheet covering the tall object, like a ghostly emanation. Something made a slight noise under the cover.

Click!

The sheet began to move. It slid over the contours of something smooth.

Brady peered around the back of the chair. That's when he saw it. Lying on the floor was the arm he had seen from the window. Otto Hahn's arm. Brady began to choke. The smell of incinerated flesh was powerful here. He moved the chair aside, then gagged at what he saw.

There was very little left of Otto Hahn. His arm ended in a small pile of smouldering ash. His head and half his face had been reduced to charred bone. His body was still smouldering and the immediate floor area around it was blackened. It was as if a bolt of lightning had struck the old man. Brady reached out and picked up the thin wire spectacles, which were still perched on what had been his nose. He gasped with pain and dropped them. Brady half stood, staring at the remains of his mentor. He was crying, but he could not sob. His breath had seized somewhere within him.

Click!

Slowly, Brady turned.

Click!

The drape had slid halfway down. A woman's arm was outstretched, finger pointing directly at Brady. As he stared at the apparition, its arm moved downwards making a clicking sound.

As Brady watched incredulously, the sheet responded to the call of gravity and slid from the object. Brady's eyes widened in surprise, wonder and terror. Staring back at him was a doll so lifelike that he was not entirely convinced it wasn't real.

'My God,' croaked Brady, 'you're bloody perfect.'

He was reminded immediately of the Bellmer dolls he had seen in Paris. This was no shop-window mannequin. This was a faithful replica of the multi-jointed dolls made famous by the German eroticist. But it was constructed from a flesh-like material. Even its fingers were jointed. It was as near human as you could get. Brady approached the doll, staring into its face. In the flickering darkness the face looked hauntingly familiar. He touched the doll. It felt cool and the material had the familiar plasticity of flesh.

A new expression registered on Brady's face. His customary emotional control had dissipated. Now his face was filled with desire, fear and fascination: his was the face of a man obsessed.

He noticed a small object sitting on a table nearby. A controller. Gently, almost reverently, he picked it up and aimed it at the doll. He experimented with a number of buttons. The doll began to move. Brady found he had limited control over the movement of the doll's limbs. He could make them bend, stretch and turn. The doll could not walk or, at least, he couldn't make it do so. Even its mouth could move.

As he was playing with the controller, he noticed, with a heart-pounding wrench, that the doll's limbs could be removed and fitted to other parts of its body, just like the Bellmer design.

'Otto, you have excelled yourself. What an epitaph.' Brady

turned and once again almost wept at the sight of the charred body.

'How,' muttered Brady, 'how did this happen?'

He looked at the doll as if for an answer. For a moment, he had half-expected the doll to speak.

Brady was now filled with a sense of purpose. He knew exactly what he had to do. All those hundreds of photographs of Jordan would prove their worth.

Suddenly, he was thinking clearly. He picked up the sheet and covered the doll, then slipped the controller into his pocket. With a final glance at the remains of his old friend, he picked up the doll and made for the front door. He opened it and peered outside. All was quiet. Brady walked casually to his electro-turbo and placed the doll in the passenger seat. On an impulse he removed the sheet and threw it into the back. Then he climbed into the driver's seat and looked at his passenger. It was incredible, so lifelike, as though all it needed was a human heart to bring it into being.

He drove home slowly, savouring the company of the doll. No one gave them a second glance even when they stopped at traffic lights.

When Brady got the doll back to his apartment he took it straight to his sanctum. There he positioned the doll on the chair in the centre of the room, surrounded by images of Jordan. Frantically, he ran for his camera and began to photograph the doll from every angle. He experimented, moving her limbs, using a combination of the controller and physical re-assembly. His fingers traced the contours of the doll's body. He was sweating profusely now and he moved in short jerks and bursts of energy.

He put the camera down carefully and stood in front of the doll. It stared at him without feeling.

'I'll make you feel something, you bitch,' he croaked.

He began to stroke the doll's inanimate breasts, running his thumbs over her nipples.

'Wait till I've finished with you,' he hissed at the doll. 'You won't recognize yourself.'

*

That night Jordan was alone. She had been working late and when Johnny had called they had both agreed to get an early night. He had sounded tired and wound up.

It was nearly midnight. She considered taking a pill to help her sleep but decided she would not be beaten by any nightmare. She emptied her mind and began to drift into semi-consciousness.

A vivid image of Frank Brady entered her mind. It was so vivid it felt like someone had run a sword through her brain. It was only the briefest glimpse. She had not been feeling well. She put it all down to overwork and stress. But now she felt weak and she began to sweat. Her skin started to crawl. She sat up, switched on the bedside light and examined herself. She could see nothing out of the ordinary. Her breasts were heavy and her nipples were proud and erect. But she had the distinct feeling they were being caressed. Goose bumps had erupted all over her breasts as the familiar feeling of arousal began. Her skin was crawling, as though millions of insects were running over her body.

'What's happening?' she cried.

Instinctively, she got up and ran to the shower. The spray jets pulsed warm water which cascaded over her body. She rubbed her breasts, massaging them madly. Gradually, the feelings began to ebb. She slumped against the shower wall and turned off the water. With difficulty she stepped into the bathroom. A feeling of intense weakness had washed over her. She stood for a moment, staring at her reflection in a full-length mirror.

'God, you've lost weight,' she mumbled to herself, 'and you look like shit.'

It was true. Her face was pale and her skin was slightly blotchy. She ran her fingers through her hair, then stared at her hand. A small clump of hair had come away from her scalp.

'What the hell's happening to me?' She bit her lip and suppressed a choking sob.

When she went back to bed she reached for the little bottle of pink pills.

*

The next morning Johnny arrived early. When he saw her his face clouded over.

'What's up? You really don't look too good.' He reached for her and held her close.

'I don't know,' she replied weakly. 'I think maybe I've got some kind of wasting disease.'

He held her shoulders at arm's length. 'That's not funny. Have you seen a doctor?'

'No.'

'Well, book an appointment. We pay a fortune for medi-care so we may as well get our money's worth. Take the day off and get yourself over to the clinic. I insist.'

She smiled up at him weakly. She did feel tired and washed-out. She wasn't sleeping well and even when she did bomb out with the pink pills she did not wake up refreshed. What with the nightmare which recurred several times a week and now the odd feelings linked to Frank Brady, she was beginning to worry. She decided not to tell Johnny about the Frank Brady connection. It sounded absurd.

'Maybe you're right,' she said submissively.

'Of course I am,' said Johnny. 'Now, I'll fix breakfast while you sit in the sun.'

She allowed herself to be shepherded to the balcony while Johnny busied himself in the kitchen. He had decided not to mention the slimy attack of yesterday. He didn't know what to make of it himself. Instead, he put on his bright, good-morning-America voice.

'Maybe you should try some meditation?' he called from the recesses of the apartment. 'Might help you to relieve some stress.'

She gave no reply. As she sat in her cool white chair on her sixth-floor balcony she had the distinct impression of someone or something touching her between her thighs. Without knowing why she glanced at the apartment opposite. There was nothing unusual about it. The windows were dark. As she stared at them she began to experience a palpable feeling of menace which she knew emanated from behind the windows. Something was watching her. She shook her head to clear the illusion. Get a grip, she told herself angrily.

Just then Johnny arrived with a breakfast tray and placed it carefully on the white table. He looked at her with some concern.

'I don't want anything bad to happen to you, Jordan. I couldn't stand it you know.'

He sounded so child-like and lost at that moment that Jordan's heart opened and went out to him. He bent to hug her and she held him desperately.

'Nothing's going to happen to me. I've got you to take care of me, haven't I?'

'You bet,' he said.

Brady had not slept. He had sent Satoko away for a while. She would return in time to organize his pre-exhibition party. For the moment he was alone with his new creation. Carl Meissen, his agent, had called several times insisting they meet to discuss offers and projects. Brady had told him to refuse everything until the exhibition was over. And then he wanted to take stock, see where he was going next. Grudgingly, Meissen had seen the logic in this, although he could see his percentage, and his meal-ticket, slipping out of his grasp.

Brady was now working in overdrive. Inside the sanctum, photographs and snippets of photographs littered the floor. Brady was hard at work, turning the doll from an essentially featureless female mannequin into something which would almost look human. If only I could breathe life into her, Brady thought as he worked. And his mind was conjuring up magical practices he would use to push back the barriers of eroticism till he made contact with the infinite.

Right now he was turning the doll into a replica of Jordan Semiramis. He was carefully making a photo-sculpture by pasting down life-size cut-outs of photographic images on to the contours of the doll's body. The result at first looked vaguely cubist.

Brady was breathing heavily, exhausted by his work. He had not eaten or drunk anything since he had started. Gratefully, he opened a bottle of champagne and smeared a slice of black bread with truffle pâté. Then he relaxed and studied the result of his creative efforts.

He played with the lighting, shifting from dazzling brilliance to near darkness and watched the way the doll altered and changed expressions. The features were not regular. There was a patchwork quality about the result. Brady played with the controller, noting how the limbs moved now that they had been papered over. He had painted the doll with a light cellulose-based liquid that formed into an ultra-thin membrane. This acted as a seal. The limbs could still be detached and positioned elsewhere to give the potential of a variety of postures and poses. Brady could hardly wait to start. He intended to photograph the Jordan doll on location all over the city and across the river in the Badlands.

But, before he did, there was one more little job to finish, one stroke of genius to complete. Something of which, Brady was sure, Hans Bellmer himself would have been proud.

He stood up and went to his camera store and selected a tiny motorized Fuji with compu-link. Then he approached the doll. Kneeling down almost reverentially in front of the doll, which had been positioned in a casually erotic pose, Brady touched the doll's navel. A small flap opened and inside was a miniature electrical housing. Delicately Brady fitted the camera into the housing and connected two tiny wires to the two other male connections. They were self-soldering. Brady had been holding his breath. He relaxed, exhaled and replaced the flap. Inside the doll's navel, the tiny lens winked.

Brady stood and undressed slowly.

'Right my little darlin',' he smiled, 'take a look at this then.'

A whirring sound came from the doll's stomach. Its arms were stretched into anatomically impossible positions. Its head was twisted halfway around its neck but Jordan's photographic eye still stared bleakly at Brady as he began to pose in front of it. He moved lithely like a dancer, pressing the controller at random. Muted clicks came from the doll's navel as the camera shutter opened and closed.

Hours later, Brady and the doll were driving over Queensboro Bridge. ZeePee security had got used to his regular appearances.

It was not forbidden to enter the Badlands but it was positively discouraged. Still, quite a few desperadoes attempted it. Some never returned. Some stayed, finding a home from home amid the anarchy. And others were forcibly exiled into the urban jungle. These were the failures who went bust and couldn't maintain their taxes and compulsory security payments.

Brady had hidden the doll in the back of his sloop jet. Tonight he wanted to remain inconspicuous, although he knew the very sight of a sloop jet spelt Manhattanite. Captured sloop jets were a great prize. That was why, when parked, they could be placed in anti-tow mode. The exterior was so smooth there was nowhere to hook a tow line, and the Lexus system could be primed to fire if the vehicle was touched. Only voice-activated control could disengage the system.

Brady turned his lights down to dim and headed east. Avoiding the areas he knew would be crowded, he stayed close to the river till he found what he was looking for.

He parked in darkness next to a ruined factory. Carefully, he stepped out of the jet, carrying the doll and a number of cameras around his neck. He set his security systems, checked his pulse pistol was in place and, taking a small torch, checked out the location. It was a tomb, filled with rusting and ruined machinery. And it was perfect. In one corner stood the remains of an old automobile, corroded and lifeless. Brady was sweating with fear and excitement as he posed the doll amid the rusty metal. He would have to be careful. His bursts of flash might be noticed. There were things lurking in these dark buildings that he did not want to be on first-name terms with. Brady was reminded suddenly of the expression on Marcia's face before she fell. She had seen something that had terrified her to the point of death.

Brady worked feverishly, using the controller to move the doll into different positions. If he had listened he would have heard another noise. The soft whirr of another camera was coming from the doll.

Brady did not stay in one location too long. He found another building with a staircase still intact. It stood alone and ended abruptly in mid-air. Brady disassembled the doll and placed its limbs, head and torso on different stairs. The bizarre combination excited him. Something about the configuration of the limbs was deeply sexual. He felt close to Hans Bellmer at that moment. He was probing into areas of the sexual psyche that few had ever done. He took more photographs, switching limbs, torso and head into different combinations.

Then he heard it. It was faint at first but it gradually grew louder and closer. It sounded like the cry of a small child, pitiful, seeking protection. Sweat had congealed on Brady's body. His skin was clammy and he fumbled helplessly as he slung his cameras around his neck and began to gather up the doll. There was no time to assemble it. The whimpering sound seemed to come from everywhere. It was like the very air was crying.

Brady looked over to where he had parked the sloop jet and saw a shadow pass across the vehicle. His blood froze. Desperately, he started to climb the staircase. The structure shivered. Brady knew it was on the point of collapse. He tried to spread his weight and hold the doll at the same time. This is crazy, he thought. I'm trapped here. There is no way out except to jump down to the ground into the darkness. He remembered Marcia and began to shake. He reached the top of the staircase and gazed into the semi-darkness. He felt foolish. Here he was, perched at the top of a staircase which ended in nothingness while some unknown creature of the dark had him at its mercy.

He could see the shadow. It was denser than the surrounding darkness, almost as though it had detached itself from it. The whimpering whisper was growing louder. The shadow was moving towards the staircase. Brady reached very slowly and deliberately for his pulse pistol. As he started to take aim, the staircase gave a shudder and pieces of masonry fell to the ground with a clatter. The shock caused Brady to lose his grip on the pistol and it fell into the darkness. He cursed. Now he was really frightened. He had no protection, except his camera. With sudden hope, he remembered the camera flash. Maybe this thing could not stand bright light. It was a possibility. It made sense. It was his only chance.

That was when he heard the voices.

There were at least three of them. One of the voices was weeping and begging the others. They were approaching from the other side of the building. Brady tried not to breathe. He was counting on not being seen. He glanced down at the shadow and saw nothing. The muffled keening sound had ceased. Brady twisted his head and saw them. It was difficult to make them out but it was clear what was taking place. One of them was about to die.

The victim was struggling in the grip of the other two, begging and crying to be set free. He was fighting for his life but his captors were laughing cruelly. They reached the base of the staircase and stopped. Brady could make them out now. Two highly painted street warriors were holding a short, stocky man prisoner. They were all grotesquely ugly. The heavies were brutally scarred and carried an array of weaponry. The prisoner was bleeding profusely. His face was obscured by blood and dirt.

'This'll do,' snarled the bigger of the two. 'Tie him to the railings.'

With the stocky man gradually resigning himself to his fate, he was roughly tied to the bottom railing. The whole staircase shook and Brady prayed it would not collapse. Then he prayed they would not spot his pulse pistol and, more importantly, the sloop jet.

'There's gonna be pain and pleasure, Menko,' the smaller one spat at his victim.

'Yeah!' snorted his companion. 'You're gonna feel the pain and we're gonna get all the pleasure. Isn't life a bitch?'

'Please,' begged the older man, 'please, don't do it. I promise I'll deliver, just give me a coupla days more.'

'Time is an illusion,' said the bigger thug, taking a metal spike from his belt. 'Besides, we don't feel like givin' you any more. We feel like killin' you. Now, what's wrong with that, Menko? Can you come up with a persuasive argument?'

Menko began to blubber uncontrollably. Brady wrinkled his nose and tried not to breathe. The man was so terrified he had crapped himself.

'Aw shit, Menko,' the smaller one smiled, 'couldn't you wait?'

The bigger warrior approached Menko and held the spike to his eye.

'You've got to learn to see the truth, Menko. Maybe this'll help you.'

Menko screamed. Then Brady saw the two warriors take a step back and look to the side.

'Holy fuck, what's that, Chivas?'

The big one with the spike dropped it and backed away.

'I dunno,' his voice was charged with sudden fear.

Then the whimpering, keening, child-like wail began again. This time closer. Now at the base of the stair. The two warriors backed off, then screamed and ran stumbling off into the dark.

Brady gazed down at the figure slumped below him and saw Menko look up at the shadow. His strangled cry was short-lived. The shadow began to take shape. Brady could see a small, goblin-shaped creature, part human, part animal, standing in front of Menko. It was crying like a baby. Then Brady realized it was a child. It began to climb up Menko's body, digging large claws into his flesh and hooking them around his ribs. Menko screamed until his larynx was pierced. Then he gurgled help-lessly. Brady saw the child mutant reach Menko's head. It placed its hands on both sides of the man's head and began to squeeze. With seemingly little effort it crushed Menko's head, squeezing the inside of his skull from the bursting crown of his head like toothpaste. It began to eat the blood and brain tissue. Brady urinated. He could not hold back. He held on to the doll and fought against his fear and his nausea. He clenched his eyes shut.

When he opened them again the creature was looking directly at him. Then it began to climb the outside of the staircase.

Brady did not hesitate. He grabbed his camera and fired.

The explosion of light burst into life, illuminating the shadow creature for a split second. The creature screamed and fell back into the darkness. Brady moved. He was down that staircase and running for the sloop jet. Behind he heard the child-like wailing again and the sound of pursuit. He was yards from the sloop jet now. Then something hard and sharp caught his ankle. He stumbled and his flesh ripped. Pain shot through his leg but he kept going. The password. What was the fucking password? The sloop jet was directly ahead. His brain was racing.

'Deva!' he screamed, and almost wept as the doors slid open.

He dived for the entrance but something caught his foot. He twisted and kicked out with the other. The goblin child was on him, he could see the grossly inflated child's head with the baby blue eyes. But the mouth was distorted, a huge maw with rows of five-inch teeth. Its breath hit Brady like a sewage conveyor.

Brady lunged backwards, wriggling into the sloop jet, desperately searching for his spare pulse pistol with his other hand. The creature paused, then stared. Brady saw that it was gazing at the doll's head which he still cradled in his arms. His legs were dangling outside the vehicle door. He didn't need a second invitation. He hauled himself inside with demonic strength.

The creature backed away, still staring at the photo-sculpture head of Jordan. It howled and cried as though in agony. Brady did not stop to ask why. He was inside now and the door was sliding shut. Unceremoniously, he dumped the doll in the back and slammed the car into drive.

The press conference was over. Johnny Raine stood up and started to leave. This was a routine event but tonight had been a little different. He had fielded suicide questions in one guise or another for most of the conference. Alex Hamlisch was proving to be a thorn in the side of the Channel. But, until they could make an official announcement, the policy was say nothing, neither confirm nor deny.

The routine press reception was held for all the Channel's top programmes. Sapphire O'Hara was holding court as Johnny left. He was quite happy. She was gold dust right now. Johnny looked back to the cluster of hacks clucking around her and sighed. He could remember when he had been in that position. He still was in some ways. But he didn't have the equipment that Sapphire had. He actually liked her. They had posed together for many a magazine article – Mr and Mrs Boom Boom they were called. But it stopped there as far as he was concerned. There was only one woman in his life at the moment and for the foreseeable future. And he was going home to her right now.

But not before Hamlisch buttonholed him. 'What do you think

of all these suicide rumours, Johnny,' he asked him quietly. 'We're all getting a bit tired of the denials.'

'What denials, Alex? By the way, what was that you said about suicide rates?'

'Oh, I've been doing some digging. Manhattan is not the placid place it appears on the surface. It all started last month; that's why I'm pushing you for a yes or a no on the suicide idea for the show. There have been a spate of suicides all over town. It's the same story out on Long Island. And my sources inside the Zone Police tell me there is more unrest than usual over the East River. Maybe the cauldron is bubbling over. So, I ask myself, how come the top show in the country is considering putting live suicide on prime time? It's a valid question, Johnny, don't you think?'

'I think you're a harbinger of doom, Alex. I've got to go. Goodnight.'

Johnny left the building hurriedly, but what Hamlisch had said disturbed him. He wasted no time in getting down to Lexington. He knew something was wrong the moment he put his spare key into the lock and opened Jordan's door.

It was dim inside but it was obvious the room had been trashed. His heart jumped into his mouth.

'Jordan,' he whispered, then he screamed, 'Jordan!'

There was a crash from the bathroom. Johnny bounded across the living room and burst in. He was knocked backwards by the force of the attack. Jordan's hands were around his throat and her eyes were wild. It took her several seconds to realize it was Johnny. She released him and trembled in his arms.

'Darling.' Johnny held her. 'What's the matter, what's happening?'

Before she could reply, she lurched around the room clutching her body. Her face was thin and drawn. Her eyes were bloodshot and blood was trickling from her mouth where she had bitten her tongue. She collapsed on to the floor in a foetal position and howled. Johnny almost had hysterics. He punched in the medi-care number on the vidi-phone and barked instructions.

Then he ran to Jordan who was staring into space. Johnny put his arms around her. She was whimpering. He held her for a long time, then managed to get her on to the bed and cover her with a sheet.

She tried to speak between huge gulping sobs.

'I don't know what's happening. There's something inside me. 'I'm scared.'

'Hush,' he comforted her, but his pulse was racing. 'I'm here now. I'll never leave you. You're going to be all right.' Her convulsions began again, but they were weaker now. She stared at Johnny helplessly.

'What's happening to me?' she whispered.

He had no answer. Then the medi-team arrived with their portable equipment. The doctor in charge sized up the situation and gently ushered Johnny aside. They went to work, running what tests they could. Jordan seemed calmer now. They gave her a sedative and took a blood sample. When she was asleep, Johnny spoke to the doctor. 'Well, what's wrong with her?' he demanded.

'Can't give an instant diagnosis,' the doctor replied with practised calm. 'I want to run some more tests. Hysteria and delirium can be caused by a number of things. She looks run-down. Maybe she just needs a holiday. Look, I want her to come in for some more tests. Don't worry, we'll get to the bottom of it.'

Johnny felt only partly reassured but he knew the doctor was right. They had done all they could without taking her in. He looked over at her. She was sleeping like a baby.

He sighed deeply with a mixture of fear and anxiety and began to tidy up the room.

Chapter Fourteen

The waiting room inside the medi-care centre was spotlessly clean. Comfortable chairs were placed around the area with casual precision. Soft music and even softer aromas were kept at discreet levels. The intention was to breed an atmosphere of calm efficiency.

Residents of every credit level could make use of the network of centres located in various parts of the island. Health care rivalled security as the top compulsory taxation sector. There were no tax dodgers in Manhattan.

The centre, near the old Chelsea Hotel, was half empty. About a dozen or so people were waiting. A large circular desk dominated the waiting room. Well-groomed medical staff moved to and fro serenely. No one ran anywhere here. Johnny sat bolt upright in his chair and clasped his hands together. A tall, middle-aged and impeccably groomed, white-coated receptionist regarded him sympathetically. Her dark skin gleamed under the even light cast from the ceiling panels.

'I'm sure she'll be perfectly all right, Mr Raine.' She spoke with a soft southern accent. He smiled at her. She continued cheerily. 'Ms Semiramis is just in for a check-up, that's all. It might surprise you to know just how many people get run down living in a place like this. It's not the holiday resort people outside think it is.'

Johnny was interested in spite of his concern about Jordan. 'What do you mean?' he asked her.

'Oh, you must see it on your show all the time. That's what makes "All The Way" such a great escape valve.' She leaned forward as if about to betray a confidence. 'People think we're all free here, right? Seen the Brooklyn Bridge lately? It's like a separate State all by itself. There's more military hardware around that bridge than some countries have in their whole army.'

'It's for our protection, isn't it?' said Johnny.

'Oh sure, don't get me wrong, Mr Raine. I know what it's for. I was just talking about stress levels.' She chuckled ironically. 'It makes you wonder who the real prisoners are – us or them across the river.'

Johnny stared at her. Then he saw Jordan walking towards him along a corridor. Accompanying her was a tall, slim, dark-haired doctor. Johnny jumped up and ran to her. The doctor smiled.

'Mr Raine, it's good to see you. I just love your show . . .'

'To hell with my show, doctor,' Johnny interrupted. 'How's Jordan?'

'I'm fine,' said Jordan.

'There's nothing medically wrong with Jordan, Mr Raine. We've run some comprehensive tests and can find nothing. But I have to say that this kind of malaise afflicts quite a large number of people here. Some of us have given it a name: MS, Manhattan Syndrome.' He smiled at the medical joke. 'So I suggest, Jordan, that you cancel all appointments, pack up your computer and tell your clients you're taking a vacation, on doctor's orders.'

Johnny looked so relieved that Jordan laughed. 'Come on,' he said, 'I'm taking you to lunch.'

It wasn't until they were seated comfortably in the rear seat of an open-topped electro-cab that some of his worries returned.

'Johnny, they found nothing because there is nothing to find,' said Jordan. 'How do you find a nightmare? How do you trace feelings of despair? Something is trying to crawl inside my mind. And what about your nightmares? Maybe there's a connection. Maybe we're looking in the wrong place. Look, I know all this must sound like mild psychosis but it's none the less real for that.'

Johnny looked at her. She was thin. She must have lost more than a stone. Her skin had lately acquired the first touches of that stretched and translucent appearance. She had combed back her hair severely and he noticed with dismay how thin it had become. His earlier relief in the medical centre started to evaporate.

'I've got to get you away from this place,' he said bitterly. 'Just trust me, darling. Maybe we should try another kind of doctor.'

'I stopped seeing shrinks years ago,' stated Jordan bluntly. 'All they did was shrink my credit balance.'

'I wasn't thinking about an ordinary everyday shrink,' Johnny told her.

'What do you mean, a witch doctor?' she remarked as they got out in the Village.

They strolled across a leafy square and entered a little French restaurant they used to frequent when they first met. There was a shaded balcony and they took a table which gave them a view of the square. They said nothing for a while. Jordan just drank spring water. Johnny stuck to beer. Already she seemed tired and worn out, he thought, watching her closely.

'There's a party this afternoon. Frank Brady's throwing a pre-exhibition bash at his apartment. I thought I might go,' Johnny told her.

'Count me out,' sighed Jordan as the waiter served light chicken salads. 'I'm not in the party mood. And there's something fishy about that man. I can't put my finger on it.'

Then she caught sight of her reflection in a mirror opposite. She put her hands to her face and stared at herself.

'Oh my God, look at me. I look like a refugee from some prison camp.'

'You look fine, you're just rundown, that's all.'

'How would you know?' she responded angrily. 'How the hell would you know how I feel? All you're concerned about is your precious show and the obscenity of public suicide. I sometimes think you're as crazy as those freaks you seem to worship.'

Johnny sat back and could not find any words to say. Almost immediately Jordan clutched his hand.

'Oh, I didn't mean that. I'm sorry. It's just that I've been going through a lot lately. I'm getting twisted up. I know you're just doing all this so that we can get out. It's just . . .'

'I know, honey. Don't worry, I understand,' said Johnny. 'Just a couple of weeks more, I promise, and we'll be taking a one-way ticket to sanity.'

Johnny dropped Jordan off at her apartment and, after making sure she was comfortable, he left to get changed for Brady's party. Jordan smiled as he left, watching his tall figure appear at ground level from her sixth-floor window. Maybe the doctor was right. Maybe it was all just the result of overwork and stress.

She sat in her favourite balcony seat and tried to relax. After a moment or two her eyes were drawn to the window opposite, on the other side of the street. She looked at the window curiously. Was she imagining things or was there someone watching her? It was hard to tell and, even if there was, what was wrong with that? It was their apartment. It was a free country.

She started to turn away when a shiver of recognition ran through her and her gaze was pulled back to the window. Was that a camera lens she could see? The window was slightly open. It was too far away to be certain but something was glinting in the early afternoon sunlight. A light breeze was causing the curtains to move. The gleam behind the window became more pronounced. There was something there, she was sure of it.

She started to rise to go inside when a moment of paralysis rendered her immobile. She opened her mouth as the familiar nightmare rushed towards her. Standing behind the curtains watching her was a figure. She could not make it out clearly. It was partly obscured by the curtains and it was on the other side of the street. But what caused her to catch her breath and try to quell her rapidly rising pulse rate was the jolt of recognition.

Jordan was staring at herself.

She was finding it hard to breathe. Although the figure in the window must have been more than a hundred yards away, she was staring directly into its face when it became visible behind the shifting, breeze-blown curtains. And it was her face. But it was distorted, almost disfigured. Even in her fearful state, Jordan was determined to try to rationalize what was happening to her. Was it her double? She'd heard that everyone in the world has a double. No, she didn't believe that; this was no double. She was a logical woman. She believed in the here and now. But she had to admit to herself that ideas such as possession frightened her in a way she could not explain.

The thing that was watching was her but it was not her. It was not human, Jordan was certain of that. It was some kind of replica. Jordan had never prayed before. But she made some

kind of spiritual plea at that moment. Gradually, she forced her
eyes away from the empty gaze of the watcher. Her limbs were
shaking. She felt nauseous again. She was determined to get to
the bathroom without being sick on the carpet. She almost made
it. She found she had to crawl painfully along the floor because
her limbs were not responding. One part of her mind was now
icy cool. It could regard these events dispassionately. She was
going to be sick and dizzy, she knew it. Then the sweats would
start. She made it to the bathroom and threw up on the tiled
floor. Now she could hear a voice. It was a voice that echoed
down corridors of time from a vast distance. Now that she had
heard the voice, she knew it was not going to leave her. At that
moment she believed she was starting to go insane.

Johnny knew many of the guests who were disporting themselves at Frank Brady's party. There was an excess of food, a
mixture of middle-eastern, Chinese and kosher. This, thought
Johnny as he sipped a glass of spiced wine, this is a pretty good
cross-section of Manhattan's elite.

There were big media names here and some who were up-
and-coming. And there were some well-known music superstars
as well. He could see Pandora Yamani flashing her eyes at the
newest black star, Joshua Benn, whose powerful muscles could
be seen rippling through his shirt from across the room.

Johnny spotted Frank Brady, looking a little pale but in good
spirits, dispensing *bonhomie* and charm in that slightly brittle
accent of his. Johnny recognized Carl Meissen, Brady's agent,
with his arm around a thin but attractive woman. Johnny knew
her to be a leading vidi-novelist. She wrote trashy sagas for the
massive women's market and was hugely successful.

In one corner of the room, a huddle of media types and
actresses were gesticulating and talking loudly about deals and
testing. Another group was unmistakably the seedy and rapa-
cious Manhattan art crowd. They adopted a more disdainful
attitude and spoke quietly while appraising the female and male
talent on show.

Johnny was interested in the apartment. Brady seemed to have
collected objects from his travels as a merchant seaman. Many

were exotic and unusual, some were primitive and disturbing. One series of photographs caught Johnny's eye. They depicted a strange, wooden-like female form contorted into impossible shapes. They were distasteful yet compulsive, like devil dolls.

The party was awash with journalists. Brady had always made good copy, particularly as he was one of the few who ventured publicly into the Badlands. Johnny felt a kind of affinity with Brady when that thought struck him.

Satoko glided up to him carrying a tray of dim-sum. She smiled at him enigmatically as he speared a couple of dumplings. Johnny smiled at her and then looked up. A rather exotic-looking woman was watching him. Before he could move he was buttonholed by Fred Mason, an executive from CyberTel.

'Johnny boy, how's it going?' shmoozed Mason.

'Great, Fred, just great,' Johnny replied.

'That's not what I hear, old buddy,' grinned Mason.

'What are you talking about?'

'From what I hear "The Hot Love Show" and "Dreams Come True" are breathing down your neck, Johnny. "All the Way" could be going all the way down. And, before you say anything in your defence, old buddy, we've all heard the live suicide rumours. Crap! It's bullshit. You know and I know it's old man Freiberg fighting to save his ass. Isn't that right?'

'I can confirm or deny nothing,' Johnny smiled, 'so do me a favour, Fred.'

'Yeah, what's that?'

'Shut the fuck up.'

Fred Mason laughed heartily and slapped Johnny on the back. The exotic-looking woman was still watching. Mason noticed her.

'Would you look at the mouth on that? She can irrigate my sensory ducts any time. I think I'm about to score a hit, Johnny boy.'

'Oh yes?'

'Oh yes. Think dirty, my friend, think dirty. You're in the media after all, it's your sworn duty. Wish me luck.'

Fred Mason cruised over to the exotic woman and Johnny decided to go walkabout. He slipped away from the main party and shuffled through the crowd along the hallway. He noticed a small passage leading to other rooms. He was curious to see how Brady lived. He glanced around. He was clear. No one was watching. He padded quickly along the passage and tried the door at the end. It opened and he darted inside.

When his eyes became accustomed to the darkness and the red flickering light he realized he was standing in Brady's darkroom. It was large and well equipped. At the far end were lines of viewing light-screens. Old-fashioned negatives hung in rows and there were a number of large workbenches stacked with the latest laser-disk processing equipment. Johnny wandered around idly, then noticed another door at the far end of the darkroom behind an L-shaped alcove. He walked over, glanced around once more and tried the door. It was open. He pushed it slowly and it opened fully. It was another room, a large one. It was completely dark. Johnny entered the room, feeling for a light switch. For a couple of seconds he flapped his hand against the wall. The room seemed large in the darkness but it wasn't until he found a dimmer switch and turned it up that he realized quite how big.

It felt like a small church. It had a high, vaulted ceiling and all the windows were shuttered up. The room was painted white and in the centre was a single swivel chair. Apart from a tall shape covered by a black drape standing in a dark corner, it was the only object in the room.

Except for the photographs. It took Johnny several seconds to realize who he was looking at. Then he gulped. He was looking at a giant blow-up of himself. It was grainy. He was naked and his mouth was open. The shot had been taken through a car window. But the figure that filled him with fear and pleasure, as well as total shock, was Jordan. She was naked, her breasts were prominent and swollen. Her head was thrown back and her tongue was fully extended. She looked like a rampant vampire.

When Johnny managed to rip his eyes from the image, he began to shuffle around the room. Jordan was everywhere. Huge blow-ups hung side by side with action stills in sequence. The floor was littered with torn photographs, snippets and cut-outs. Johnny was amazed and totally shocked. What the hell was

Brady playing at? When had all these shots been taken? And did they have any connection with Jordan's illness?

His mind raced with possibilities. Connections and remarks started to fall into place. Everything that had been happening lately seemed to be focusing upon one single point, here in this mausoleum. This must be the connection. Brady was involved in a way Johnny could not fathom. What had Jordan said that morning, something about witchcraft? Well, now it did not seem so far-fetched. Brady was clearly obsessed by her. But, reasoned Johnny, he was a photographer after all, and an artist. Johnny had seen Brady at work. He often photographed his subjects in the raw. He was a fly-on-the-wall photographer. But how could this mausoleum be explained? Maybe it was just the way he worked. No, something about this was different. This went much deeper.

So, what now? Should he confront Brady? That would seem the obvious thing to do. Should he tell Jordan? Would it make her even more unwell? He knew one thing for certain. He did not want to leave Jordan alone for a second. But he knew he had to. He would have to see this suicide thing through. Meanwhile, he would tell Jordan. She had to know. Then maybe he should confront Brady, ask him just what the hell he thought he was doing. Getting it all out in the open just might blow away a few mysteries, force the issue. If Brady was trying to harm Jordan he would kill him. From now on he was going to take matters into his own hands. He had never been the type to be pushed around or manipulated and he felt Brady had been playing some secret game, and that made him mad. He knew Channel Boom Boom was playing its own corporate game and that made him mad too. But above all he felt vulnerable. He was going to persuade Jordan to see Grohmann. He was the only person who might be able to unravel the nightmares and the wasting illness which appeared to be afflicting her. She wasn't just run down. It was much more complex than that. Who knew what other arcane or mysterious practices Brady might be capable of?

Slowly, he retreated from the room, unprepared to turn his back on the images. He switched off the light and retraced his steps. He grabbed a drink and blended with the crowd.

A little later he noticed Brady watching him. The Englishman was not smiling. He knows something, Johnny thought. Well, fuck him. He can know what he likes. Whatever he's doing he's going to stop, one way or another.

It was while he was talking to Joshua Benn that he felt a tap on the shoulder. He turned and there was Frank Brady smiling at him.

'Enjoying yourself, Raine?' he said.

'Great party, Brady,' Johnny replied, 'let's hope your show is as good.'

'Oh it will be,' he replied. 'I insist you come, and bring the delightful Jordan. Where is she, by the way? I thought she would be here with you.'

'She's not well. But I think she'd have to be on death's door to miss your exhibition.'

'I think it might surprise you.' The photographer smiled.

Johnny was tired of being manipulated. He went on the offensive but kept his voice low and personal.

'I've seen it, Brady. I've seen your secret room. I've seen your portrait gallery. What kind of sick fuck are you, Brady? What are you up to? If you wanted to take pictures of Jordan all you had to do was ask. And I object to being the subject of your sordid imagination. Those shots in the car park. You were following us. You were sneaking around like a cheap journalist. OK, if that's what you call art, maybe I'm a philistine, but I draw the line at intrusion of privacy. And if you're practising some kind of black magic . . .'

Brady had gone pale. His lips had compressed into a straight line. Johnny didn't show it but he experienced a pang of fear at the barely controlled anger in the saturnine face of the photographer.

'You've been prowling around my apartment,' he hissed. He glanced around at his guests. He was being beckoned by admirers from all around the room. He turned to Johnny impatiently and the younger man could see he was almost shaking with anger.

'You talk to me about invasion of privacy. You know nothing. Black magic! There are things in the universe that put black magic where it belongs, in kindergarten. You are like a child stumbling through a forest, matey. You're lost like all the others. You can set your mind at rest. If I had designs on your girlfriend's body I would have had them well satisfied by now, believe me. Don't forget, Raine, you owe me. One of these days I'm going to call in that marker. In the meantime just take one thing on board that single-track media mind of yours. There is something taking place which is more powerful and more dangerous than anything you have ever experienced. You are directly involved, old son. And so is Jordan. And, as far as my art is concerned, I will do what I like, when I like and with whom I like. Do you understand me?'

'What do you mean, we're involved?' whispered Johnny.

'You'll find out. There is only one person who might have an answer and its not our mutual friend Grohmann. Tell me straight. When you were snooping around did you see anything other than photographs?'

'You're talking in riddles,' said Johnny. 'No, I saw nothing else. The photographs were quite enough to tell me that something you're doing is making Jordan sick.'

'What kind of sick?' asked Brady.

'I'm taking her to see Grohmann. He must have some idea about the powers of the paranormal,' Johnny replied.

'You're wasting your time. I've told you, there is only one person who might have an answer and she is over the other side. Now, I'm wasting my time. I've got guests to look after. See yourself out.'

Brady slouched away into the chattering crowd. Again Johnny had the feeling that he had come off second best against the Englishman, but for the life of him he couldn't think why. Right now all he could think about was Jordan. He knew there was a direct link between Brady's secret room and her sickness. But he couldn't prove anything. Then again, what was there to prove and what exactly was the connection? A bunch of photographs on their own proved nothing. There had to be something else. Brady had been edgy and off-balance. He gave the impression he was acting under some kind of compulsion.

Johnny wriggled his way through the crowd. Jordan wasn't

the only one who had been experiencing bad dreams. He too had had a hard time sleeping lately. He kept remembering the two freaks he had killed outside the club. And Jordan's description of her nightmare ... It all struck a familiar chord somewhere deep in his subconscious. Maybe Brady was right and they were all involved with something none of them understood. He left the apartment feeling light-headed and almost ran the four or five blocks to Jordan's place.

That night Brady sat and meditated for a while to clear his mind. Then he went into his bedroom. He had positioned the doll by the French windows which he had left open. A light breeze brushed the curtains and echoes of faraway music drifted in on a stream of Spring-scented night air. Brady undressed, breathing heavily. He lay on the bed and played with the controller to make the doll move in tiny jerks. The effect was surreal. Jordan was staring down at his naked body, he was sure of it. What did a guy like Johnny Raine know about the subtleties of sexual magic? Brady had studied tantric methods of magic. He muttered a repetitive mantra under his breath and watched his erection rise till it was swollen and pulsing. From the doll's stomach came the whirr of an electric motor and the click of a camera shutter.

Brady was not interested in Jordan for herself. She represented something powerful, ancient and unknown. Brady knew also that the time was coming when everything would be ripped asunder. Maybe Bobby Bolero was right about Guru Lennon. Maybe happiness is a warm gun. Brady ran over the connections again. There was Angelica. Then there was Jordan and Raine. Somewhere in the equation Marek Grohmann also figured. He had to. Despite what he had told Johnny, Brady knew Grohmann as a man of unusual insights. Something he had said at the time when Brady had consulted him about the nature of his obsessive personality flashed like a knife blade. The Purple Zone. It was real all right. All Brady's esoteric study and magical practice convinced him of this. And hadn't Raine also consulted him? Brady slouched around the apartment and fixed himself a drink. What or who had killed Otto Hahn? He glanced at the doll as if seeking an answer. It had been a witness. Or perhaps worse. His violent death was no accident and yet Brady was convinced it wasn't a simple case of murder. No, the wheels were turning. His own dreams had been disturbed. Maybe Bolero was right about the force too. Maybe something was on its way.

The doll stared impassively back at Brady, framed by the glittering lights of the city. It kept its thoughts to itself.

Not far away Johnny Raine was holding Jordan down on her bed as she fought against invading demons. She was screaming.

'It's inside me, it's inside me.'

She was fighting something she could not see. Johnny was crying hot tears as he tried to prevent her doing damage to herself. She was fighting him with tremendous strength. Her eyes were wide and dilated, her hair was straggly with sweat and she was losing clumps of it. Her skin was peeling in places.

Then, as suddenly as the fit had begun, it abruptly ended. Jordan lay panting on the bed with her eyes closed, utterly exhausted. Johnny looked down at her, noticing how prominent her ribs had become. He rolled over on his back, gulping deep lungfuls of air as he sought to lower his heart rate. He was drenched in sweat.

He had made up his mind. Tomorrow first thing he was going to call Marek Grohmann. Johnny looked over at Jordan. Her eyes flickered open and she smiled at him weakly.

'Sorry,' she murmured.

'Nothing to be sorry about. I'm worried about you, honey. How are you feeling now?'

'I'm OK, 'she said as she raised herself on one elbow, then she laughed sadly. 'Sorry about the disappearance of our sex life.'

'That's not important right now. Look, do you want to talk about it?'

'It's simple really,' she said sitting up and rubbing her face in her hands, 'I'm falling apart, that's what's happening. Now I hear voices, or rather, one voice. It's quite clear and unequivocal. Johnny, I don't know what that voice is or where it comes from but if it doesn't stop soon I'm going to go insane. That's about the size of it. These attacks are getting more frequent. Right now

I feel fine. I'm worn out, but I'm OK. Earlier today, after you left, I was looking over at the window across the street and I saw myself. I was standing in the window watching me over here. Now, OK, most people would say I was dreaming. Well, I wasn't fucking dreaming. It was real. It was as real as these nightmares and now this voice. It's incredible really. Going insane is such a rational process.'

'Go and take a shower. I'll make some coffee and a snack,' Johnny said, his voice filled with compassion.

Jordan leaned over and kissed him tenderly. 'You know, most guys would have just run away from all this. Having a nice relationship with lots of lovely sex is great. But sticking around while someone loses their mind can't be a bundle of laughs.'

'You're not losing your mind,' Johnny insisted. 'Now, go and do as you're told. I've got some things to tell you.'

Wearily, Jordan complied. She really was thin now, Johnny thought to himself as he stumbled into the kitchen and put some coffee on. He made some toast and spread it with cheese and tomatoes and some nuts. He returned to the dining room, left the tray on the table and went for a shower. Jordan was towelling her hair dry and holding back tears as more strands came away. Johnny showered quickly and joined her. She appeared remarkably calm. She sipped her coffee gratefully and gazed at him expectantly.

He decided that there was no point beating about the bush. He told her everything, about the party and the gallery full of her photographs and his conversation with Brady. She said nothing for some time. She was thinking deeply.

'It makes sense,' she replied at last. 'Somehow he's doing something, whether he's aware of it or not, which is screwing my mind. It's the only conclusion I can come to.' She paused then looked directly into Johnny's eyes. 'Maybe we'll just have to kill him,' she said.

Chapter Fifteen

Lieutenant Mike Schroder was dying for a smoke. But he knew he couldn't light up in the full glare of the vidi-cameras. It wouldn't go down well at City Hall or at the central precinct of the Free State of Manhattan police force. Homicide and death under unusual circumstances belonged to the bad old days. Sure there was still the occasional murder, rape or suicide, but nothing like it used to be before the Isolation.

He stood outside the old man's house contemplating his pension. Just another six months to go and he would be free. He and his wife had their hearts set on a little place on the retirement island of Cuba. Maybe he'd run a little bar near the beach and spend the long summer evenings philosophizing and reminiscing with all the other expatriates.

He sighed deeply and locked away the fantasy in his mind.

Right now he was doing his best to fend off the horde of reporters which had gathered around this quiet Morningside house. He'd put his deputy, Elmore Hunt, in charge of bamboozling the press.

Why the old man's death had caused such a stir he could not figure out. Sure, the circumstances were unusual, to say the least. An old man by the name of Otto Hahn had been burned to death. There was no sign of a struggle. Nothing looked as if it had been disturbed. Nothing had been taken as far as it was possible to judge. There was, of course, the broken window and the traces of earth and gravel on the carpet which indicated a break-in. Maybe some crazed bankrupt had picked on this unremarkable house at random. You're getting old, he chided himself. There had been a break-in, no doubt about it. The trouble was, that didn't explain how the old boy had met his end. He looked as if he'd just got back from hell. Schroder had studied the precinct reports as part of his routine meetings with the State police department but statistics could be used to prove anything. Schroder preferred old-fashioned instinct. A blip on the computer figures didn't prove that they were facing a new crime wave. But it could not be denied that every precinct had reported increased figures. Oddball suicides were not unheard of, particularly if someone was facing the final ignominy of banishment. He'd seen suicide notes that would make you weep. Fear of bankruptcy and the shame of public humiliation seemed to weigh more heavily than the prospect of being kicked out of Manhattan for good. Sometimes they had enough stashed away to pay for an air ticket out. If not, they had to make the final walk across the bridge. Schroder shivered at the thought.

Apparently, old man Hahn had been some kind of artistic icon, not very famous when he was alive but now he was being built up into a very profitable property by the art sharks. Schroder had seen it all before.

Hahn had had some connection with the film industry, which, in Manhattan, rivalled finance and leisure as the main preoccupation of the media. He had been something of a bizarre genius and his even more bizarre demise had kindled a flame of front-page interest amongst the hacks.

A small crowd had gathered, watching quietly. At least three anchors were presenting their accounts to camera. Elmore Hunt, black and massive, stood watching events with elephantine cool. He was supervising the police operatives and the medi-team, keeping the small crowd at bay and ensuring a clear passage from the house for what was left of the body.

An attractive journalist, Tessa Vane, sidled up to Schroder, smiling with encouragement.

'Lieutenant Schroder, Tessa Vane, Central News Features. Do you have any comment about what's happened here? How long has Otto Hahn been dead, for instance?'

'The best part of three days as far as we can make out.' Schroder glanced angrily over at Elmore Hunt.

'Do you have any ideas? Was it an accident or murder?'

'I really cannot comment until I've seen the autopsy report,' said Schroder.

'According to the neighbour who found him he was unrecognizable. Are you certain it was Otto Hahn, the artist and model-maker?' the journalist persisted.

'We're as certain as we can be until we carry out a full autopsy and check his dental records. Now, will that be all?'

'Our viewers would like to know, Lieutenant, what the Free State of Manhattan is doing about the sudden increase in violence. Some people say the old days are coming back. What's your opinion?'

'I don't think the old days will ever come back,' Schroder replied with a trace of regret.

'Have you any comment to make about the brutal murder of a prominent financier, Mr Bruce Willard, by what can only be described as a monster from hell, or from the Badlands?'

'It's not my case, Ms Vane. Now, if you'll excuse me.'

Schroder shoved past Tessa Vane. She raised her eyebrows quizzically to camera. 'That was the voice of the Free State of Manhattan Police Department. The strange and frightening death of Otto Hahn is another in a growing number of brutal attacks on innocent and defenceless citizens. City Hall is not saying much. Commissioner Halloran plays down these events. But how many go unreported? It seems eighty-year-old Otto Hahn was burned beyond recognition. Cases of self-immolation have been known to happen. But isn't it really the case that, far from receiving the protection the citizens of Manhattan pay a high price for, it is becoming easier for rapists and murderers to attack us in our own homes than ever before? Is this, as some believe, the thin end of the wedge, the beginning of a new wave of violence? Can the denizens of the Badlands be kept out for ever? This is Tessa Vane, for Central News Features, Morningside.'

Mike Schroder strode over to join Elmore Hunt as the medi-team brought out the remains of Otto Hahn. There was little to carry. Schroder glanced at Hunt who shrugged his shoulders with a puzzled expression. Schroder saw Dr Liam Finney bring-ing up the rear, ushering his team to get what was left of Otto Hahn into the ambulance. The crowd meanwhile was beginning to lose interest and the vidi-crews were wrapping.

'How's it going Liam?' said Schroder.

'Hi, Mike,' replied the fresh-faced Irishman. 'Well it's a strange one, I don't mind telling you.'

'What do you make of it? Cause of death, I mean?'

'We might as well have removed what's left of the poor bastard in an urn and read him his last rites. It was like he was put through an incinerator, Mike. But the puzzling thing is there was no damage around him except the burn marks on the floor underneath the body. What do you make of it?'

'Murder?' suggested Schroder. 'Could be. Douse him with petrol and set light to him.'

'Hmm! Somehow I don't think so. No smell of petrol and you'd expect to find something actually left. This old fellow was mostly a pile of ash. If you sneezed he'd have blown away.'

Mike Schroder shook hands with Finney and turned slowly and thoughtfully around and walked back to the police electro-turbo.

Marek Grohmann tapped his fingers gently on his massive desk. The call he had received from Johnny Raine had set his juices running. The star presenter's therapy sessions some years back had been a qualified success. He had managed to dilute the anger, pain and resentment he had felt following the death of his wife. Grohmann remembered Angelica. She had been a rare beauty and Raine had been intoxicated by her. Grohmann had been able to expose Raine's raw nerve, dig deep into his feelings and, partially, restore his feeling of self-worth.

This morning he was preparing to meet Jordan Semiramis. Raine had explained his worries and concerns about the strange dreams and the wasting disease which had suddenly afflicted her. He had told him also of his own nightmares. Grohmann was disturbed, yet stimulated; cautious but driven by an insatiable desire to explore the unknown. His greatest fear was that he had unwittingly exposed Raine to powers which could only be imagined or which were hinted at in the magical grimoires he cherished. He took a deep breath and found his still centre. He would be prepared. Minutes later he was jarred out of his reverie by the voice of his receptionist announcing the arrival of his next appointment.

Jordan held Johnny's hand nervously. It had taken a great deal of persuasion to get her this far. Just being in a place like this showed that she recognized something was wrong with her. And she did not want to admit it. As she sat there stiffly with Johnny, the receptionist appraised her in preparation for her usual briefing to Marek Grohmann. He liked her to provide him with instant and instinctive reactions to new clients.

Poor thing, thought the receptionist. She looks like she could use a square meal rather than pay the huge fees Grohmann charged for a consultation. In this case though she knew he was making an exception as he was extremely curious. Johnny Raine had discussed it with him and he had been intrigued. Hmm, she sighed, he's every bit as good looking as he is on television.

Johnny turned to Jordan and smiled crookedly. 'You OK?' he said.

'That's a dumb question,' she answered. 'I don't know about this, Johnny. I've told you, I quit seeing guys like this years ago.'

'He's got a brilliant reputation,' Johnny argued, 'and, whatever you think, he has helped me. He's our best hope.'

Jordan remained unconvinced, but she was prepared to go through with the interview for Johnny's sake if not for her own.

'What was it you said Brady told you?' she asked. 'About there being only one person who understands what's going on and she's on the other side?'

'That's what he said, but I don't know what he was talking about. We weren't exactly making polite conversation.'

A quiet buzzer sounded somewhere on the receptionist's desk. She picked up a telephone receiver and spoke quietly for a couple of moments. Then she came over, smiling, and extending her hand to Jordan. 'Doctor Grohmann will see you now, Ms Semiramis.'

Jordan stood up and Johnny stood with her. The receptionist looked at Johnny questioningly.

'I'll have a word with Marek first, if I may,' he smiled.

She said nothing but led them both to a large, heavy oak door, opened it and ushered them into Marek Grohmann's consulting room.

The psychiatrist was standing by his desk, waiting. He smiled benignly at Jordan as he shook first Johnny's hand then hers. He noticed her weak grip.

'Johnny, nice to see you again. And Jordan. It is a pleasure to meet you, my dear.'

Jordan smiled weakly but said nothing.

'Thanks for doing this, Marek,' Johnny said with disarming charm. 'I know you're very busy. But this is special, and so is Jordan.'

'You know that I cannot let you stay during our conversation,' Grohmann told him, all the time looking at Jordan reassuringly.

There was a nervous silence. Jordan clearly objected to being discussed as though she wasn't there.

'Let's get on with it, shall we?' she said sharply. 'I'm starting to feel tired.'

Johnny kissed her on the cheek tenderly, then turned awkwardly and left the office. For a moment Grohmann stood watching Jordan, then he indicated two comfortable armchairs.

'Would you like some coffee or tea?' he asked.

'No, no thank you. Look, I'm not sure if I'm going to be any good at this kind of thing. Johnny said you might be able to help. Frankly, I'm sceptical.'

'And so you should be,' Grohmann said as they both sat down. 'Scepticism is a perfectly natural and healthy reaction when face to face with an old dinosaur like me.'

Despite her reservations, she smiled. There was something unaffected about this man. He was not threatening in any way.

'So,' continued Grohmann, 'Johnny tells me you became ill very suddenly and for no apparent reason. Your medical records show that you are quite disgustingly healthy, if a little run down. You're an intelligent woman. Is there anything wrong you wish Johnny not to know?'

Jordan shook her head and appeared a little tongue-tied. Finally she blurted out, 'I find it difficult to talk about. I'm not sure this is a good idea.' She started to rise but Grohmann just smiled and casually raised his hand. She sat back in her chair.

'Semiramis. That's an unusual name.'

'It's Turkish originally. My father was from Istanbul. My mother was American.'

'Let me tell you something, Jordan,' said Grohmann quietly. 'I have a confession to make. I too am always nervous when faced with a new client. What secrets will they reveal? What horrors of the mind will they share with me, a complete stranger? And the client, can they trust this old goat? What does he know? But that is the excitement, don't you see? By just being here you have taken the very first faltering step on a journey. You have started a process. Who knows where it will lead. Now, in your own time.'

Jordan took a deep breath. Suddenly, telling this comfortable, avuncular man her innermost thoughts seemed the most natural thing in the world. It was their secret. She knew instinctively she could trust him. She let it all out. She told him about her dream in detail, even about Angelica. She told him about the voices and the sense of being intimately touched. She described coming face to face with her distorted double and she wept quietly when she talked about her weight and hair loss, her fear of sleeping and her inexplicable fear of a man she had met only a couple of times, Frank Brady. Grohmann made a particular mental note of this and suppressed his own fear at the connections which were falling into place with the terrifying precision of an alien jigsaw.

'It sounds crazy,' she told him, 'but it feels like something or somebody is just sucking the life out of me. It started with a feeling of listlessness, lack of energy, loss of interest in my work, in sex, in everything. Then I started having the dream. I can't explain why Angelica should be part of it. You know that we were friends at school, long before she met and married Johnny. It's just an odd coincidence. Later, Johnny told me that Frank Brady has been photographing me secretly. He has some kind of temple set up at his apartment filled with photographs of me. So what, I hear you saying, he's a photographer after all. That was my first reaction but it still doesn't make sense, does it? I felt strange the very first time I met him and I know he felt the same. It was as though we had met before, although we hadn't. I can't explain. God, this must sound really stupid.'

She paused. Grohmann seemed only half awake. The room had darkened. He reached out and switched on a table lamp.

'No, stupid is not what it sounds,' he murmured low, like a

priest in a confessional. 'Of course, there is nothing wrong with a photographer taking photographs; however, in this case, it does appear that there may be a connection. Or, indeed, it may be something else entirely. Every phenomenon has a cause. Sometimes it is obvious, sometimes obscure and sometimes it is buried deep within the psyche and cannot be approached in the normal way.'

'What do you mean?' she asked.

'Would you let me hypnotize you?'

'What for?'

'It's part of the process of elimination. Maybe it will show us nothing, or perhaps all will be revealed and you will know how to combat this strange wasting disease. It may be, perhaps, that a traumatic event in your past has cut an invisible psychic cord. Trauma can do this. It can separate and protect experiences. The mind can protect itself from pain by dividing the ego. So, I would like to put you under hypnosis. It's a perfectly safe procedure and has been part of standard medical research for years. I feel that the answer to your present crisis lies deep in the past. I would like to regress you to your early life. Will you cooperate?'

'OK, why not?' sighed Jordan.

'I am going to give you a card, Jordan. On the card are some words. They will mean nothing to you. They won't even make any sense. They are just sounds strung together. It is a mantra. I discovered it a few years ago and it is particularly effective in calming the mind, dispensing with random thoughts and helping to focus upon your inner self. When I tell you to I want you to repeat the mantra over and over quietly to yourself.'

He handed her the card.

The room was now distinctly gloomy. Jordan had the impression that Grohmann was fading into the background. He was talking to her. She saw a light shining and then it became a white field of snow. She could still hear Grohmann's voice, reassuring her just like her father used to do. She glanced at the words on the card and began to recite them in a low monotone. Soon all she could hear was the sound of the words reverberating inside her head, penetrating deep into her psyche. Her hand drooped and the card fell to the floor. Still her lips moved as she fell into a deep trance. Finally her lips ceased moving.

Grohmann looked at the thin but beautiful figure lying slumped in the armchair opposite. He picked up a phone and whispered to his receptionist. He checked that Johnny Raine had gone and would return later. He also made sure that his next appointment was delayed for half an hour. This case was decidedly more interesting than the run-of-the-mill Manhattanite angst he normally dealt with. There was something intriguing about the situation and about the woman. Johnny had showed him a photograph of Jordan taken only two months before. He would hardly have recognized her as the same person. The medi-centre had run all the routine tests. Nothing! He was sure as he could be that behind the dreams, hallucinations and distress of the three people, Johnny Raine, Frank Brady and now Jordan Semiramis, a powerful current was flowing, as inexorable as an ice-flow. By some arcane sorcery, something had focused its spiritual eye on these three people. He only hoped he would be able to remove them from its influence. What the consequences might be for all of them if he didn't, he dared not even contemplate. Now, as he watched her, Jordan began to stiffen and move. Her face began to twitch, a little at first then with increasing rapidity. She mumbled incoherently.

Grohmann pressed a button and a discreetly positioned camera whirred into life.

Grohmann spoke to her softly but firmly.

'Jordan, can you hear me?'

'Yes,' came the muffled reply.

'Jordan, I want you to listen to me. I want you to tell me about your childhood. Can you see your father?'

'Yes, in room. Happy.'

'Were you happy as a child?'

'Yes, oh yes. Daddy, daddy.'

'Is your mother there?'

'Yes, she is.'

'Do you love your mother?'

'Yes.'

Jordan could hear Grohmann's voice. But now another voice

was talking to her, blotting his out. It was an ancient voice and it was linked to her in a deeply personal way. She was tied to a supernatural twin who felt as she did and knew what was in her mind, yet had a mind of its own. There was a coldness about the voice, a chilling soullessness. The voice was indistinct at first but then she heard it with startling clarity. What it was saying filled her with dread.

'You are mine,' said the voice, 'you are mine, you are mine, you are mine . . .'

Grohmann was worried. He was losing control. Jordan was muttering in a deep, guttural voice. Still he kept his patient, modulated voice calm and persistent.

Jordan was wandering through familiar corridors. She knew what was to come. Somewhere her father's voice was calling her. Then at times another voice spoke, a calm and reasonable voice. And then yet another voice floated along the canyons of her mind, a harsh inhuman voice. She knew that the voice belonged to whatever was behind that door.

She entered the room and saw the three doors. Fearful now, she opened the first. She was powerless to prevent her actions. There was the pale figure of Angelica staring at her with her impossibly blue eyes. She recoiled from the sight of the purple web siphoning her blood like some organic vampire. When the blood spurted and trickled towards her she retreated. She knew what was behind the second door just as she knew she had no choice but to open it and flee from the membrane behind which dwelt some awesome creature of chaos.

And she came to the third door. At first she could hear her father's voice imploring her not to open it, but now there were two other voices competing for her attention. She put her hand on the door knob and froze in fear as always. She heard the voice repeating, 'You are mine . . . you are mine . . . you are mine . . .'

This time the door knob began to turn and the door opened very slowly. A wave of nausea swept over her and she shrieked. But the shriek was not a high-pitched female call. What emanated from her larynx was a deep, powerful, vibratory animal bellow. It reverberated through her, shaking her to the core. The voices were screaming at her now, calling her name, fighting for her attention.

Grohmann sat wide-eyed, looking at Jordan. The room was vibrating with the bass resonance of an animal-like roar booming out of the frail figure on the couch. It struck fear into Marek Grohmann's heart. This was a case of possession, he was certain of that, yet it had singular and unusual aspects. The woman before him was speaking in tongues, or at least in an utterly inhuman and incomprehensible language. Jordan babbled violently. As Grohmann watched with gathering disbelief and shock, Jordan began to shake. Her skin began to ripple and her mouth sprang open. She hissed and spat. Her fingers dug into the fabric of the chair and ripped it. And still the demonic voice ranted at the world.

Grohmann was now visibly worried. He had to get Jordan back. He leaned forward and spoke forcefully and directly to her, calling her name, calling her back. At first he had no success. Jordan was writhing now and rocking the armchair to and fro with the power of her convulsions.

But he persisted and gradually the voice and the paroxysm subsided until she lay in the chair totally exhausted. He called her back and she responded by opening her eyes. Grohmann switched off the recording and increased the lighting. He was breathing deeply. Finally, he sighed heavily.

'What happened?' said Jordan.

'You've been on a little trip, Jordan,' said Grohmann, 'and now you are back safe and sound. How do you feel?'

'Exhausted. Like I've been through a shredder. Have I been under long?'

Grohmann glanced at his watch and grunted in surprise. An hour had passed in the blink of an eye.

'Not long,' he said.

'You mentioned coffee,' she said.

'Yes,' he replied, 'I'll arrange it. And I'd like to arrange another appointment very soon, this week.'

'Look, I'll be honest with you, Doctor Grohmann. I'm trying to save my credits at the moment.'

'Don't worry about my fees,' said the psychiatrist.

'That's very kind of you but I don't know if this is going to help.'

'I believe it can. You'll just have to trust me. I think something is happening to you and I think you are going to need all the help you can get. Now, you mentioned Frank Brady?'

'I'm certain he has something to do with it,' said Jordan.

'There is to be an exhibition?'

'Yes, "The Savage Eye" at the Lepri Gallery. It's next week.'

'I see. Perhaps I will attend. I am an old friend of Antonio Lepri.'

'I don't know if I'll be well enough. Whatever he's doing has got to stop, Dr Grohmann. And it's going to stop, one way or another.'

Grohmann helped her to her feet and ordered coffee for her in reception. He declined to join her but saw her to his office door. She looked at him.

'Thank you,' she said.

'I have some ideas, Jordan. Before I discuss them with you I want to check on one or two things. Perhaps when we meet next I will have more to tell you. Meanwhile, I would like to see you very soon, before the exhibition at the Lepri. OK?'

'OK,' she agreed.

'Right, fix up a time with Julia. Tell her it's priority one.'

She smiled at him again and walked out of the office. As soon as she had left Grohmann moved quickly. He replayed the tape and turned up the sound. Again he witnessed the transformation of Jordan Semiramis into something malevolently alien. He concentrated, making copious notes, muttering under his breath.

Possession was Grohmann's best guess as he watched Jordan's tortured face reflecting her inner turmoil. 'But it's more like some kind of psychic virus. Frank Brady, what are you up to?'

He switched off the recording, made an instant copy of the relevant parts of the soundtrack and punched keys on his vidi-phone. A tired-looking woman gazed back at him balefully.

'Institute of Mankind,' she stated in a bored voice.

'Ravish Loria, please,' said Grohmann.

'Who shall I say is calling?' she asked.

'Tell him it's Marek Grohmann.'

Without a change of expression, she pressed some keys on an unseen keyboard.

'One moment please.' The screen went blank for a moment then another face replaced the woman's. Ravish Loria was brown and wrinkled as a walnut, with cascading white hair. His face was wreathed in smiles.

'Marek, my dear friend, to what do I owe this unexpected call? lt's been too long.'

'Ravish, you old devil. I've just read your paper on Qabbalistic symbolism and Moses Cordovera's doctrine of evil. It was heady stuff.'

'Such praise. You must want something pretty badly, Marek,' laughed Loria.

'I do have a favour to ask.'

'I thought so. First you soften me up, then you plunge in the knife. So ask. What does it cost to listen?'

Grohmann explained about the tape and the sound bites of an unknown language and gave the essence of the case to his friend. He did not mention Jordan's name but implied that there could be some kind of arcane sorcery involved. That was probably a wild supposition but it had to be considered. As he spoke, Ravish Loria's expression lost its playfulness and became serious.

'And you would like this translated overnight? Do you have any idea of how long something like this might take?' he said.

'For a genius like Ravish Loria time does not exist,' smiled Grohmann. I really need this in a hurry, Ravish.'

'Well then, you'd better get it over here right away. What's keeping you?'

Grohmann smiled at his old friend and switched off the vidiphone. He called his receptionist and told her to hire a cab right away.

Ravish Loria worked till the early hours on the rough tape, keeping his hard-pressed computer operator busy as he broke down the sound bites and fed them through the analysis procedures. At about two o'clock he called Marek Grohmann.

The psychiatrist was not pleased at being disturbed, until he discovered who was calling.

'I think we have broken a record,' said a tired-looking Loria from the vidi-phone, 'and I do not feel in the least bit guilty about getting you out of bed. Do you want this information now, or do you want to buy me lunch tomorrow?'

'Both, Ravish. Give me what you have now. Tomorrow I'll buy you the best lunch in Manhattan.'

'That sounds like a good deal.'

Grohmann was now wide awake. He cleared his bedside table, found a note-pad and waited expectantly.

'I'm sorry to tell you, Marek, that we've drawn a blank. The words or sounds uttered by this man come from no known root. However, I do have a theory, but it's way out of left field.'

'Go on,' Grohmann said.

'Aspects of the dissonances and the rhythm patterns struck a chord in my memory. I'm surprised it didn't jog your ancient brain cells, Marek, but then you are older than me.' He chuckled, then continued. 'I remembered the theory of celestial zootypes and the theory of ancient currents which emanated from distant stellar influences when the universe was young. There is a group of spiritual entities, one of which in arcane lore is called Ayvas. The sound this spiritual zootype is apparently associated with is a kind of insect-like buzzing. Some say mankind will be replaced on earth by insect intelligences, beetles to be exact. But, I digress. My theory is that you are listening to some kind of spiritual message, rather like the old "Book of the Law". Or it may be something more alarming. Ayvas is also associated with groups of demons which inhabit the lower planes of awareness and who are supposed to have been brought into existence by mankind itself, created from the sum total of accrued evil. I met someone many years ago who had a powerful gift and who claimed to be able to penetrate the pathways beyond the Guardians, and return unscathed. But don't ask me her name.'

Grohmann was plunged into a deep silence. Loria interrupted his reverie.

'I'm going to bed now, Marek, that is, as long as there is nothing else I can do for you – a translation of the Aztec scriptures for instance.'

Grohmann shook his head. 'I really am most grateful, Ravish.

You have excelled yourself. Let me say that the only thing which will excel your work will be the sumptuousness of today's lunch. I will see you at Grey's.'

'I look forward to it. Goodnight, Marek.'

Grohmann poured himself a drink and pondered Loria's analysis. There had been other, similar, documented cases, examples of automatic writing, speaking in tongues, prophecy and so forth but he had never expected to witness anything like this. And Frank Brady. He did not know what to make of his involvement. A sanctum in his apartment? One thing was certain, Marek Grohmann was going to be at the opening of "The Savage Eye". Something told him that this exhibition would be a turning point in some way. Call it instinct. It wasn't very scientific, but Grohmann believed wholeheartedly in trusting his instincts.

The demon probed the world with its new-found awareness. For aeons it had waited. Time meant nothing. Time did not exist if space did not exist. Now it was approaching sentience. It luxuriated in the power surges of the individualities which had given birth to it. These wretched beings from the mundane world of material existence were searching in their primitive way to discover it. But the demon was not ready. It was carefully digesting the life-force of the female. It was using the necromancer to create a temporary host and it was savouring the psyche of the other male life-form.

When it finally emerged into the light of the world, it would destroy the trio who were now so intimately entwined. It would feed on their life-forces and eat their hearts.

The host was crude but useful. It had no brain or mind or conscience. It would suffice for the moment until the blindness which affected the demon was fully lifted. Then the world would see such concentrated evil.

The demon experimented with its host, exploring its primitive control system.

Click!

Chapter Sixteen

In a city starved of genuine cultural or artistic development, where television and film reflected the popular appetite for shallow and crass entertainment, "The Savage Eye" came as a breath of fresh air. It had been publicized with dignified restraint but nevertheless was guaranteed to attract thousands of visitors. There was simply nothing else like it. Other exhibitions were safe and predictable. This exhibition reflected Frank Brady's status.

There had been considerable overseas interest in the exhibition, and Manhattan's hotels were receiving visitors from many countries who had come, not just for the exhibition, but to see the Isolation city for themselves. Temporary credit facilities had been granted to the many British, Japanese and European tourists who arrived at the heliport after their short ferry flight from Staten Island airport. The proximity to the notorious Badlands added a certain excitement to the trip.

Outside the Lepri Gallery, the sidewalk was heaving with guests and VIPs, the rich, the super-rich, the press and the artistic community.

For the gallery this was one of the big exhibitions. Everyone who was anyone in Manhattan would be sure to have their photograph taken for the social columns in and around the Lepri Gallery.

Inside, the atmosphere was redolent of perfume and the unctuous smell of success. Pampered multimedia artists mixed with heavy-drinking journalists, media-web and film stars and hopefuls jostled with serious writers, industrialists and the usual flotilla of financial heavyweights and pulp-fiction writers.

Antonio Lepri welcomed his guests with a smile and a witty remark. Waiters circulated with drinks and canapés and Frank Brady was standing in the centre of a clutch of admirers. He looked elegant in a loose-fitting dark-blue suit and white crew-necked shirt.

Among the early arrivals was a group from Media City, including a team from Channel Boom Boom led by Maurice Freiberg. Johnny arrived with Jordan on his arm. She had done a remarkable job on herself. She wore a long black dress, high at the collar with a sashed waist and a dark ruby cape. She had worked on her hair to disguise the ravages it had gone through and had spent hours on her face. The result was stunning. She was dramatically thin and tired but had perked herself up with a little blue pill before setting out.

Almost unnoticed, Marek Grohmann arrived, wearing a conventional tuxedo. His second session with Jordan Semiramis had been largely inconclusive. He had established details of her early life and of her love for her father. Her mother and sister, who lived now in Canada, appeared less important to her. There had been no breakdown in those relationships; her sister seemed very attached to her mother and Jordan had simply gone her own way. Grohmann had wondered why it had been so many years since they had seen each other but that was another issue. Right now it was her wasting disease which preoccupied him. She appeared to be sustaining herself by taking quantities of mild stimulants. There was nothing wrong with that to Grohmann's mind but it only served to disguise the real, underlying malaise that afflicted her. Today he intended to have a serious word with Frank Brady. They once shared a common interest in the occult until Brady proved himself to be too emotionally unreliable. Grohmann had helped Brady several years before when the photographer was going through a particularly bad patch. During those therapy sessions, Grohmann had first tried the mantra regression technique. It had been a spectacular success, with one exception. Grohmann became aware of the entrance to a nether world present within every human being but which remains hidden to the vast majority. Very few enlightened ones have ever explored the non-conscious world. Whether this world, like its material counterpart, was just another illusion constructed by the mind he did not know.

When Brady returned he had undergone an infinitesimal change or alteration. Grohmann had almost missed it.

As for himself, standing amid the glittering gathering in the gallery, he had undergone a shift of perception. His earlier premonition of death was still imprinted upon him but he had come to terms with death many years before. If he was wrong, and death was not the threshold of another set of experiences, then oblivion would be irreversible. These gloomy thoughts could not quite quell the feeling of euphoria he was starting to experience. His life had been full. He had come to America full of hope. He and Imelda had been so much in love. His only regret was that the sweet taste of that love had faded and could never be experienced again. After Imelda had been killed he had gone through a number of arid affairs. He had been establishing himself in his career and there were certain women who had access to the kind of connections he desired.

Now, in the darkest of nights, he felt so alone; despite his beliefs and despite his transcendental journeys. Without his interest in the paranormal and esoteric dimensions of existence, his life would be mind-numbingly dull. Seldom did he come across a really interesting case. He had no family to speak of. His social life was active but boring. Only sailing off Long Island Sound and exploring the cosmic potential of his mind provided the satisfaction he craved. Putting it simply, he longed for some excitement. Whatever the consequences of what he described as the Purple Zone, whatever it concealed, whatever the fate of the three people involved with this haunting, obsessive possession, at least it wasn't dull.

Grohmann shook himself out of his reverie and moved through the crowd, smiling and shaking hands, making his way towards the main exhibition hall.

The noisy, chattering crowd was swirling and laughing in the main concourse. Cameras flashed like Christmas lights and several vidi-crews were battling for both space and interviews.

Also battling for space in the crowd were twin dwarfs, identical in their dress suits and shrivelled expressions.

Marcus and Theodore Papadakis were two of the most successful currency brokers in Manhattan. Unknown to many, they also ran an undercover supplies business to certain wholesalers in the Badlands. By a circuitous route, raw materials, food and other supplies found their way to the anarchic markets of

Brooklyn. The fact that certain senior Zone Police officers were paid handsomely to turn a blind eye was not a matter of public knowledge. The dwarfs were paid the utmost respect by those who knew what and who made Manhattan really tick. Right now they were sipping champagne cocktails and gazing around with the amused and slightly cynical expressions of those who share a special secret.

'Hideous creatures, aren't they, Theodore?' said Marcus to his brother.

Theodore looked up. 'Experiments that went wrong, Marcus, all of them. They're too far off the ground, that's their trouble.'

Marcus chuckled. 'The last of the line always are, my dear, quite exceptionally hideous.'

'There are always exceptions,' Theodore growled. 'She, at least, is quite divine.'

The two dwarfs turned to look at Jordan as she walked by. They sighed in unison. Just then, Antonio Lepri mounted the stairs to the first floor clutching a microphone. He cleared his throat and the audience grew quiet.

'Ladies and gentlemen,' he began, 'ladies and gentlemen; and members of the press.' There was a ripple of predictable laughter. Lepri continued. 'It gives me very great pleasure to welcome you to the Lepri Gallery this afternoon for what, I believe, will be regarded as one of the most important artistic events of recent years. It is not very often, in the strange times we live in, that an artist touches the nerve-endings of an entire society. Such an artist is Frank Brady. I will not spare his blushes because I believe his work turns the spotlight not only on the external world, and in particular a world that few of us wish to contemplate or understand, but just as importantly, on ourselves. His photographs have been published and exhibited all over the world. Again, I will not spare his blushes when I tell you that Frank Brady, the lad from Liverpool in England as he likes to think of himself, is probably the most famous photographer in the world.

'"The Savage Eye" will disturb many of you. It will frighten some of you. There are those of you who will turn your eyes away from the images he has captured. There are many of you who will simply not believe what you are about to see. Today you are all part of an experience. You are about to see life as it is lived by millions of people in many parts of the world. You are about to see the hard underbelly of society, the poetry of poverty and the vitality of violence,' Lepri paused. 'Frank has asked me to tell you that during the exhibition, in about half an hour's time, a very special exhibit will be brought in. You will find a roped-off area inside. Please don't tamper with this because that is where the special exhibit will be unveiled by Frank Brady himself. Now, my directors would never forgive me if I did not make my usual pitch. The sales desk will be open if you wish to order prints of any of the photographs you see. On sale also is a beautifully produced book of Frank's work with notes by the artist. It's called *The Savage Eye*, what else? Now, I invite you to make your way to the gallery.'

There was a ripple of applause and a rumble of anticipation as the crowd moved in a multi-coloured mass towards the gallery itself.

Inside the gallery, Brady's work had been sectioned off to facilitate a natural audience flow. Brady found Lepri in the crowd and took him by the hand.

'Thank you, Toni,' he said warmly, 'for a wonderful opening.'

'Frank, it is I who should be thanking you. Look at this crowd. It's fantastic. Come on, it's time you circulated.'

In spite of his smouldering dislike of Brady, Johnny had to accept that the man was brilliant. Each section was devoted to a group of photographs, sometimes sequences, connected by a general theme. So there was 'Africa', 'Daughters of the Dark', 'Death Style', 'Badlands', and 'Higher Society'.

The crowd began to circulate and the soft murmurs of appreciation began to turn to gasps of incredulity and abhorrence as the bleak, violent and decadent images stared out at the sophisticates. Close to Johnny and Jordan, a tall woman sailed by on the arm of a thin, seedy and effeminate man in his middle thirties.

'Justin,' remarked the woman with a tremble in her voice, 'these circumcision pictures are enough to turn you vegan.'

'Oh, I don't know,' her companion replied, 'I think they're quite mouth-watering.'

Jordan stopped by the Marcia sequence, unable to tear her eyes away. A crowd had gathered around the series of death shots. Everyone was silent. Marcia's screaming face, destroyed and distorted by the point of the girder as it projected through her skull, had a riveting power. Other sequences caused Johnny's blood to run cold. There were shots of him taken with the Feeks and Farooks, and others of him firing his stun pistol, his face caught in an expression of absolute fear. Johnny had not expected to see his own face hanging on the wall of the Lepri Gallery.

Dominating a complete section was an enormous blow-up of the Plater's disintegrating head. Caught in a time frame, it resembled a true Cubist construction. The eyes had exploded like bullets and had been caught travelling in opposite directions. The lower jaw had separated and shattered and the tongue seemed to hover in mid-air. Jordan clutched Johnny tightly as they drifted with the crowd. In the centre of the gallery was an arrangement of photographs that caused her to weaken. A figure had been caught in various positions. It was a woman yet not a woman. It looked like Jordan, yet it was not Jordan. Its limbs were twisted and distorted and, in some of the shots, detached from the body completely.

Following close behind, with one eye on the photographs and the other on Jordan and Johnny, Marek Grohmann noted her reactions.

When he came to the distorted, broken images of the female figure, he could not take his eyes from them. He was put in mind of Hans Bellmer's famous doll creations. These were equally disturbing.

A silence had hushed the crowd. The earlier social *bonhomie* had evaporated. Several women had fainted. Many of the others were looking decidedly sick. Others had walked out in disgust. The media were recording everything, soaking up the images of violence and hate like a sponge.

Johnny had his arm around Jordan's shoulders. She had turned pale and she was trembling uncontrollably. Johnny almost wept at the sight of her clinging to him.

At that moment, Frank Brady's voice rasped from the PA

system, 'Ladies and gentlemen, if you would pay close attention for a moment, I would like to unveil a new creation.'

Four men were carrying in a tall object covered with a black drape. They puffed a little as they shuffled towards the roped-off area in the centre of the gallery. The crowd moved back, watching and waiting for whatever was to be unveiled. When the object was in position, the men left and Brady walked unhurriedly to stand next to it. By this time the entire audience was standing and watching. Near the front were Johnny and Jordan. Brady stared at Jordan for a moment then gazed around at his audience. He turned and signalled to someone, then the lights dimmed, spotlights flicked on and the black-draped object was starkly illuminated. Marek Grohmann slowly made his way to the front.

'Before I reveal my latest creation, I would just like to say, ladies and gentlemen, and those who aren't sure, thank you for coming to my show. I would like to thank Antonio Lepri and his staff. They have surpassed themselves. Now ladies and gentle-men . . .' Brady took hold of the drape and began to pull. It started to slide from an oblong glass case. 'I would like you to welcome, Our Lady of Obsession.'

Posed inside the case was the doll. It had been positioned carefully to maximize its erotic potential. The photo-montage face stared malevolently out at the world. The doll was wearing skimpy Erotique underwear. A smear of blood-red lipstick gave its mouth a savage sneer.

There was a rumble of disquiet from the audience. The vidi-cameras and stills photographers bombarded it with light. Then, slowly, people began to walk towards the doll, fascinated by its anatomical dexterity and its expression of vicious insolence.

The audience could not take its eyes from the mannequin. Brady was surrounded by journalists and admirers bombarding him with questions. Across the gallery, Maurice Freiberg was looking at the doll with a vacant expression. Then, for no accountable reason, he underwent a mild asthma attack. He was immediately surrounded by a bevy of media executives. He pushed them out of the way roughly and fished in his pocket for his portable mini-nebulizer. He inhaled deeply, staring at the doll all the while. Within seconds he had recovered and was turning away from the photo-mannequin. Then a scream rent the air.

There was an immediate silence and a space cleared in the gallery. Johnny was bending over Jordan. She was out cold. Her skin was clammy and her breathing was shallow. Johnny was frantic. Antonio Lepri was at the scene in seconds. He had called the first aid team on standby for the show. They would be at the gallery rapidly. Johnny was trying to revive Jordan but she wasn't responding. He felt a surge of panic welling from his stomach. He gazed down at the ashen face and was overcome with grief. But it was a cold grief. He thought then of what Jordan had said at the apartment. Maybe we should kill Brady. That was it. Suddenly it was all crystal clear. Killing Brady had to be the only answer. He had killed for the first time outside the Ancestor Club but it hadn't seemed real somehow. To kill someone in cold blood was a different proposition. But anger and fury were racing through Johnny's veins. If Brady was responsible, and having seen the voodoo doll it was patently obvious that he was, then Johnny would kill him. Mixed in with his churning emotions was the need to exact revenge for Angelica. He had to fight to control the urge to kill the bastard right here and now. No, it had to be planned. It had to be perfect.

Johnny was cradling Jordan's head in his arms as two medics arrived with a stretcher. Johnny hardly heard the murmurs, comments and condolences that washed over him. He heard Grohmann's voice reassuring him. 'She will be all right Johnny. Go, go with her. I'll have a word with Mr Brady.'

Johnny looked at Grohmann blankly, then glanced over to where Brady was standing. The disturbance over, it was back to business. Brady looked across at Johnny without expression. Lepri had put his arm on Johnny's shoulder.

'It's probably just lack of air,' he reassured him. 'Do you want to go with her?'

Johnny didn't reply but just held Jordan's hand as the medics carried her out of the gallery. He looked back over his shoulder and found himself staring into the face of the doll. He could swear it was smiling wickedly. Johnny wanted to destroy the doll and Frank Brady there and then. The creature was hideous, the creation of a warped and sick mind.

But now his only concern was for the limp and comatose figure of Jordan lying on the stretcher. She was being rushed to the nearest medi-centre and he would be by her side when she opened her eyes.

The post-exhibition phase was setting in. This was the analysis stage when expert opinions were voiced and arguments ensued. 'The Savage Eye' was a success. The headlines on the main Manhattan news channel would major on the number of visitors who had collapsed or who had been unable to take the alternative reality the exhibition represented. Brady was receiving congratulations all round. Everyone wanted to talk to him to ask him about his experiences in the Badlands, to find out how he could put himself through such experiences for the sake of his work.

The vidi-crews and journalists had gone. Grohmann bided his time, waiting for exactly the right moment. It came when Brady walked across towards the doll. Quickly and nimbly, Grohmann appeared by his side.

'Marek,' said Brady, 'I'm sorry. I meant to talk to you earlier but you know how it is.'

'I most certainly do, Frank, Grohmann replied, 'but I'm glad of this opportunity to speak to you alone.'

'What do you think of her?' Brady touched the doll's glass case lovingly. 'She tore their hearts out, didn't she?'

'She bears a striking resemblance to the young woman who fainted,' Grohmann said. 'Who was your model, Frank?'

'What are you suggesting?'

'I'll come straight to the point. I think your superbly crafted mannequin is a glorified ju-ju doll. I can't work out whether what you're doing is deliberate or you're being driven by another one of your obsessions.'

'You think I'm a twisted, screwed-up fuck, don't you?' Brady snapped. 'You've never had the guts to go all the way, Marek. You sit in your fat office on your fat butt dabbling in a world you think you understand and you have the gall to talk to me about obsession. I am an artist. I take what I like for my material.

I go to the source. I challenge myself. Don't talk to me about fucking obsessions. You helped me once, a long time ago, but you also opened something in my mind and then abdicated all responsibility. But you did me a favour. Whatever you exposed me to has filled me with a new power. I'm tapping into something awesome. And you know what? I don't care how dangerous it is. Some of us sail close to the horizon. Shrinks like you just grow fat and old and shrivel up.'

Grohmann bristled. His face had drained. He had never felt so angry. He glanced up at the doll. He could have sworn it had changed its position fractionally. He met the doll's eyes, those lifeless pieces of glass and film. His vision swam momentarily. The eyes were alive. They were like black, glittering pools of starlight. They were empty and yet brimful of vibrant energy. He dug his psychic heels in as he felt himself surging towards those eyes. In his mind, sizzling between his ears, raced a buzzing, snapping sound, like a speeded-up tape recording. He had heard that sound before. And he knew where. He had last heard it bellowing from the fragile larynx of Jordan Semiramis. There was a deep vacuum reaching for him, sucking him in. Beyond the eyes lay a universe of possibilities where everything was simply in the process of becoming.

He staggered back and glared at Brady. 'It is you who are the dabbler, Frank. You are using this abomination to drain the life-force from an innocent young woman. You know who I mean. I'm speaking of Jordan Semiramis. I've heard about your so-called sanctum where you keep hundreds of photographs of that unfortunate young woman. Well, you're not going to get away with it. I believe you were instrumental in the destruction of the last woman you were obsessed with. Remember Angelica? How could you forget? I know about the connections. I know Johnny Raine is involved but I don't know how, yet. Neither do I know if you are a real magician or just a plaything of some higher power. But I'm going to find out. Be careful, Frank, I'm warning you.'

Brady poked the heavier man in the chest. His anger was about to overflow but he held it in check. They were in a public place. What he had in mind required secrecy.

'Look, shrink,' he snarled venomously, 'if you want to know what's really inside my mind, get your fat backside over to my place tonight. If you think I'm practising some kind of hoodoo or witchcraft then come and see for yourself. You know where I live. And count yourself lucky I'm prepared to give you the time. But now, get out of my face.'

Brady pushed past him. Grohmann's heart was beating quickly and his blood was rushing through his veins. One thing was certain. He would keep the appointment with Mr Frank Brady.

As he shuffled off to join the last of the throng leaving the gallery, something was watching him. Something had tasted him and had savoured the confrontation between himself and Brady.

The doll appeared to move its head, just by a centimetre or so. Antonio Lepri was ushering the stragglers out of the hall to a little reception he had planned, when he glanced back at the doll and shivered. My God, he thought, in this light and at this distance it seems alive. Something about the doll looked different. He shook his head. That was impossible.

Johnny sat by Jordan's bed in a room filled with subdued light and silent, flashing electronic monitors. They had run tests and she was OK, they said. She had had a shock, he was told.

He was watching her when she awoke, disorientated at first, then she saw him. They had fitted her up with a drip and she looked healthier than she had done for weeks. When the memories flooded back, however, her face clouded over.

'Johnny, darling, what happened ... The gallery ... That creature ...' She tailed off.

'Don't you worry about anything any more. I'm going to take care of things.'

She sat up, looking remarkably recovered, although thin and pale. 'What do you mean, take care of things?'

Johnny shifted in his chair. 'I'm going to do what we talked about. I'm going to kill him.' She stared at him. 'What have we got ourselves into?'

'I don't know and, frankly, I don't care. I only care about you and me. I have no choice. It has to be tonight.'

'I'm coming with you,' she said.

'Are you kidding? You're in no condition to do anything.'

'I want to destroy that doll creature. Then I want to destroy Brady. I have to go. Don't you see, I have to be there.'

Johnny started to argue with her but she was adamant. There was fire in her eyes again. Reluctantly, he agreed. Her point was that by tomorrow it might be too late. She felt all right, weak and light-headed but all right. She would take a couple of little pink pills. They would keep her going till it was over. When Johnny stood up to leave her, he felt an icy calmness enter him.

'Right,' he told her when he had kissed her tenderly, 'I'll go back to my apartment and get prepared. You discharge yourself and I'll pick you up later at your place. Then we'll head for the gallery. We'll have to find a way to break in. Are you sure about this?' he asked her.

'Perfectly sure,' she told him, 'and getting into the gallery might be easier than you think.'

It was just getting dark. Rolling thunder clouds were piling up, pushed by an ocean wind. Marek Grohmann drove his old convertible towards Central Park. He could hear explosions coming from the direction of the East River. Glancing over he saw the throb of pulsed lasers and intermittent flashes of gunfire. He sighed. The Zone Police were being kept busy these days. Perimeter battles were becoming more frequent. He turned off towards the secluded district where Brady lived. Grohmann took a deep breath. This was going to be interesting.

Johnny approached the entrance to his apartment and stopped dead in his tracks. It was that smell. He looked down and saw the paving stones streaked with slime. He remembered that smell and he remembered the slime and he remembered the insane fear he had felt that night. He looked around him carefully. It had been just over a week since he had received the terse message from Shell. People were waiting for him to do something. And he was completely in the hands of this strange, misshapen creature. Two million credits and freedom rested upon her cooperation. If it came to it, he would do without the credits and just get out with Jordan. But life would be that much more comfortable with money. Either way it would all be over soon. If the TV suicide did not come off, that was just too bad. He had discovered an ice-cold side to his nature. No one would ever suspect Johnny Raine of Brady's murder. Unless, of course, someone noticed the similarity between the doll creation and Jordan and discovered their relationship. Grohmann knew, of course. To hell with it, he thought. Let's just do it and get out.

At that moment his nerves were on red alert. He flattened himself against the side wall of the apartment block, glanced up at the tumbling, evening storm clouds and began to move towards his front door. He was scared. He had no weapons. His only chance was to get inside the apartment and reach his pulse pistol. His senses told him that whatever had been here had now gone. The door was yards away. He held his compu-key like a weapon. He moved closer to the door and saw it had been covered in the sewage-like slime. He fought hard against retching, then saw that something had been written in the morass. Bolder now he stepped up to the door.

A glutinous brown mess covered it. Trails of slime led back out to the street. A message had been scratched into the rank, mucus substance, which was coagulating into a carapace-like material. It said 'Tomorrow night, Shell.' That was perfect. That gave them a day before the first recording. Johnny aimed his compu-key at the receiver above the door. He would call maintenance about the mess. Right now he had to move fast.

He changed into his black, one-piece outfit and checked his weapons. He stuck a pulse pistol into his belt and slipped on a jacket. Then he made a number of calls. The first was to the studio. He called Clark Taylor, head of Channel Boom Boom PR. Taylor had left for the night so he had him message traced. Then he called the number Solo had given him. The security chief was still at his desk. Johnny was impressed despite the instant dislike he had taken to the man. He did not waste words. He told Johnny to expect a small, reinforced personnel carrier to be delivered to his address the following night. Johnny declined the offer of a security operative to accompany him. The RPC, Solo explained, was a larger version of the sloop jet, carried more weaponry and had space for around four people in its high-security compartment. It was used normally for transporting prisoners, alive or dead. Solo would make all the necessary arrangements. It all sounded so simple and civilized. Next, Johnny called Lloyd at home. He had clearly disturbed him because the producer sounded breathless and tearful. He did not switch on vision so Johnny could not see him. When he received the news he became excited. OK, he told Johnny, leave everything to me. He would make some calls and alert production and Media City security. Johnny could hear voices in the background and the unmistakable sound of leather striking flesh. His last business call was to leave a message for Stan Michaels. He wanted access to those credits fast.

He called the medi-centre and checked that Jordan had discharged herself. She was weak but very determined, the receptionist told him. He smiled, then called her at home. She sounded a little lost but filled with resolution. Now they had decided on a course of action, they both felt better. However, they had to stop and think just how they were going to break into the gallery. Security of major buildings in Manhattan had, strangely enough, become lax during the Isolation. It was generally felt that people and property were safer now. That was not strictly true and a building like the Lepri Gallery would have its own security system. Johnny was relieved when Jordan told him that she had worked on the original compu-key code system and could probably produce an over-ride code from her original files. If the system used at the gallery was an older version, then it just might work. It would not take her long to carry out a search-and-find program then produce a replica of the binary ID code. The gallery did not employ full-time security guards. So, if they could get inside, the only obstacles they might face would be the possibility of a remote sensor system.

'I want to make one visit on the way over,' Johnny told her, 'then I'll pick you up.'

'Love you,' was all she said as her image dissolved. For a moment, Johnny just stared at the screen. He wanted to cry at the sight of her. Her cheeks were hollow and her skull was now visible through her skin. It also filled him with a cold fury. If he needed justification for his actions it was all there in Jordan's face.

Before he left the apartment to collect his electro-turbo he selected a thin, strong alloy bar. They needed some way of smashing that glass case and destroying the sick doll creature inside.

Grohmann turned off the ignition. Outside, a breeze had picked up and, when he opened his car door, the first drops of rain were falling. He was standing in a quiet street lined with trees, caressed by a gathering wind and dappled by streetlights. There was an old-fashioned feel to the area. The houses and apartments were discreetly positioned within the greenery. It was a civilized place, the kind of place he remembered from his childhood; the kind of place where people felt safe and where nothing ever happened. Grimly, Grohmann began to walk towards the tall apartment building where Brady lived. As he approached the ground floor he noticed that the outside door was slightly open. Inside was a softly lit lobby. He looked up at the ten-storey building. It was dark except for lights coming from the fifth floor. He slipped inside and walked across the lobby towards the elevator.

Antonio Lepri was satisfied. It had been a wonderful day. The exhibition had been a great success. The demand for Brady prints had almost overwhelmed his sales staff. He was among the last to leave, tired but fulfilled. He took one last look around the gallery, switched on the computer alarm system and went to meet his wife for dinner.

The gallery was quiet, except for the murmur of the air-conditioning system. Subdued lighting bathed the rooms in soft pools. Shadows danced on walls as the atmosphere in the gallery changed. When everyone had gone, the building enjoyed a secret existence. Sculptures loomed like predatory monsters in the dimness. Paintings and drawings, images on flat canvas and wood, photographs and frescoes, tapestries and tinted miniatures began to breathe with a life of their own.

Images of crucifixions and violent death, images of the Badlands throbbing with life, awash with soft light, now seemed to come alive. Only one pair of eyes watched them vacantly. The doll stared, unmoving, gazing blindly into nothingness.

Then there was a sound. A soft, whirring sound. Then there was a movement, undetected and unseen except by the faces which stared out from the walls.

Click! Something moved, a finger, an eyelid.

Click! The mouth twitched.

Inside the doll its electronic conduits were being explored intimately. Power was gathering itself together out of nothingness. This was where the spirits gathered. This was the repository of a life-force, enough to provide a home for the spirit. And the spirit had been waiting a long time for this moment.

The doll moved.

I am here. I am now, said the spirit. It was restricted, imprisoned in a man-made machine. The host would suffice for the moment. The spirit had been feeding well. The woman had provided a vibrant source of energy and life-force. She was still alive, but only just. Now, to continue to become what it was destined to become, the spirit recognized itself. It was the crucible of all the accumulated hate-force of human life.

And it hated human life.

Its sole purpose was to absorb all its energy, all its life-force. The husks, shells or bodies could be dispensed with. They were just unnecessary appendages, destined to rot back into the material universe as if they had never existed.

I must continue, the spirit told itself. I must complete the cycle of entry. What has begun must be finished.

The doll moved again.

Chapter Seventeen

There was one thing Johnny had to do before he called for Jordan. Call it compulsion, since he had no reason to go there. He just wanted to see the crucifix machine again. The awesome creation was housed in a warehouse behind the Media City building. Access was restricted to the very few who knew about it. So far, its existence had not been leaked to the press. For over two weeks now, speculation about suicides on TV had been rife. Soon they would be dismissed as Channel Boom Boom hype, designed to put the fear of Freiberg into the hearts of Jack Silverman and other senior executives of the top three US channels.

Johnny gained access easily. He walked slowly around the edge of the warehouse, keeping to the shadows. In the centre of the building stood the crucifix machine. Two of the designers were putting it through its paces. Something told Johnny to stay back and just watch. What kind of warped mind could design a thing like this, he wondered? He recognized Vere Nixon, chief designer. Johnny had always regarded Nixon as being creative but level-headed. It must be the madness of Manhattan that enabled rational people to disengage whatever moral or humanistic instincts they had. Nixon was standing at the side of the machine, holding a controller. His colleague watched as the lights raced around the frame like the entrance to a circus. Nixon pressed keys on the controller. Positioned on a small pad in front of the frame and underneath the hanging skullcap was a dummy. For an instant, Johnny was reminded of the doll in the gallery. The dummy was man-sized and weighted to replicate the human body. Suddenly the skullcap descended. It happened so quickly that Johnny was surprised. The skullcap snapped into position at the top of the dummy's head. Johnny knew that inside the skullcap a powerful pneumatic headband was gripping the dummy's skull. Small titanium needles had penetrated millimetres into the skull all around the headband. As Johnny

watched, the dummy was lifted off its feet and hung suspended
and swaying, reflecting the flashing lights from the machine. The
whole process had taken less than three seconds. Nixon called a
warning to the other technician and pressed the controller.

Instantaneously, the dummy was electrocuted. The lights that
were playing around the frame of the machine changed direction
and poured along the pendulum arm and down into the skullcap
like a molten river of light. The dummy exploded in a burst of
flame. Simultaneously, there was a loud, metallic snapping
sound as, out from the side frame flashed a ten-foot long blade,
thin but razor sharp. The blade was hinged like a flick-knife. It
decapitated the dummy and snapped back into its housing before
Johnny had taken a breath. The speed of the operation was
terrifying.

All that remained of the dummy was a pile of smouldering
ashes while the decapitated head swung gently to and fro, still
held by the skullcap. Nixon grunted with satisfaction and
released the skullcap, allowing the head to drop to the floor.

Johnny had seen enough. Slowly and thoughtfully, he retraced
his steps. He was shaking his head. This whole hideous operation
had nothing to do with television or with entertainment. He was
going to have to force himself to go through with the first one.
And the first one would be his last.

Jordan was silent as they drove through the Manhattan streets,
now slick with rain. The night sky was illuminated with
occasional flashes of light. The laserjets were in operation again.
As Johnny drove towards the Lepri Gallery, Jordan watched him.
His jaw was tight with tension. His normal, ironic smile had
been replaced with a grimace.

As for herself, she was dying. She knew that now. The doctors
and medics would find nothing. There would be no explanation
for her death. She was wasting away. She wore a tight-fitting hat
to disguise what was left of her hair. Oddly, she felt remarkably
calm. This was her only chance of survival. She was not certain
it would succeed. They could all be totally wrong and Brady and
his doll creation could be innocent. Deep inside her, however,
she knew they were at the heart of her problem.

Johnny parked at the back of the gallery. They waited until the streets were relatively clear, then left the electro-turbo and made their way to the rear of the building. It was quiet and a warm Spring rain was drizzling. There were few people about. The building appeared quiet and serene. Low-level lighting shone dully from the windows as they located the rear staff entrance. Johnny checked his pulse gun and gripped his alloy bar tightly. They sidled along a wall, instinctively ducking below windows, although the effort was almost too much for Jordan.

The rear door was standard office design. At the side was the compu-entry machine. Johnny held out his hand. Silently, Jordan handed him the thin metal strip which contained an imprint of the override systems code. She was praying it would work. If not, they would have to break in, risking the alarm system, destroy the doll and get out before the State Police arrived. Some chance, she thought. Johnny slid the strip into the optical recognition slit. Normally, the response would have been immediate and the door would open. Nothing. Johnny clenched his jaw and looked at Jordan. The strip popped out after several seconds. Then the door opened. They looked at each other with relief. Johnny slipped the strip into his jacket pocket.

Then they were inside. They prowled slowly along corridors, passing numerous offices and other corridors and galleries. In the darkness, the gallery seemed enormous. The atmosphere was unwelcoming; the gallery seemed charged with a life of its own. And it didn't like visitors. They reached the main reception area. Jordan gripped Johnny's arm. He reached for his pulse pistol and they crept silently towards the Brady exhibition gallery.

The atmosphere was more oppressive here. Johnny had the distinct impression that they were being watched. Something unseen was lurking in the shadows. Jordan was breathing heavily. There was something here, Johnny could sense it. Still they padded forward towards the entrance to 'The Savage Eye'.

Total silence descended like a thick black blanket as they entered the exhibition. They stood looking at the barely discernible images. In the darkness and the flickering light from an outside neon sign, the images took on an altogether more sinister appearance. They seemed alive. Jordan almost fell at the sight of the Marcia picture. She tore her eyes away.

They crossed the gallery towards the looming shape of the glass case. It was dark, almost black, save for reflections from the neon light. As they crept towards it they heard a sound.

It came from behind them.

They froze. Nothing. They had reached the glass case. They were within a few feet of it when they heard the sound again. It was clear but soft.

Click!

Johnny was sweating profusely. His grip tightened on his pistol. He swivelled round, pointing the laser snout into the gloom. Brady's fractured images watched him impassively. Jordan seemed transfixed. In the striated light she appeared like a skeleton or a corpse. She moved around to the front of the glass case and staggered back, gasping and clasping her hand to her mouth. Johnny was with her in a second. He turned to look at the doll, gripping his alloy bar in one hand and his pistol in the other.

The doll had gone.

The front of the glass case had burst open. Shards of glass were strewn all over the floor. Johnny stood with his mouth open. What the hell was going on? Someone had been here before them and taken the doll. Who? Then came the sound again.

Click!

Nearer this time. Jordan was shaking like a leaf. She was trying to speak, to implore Johnny to run. He held her and they turned to face the way they had come.

Nothing.

But they were being watched. The temperature had plummeted. Johnny was shivering. His blood was turning to ice. The temperature in the gallery had reached almost arctic depths.

With the precision of a frozen needle making an incision, both their minds were invaded. They tried to resist, but images like fire and ice raged inside them. Within the maelstrom of paralysing numbness something had concealed itself. Johnny held Jordan in a frantic death-like embrace. If they were going to die they would be together. The newsreel of his life unwound between his frontal lobes. It had been a pathetic existence, riddled with weakness and indecision. He knew with startling certainty that most of his life had been wasted upon futile ambition and ego-centred desire.

It was hopeless. His spirit was facing defeat. What was the point of living in this hell world? Human beings were shit; human life was a mountain of detritus and excreta. And love. What was the point of love? A momentary orgasm in the huge span of existence.

Jordan too was weeping. Despair was filling her soul.

Johnny held his pulse pistol. What was the fucking point of it all? Why not end it now? The two of us could die here, together. In a week, even our memories would be as dust in a windstorm. He raised the pulse pistol to Jordan's temple. Only hate existed, he knew that now. Hate was the primal force, not love.

Click!

The sound was sharp. It shook Johnny out of his malaise. His immobilized legs began to move. He took Jordan by the hand and ran. Screaming and oblivious of detection, they raced back out of the gallery.

They burst through the rear exit. Jordan had to stop. She was too weak to go much further. Johnny picked her up and carried her to the electro-turbo. He got her inside and strapped her in. Then he leaped in by her side.

'Take these,' he ordered, handing her some little blue pills.

She grabbed them and crammed them into her mouth hungrily. He gunned the electro-motors and the car whined away into the night.

Johnny was aware enough to obey the speed limit. Slowly, Jordan began to recover a little. The blue pills were doing their job.

'Where's it gone?' she croaked. 'Where's that hell-bitch gone to?'

'I don't know,' Johnny said. 'I just know one thing. It's Brady. It must be. We can't let him live.'

Johnny had never experienced such overwhelming despair as he had in the gallery. It had hit him like an avalanche. There had been no time to think or to evaluate or reason. He was trembling as he headed across town towards Brady's apartment and praying also that the Englishman was there. Well, if not tonight, then tomorrow, he didn't care when. He had never felt a power like it. Something had caught hold of his mind and squeezed it till the neurons rattled. He had been lucky to get away. Next time there would be no escape. He had almost pulled the trigger. He had been a light-beam away from killing Jordan. As for her, it was a wonder she could walk. He glanced at her, with a shock, remembering that it was only a week ago that she had started to feel unwell. He knew one thing for certain. He was going to fight all the way for her.

Johnny parked in a shadowed stretch of road near Brady's apartment. As he and Jordan got out of the electro-turbo he noticed an older vehicle parked some way up the street.

Johnny took Jordan into his arms. She held him weakly, showering his face with kisses. She felt like a bag of bones.

'Whatever happens, Jordan,' he said to her, 'remember I love you.'

She didn't or couldn't reply. Gently he detached her arms from around his shoulders and looked into her eyes.

'We've got to do this. You know that, don't you?' he said.

'I know,' she smiled at him, 'otherwise I won't be around much longer.'

She began to weep, huge gulping sobs. He held her until they subsided.

'Now, let's go do it,' he said, 'before I lose my nerve.'

Jordan's tears had ceased. Now she was calm and totally focused. She felt emotionless and cold.

They crossed the street towards the building. Once inside, they made their way to Brady's apartment on the fifth floor.

To their surprise, the apartment door was open. They padded inside, slowly and carefully, nerves straining for the slightest sound or movement. Johnny gripped his pulse pistol, set to maximum power, enough to blow Brady into the galaxy. Inside the apartment it was dark. Johnny was trying to recall the geography. Somewhere a ponderous clock ticked. Jordan followed Johnny along the hallway and into the main living room.

They paused, watching and trying to sense Brady's presence. The room was empty. A light was on in one corner, enabling them to see enough of the room to make their way across it without stumbling into furniture. Johnny could hear Jordan's breath painfully rasping in her lungs. He remembered where he was. This was where the party had been held, so over there must be the small passageway that led to the darkroom and to Brady's secret sanctum.

As in the gallery, Johnny had the distinct feeling of being watched. Nevertheless, he moved forward, with Jordan clinging like a shadow behind. They moved into the passageway. There were some wall lights glowing softly, so they could see the entrance to the darkroom ahead of them. A tap dripped somewhere ahead in the darkness. They seemed to adjust the pace of their footsteps to the rhythmic plink-plunk of the drops of water. Neither could bear to speak. An overwhelming sense of foreboding filled the apartment. Jordan especially could feel the psychic vibrations emanating from the very walls. She swallowed her fear, reminding herself that her life was hanging by a very tenuous thread. They pressed on, through the darkroom, heading for the room Johnny had discovered during the party. He knew that this was where Brady would be, if he was in the apartment at all.

Johnny knew where the light switch was. He opened the door slowly, pulse pistol at the ready. The room was in darkness. Something was creaking inside, a regular, rhythmic creak like a faulty wheel-bearing. Undaunted, he held his breath and stretched out his left hand to find the switch.

His fingers touched the dimmer and he turned it clockwise. Slowly, lights came up around the room. Jordan moved in from behind Johnny's back and saw that the walls were still partly covered by photographs of her. Many had been removed and were lying scattered on the floor, others had been torn into shreds.

The creak came from an unoccupied chair in the centre of the room, which was revolving as though its occupant had recently vacated it.

Johnny and Jordan were both staring at the end of the room,

where the largest photographic blow-ups had been mounted. Johnny had seen this before, but Jordan was dumbstruck. It came home to both of them how much she had changed in such a short time. Her beautiful, healthy face and body were now thin and haunted. Her once-glowing skin was patchy and flaky.

They walked slowly forward. Then the stench hit them. They cried out, then turned to their left to see what could be causing the unholy and putrid smell.

The first thing they saw was an intricate shadow cast on the floor. When they saw what was casting the shadow, Johnny fell to his knees, vomiting uncontrollably, while his eyes opened and he tried to scream at the same time. Jordan was frozen rigid with fear. Her limbs had turned to stone.

'Oh!' Johnny was moaning, 'Oh, my God.'

Jordan began to walk towards it.

In front of them was a large, geometrical metal frame in the form of a cage without bars. The frame was covered in magical symbols and images of mythical beasts. Inside the frame, pinned to it by thin, silver spears, was the naked and mutilated body of Marek Grohmann. His mouth was held open by a metal spike. His body had been systematically carved, like a sculpted figurine. Chunks of flesh had been carefully removed, creating a pattern of holes in his torso. The bloody recesses formed a sort of altar. Placed in the flesh-holes were tiny idols, figures of creatures and demons. Also in each flesh-altar was a coloured candle flickering obscenely, reflecting from the exposed ribs of the psychiatrist. Some of the ribs too had been cut to shape. His penis had been amputated and in its place a black crucifix had been rammed inside his scrotal area.

Johnny was still retching as he got to his feet. Jordan had walked forward towards the sacrificial remains of Grohmann as though attracted to it. Johnny stared at her and recognized a similar expression on her face to the one he had seen on the day the model had been so brutally killed.

The floor around the carved carcass was awash with blood. It had partly congealed. Johnny's mind was racing. He still held his pistol. He approached Jordan just as she had stretched out her hand to touch one of the idols, a winged beast.

'No, don't touch it,' Johnny shouted, 'we've got to get out of here.'

Johnny sensed, more than heard, someone behind him and to the right. Grabbing Jordan by the shoulders he swung round in one movement. Before he could raise his pistol to the firing position Brady was upon him. He was saturated with blood. His eyes were wide open, staring, demonic, totally mad. He held in his right hand a long, thin, obsidian knife. Johnny fired and missed. A hole appeared in the sanctum wall and the blast threw Brady forcibly on to Johnny. He swung Brady round using the older man's impetus to throw him against the back wall. In the struggle his pulse pistol was sent skittering across the floor. Brady stared up at them then began to sing to himself, all the while chuckling with a sort of hopelessness. He started to get to his feet.

'The big ship sails on the alley alley-o, the alley alley-o, the alley alley-o. The big ship sails on the alley alley-o,' sang Brady.

Johnny grabbed Jordan's hand and they fled the room. She was screaming and trembling from the sudden exertion. They ran through the darkroom and back into the living room with Brady in pursuit.

Fear had caused an evil-tasting bile to rise inside Johnny's throat. He saw Brady rushing towards him, knife raised, hissing his song between his teeth. Then, suddenly, a murderous calm came over him. Brady seemed to be moving in slow motion. Johnny kept his eyes firmly on the knife hand. Brady was strong, stronger than Johnny had imagined. He knew it was life or death for one of them. At that moment, sheer hate and fear combined to fill him with an icy coldness. Survival was all that counted. He remembered his martial arts basics and adjusted his weight. As Brady lunged, Johnny dropped his left shoulder and parried the knife-arm thrust. At the same time he hammered his right fist into Brady's solar plexus. The photographer crumpled, staggering towards the balcony. Jordan meanwhile was holding one of the blood-soaked idols from Grohmann's body. She threw it at Brady with deadly accuracy. It struck him on the temple and he dropped the knife. Johnny rushed for it but Brady was too quick. He picked up the knife and slashed upwards slicing through Johnny's sleeve and cutting into flesh. Blood spurted from the wound and Johnny screamed with shock and pain. He lashed out and caught Brady on the jaw with a scything hay-maker. Then the two men were locked together in a deathly embrace. Brady got his hands around Johnny's throat and was forcing him over the edge of the balcony, leering into his face, his eyes wide. Johnny fought back, trying to use his knees to dislodge his assailant. Gradually, Brady's strength began to prevail. Johnny was nearly halfway over the balcony; wind and rain caught both men's screams and scattered them across Central Park. Below, all Johnny could see was blackness. The fall would kill him, he was certain. This gave him renewed strength. He clawed at Brady's eyes but Brady sank his teeth into his wrist. Johnny tried to scream, but his windpipe was being squeezed. His face began to turn blue.

Suddenly, Brady's head exploded in cloud of blood and bone. Jordan staggered back, dropping the tripod she had found. The effort of the blow drained all the strength out of her and she collapsed.

Brady released Johnny and fell backwards, his weight taking him over the balcony edge. One hand stretched out and fastened on to the balcony railing. Johnny pushed himself free as Brady began to fall. Jordan had risen and was walking towards the railing when Brady's other hand suddenly shot up and grabbed Johnny's throat. He released his grip on the railing so that now he was hanging from the fifth floor balcony and pulling Johnny over with him, choking him at the same time. Johnny fought, grabbed Brady's wrist, but the photographer had found the strength of ten from somewhere.

Johnny was going over with him. Black stars flashed in front of his eyes. He knew he was going to die. A million memories surged through his mind like they were on a strip-film moving at hyper-speed.

Jordan had picked up the tripod and staggered to the railing. She raised it high above her head and brought it down with all the force she possessed on to Brady's wrist. Bone snapped. His grip slackened, then his hand opened.

He fell without a sound. Johnny reeled back, choking and

gasping for air, ears pounding. He turned to Jordan and held her. They were both shaking, unable to speak.

They collapsed to the floor, letting the windswept storm revive them. They were soaked with rain, sweat and blood. But they were alive. It was done. The spell had been broken.

Gradually, their ability to think rationally returned. Johnny raised Jordan to her feet and they started to walk back into the living room.

'We can't leave him there,' said Johnny. 'We've got to get rid of the body.'

Jordan said nothing. She could hardly walk. Far from being released from whatever spell had been cast, she felt weaker than ever. Her heart was pounding and her chest felt as though it was caving in under a great weight. She felt pain shooting up through her chest and paralysing her. She couldn't speak but she managed to stumble blindly after Johnny as they left the apartment and walked carefully to the elevator.

No one had seen them, and no one must. Johnny held her as they descended. She looked awful, like death itself. Jordan couldn't bear to see Brady's body lying broken and smashed on the grass outside. She was becoming rigid with fear at the prospect.

The elevator door opened. Johnny took a step back. The figure watching them was in partial darkness. For a moment it stood there, then began to walk into the elevator. Johnny drew back his fist as the figure entered. The man was about Brady's size.

Johnny stared at the face. He was about to let fly when he stopped. It was an elderly man, slightly stooped, wearing a pair of large sunglasses which partly obscured his face. He held a thin white probe-sensor in his hand.

Johnny realized with a relieved shock that the man was blind.

The blind man turned his head, sensing their presence.

'Good evening,' he said, with a rattle in his throat.

Johnny made no reply. Instead he took Jordan and half carried her out of the elevator towards the front door.

Once outside they breathed deeply. Jordan was now pale and clammy. They started looking around the base of the building.

Johnny checked the ground carefully. It was a clear grass area surrounded by shrubs and bushes.

It was empty.

Johnny propped Jordan against the wall and searched. He could find no trace of Brady's body.

A dark void opened up inside Jordan's head. The pain was short-lived but excruciating. As she collapsed, she knew with a sudden clarity that she was having a heart attack.

Johnny rushed to her, crying and weeping. But her heart had stopped.

He bent over her prone body lying in the wet grass. The rain increased in force, and thunder came rumbling over the park towards them. They were soaked through. Jordan's thin body was lifeless. Her lips were turning blue. Desperately Johnny placed his hands on her chest and pumped, trying to stimulate her breathing. He opened her mouth and gave her the kiss of life but all he could sense from her lips was the taste of death.

He cried out, screaming into the gathering storm. Frantically, he lifted her into his arms and ran to the electro-turbo, heedless of being seen or recognized. He forgot about Brady and what they had just done. He forgot about Channel Boom Boom. There was only one thing in Johnny Raine's mind at that moment and that was to save Jordan's life. Instead of reversing her wasting disease, Brady's death had made it worse. It had tipped her over the edge.

Gently, he placed her drenched body on the back seat, covered her with a thick blanket and leaped into the driving seat. Then, ignoring Manhattan's tight speed limits, he hit the accelerator and screamed off into the night heading for the nearest medi-centre. Every second counted. The thought of losing Jordan filled his every fibre with such an intense remorse that his entire body ached.

He knew then that he couldn't live without her.

Chapter Eighteen

Mike Schroder was sitting at his desk in Central Park precinct while his comfortable world collapsed around him. Retirement seemed a long way off now. There had been ten murders in the last three hours, a senior city official had thrown himself from a twenty-storey building near Wall Street and reports of violent outbreaks, assaults and more suicides were pouring in. The last couple of days had seen the crime rate turn somersaults. The press was building up the increase into something approaching Armageddon. It was getting just like the old days, Schroder thought to himself. No one could figure out the cause. Manhattan was generally peaceful.

But what was worse was the increased activity down by the river. Schroder had never had much time for the Zone Police. Overdressed and overpaid, he called them. They were a private army and there was a strict demarcation between their role and that of the State Police. The ZeePees had no real authority. They took orders from the State boys. They had to.

Schroder shook his head. What were the media boys getting up to? Live suicide on that Johnny Raine show. First time on TV. Schroder could hardly believe it. Six months and he'd be out of this madhouse. He'd been looking forward to cruising towards retirement. That dream had been shattered when Captain Andrews barked his instruction to double the number of patrols on the streets. They had to contain this situation. It had by no means got out of hand but what if it continued and got worse? Now he was back to cruising the streets, the normally peaceful and untroubled streets. He wasn't looking forward to it.

The Zone Police had moved into a serious alert mode. There had been steadily growing unrest within the last twenty-four hours. Intelligence reports flooding into ZeePee headquarters at Brooklyn Bridge indicated a possible organized assault. The Badlands were coming to the boil. Nothing in particular had triggered any incidents but gangs of ragged mutants had been seen massing by Washington Bridge and over by the Bronx, where the largest concentration of ZeePee fire-power had always been. A massive garrison stretched along Harlem River Causeway. Isolated gangs, looking for excitement and martyrdom, would sometimes take on the ZeePees. There had been reports coming in of more concentrated attacks as the hordes of the hopeless sought their piece of the Big Apple. Fifteen attacks had been reported in the last twelve hours.

Every light was burning in the Media City building, and over at CyberTel headquarters and in the newsrooms of the local and regional cable and satellite offices. Digitized live-action sequences were being patched together with news reports via editorial neural network architecture. There was no sense of panic, just a fragile awareness of how rarefied life actually was in Manhattan. The State, through Commissioner Halloran, was playing it down. Sure, there would always be a certain number of murders and suicides. That was part of life, after all. There was nothing for the citizens of Manhattan to worry about. They could sleep easy in their beds. But the media was on the alert, checking out every whisper of an attack, camping on the steps of police precincts, stopping police electro-turbos in the street.

Channel Boom Boom was popping with hyperactivity. News apart, the biggest show in its history was in preparation. The only person missing from the building was the show's star, Johnny Raine. Maurice Freiberg had already had two asthma attacks in the past five hours. Where the fuck was Johnny Raine, he asked every ten minutes. Ever since Johnny's phone call to Lloyd and State security, the 'All the Way' production team had been pulling out the stops. Severe-looking security personnel had arrived and started checking out the building. Solo had turned up and his brooding presence was giving everyone the jitters.

Some dressing rooms had come in for special attention. A team of silent and unsmiling workmen spent the night reinforcing them to give added protection. At midnight the crucifix machine had been moved from its hiding place and set up on stage. Freiberg felt his control slipping and he didn't like it. He had already had a couple of run-ins with Solo. They had locked horns when the programme chief objected to the small army of well-armed special security operatives who were strolling around and getting in everyone's way, disturbing some of the more creative and delicate media types. Since then they had been discreetly withdrawn and had melted into the shadows.

The press room was the busiest it had ever been. Clark Taylor was on permanent call and Freiberg, Lloyd and other members of the production team had been giving interviews around the clock. The press wanted Johnny Raine. In one sense, Freiberg was glad he was not there. It added spice to the suspense. But the frantic press interest, coupled with the floods of vidi-phone calls from all over the country either condemning or praising the suicide show, as it had been dubbed, was causing tempers to fray. But the hype was building up. Freiberg lit a cigar and gazed out over the troubled city and sighed. Raine had better deliver or else. There was too much riding on this show now. Halloran had been over, with the top Media City brass. Freiberg's original alternative plan to replace Johnny Raine if he didn't deliver and make that the big surprise story just wouldn't wash. Raine would be finished all right. But so would Freiberg, and he wasn't ready to go yet. He had also held off authorizing Raine's credit deposit. The moment those freaks arrived at the rear entrance to the studio he would call accounts. Freiberg was a man of his word.

The doll was dreaming. It stood in the shadow of a shop doorway on Broadway. Images of stars and ancient landscapes coursed through its crude electrical system. The demon now inhabited the elementary neurons. The demon was the dream. It was immersed in the process of regeneration. It was becoming self-aware. It was becoming conscious of the millions of human minds outside itself. It was reaching out and touching those minds. And it was dreaming, inside this multi-jointed mannequin.

It could feel the woman known as Jordan clinging to her crude life-force. It probed gently into the cerebral cortex, experiencing the pain and tasting it with its mind. It was delicious. It saw images from her memory bank. There was sunlight and peace and great joy at being in someone's arms. The demon recoiled but the images remained. There was laughter, echoing down through time, but as fresh now as it had been then, for there was no time, no real time. The demon probed deeper, back through darkness, and encountered a feeling of immense peace and well-being.

A businessman in a dark suit stepped out into Broadway from Ronnie's bar and swayed happily. He tightened his grip on his briefcase. Wouldn't do to lose that, he told himself. He looked around. Everything looked so normal. What was all this end of the world is nigh shit on the web. Who believed a word of that crap anyway? People were strolling along Broadway just like always. Cabs and electro-turbos were cruising up and down. Nothing unusual about that. Somewhere in the background he heard a siren. Then, in the distance, what sounded like scream-ing. So what, life was still pretty safe in Manhattan. There were lights coming from the river. Just those ZeePee shit-heads making a name for themselves, he thought tipsily. They had to do something for the money they got paid.

He belched, and a cloud of whisky-flavoured breath left an aftertaste. Boy, could I do with a fuck, he thought. The old lady's not what she was. Probably screwing around, like everybody else. As long as you got your HIV clearance you were OK, weren't you? He gazed across the street and that's when he saw her. She was standing in a doorway, looking vulnerable. Even from here he could tell she was a looker. She was wearing what looked like a long cape, opened at the front. His heart missed a beat. Was she just wearing underwear beneath the cape? Shit!

As he watched, the cape closed. He lurched forward and crossed the street. A couple of horns blared at him but he ignored them. He approached the woman who was watching him strangely. As he got closer to her he saw she was beautiful. Her face seemed to alter its shape as she turned her head. The cape opened. He could see naked flesh underneath and the skimpiest of underwear. His libido cranked into overdrive.

'Hey, baby doll,' he breathed, 'this is your lucky night.'

The doll watched him impassively. He moved closer. He

stretched out his hand, his fingertips touched the edge of the cape. He began to sweat and blubber a little as he pushed the cape aside and reached in, fingers extended. His hand closed around the doll's breast. A confused look creased his face. The breast was not soft and succulent as he had expected. It was hard, like wood or plastic. He raised his head and looked into the doll's eyes. They were empty, like the universe, except for a pinpoint of red fire which grew like an approaching comet. When the madness hit him it scrambled his brain cells in seconds. The expression of terror lasted for the same amount of time. The demon tasted the man's fear and savoured it, sucking his psyche and absorbing it into itself.

Passers-by screamed as they saw a man in a dark suit with a briefcase by his side suddenly ignite and burst into flames. The intense heat blackened the sidewalk where he stood.

A small crowd had gathered, shielding their faces from the inferno. The fireball was screaming. But not for long. Within ten seconds or so all that remained was a pile of glowing ash and charred bones. The man's eyeballs had rolled a little way and came to rest, staring up at the crowd.

The horrified onlookers stared at the doorway. It was empty. The man had just self-immolated. Further along the street, a figure paused and looked back over its shoulder. It pulled its cape around its body and paused for a moment before walking away.

As the doll walked along Broadway, fights erupted spontaneously. A woman was hit by an electro-turbo as she was thrown into the street by her husband. A well-dressed man suddenly turned to a business colleague, picked him up by the lapels and threw him bodily through a store window. Then he blinked and shook his head in disbelief at what he had done.

Jordan was rushed to the coronary intensive care unit at Central medi-centre. Johnny had to be forcibly restrained from following her. He was allowed to watch through an examination window. She was immediately hooked up to an IV, and an oxygen mask was clamped over her face. Three main electrocardiograph leads were attached. Dr Franklin administered four milligrammes of morphine. He looked down at Jordan with compassion. He hated to lose a patient and he was damned if he was going to lose this one even though she looked like a skeleton. He decided to try a diuretic, then hydralazine to reduce pre-load on the heart, followed later by nitroprusside. The greyness had left her face. It took about fifteen minutes to stabilize her but she still had not regained consciousness. The bleep on the EEG was faint but regular. Johnny's mouth was dry. His pulse was racing but he felt almost detached from the events taking place, in shock. He stood up from his slumped position with his face rammed against the glass, as Dr Franklin came in.

Jordan was travelling through corridors and into rooms. Her nightmare was replaying itself but at double speed. This time it was different, she knew it. This time she would open that door. Angelica. She was different. Now she had Johnny's face. He was laughing. She recoiled and opened the second door. The purple mist enveloped her. Inside the room she could see Frank Brady. He was covered in blood. His skin was puckering with sores and boils. His wrist was hanging limply by his side and his head was lolling on his shoulder. There was a gaping wound in his neck. He stared at her.

The third door was now in front of her. She grasped the handle and opened it. It was dark at first, then light began to filter in. There was something in the room. Something alien. Something hideously evil. The figure in the room walked towards her. She retreated and panic began to overcome her. The figure in the room was herself.

She was distorted and twisted. As she watched, the other Jordan removed one arm and attached it to her waist. Her other hand removed her head and held it out in front of her. Then, in a bizarre display of impossible dexterity, the whole figure changed shape like a contortionist gone wild. She was looking at the creature, which now resembled an insect. The head was bobbing up and down, somehow attached to its navel.

Jordan backed away, retreating back along a dark tunnel. And the tunnel was filling with purple fire.

'She's in a stable condition now,' Dr Franklin told Johnny with professional calm. 'From what you've told us she leads a pretty healthy lifestyle and there is no history of heart disease in her immediate family. She must have had one hell of a shock.'

It was not really a question. In any case, Johnny had no intention of trying to explain. He just nodded. The doctor continued, as he helped himself to a cup of coffee from the vend-robot, 'Her physical condition, however, does give some cause for concern. When she recovers I'd like to keep her in and run some tests. If you don't mind me saying so, Mr Raine, I've seen this lady before, with you, and she looked fit and healthy.'

'I can't explain it,' replied Johnny. 'She's going to live, isn't she?'

'I'm sure she'll pull through this crisis. What her condition will be like then, physically or mentally, we must wait and see.'

Johnny knew that Jordan was beyond the help of little coloured pills. She was in the best hands in town. Franklin had a reputation for compassion. He was a good doctor.

Johnny realized he could do no more for Jordan. He suddenly felt drained and weak. Franklin noticed.

'My diagnosis for you, Mr Raine, is go home and get some sleep,' the doctor clapped Johnny on the shoulder as he slouched out of the room.

Johnny got to his apartment and fished for his compu-key. Tomorrow night he was going back into the Badlands. By the weekend the first suicide show could be going out live, assuming he was successful. By the following week he would be doing a credit deal to skip Manhattan. His sudden disappearance would cause a short-lived furore but Johnny knew he was not irreplace-able. There were any number of young hungry presenters snapping at his heels.

He paused and looked around as he reached the apartment. He saw the flashes of light from the laserjet perimeter-protection installations along the riverfront. There was something in the air, he could feel it. Nearby he heard a woman screaming and it wasn't with pleasure. He shivered, letting his exhaustion wash over him. As he turned to walk to his front door, he froze.

From the north Bronx as far as once prosperous Riverdale, where the Badlands gave way to Westchester, down to Coney Island, where black-market supplies landed and the alternative distribution organizations took over, rebellion was rife. The Badlands were boiling over. In Flushing Meadow Park, Bobby Bolero addressed a huge crowd of devotees. This was the biggest spontaneous gathering ever seen in the Badlands, where gangs came in bite-sized pieces and ruled territories. Bolero's influence and unmitigated violence, together with his passion and oratory, were turning him into a saviour figure.

He roared into a makeshift microphone, his voice crackling over the twisted and distorted faces of the hopeless and the soul-dead, heavily protected by his elite guard. He stared in the direction of Manhattan. His eyes were filled with messianic fervour and his head was filled with the voice. It was the voice of an angel, then the voice of a demon. It spoke to him. It told him the time had arrived for him to follow his true destiny. He would lead the slithering, deformed and disenfranchised masses to take back what belonged to them. The good life could be theirs. He could be the Prince of New York. Bolero knew that the spirit lived within him and now was talking directly to him.

'The time has come,' he screamed hoarsely. 'The one has arrived. The one I promised you would come is here. And I, Bobby Bolero, will lead you to a new life. How d'you feel about food, real food? How d'you feel about heat and light and air conditioning? How d'you feel about all of the lonely people?'

The crowd was screaming back.

Bolero raised his voice to breaking point. 'How d'you feel about Lucy in the Sky with Diamonds?' He staggered back under the impact of the idea. 'She is here, she's here now, and she's waiting for us. She's waiting for us in the capital of credit, the city of illusion, the poisoned apple. Do you want some? Do you really want some?'

The crowd pounded the ground. And from the darkness of the burnt-out buildings surrounding the park, the nameless were also listening. And the word was spreading through the sewers.

'We have been given the sign,' Bolero lowered his voice. 'They're gonna put death style on TV and I want everyone watching.' He was building up to a climax now. 'That's our sign, that's our fuckin' sign.' Bolero staggered back under the weight of his emotion into the arms of his minders, like an old-style evangelical preacher.

She was looking at him from the small garden, dappled by streetlights and the gently waving branches of a small acacia tree. It couldn't be. He had just left her at the hospital. How could she be here? Johnny's love for Jordan simply overrode logic. He stood, holding his compu-key in his hand, staring at the figure of Jordan and his heart opened up to her. At that instant, piercing fear and despair filled him. No, it must be her ghost, her spirit. Jordan is dead. There is no point going on. Suicide. That was the only answer. Why not? Why not just get out of all this? What the fuck was the point of it all? Why bother waiting for it to appear on the web? Jordan was waiting for him. Death was fine, it was all right, it was our true destiny after all. Why fear it? God, she was beautiful. Just like she used to be. Why was she just smiling at him? Why didn't she speak?

Click!

Jordan began to walk towards Johnny stiffly. Her eyes were like red coals. They pinned Johnny back against the wall. He felt his insides melting. He felt his mind melting. He wanted to embrace her, yet he couldn't move. Fear had gripped his heart like a lemon squeezer. The urge to die was almost overpowering. It all seemed so natural. Jordan wanted his life-force. She was welcome to it. She must have died after all. And she wanted him to be with her.

The doll moved closer to Johnny. Its cape fell open, revealing the contours of its body, its full, round breasts and bulging crotch. Its hair was rich and full, dark and sculpted.

The illusion snapped. Johnny felt a searing pain in his brain. Jordan was dying. She was at the hospital. He had just left her. This was Brady's evil creation. With every ounce of willpower he possessed, Johnny pressed the button on the compu-key and moved towards the opening door. But his feet felt like lead. His mind was filled with fire and demons. He looked into the abyss where no human should look. And he knew the true meaning of oblivion.

Jordan who was not Jordan was approaching. She was smiling

at him. Every impulse within him told him to run. There was a power here he could not resist. He knew it was being held in check by something, some barrier. He lurched for the door, his breathing shallow, painful. Something touched him, fingertips sliding down his back, leaving a fiery imprint. His back was burning. Rivers of fire raged where the fingertips had lightly touched him. He saw the door. He wrenched at his muscles. He willed his body to move. He was going to die. He knew it. He had to get away. With an effort of will, he threw himself inside the door and kicked out with his foot. The door slammed shut. Crying with fear and pain, Johnny hauled himself up a flight of stairs, eyes staring at the door. He could feel the emanations. They were calling him back. Embrace me, they were saying. Embrace me and embrace death. Death is all there is. Peaceful, drifting, wonderful.

Gradually, the feeling of fear and dread subsided. Johnny crawled into his apartment and stood up shakily. He stumbled to the window and looked out. The streets were busy. People were walking quickly, sirens were blaring, cops seemed to be everywhere. He saw a figure crossing the street. When it reached the other sidewalk it turned and looked up at him.

Johnny did not believe what he was seeing. The doll was simply a mannequin made up to look like Jordan for some sick reason. Now it was walking. It was alive. The doll had disappeared from the gallery. Brady had disappeared. What the hell was going on?

He collapsed into bed. The vidi-phone rang. Cursing, he sat up and jabbed a control for voice only. Lloyd sounded anxious.

'Where the hell have you been? Freiberg's going through the roof. You called to say it was all systems go then we don't see hide nor hair of you. What's happening, Johnny?'

'I'm going over tomorrow night. We'll get a production meeting underway tomorrow morning, OK? I told Freiberg there were no guarantees. I'm putting my life at risk here, just remember that, Lloyd. I don't see anybody volunteering to go in with me.'

Lloyd was silent for a moment. 'OK, Johnny. Look, the

publicity machine's moved into top gear. We've just got to get these freaks over here for Saturday's show. Especially now.'

'What do you mean, especially now?'

'Have you been asleep? Things are going crazy. There have been murders, suicides, fights everywhere. Newsdesk is making a big thing of it. Oh yes, and some psychiatrist or other was found mutilated in that photographer's studio, you know, the English guy. That's making headline news, especially as he's disappeared. Look, Johnny, I'm getting a lot of pressure from upstairs. You know this suicide business is totally sick. But there are some big names behind it. Somebody wants a show of strength.'

'I know,' said Johnny wearily. 'Look, there's nothing we can do about it now, Lloyd. I'll see you tomorrow first thing.'

Johnny snapped off the vidi-phone and collapsed on to the pillows. He was just drifting off into a disturbed sleep when it rang again. Cursing violently, he thumped the control panel and a hoarse, panting voice filled the room. Johnny suddenly came to life.

'Brady!' he breathed incredulously.

'Hello, matey, did I wake you?' Brady sounded on the edge.

'Where are you?' whispered Johnny.

'That's for me to know and you to guess. You thought I was dead, didn't you? Thought you'd done a good job,' he coughed painfully. 'Well, you almost succeeded. I don't know how long I've got.'

'You bastard,' hissed Johnny, 'if I could get my hands on you.'

'But you can. That's why I'm calling you. I don't have much time and it's difficult to speak so you'd better just shut the fuck up and listen. I can understand you wanting to kill me, but what you don't know is that there is something bigger than any of us out there. Why do you think the whole place is falling apart? I'm going to die soon, Raine, one way or another. I've been obsessed totally and utterly by your girlfriend, Jordan. She and I and you are involved together . . .'

'If you're talking about witchcraft and that mumbo-jumbo . . .' Johnny butted in.

'Don't interrupt, Raine.' He coughed and then cried out in

pain. 'Holy shit! Look, it took a lot to call you, so just listen. You've got to find the one they call Speranza. She's on the other side. She's helped me before. She's special. Not of this world, believe me. And you can believe whatever she tells you. I'm not talking about witchcraft. I'm talking about obsession and a power none of us is strong enough to withstand. It's all in our past, Raine. And Grohmann was at the centre of it. Right now he's finding out the truth firsthand. I've got to go, can't talk any more. Can't move much either. If you want to know more, meet me tomorrow evening. If I'm still alive I'll be at the gallery. I've got some preparations to make. If I'm going to die, then I'll do it in the right place, surrounded by my work. That's where I'll be. Six o'clock Raine. Be there.' The line went dead.

Johnny collapsed once more, his limbs like lead, his mind racing. Brady was alive, just. His initial anger at Brady had subsided but he still knew that as long as he lived Jordan would be in danger. If Brady was at the gallery tomorrow night then he would have to finish what he'd started. He thought about the doll. Did Brady know it had suddenly come alive? The very thought of it was preposterous. Now, as a disturbed sleep beckoned, Johnny found it hard to believe. He must have been hallucinating.

Speranza! The name seemed hauntingly familiar. He had seen that name before somewhere. What was Brady talking about? Not of this world. Obsession. We are all involved. Too many questions and no answers. Tomorrow would see some questions answered. First he would sort out Freiberg and get those credits organized. Then, as promised by Solo, he'd pick up the RPC. First off was Brady at the gallery, then he'd try to locate Shell. Maybe she knew who Speranza was? Lastly, pick up the Feeks and the Farooks. It all sounded so simple. The actual production would have to take care of itself. This programme would set new viewing records, of that he was sure. Whether the suicide business and the crucifix machine would survive for a second week was doubtful. But by that time he and Jordan would be long gone.

Chapter Nineteen

When Johnny strode into the Media City building the next morning he had to push his way through a large crowd. There were delegations from the Church of the Risen Christ, the Evangelical Eyewitnesses, the Euthanasia Society, the Catholic and Jewish Missions and minor pressure groups of every kind. And the press was there in force.

Alex Hamlisch spotted Johnny before he was mobbed. The reporter hung on to Johnny's arm, heaving the shouting, placard-waving crowd out of the way as security battled to clear the reception area. Hamlisch squeezed into the elevator beside Johnny.

'You don't miss a trick do you, Alex? Make it quick because you're taking the next car down.'

'Is the suicide show definitely on, Johnny? Yes or no? Channel Boom Boom's gone public, you know that.'

'It's on if I can get some of the freaks over here,' Johnny told him.

'When, Johnny, when?' Hamlisch persisted.

'I'm going over tonight. First show should be tomorrow night.'

'How do you feel about seeing people die on TV?' asked Hamlisch.

'I'll tell you afterwards, Alex.'

The elevator stopped at the atrium floor. Hamlisch tried to follow Johnny out but was pushed back in. With a sigh he pressed the button for the ground floor.

There was almost as much commotion on the atrium floor as there was below. Freiberg saw Johnny arrive and steamed over.

'Well? Where were you yesterday? I've had seven shades of shit poured all over me. The city's gone crazy. It's like the show is some kind of prophecy. Well, come on, Johnny, is this thing for real or not?'

'I'll know tonight, Maurice. I'm going over to bring 'em back tonight.'

Freiberg calmed down a little. Johnny motioned that he should join him in his office. When the programme boss entered, Johnny closed his office door, much to Veronica's disappointment. She had a list of calls for her boss as long as her arm. She went off to make his morning coffee, just the way he liked it. Meanwhile Freiberg eyed Johnny with his pale gaze.

'Well?' he said.

'Maurice, you mentioned two million credits. I've checked with Stan Michaels. The go-ahead hasn't been given yet.'

'I told you, Johnny. When you get the first show over then we'll talk a million, with another million two months from now.'

'Not good enough, Maurice. I'm as close as I can be to pulling this off. Those freaks will be here tonight. The show goes out tomorrow night. I'm risking my neck for your bonus. You could dump me any time you liked. You're safe, Maurice. Even if the board sacked you, which they wouldn't, you've booked your place in the sun over in Long Island or Miami or Jamaica or wherever and you've got your private heli-jet to get you there. Oh yeah! I know all about that. Not many people do. So, the deal is: you authorize the two million right now, straight into my security account. That way no one can have second thoughts. Then I'll go over tonight. If I don't come back . . .' Johnny shrugged and picked up the internal phone then held it out to Freiberg. The programme controller looked at Johnny coldly for a couple of seconds, saying nothing, then he took the phone from Johnny and punched in a code.

'Stan, Maurice here. I want you to do something for me.'

For the second time in a week, Mike Schroder found himself fending off journalists and trying to keep the lid on a particularly gruesome murder. This one was especially bad. It looked like the work of a real screwball, some kind of religious nut. Schroder had seen some pretty bad things in his time, but, since the Isolation, crimes of this type and on this scale had largely stopped. In this case a minor celebrity was involved, well, two minor celebrities if you counted the psychiatrist Grohmann. The photographer, Frank Brady, whose apartment Grohmann's body had been discovered in by a neighbour, had vanished. Ironically, as it turned out, he had an exhibition running at an upmarket gallery. Apparently this guy went in for photographing hideous, decadent death scenes, especially in the Badlands. Maybe he had decided to give up the camera in favour of a scalpel.

Schroder was idly walking around Brady's apartment as they brought Grohmann's body out. The medical team looked pretty green around the gills. Elmore Hunt lumbered out after them.

He went to the balcony for some fresh air. More bloodstains had been found on the balcony and on the living-room floor. Strands of human hair had also been found. Elmore's black skin looked pale. Schroder gazed at the weird artefacts in the room, in particular the photographs of a distorted doll-like creature. He shivered. The guy was clearly a fruitcake. Schroder didn't know what to make of the photographs that decorated the studio walls. She was beautiful. And she looked familiar. Oh well, forensic would check out all the blood samples and compare them with the HIV blood-group records. That was one advantage of the rigorous anti-AIDS campaign. Everyone by law had to register a blood and urine sample. It helped narrow down the search time. Schroder put his arm around his partner's massive shoulders.

'You OK, Elmore? You look as if you've seen a ghost.'

'What kind of sick fuck could do something like that?' He choked out the words. 'I've never seen anything like it. Looks like some kind of black magic rite.'

'Yes,' remarked Schroder as he and Elmore left the apartment, 'that's exactly what it looks like.'

The day passed in a dream for Johnny. The morning production meeting had been edgy. Wilma Rubenstein confirmed that the crucifix machine had been put in position behind a drape on the 'All the Way' set. The show was a sell-out. Half of Manhattan had been trying to get tickets. They were being allotted in a rota system with non-acceptances being passed down the line. For the first time ever, people were bidding to buy tickets. Some had offered ridiculous money just to be at the show. Jack Carey had prepared script alternatives and Phil Razzman had lined up a couple of surprise victims just in case the freaks did not show up. No one mentioned what contingency plans had been made in case Johnny did not return. When he raised the question there was an embarrassed silence. Lloyd blurted out that they had had to make some arrangements. Freiberg had favoured a presenter who was trying to defect from CyberTel, Fred Mason. Johnny couldn't resist an ironic smile. He could just see Mason worming his way into Freiberg's confidence.

The atmosphere was muted. Several of the camera crew had refused to work on the show. The press office had received fifty death threats. Top of the list, of course, came Johnny Raine. Security had been doubled and the production team, camera crew and office staff just had to put up with the presence of security guards. Solo had been sniffing around for days. The show was getting a reaction. Like it or not this was real television.

Solo interrupted the production meeting to run through security arrangements again. He held Johnny with a lidless gaze as though he had a sneaking admiration for anyone who would go to the Badlands alone at night.

Johnny managed to get a call into the central medi-centre. Jordan was improving. She had drifted in and out of consciousness, which was a positive sign as far as Dr Franklin was concerned. They were feeding her intravenously and she looked a little healthier. The prognosis was cautiously optimistic. But she wasn't out of the woods yet.

At about five o'clock Johnny prepared to leave his office. He felt remarkably calm. The reinforced personnel carrier had been delivered on time, as promised. Johnny went over his plans. He would go back to the apartment, soak in a hot bath, microwave some pasta and drink a bottle of Chardonnay. Then he would get dressed, check his spare pulse pistol and leave. He would have checked out the RPC already. Solo had told him it was a cinch to drive. It had some sophisticated weaponry on board and automatic rear-door locks. This meant he could open and close the rear compartment without leaving the security of the vehicle. In appearance it was very like an inflated sloop jet. Solo had also given him a special pass and the guards on the bridge had been notified.

Then he would drive to the gallery. He still had Jordan's

override pass. Last night's mysterious disappearance of the doll would have caused some concern. Brady must have some way of getting in. Maybe he had a special key. But what condition was he in? Johnny was certain they had killed him. He had sounded almost at the end on the phone. But he was a strong man, mentally and physically. What if the gallery had changed security codes or made new security arrangements? He would just have to take that chance.

He had steeled himself to commit murder. He told himself it was for Jordan's sake. It was ironic. Here he was about to preside over a suicide show on TV and to kill another human being in cold blood. The last few weeks had uncovered some parts of Johnny Raine that he didn't like. He would get it over with quickly and get back to the RPC, then head straight for the bridge and into the Badlands. He only hoped he could remember where Shell lived. He shivered at the prospect of going back into that hell-hole.

As he left his office, he noticed the sudden lull in the usual babble of noise. They were watching him. Their faces said it all. You're plain crazy. You've got a lot of guts, kid. Veronica dabbed her eyes with a handkerchief as he passed by her desk. Freiberg came over and clapped him on the shoulder.

'Good luck, Johnny,' he almost yelled, 'go get 'em.'

Johnny paused and looked around at the faces he had known and worked with for the last three years. He felt a tug of emotion at some of the memories. But he just gave a little wave and strode to the elevator.

It was like a replay of the previous night. Johnny cruised noisily past the front of the gallery. Nothing seemed to have altered. The area was busy. There were a lot of people about and the RPC caused a few heads to turn. Johnny hadn't bargained for being so conspicuous. He veered down a side street and parked in shadow. He checked his weapons, left the vehicle and made his way to the back entrance.

He kept to the darkened shadow of the building and came eventually to the rear entrance of the gallery. Like before he tried the override card. It worked. He slipped inside the building and drew the pulse pistol. The gallery had lost none of its spooky power and Johnny prowled quietly towards the Brady exhibition, nerve-ends jangling, eyes flitting this way and that.

He came to the gallery entrance and was about to enter when he noticed the tiny red light at about waist height. Laser sensors. To walk through the beam would trigger an alarm. He took a deep breath and called out.

'Brady, Brady, can you hear me? Come on out.'

The silence was almost tangible. There was only one light-beam sensor. Johnny switched the pulse pistol to low power and took aim. A bolt of high-intensity light exploded on target and the sensor disintegrated. Silence. For all Johnny knew, the gallery had been rigged up with the latest security devices, the ones that can virtually count your molecules and have your life history on file before you could blink. An alarm could have alerted the nearest precinct house already. He shrugged. He would just have to take that chance. He hadn't much time. He moved cautiously into the gallery. Again the bleak images on the walls had the power to fascinate and frighten. Holding the pistol in front of him, Johnny walked into the gallery. He called Brady's name again. There was no reply. Maybe the bastard was dead. Johnny still could not figure out how he had survived. Although he was inwardly terrified, he decided on a show of bravado. He was no natural-born killer. He knew, when this was all over, his conscience was going to make him pay.

He gazed around the gallery. The glass case which had contained the doll was gone. But there was something in the gloom. Johnny couldn't make it out. Nervously, he made his way towards it. As he got closer, the shape began to resemble a human figure. Johnny started to breathe heavily and sweat. He called out again, louder this time, more defiant. Still no reply.

Johnny approached the shape at the far end. His finger trembled on the trigger of the pistol. Then he heard the sound. It was a barely discernible moan of pain. This was pain of an excruciating kind. It was muted, as though being forced through a ruined larynx. Johnny was within a few feet of the figure. He could see it was standing flat against the wall, right up against the huge, life-size photograph of the Badlands crucifixion. At that moment, the moon emerged from behind a bank of cloud and shone bleakly through the windows in the roof, flooding the gallery wall with light and etching the scene with dramatic impact.

Johnny clutched his stomach to prevent the bile rising. Brady had been crucified, matching the figure in the photograph. Spikes had been driven into his hands and into the wall. His legs from the knee down were burnt beyond recognition and his boots were dangling on bone. Several fingers from both hands had been severed and were lying on the floor and his stomach had been slashed. Smoke issued from the inside of his body as though his entrails were burning. He opened his eyes and moaned. His head was covered with congealed blood and a skewer had been driven into his gaping mouth pinning his tongue to the wall through his cheek. Johnny almost cried at the sight. Brady's eyes implored him to do something.

On the floor nearby some photographs were scattered. Johnny could not speak. His throat had snapped shut. Without thinking, he picked up some of the pictures and looked at them. He was hit by another shock to the solar plexus. He couldn't believe what he was looking at. The photographs showed Brady in various erotic poses. Disgusted, Johnny threw them down, all except one which riveted his attention. It showed the doll, but not as a doll. The creature in the photograph was more like a devil from hell. Its eyes were blazing. Its mouth was open in a frozen scream of evil and a kind of aura surrounded it like a halo. Johnny tossed it to one side. Brady was making a desperate effort to communicate. He clearly had a short time to live. Suddenly Johnny began to tremble with a mixture of fear and compassion. He held his breath, tucked the pistol into his belt and grasped hold of the skewer pinning Brady's tongue. He pulled. Brady screamed, and festering organs from his stomach oozed slowly out from his insides. The stench was overpowering. Using all his strength, Johnny withdrew the spike from Brady's mouth. As it emerged and his tongue flapped free Brady screamed from the depths of his soul. His voice regained a little strength but he could barely talk.

'Who did this to you, Frank?' Johnny finally found his own

voice. Brady was making a huge effort to speak. Words came but they were distorted.

'She ... came,' he breathed. 'Victim ... didn't know ... you ... me ... time ... see Speranza.' With this final effort Brady died. He slumped forward, hanging by his pinned hands. Johnny couldn't bear to see Brady like this. Grimly, he stepped back and drew his pistol. He aimed at the wrists and fired, severing both hands and leaving them skewered to the wall. Brady's body crashed in a bloody, steaming mess. Johnny threw up and staggered back. In the distance he heard a siren and his mind was forced back to reality. He turned and ran from the gallery for the second time.

Panting and sickened by what he had seen, he climbed desperately into the RPC and strapped himself in. He knew instinctively that both he and Jordan were in terrible danger and the recent disturbances, suicides and Badlands uprising had something to do with that hideous creature, that doll with a life of its own. But how could it be alive? What was inside it? Maybe this Speranza person had the answer.

He headed for the Queensboro Bridge and into the sound of gunfire and laserjet explosions. He truly feared at that moment that he might not return.

Chapter Twenty

The Zone Police on duty at the bridge looked at him as if he was out of his tree. They had been fully briefed but the thought of this media performer going in alone struck them as little short of insane. They told Johnny there had been isolated outbreaks of intense violence. Some of the other bridges, particularly up near the Bronx, had seen action. Inside the Badlands a major war was going on. Bobby Bolero was fighting for dominance against two other tribal leaders.

'You should be OK as long as you stay inside this baby,' said the ZeePee sergeant, giving the RPC a good luck pat on the roof.

Everything was moving too fast for Johnny. He hardly had time to think of Jordan.

He hit the bridge at speed and hurtled into the ravaged landscape under a moon-filled sky. He hadn't driven fifty yards when a shell exploded on the side of the RPC. Johnny fought for control, swerving to avoid rubble and fallen masonry. More shells hit him. He returned fire, seeing nothing to aim at except shifting shapes and flickering lights. His brain was racing, trying to remember the building. He tore down ransacked streets. From one, a wall of light emerged. He was almost blinded by the intense glare but he rammed his foot on the accelerator just as a swarm of shells exploded all around him. He was hit several times and the RPC was rocked by the power of them. In his rear mirror Johnny saw the river of light begin to follow.

Desperately, he raced through streets filled with deformed people. He turned left, recognized a landmark from last time and eventually saw the building. He swore with relief. He had gone over and over the route from memory. Luckily, there were few people around this part of the neighbourhood. Behind, in the distance, the lights were getting closer. Johnny switched off his headlamps, relying on moonlight to pick out the tall, encrusted building. As he approached it he saw a kind of ramp.

He drove down under the building and swerved into a corner, killing the engine. For a long moment he waited, sweating with fear. He didn't have to wait long. A wave of light and roaring engines went by, ignoring the ramp. Johnny was staring through his rear mirror. If they decided to come down here he would be well and truly trapped. He realized that the wall of lights came from a battalion of motorcycles. Johnny remembered the first time. He remembered the hybrid built into the structure of the bike. He had been truly fearsome, an empty face devoid of any human qualities. There must be a hundred of them outside. Johnny's heart was racing. It seemed like an age before the last lights passed by and the roar of their engines faded into the distance.

He gazed around the subterranean car park. He could see nothing. He listened intently through his two-way microphone. He could hear nothing. But who could guess what was hiding in the darkness? Then something moved. He saw it out of the corner of his eye. It was approaching the RPC. Johnny grasped the trigger of the Lexus and slowly trained it on the approaching shape.

Then a voice spoke in the darkness.

'Hello, Johnny Raine. Come out quickly. You will be safe.'

The voice was sharp and metallic. With a shivering sigh of relief, Johnny opened the RPC, slipping it into voice-activated mode. He stepped down and the door slid shut behind him. He suddenly felt terribly vulnerable, aware that at any instant his life could be terminated.

Out of the darkness, Shell materialized. Johnny took a step back at the sight of the half-child, half-monster. She was about a foot shorter than him and her body was covered in scales and boils. As before, however, it was the half-metal, half-little-girl face that fascinated him.

'Who were they?' Johnny croaked.

'Furzis,' Shell replied with a hissing sound, 'the most dangerous of all. We can't stay here. Come up to my apartment.'

'Apartment?' Johnny couldn't help smiling. Then he was following the creature into the darkness.

They came to a wall of rubble. Delicately, Shell started to

climb. Johnny followed. About halfway up there was a hole in the wall. Shell must have collected a flashlight from somewhere because a beam of light revealed a long-ruined elevator with the twisted metal doors still hanging from it. Shell walked to the elevator shaft and stepped in. Johnny's heart jumped. He ran forward and there she was, standing on a wooden platform. Carefully, he stepped in and felt the platform swaying.

'Help me pull,' ordered Shell, reaching for a loop of rope in the centre. Johnny stepped closer to her and they both took hold of the rope. They began to pull and the platform began to rise. Counterbalanced weights made the exercise easier but still Johnny was panting by the time they had reached the top floor.

Shell looped the rope over a hook and led the way around what used to be a corridor. Moonlight flittered in through holes in the roof, patterning the area with pools of light. They went through a hole in the wall into the most amazing room Johnny had ever seen.

Everything in the massive room area had been made from recycled trash, waste materials and old car parts. A huge bed had been built from organ pipes and was covered with springs. Johnny was reminded of when he was a kid, playing with toy construction sets. A pile of cushions was spread out on the bed with more strewn around the room. There was a surreal feel to the place. Makeshift furniture was distorted, twisted and fabricated from a remarkable assembly of junk. There was a stripped-down pool table upon which candles flickered. The table had been laid and there was a bottle of wine and two glasses twinkling in the candlelight. Johnny walked around the room, touching things, then he gazed out over the panoramic view of the Badlands towards Manhattan. The windows had been improvised from clear plastic material. He turned to say something to Shell, then stopped. His jaw fell open theatrically. He tried to speak but his voice was out of action.

Shell was coming apart. Her taloned, part-metal fingers had pressed a lever of some kind at the side of her head. A crack appeared, running down the centre of her skull, neatly separating the metal and the doll faces, and went as far as her groin. Slowly the crack widened as she prised herself apart with her hands.

Johnny watched as something began to wriggle out of the suit of cleverly designed body armour.

Like a butterfly emerging from its chrysalis, a young dark-skinned nymphette climbed delicately and nimbly out and stood before him. She was beautiful and she was naked. She smiled at him, showing no embarrassment.

'I hope you're hungry,' she said with a smile. 'I've gone to a lot of trouble. Or perhaps you would like sex first?'

Johnny just stared. Her head was shaven and her eyes were large and limpid. A trickle of sweat ran down between her well-shaped breasts, sliding down over her stomach. She smiled at him again.

She walked towards him, took him by the hand and led him to the bed. Johnny was mesmerized by her. She helped him undress and regarded his body with admiration. Slowly and without a word they sank on to the bed. They came into each other's arms and Johnny could feel his passion rising like a thermometer in a sauna.

'Do not worry about catching anything. I'm clean,' she promised him.

At that moment all thoughts of Jordan, TV shows, demon-dolls and escape melted from Johnny's mind. Gently, she pushed him back on to the bed and began to run her mouth and tongue over his body and down around his stomach. His pulsing member stood proud and erect. For a while she ignored it except for a brief touch which drove Johnny even crazier. Finally she slid her hand down, pulling his foreskin hard, and slipped her lips over the tip.

'This is the hors d'oeuvres,' she mumbled between mouthfuls, 'the main course comes later.'

Johnny moaned with passion as her fingers traced patterns under his groin. She slid her body up along his till her lips were pressing on his mouth and their tongues danced a bossa nova together. He stroked her body constantly, touching trigger points which made her squirm. Finally, side by side, he made love to her, watching her dark skin shimmer as the moonlight flooded through the plastic windows.

Later, totally satiated, they sat and ate, gazing at each other over the candlelight. She had prepared some kind of stew. Johnny didn't ask what it was. It tasted delicious. From somewhere she had obtained a bottle of claret. Johnny looked at her in wonderment. Then, with a sudden start, like a man who has remembered an appointment, he sat up.

'What's the matter?' she smiled at him.

'This is crazy,' he said. 'In a world of freaks you appear like an angel. Look, someone I know is dying in Manhattan. I've been told to find the one they call Speranza. Have you heard of this person?'

'The one who is dying,' Shell enquired in a low voice, 'do you love her?'

Johnny hesitated. 'Yes, more than anything.'

Shell was silent, but took a sip of wine.

'Yes, I know Speranza. She is with the circus,' she said finally.

'Can you take me to her?' Johnny asked.

'Yes. But things are really breaking down here. It's always been a question of survival but something new has happened. There is a war on and I think they will attack the Rotten Apple.'

'They'll be mown down like grass,' Johnny snapped.

'They won't care. They don't care about death.'

'What about the ones you promised me? The ones who will appear on the show?'

'Oh yes, they will be here tonight, at midnight. Since it was on the media-web that it was really going to happen, they all want to go on the show. That is, if they're still alive.'

Johnny was reassured. Then he studied her for a while. 'Tell me about you,' he said. 'You live here, you wear that obscene disguise. Why the hell don't you live in Manhattan? With your looks you could make money.'

'I was brought up here by my mother. We had no money so we were kicked out during the Isolation. My mother was good to me. We found this place and she gave me an education, using the books we had brought with us. To survive we scavenged around like everyone else. She was careful to avoid drugs. She hated them and she managed to prevent me from getting hooked. It got so dangerous and there were so many mutations and deformities occurring that we had to disguise ourselves. Anyone who looks normal here doesn't live long. So, we built freak outfits for ourselves. It seemed to work. The worse you look and the more deformed you are, the more respect you get on the streets.'

'What about your father?' Johnny asked, sipping wine.

'He left when I was very young. I never really knew him.'

'I'm sorry,' he said. 'How come you live here without attracting trouble?'

'There are a lot of places like this around. There are things living in some buildings that, well, you just don't want to even think about. Places like this are no-go, even here. I've got a natural defence force. We kind of cohabit, you might say. I take precautions and I'm pretty cut off here. It's just like Manhattan really except this is not the best part of town. The best parts are where the power is, electric power,' she laughed at his expression. 'I'm pretty safe here. The building is a total ruin most of the way up and I have a method of disguising the elevator.'

Johnny chuckled, then his expression hardened. 'You think there's something weird going on here, but it's even worse on the other side. Some kind of force has been let loose. It's hard to explain but it involves this person I was telling you about and Frank Brady. I've got to find Speranza. According to Brady she can tell me just what the hell's going on.'

'How is Frank?' Shell asked him.

'He's dead,' Johnny said bluntly. 'Something killed him before I did. We had a fight. He had gone crazy. It was him or me. I thought I'd killed him until I got a call from him. He was in a pretty bad way. I thought he was behind all the weird things that had been happening but I think now he was a victim of something far more powerful. He wanted to see me. That really was the crazy part, ringing up a guy who's tried to kill you and arranging a meeting. I don't know how he could walk, let alone make a call. When I got to the meet he was dead. He'd been torn apart, crucified. Can you believe it?' Johnny sat back, overcome by the memory.

Shell had remained silent through this. A tear ran down her cheek.

'Poor Frank,' was all she could manage.

Johnny looked at her. 'How well did you know him?'

'As well as anyone ever did,' she said. 'No one ever really knew Frank Brady.'

Abruptly, she began to clear away the dishes and placed them in a basin.

'When we get to Manhattan,' she said, 'I don't want to come back to all this.' She turned to him and he could see a light in her eyes. 'But I can't stay without credit. However crazy you say Manhattan is, it's got to be better than this.'

'I'll fix something up,' Johnny promised, 'don't worry about that.'

She walked over to him. She was wearing a Chinese silk robe. She allowed him to slip his hands inside, encircling her waist.

'I could get to like you,' she smiled.

'Likewise,' he murmured, 'but . . .'

'I know. What time is it?'

He looked at his watch. 'I make it ten thirty.'

'They said they would be here at midnight. But time here is uncertain. To find Speranza we have to go across town.'

'Who is this Speranza?'

'Oh, just part of the circus. It's a hoot, that circus. There are more freaks in the audience than there are in the parade ring.'

I don't get it,' said Johnny, 'how can a circus survive in a place like this?'

'It's the only entertainment there is, except for the media-web. Believe me, if people didn't want it, it wouldn't survive.'

She stepped into her body armour and Johnny marvelled at the construction of the suit. It had been cleverly designed to include a voice-distorting two-way microphone. Shell looked out at Johnny before she began clipping the front of the suit together.

'I enjoyed that, Johnny Raine. I would like more.'

'I enjoyed it too,' he told her, 'it was incredible.'

She smiled at him as she disappeared inside the suit. Johnny shivered at the sight of the disfigured creature she had become. The transformation was totally convincing and, as before, he found her appearance mesmerizing.

He checked his pulse pistol, zipped up his jacket and waited until she was ready. Her taloned hands looked as if they could rip flesh to pieces in seconds. She walked towards him with her talons extended. Johnny recoiled, then relaxed as he heard Shell's muffled, tinny laughter.

'Time to go, Johnny Raine. Are you ready?'

He followed her to the elevator. She unhooked the ropes and handed one of them to Johnny. He almost overbalanced as the platform began to descend. He watched her as she controlled the descent, like a mountaineer abseiling down a cliff. He synchronized his movements with hers and the platform moved slowly downwards, past dark, ruined floors filled with the stench of decay and death. As they lowered themselves down he could swear they were being watched by a lurking presence. This business of being watched was starting to get to him. An intense and palpable feeling of malevolence surrounded both of them; it seemed to be breathing in the gloom.

They reached the ground floor. Shell stepped out, carefully indicating that Johnny should keep hold of his rope. When they were both standing on the rubble, she instructed him to pull the rope again. The platform rose to above head height. Shell showed Johnny how to hook the ropes to the frame of the elevator. The platform now became the ceiling. It was a clever disguise. Unless you knew it was there you would just assume the elevator shaft descended below into an abyss.

A noise was echoing up from the depths of the shaft. It was faint at first but, gradually and inexorably, it grew louder. It sounded like the chattering of an island full of birds, but Johnny realized this had to be impossible. Shell touched his arm urgently and they moved towards the hole in the wall. It was so dark that Johnny had to hold on to Shell's arm to guide him. He was sweating and stumbling over bricks, rubble and old iron girders. The chattering noise now seemed to come from everywhere.

'We must be quick,' he heard Shell's metallic voice say from somewhere in front.

Now he could hear the sound of running feet, small, quick, urgent feet. They squeezed through the hole in the brickwork. The light was a little better here and Johnny could just about make out the contours of the underground car park where he had hidden the RPC. The noise was louder here, much louder. Shell signalled him to stop. Something brushed against his foot;

something furry. His eyes strained to see in the half-light. He could just about make out the shape of the RPC. It had changed, altered. It was changing shape before his disbelieving eyes. The RPC was moving. It was now a rippling, furry mass.

'Stay perfectly still,' ordered Shell.

The noise had risen to a crescendo. Now it was loud and swelling all around them. Johnny realized at last what was causing it. And sweat broke out all over his body. It was the noise of teeth chattering; sharp, pointed teeth. Hungry teeth. A furry river was swarming over his boots. He could feel tiny legs running over his toes. As his vision improved he saw that the very ground was moving. Small wicked eyes flashed and glinted from a carpet of fur-like red and yellow flickers of flame. And needle-sharp teeth vibrated together in a rodent chorus of unrequited hunger.

'Rats,' said Shell in a metal whisper. 'They can't hurt me but they will tear you to pieces. You must remain perfectly still.'

Sweat and fear made Johnny want to shake. With a supreme effort of will he controlled his desire to run. The RPC was twenty yards away. Every inch of it was covered in a sea of rats. Johnny did not move. He commanded his body to remain rigid. Rats began to nibble at his shoes and his ankles. Seconds later his knees almost gave way as his muscles turned to water. Hundreds of pairs of claws were clinging to his lower shins. He could feel their incisors through the fabric of his jump suit.

Inexorably, they began to climb.

The room was an even temperature. It was dark and peaceful. A few lights flickered on the display monitors. Slatted blinds shut out the outside world. Jordan was floating on a sea of feathers. She felt wonderful. Everything was so bright and so warm and just filled with peace. She was experiencing a blissful, floating happiness and for once she really understood what that meant. She was old and yet young, ancient and yet newborn. It was a wonderful feeling. It was a feeling that defied death; where death became a dividing line between the intensity of her emotions.

The doctors and medical staff were fairly happy about her condition. Her coma was baffling them, however. The shock which had propelled this young woman into a semi-catatonic state must have been powerful. They were feeding her with a nutrient cocktail and already she was showing signs of improvement. But she was still severely underweight and run down. Her listlessness and muscle deterioration appeared to have a psychological basis. The endoscopy showed nothing unusual; nothing to cause her metabolism to reject protein. There was simply nothing physically wrong with her. She was strong, however. There was a ribbon of steel running through her and she would fight all the way.

When she came round, they would run more tests. Meanwhile they would continue pumping her full of nutrients, vitamins and minerals. She was on a mild morphine mix at the moment to aid her recovery.

The medi-centre had received an unprecedented number of calls. It was the same at all the centres in Manhattan. The number of violent injuries, many severe, had put members of staff in mind of the old, pre-Isolation days when the hospital corridors were often awash with blood, and when violent death was endemic in certain neighbourhoods.

Something suddenly jolted her tranquil equilibrium. Jordan felt an uncomfortable pain which wasn't physical. A black speck had appeared in the corner of her white and pleasant world. The speck was growing, mutating like cancer cells. Somewhere, in the faraway distance, a voice was laughing and she heard distinctly the buzzing of an insect, a very large insect. She was confused and resented the interruption. She knew that the voice wanted her dead and that the dividing line was close by. She could sense it. But she was not ready for this. Her resentment increased. She was angry with the speck and the voice. But she could feel its powerful emanations and she knew she would be powerless against it if it came within close range. She knew she would have to fight the voice. She found herself praying for the strength to win.

The demon was frustrated by the host it found itself occupying. This non-human form was crude and limited.

'I am alive,' the demon told itself, 'I am born.'

Yet it knew it was only part born. Its real power lay in the absolute, within the cosmos itself. The key to unlocking the gateway to existence was the ceremony. It would be performing the ceremony soon. It had been feeding on the woman's essence. It would not be long before it could dispense with her husk. It had found the sorcerer. He had fulfilled his function. The demon had enjoyed the encounter. His essence had been deeply satisfying. It had given the demon intense pleasure and increased power. Playfully the demon was enjoying other essences as they destroyed themselves with self-induced madness. When faced with the truth of its own existence this human life-form crumpled. It was weak and fragile. Soon the demon would begin its true mission. When it assumed full power there was nothing in this little world that could withstand it.

Now it was directing its primitive, non-human host towards the being whose life-essence it had been draining. The time had come to destroy it for ever, then begin the final act of the ceremony.

A young intern, Gary Thomas, saw her first, standing in the leafy shadows outside the rear entrance. In the flickering light Gary thought she looked beautiful. She wore a cape, loosened at the throat, and she was staring at him. He couldn't drag his eyes away from her. He walked over.

'Hi,' he said, 'are you lost?'

His eyes filled with pain as the woman approached him, walking stiffly. He realized too late she was not human. The doll's mouth clicked open and a deep roaring scream came from the demon.

The doll reached out and touched Thomas on the shoulder. He began to sizzle as his lungs started to boil. His bones broke, snapping one by one and his hair began to curl and dig its way into his skin like steel wire.

His body was smouldering under an elm tree as the doll entered the medi-centre and walked through the storeroom towards the swing doors that led to the main building and Jordan's private room.

Johnny moved carefully, very carefully. He withdrew his pulse pistol in readiness. His lower legs were bleeding, as hundreds of

tiny needle-sharp teeth gnawed at his flesh. Shell hissed at him.
'I will have to carry you. They cannot penetrate my armour.'

'Can you take my weight?' Johnny asked anxiously.

'I'm stronger than I look,' she replied.

'Right, I'll clear a path,' Johnny snapped painfully.

There was no way he was just going to stand here and get
eaten alive. He reached out and put one arm around Shell's neck.
Then he leaned forward and she grunted as she began to take
the strain. Johnny set the pistol for a low-power broad sweep.
He fired at the ground. Instantly a pulse of light illuminated an
ocean of teeth. The rats screeched, their cries of pain echoing
around the cavernous car park. The rats were burning and the
smell of their charred flesh was nauseating. He kept firing,
aiming at the RPC to clear the rodents from the vehicle. As soon
as a path was cleared it filled again with more screeching, blood-
lusting and angry rats. Shell was panting as she heaved Johnny
on to her shoulders and headed for the RPC. Johnny sprayed all
around them and tried to shake off the teeth attached to his legs.
The rats began to swarm up and over Shell. Johnny sprayed the
RPC with laser pulses as Shell trudged towards it through the
rapidly growing pyre of dead rats. The smell of burning flesh
and fur was rising from the smoking carcasses.

The door of the RPC became clear of rodents as they
approached. Johnny yelled the coded instruction, 'Boom, boom!'
The combination of his voice and the pre-programmed code-
word caused a sliding door to open. They were at the door now.
Johnny turned and sprayed all around them, keeping the rats at
bay. But there were more – a tidal wave of chattering teeth
swelling up in a dark mass of fury. Frantically Shell pulled rats
from her body armour. Then with her metal claws she swept
more rats off Johnny, spearing them like fish and flinging them
away.

'Get in!' yelled Johnny. She clambered in and he followed.
Rats were still biting him. He pulsed laser light above him and
around the roof of the RPC. Then he heaved himself in and hit
the security button. The door slid shut. Trembling, he fought for
control. Then he screamed. Two rats appeared on his shoulder.
Shell crushed them but not before one jumped into Johnny's face,

going for his eyes. She ripped it off and crushed it in her talons. It screamed and spat blood and gristle from its mouth.

'OK,' she yelled from her voice box, 'we're clear.'

Johnny needed no second bidding. Oblivious of detection, he gunned the engine, hit the lights and reversed, crushing rats by the hundred. Then he crashed the RPC into first gear and the heavy-duty vehicle screamed, then leaped forward. Johnny swerved into the street, rats flying from the virtually impregnable bodywork like confetti in the wind.

'Head towards the bridge,' Shell commanded.

'Get used to the weapon system,' Johnny shouted over the whine of the engine. 'You've got a multi-optic viewfinder. You can see all round you. The red switch tells you which guns you're using. You can fire in any direction. The small trigger selects the right gun. We've got Lexus launchers all around. They can blow anything away.'

Shell did as he asked, familiarizing herself with the weaponry. Johnny peered through the slatted, triple-strength windscreen. They were heading into what looked like a war zone. Guns blazed from buildings. People were running, screaming, burning and dying all around them. A pitched battle was in progress, a mutant war. Shells exploded while dust and smoke billowed in the air. Above, the full moon cast an eerie light on the scene. Johnny thought of Brady for a second. This was the kind of scene he would have loved. As a series of shells hit the RPC he realized that a photograph hanging on a wall was one thing. This was real. This was as close to death as he had ever been.

Shell started to blast a path as the RPC tore through the warring factions, bouncing and colliding with bodies and vehicles. Johnny didn't have time to think. He saw a gap in a smashed building and headed for it. As he shot through the gap and into a long straight road he was hit by an intense barrage of lights.

'Furzis!' gasped Shell.

Johnny saw them. An army of mixed-race mutants lined up like a battalion. Their bikes were not just functional. They had been constructed into fearsome shapes, beasts, apes, faces. Johnny spun the powerful heavy-duty aerojet-powered RPC on its rear wheels and accelerated away from the gang. The Furzis erupted from their formation and raced after them. Johnny handled the ten-ton war machine like a grand prix driver, hurtling along alleyways filled with garbage and wild dogs, through streets crammed with crazies all reeling and brawling, and up on to an elevated section of what used to be a rail line. The Furzis followed, firing home-made missiles. Shell replied, her metal eye glued to the image finder. She yelled with delight at each hit. Behind, Furzis were exploding in a spray of blood, metal, wheels and rubber. Johnny aimed the RPC down a long incline and over a ramp. The vehicle hung in the air then crashed down on to its suspension sending a shower of sparks flying. He raced into a disused factory, slaloming his way through debris, old machinery and pillars. Behind, the Furzis fanned out and tried to overtake. They were faster and if they got close their fire-power could do some real damage.

Ahead was a black void. Johnny peered through the windscreen. They were racing towards a ravine. This was a long-disused canal basin which fell fifty feet into a garbage tip of twisted metal and bones. The Furzis were gaining. Johnny was sweating. There was no way through. His headlights picked out the edge of the basin beyond which was a drop that would surely kill them.

'Johnny!' screamed Shell.

'Hang on,' he yelled. He slowed, allowing the Furzis to get within twenty yards of him. Then he suddenly accelerated, straight for the void. At the last second he yanked the steering wheel to the right and the RPC screamed in an agony of tortured metal. Skidding on two wheels the vehicle swerved, its wheels bumping along the very edge of the ravine. Behind, the Furzis weren't so quick. They skidded and screamed in an attempt to follow. But the home-made bikes lacked the power to manoeuvre. Crashing into each other in an entanglement of metal and flesh, with headlights dancing in a bizarre pattern, they ploughed over the edge.

Only one Furzi remained. Johnny had pulled up and slumped against the wheel. Shell heard the noise through the small speaker built into the door frame. She took aim, switched into reverse and pressed the trigger. The Furzi was screaming full tilt towards them. He met the supercharged mini-missile halfway. He exploded in every direction simultaneously. Shell sat back in satisfaction. Johnny could now feel the pain. His legs were bleeding and his back felt as though he had been in a brawl with a leopard. He tried to relax but tension vibrated through him, winding him tighter.

'How far now?' he panted.

'Not far, come on, you're OK.'

Johnny drove slowly back towards the rail ramp, then followed Shell's directions, trying to avoid the pockets of violence. They came at last to a large square. In the centre stood the circus, dark and lifeless. Around the square, people were moving but inside the circus perimeter all seemed quiet.

'Looks closed,' said Johnny.

'It doesn't get going till late,' Shell explained. 'It spends time here, then moves on to another part of town. It might not open tonight because of what's happening.'

The circus was small by normal standards and was dominated by a tawdry big top. Surrounding the tent were cages and tents and rides. Rows of caravans circled the circus. In some, Johnny could see lights flickering weakly. He was not surprised to find it closed but very surprised to discover that it appeared to be immune to the mayhem taking place, as if protected by some arcane magic. But, as he was learning, nothing was as it seemed in this hell-hole. When Johnny had last seen it, the circus had been ablaze with colour and light. At the time it had appeared incongruous. Johnny now thought that it gave the place a strange kind of normality.

'This is where you will find Speranza,' said Shell. 'It would be best to park inside the circle. They say the circus is protected.'

'How well do you know her?' Johnny asked her.

'Nobody really knows her,' she replied, 'but everyone is afraid of her.

'All the gang leaders consult her, especially Bolero. He's the most superstitious of all.'

'OK, well, what are we waiting for?'

Keeping a cautious eye out for any kind of trouble, Johnny

directed the RPC across the street and into the square. He parked near some caravans and could just make out some of the names on them. The one he wanted was a couple of vans along. Emblazoned on the side were the words: 'Madame Speranza, Fortune Teller, Clairvoyant, Palmist, Cyberpsyche'.

Johnny wondered idly what kind of future anybody had living here.

Life was too short.

When he felt it was safe, Johnny opened the door. The rank odour of animal excreta hit him full in the face. He had no idea what to expect as he helped Shell from the cabin. The door slid shut. Johnny first examined the RPC. It had taken a number of direct hits and the armour plating was blackened and pock-marked. Otherwise it looked in good shape. He walked around the back, checking the door to the rear compartment in which he would transport his prospective suicides back to the bright lights.

The moon had slipped behind some scudding clouds. As Johnny and the hideously deformed shape of Shell approached Speranza's wagon, the clouds drifted by and the moon filled the sky with its full glory. Johnny knocked on the door. There was no response at first, then a rustling noise was followed by the door being unlocked.

The door opened and an enormously fat woman regarded them warily. When she spoke her voice was incongruously high-pitched and she giggled with an innocent glee.

'We're closed,' she chuckled. The idea seemed to amuse her and her shoulders shook with mirth. When she laughed, her entire body joined in. When she had recovered she regarded Johnny with interest. She seemed to know Shell already.

'Well, you're not from round these parts,' she giggled. 'What can I do for you?'

Johnny glanced around nervously. He felt suddenly very exposed here, outside the safe haven of the RPC.

'Frank Brady sent me,' he said. 'He told me you might be able to help me.'

'Well I might,' said Speranza, 'then again I might not. Then again I may choose not to. On the other hand I may have no choice.'

Johnny smiled weakly, not knowing what to make of this strange, Buddha-like woman. She regarded him quietly for a moment.

'You're Johnny Raine, aren't you?' she said.

He nodded. 'Yes. Look, I don't know how to explain this. Something weird is going on. I have a friend, Jordan Semiramis. She's dying. It's like her soul is being possessed. And Frank Brady was involved. He made this doll. It looked like Jordan. But now he's dead and this doll, well, it's come to life. And it's evil. Nothing makes sense.'

Johnny could not make out Speranza's features clearly as she stood in the doorway of her caravan. He could not guess her age either. He felt foolish standing there, telling this quite insane story. The whole thing was a complete waste of time. This woman was probably a charlatan. How could she possibly help?

'Oh, it's all part of the eternal cycle,' she pronounced gravely. 'You may have to destroy that which you love most if you are to survive. You'd better come in if we're going to do some serious work.'

She retreated back into the caravan. Nervously, Johnny and Shell followed.

Chapter Twenty-one

Glancing around, Johnny and Shell closed the door behind them. Inside the caravan an atmosphere of deep warmth pervaded the cramped, bizarre interior. How a woman of Speranza's bulk managed to cope he could only guess. At one end was a small kitchen area and a sink filled with unwashed plates. Bottles were stacked in a corner as if awaiting collection. The curtains, cushions and small tapestries that dominated the rest of the van were richly coloured and sumptuous, and there were numerous tinted photographs showing tired, and presumably long-dead, faces staring bleakly out into the glow of soft candlelight. A cushioned bench seat ran all the way around and in the centre was a table covered with a dark ruby drape upon which were arcane images and symbols woven into a tapestry of colour and sparkling sequins; the universe compressed within an hypnotic fabric.

On the table were a tray of coloured stones, a crystal ball, an old tarot pack and a pendulum. Speranza clearly had the whole mystical kit to impress her clients. In another corner, incongruously, stood a virtual environment console, presumably for contacting high-tech spirits, Johnny thought with a tinge of amusement. But she was impressive enough without these. She had a young face, soft, plump and girlish, and she smiled or giggled constantly. Mirth lines rippled across her laughing jowls which shook each time something amused her. Johnny had the impression that she was a great deal older than she appeared. Rolls of fat ringed her neck, and her bare forearms were podgy and hung with bracelets and charms all jingling and sparkling in the flickering light. She looked slightly middle-eastern, Johnny decided, maybe she was Romany. That would be unusual enough in New York. Her eyes were small and bright blue and they sparkled with humour and something deeper. Her bulk filled the all-enveloping dark-blue robe she wore.

She indicated they sit. In the patchwork light, Shell looked even more monstrous than usual.

'If you would be more comfortable without your uniform, please take it off,' laughed Speranza.

Johnny could swear Shell was smiling. With some difficulty, she snapped off her body armour and began to squeeze out of it. But there wasn't enough room so she contented herself with just the top half of her naked body. She was glistening with sweat and Johnny felt an immediate erection start to rise.

'You won't have time for that,' Speranza told him, 'not if you want me to help you.'

Johnny looked at her with surprise. Was she reading his mind?

For a minute or so they were all silent. Johnny and Shell instinctively caught the mood from Speranza who had closed her eyes and appeared to have fallen asleep. When she opened them again she held out her hands. Without a word, Johnny placed his palms in hers and she spent a long time staring at them. As she stared, she began to breathe heavily and to hum a little tune, one of those maddening, beguiling melodies which drift away from the memory before they can be caught.

She let go of his hands. 'I want you to choose a handful of stones,' she said, indicating the tray, 'then lay them out in any pattern you like.'

Johnny selected a pile of stones at random then, with only a cursory attempt at design, laid them out before her.

She was shaking her head and smiling.

'Look,' said Johnny, 'I haven't come here to have my fortune told. I'm not one of your usual customers. I don't really believe in all this mumbo-jumbo stuff. There are things happening I can't understand. Brady said . . .' Johnny found he was whispering. Speranza didn't let him finish.

'Was that before or after you tried to kill him?" She erupted with mirth.

Johnny stared at her. Before he could splutter some response she continued. 'I know why you are here. I knew Frank Brady. I helped him on several occasions. He was a special soul, a very old soul. He had spent many lifetimes on this earth. You, Johnny Raine, are marked with fate. You have the triangle of destiny in the centre of your palm. Frank Brady had the same, though I'm sure you never had time to look. To discover the answer to your question we must go back through earthly time.' She paused, then consulted the crystal for a long moment. 'Place your hands in mine and touch the crystal with me. Then we shall see what we shall see.'

Johnny complied. Shell watched Speranza and Johnny as they formed a sort of tableau, surrounded by a halo of candlelight. The atmosphere in the caravan was changing. Shell began to feel as though the other two were moving away. She shook her head to clear the illusion but it remained. They were there, about three feet away from her, yet they looked as though they were in a different world. She felt that if she reached out to touch them her hand would pass right through their holograms.

He could hear a voice singing a lilting song. He smiled with the familiarity and comfort the voice brought him.

'As I walked out through Dublin City at the hour of twelve at night,
Who should I see but a Spanish lady washing her feet by candlelight . . .'

His father was in the bathroom, shaving. He could smell the scented soap he used and he listened for the short breaks in the song as he reached a difficult part of his face that required extra concentration. His mother was smiling at him. She smelt fresh and warm. She was pulling a vest over his head.

It was bright in the room. He had been given a new pair of eyes and he could see the fabric of his life. He could also see shadows of other lifetimes which he knew, without question or doubt, were his own.

His heart jumped when he saw the room just the way it was in his childhood.

The image dissolved like a soap bubble and now he was crying, screaming at the noise, terrified at the gunfire. He was running and panting and screaming. Just behind, his father had stopped to wait for his mother who couldn't run as fast. His father was shouting for her to catch up. He looked at Johnny and told him to run, run for his life. Before he could speak, his father and mother turned into a bloody mess. Bullets racked their bodies. He was rooted to the spot. He knew he would be next. Then he was running, running.

He was walking by the river with Angelica on his arm. Manhattan glowed like a surreal chandelier. They were blissfully happy. The darkness on the other side of the river could not touch them. They were cocooned in security and in their love for each other.

Then the image faded. Before him stood the alien shadow, lighting a cheroot. Johnny saw and recognized the face illuminated briefly by the jet of flame hissing from the silicon carbide knuckles. Angelica was suddenly whipped away from his arm in a twanging flash of flexible steel and blood. A siren blared.

He tried to move. He watched helplessly as the bleeding body of his wife, with her silent tongue dangling helplessly, was sucked down into a black hole at the creature's feet. But not before an explosion shattered its feet and legs.

A swirl of images and he was falling. Somewhere above him an aircraft was buzzing. He felt peaceful as he fell. The country below him was laid out like a rural banquet. He knew he was about to die and then to live again.

He could smell the burning flesh. It filled his nostrils and made him want to vomit. But he knew he had to keep going. Something was behind him. Something had always been behind him. Something unaccountably evil.

Peace and whiteness and glimmering pools of diamond light. He was moving. Or was it she? There was no sex here, no gender, just the tranquillity and the impression of movement. And behind, there was the shadow in the far distance, watching but too far away now to worry about. There was nothing to worry about here.

He could feel heat on his skin. Burning. The sand was hot today. He pulled on his white robe and slipped his sandals over his brown feet. The others were still walking, shimmering in the desert sun, a haze of white phantoms moving, yet still. He had to join the others. He was always being left behind. Why was he always the last? They wouldn't wait for him this time, he knew that. He would be picked off if he didn't keep up.

His tongue was dry. He needed water. They would stop for the night when their shadows were long. He knew the danger. He had been warned about lagging behind, dreaming, letting rivers of sand fall through his fingers. Always dreaming. He got up and walked after the others. Nervously, he glanced behind. They were not far away. They were never far away.

A kaleidoscope of pictures and memories flooded through unimpeded. He became aware of himself as an observer. Then the awareness would fade and he would be immersed in the image. In his observant state he knew these were not memories. Memories only existed in one dimension. Time was an illusion linked to memory and death. He found himself in a long tunnel. He was moving at great speed and the tunnel began to descend. He was falling now, falling, falling.

Noise and starlight and flames. Jumbles of coloured light. He saw the eyes staring. They were dark eyes filled with nothingness, no emotion, no grief, no pain, no love. The partly human face glared at him, spitting hate like bile. It had found him at last. It had escaped from the tunnels hidden by the Purple Zone and was here. He knew it wanted him so badly it could taste the core of his soul.

We are one, the demon buzzed. We are born. We of the stars and the lightning and the sun. We of the first born and the travellers of light. You cannot escape me. The demon was still young but its power was unlimited. Johnny somehow held himself intact. Something or somebody was supporting him, cradling his spirit. But for how long? Johnny screamed and clutched his heart. Images swirled around his mind like a crazy pinball. The pain was real. He was dying. He was crying with the pain. Then Shell was with him, holding him. He was drenched with sweat and the stench of his own fear. He could not see. He had gone blind. There were stars and galaxies forming and re-forming. Shell was weeping, imploring him to wake up.

*

His mind cleared and he could focus. Shell was holding him. Speranza had slumped back into a mound of cushions and appeared to be unconscious. She too was drenched in sweat. Her breath was laboured. The candles were almost extinguished and shadowlight was dancing around the caravan. Gradually, he became aware of his surroundings and then all his recent memories returned. He believed he had experienced the answer to the mysterious events of recent weeks but he could not explain it. It lay tantalizingly on the edge of his mind.

'Johnny, Johnny, are you all right?' Shell sounded anxious.

'I'm OK,' he managed to croak. 'What time is it?'

She looked at his watch. 'Almost midnight.'

Johnny sat up as Madame Speranza opened her eyes and giggled. 'Wasn't that a wonderful journey? I think it's time we had a little drink. I need one.' She reached under the couch and withdrew a bottle. She asked Shell to fetch some earthenware goblets and she poured them all a drink.

Remembering his last experience of Badlands liquor, Johnny was cautious. Speranza downed her shot in one. Shell did likewise. Johnny followed suit. It was a big improvement on the last stuff. It sent a charge through him. Speranza was smiling at him.

'That was one of the best regressions I've ever had. It was a wonderful journey. I love eavesdropping on other people's past lives.'

'Past lives?' Johnny sounded sceptical.

'Oh yes, dear, and one in particular holds the key.'

'What do you mean?' asked Shell, fascinated.

'Oh, my dear, it's all quite simple. There is a force trying to get into this world. If ever it reaches its full power here then it could destroy all of us.'

'You mean the devil, Lucifer, that kind of shit?' said Johnny scornfully.

'Oh no,' replied Speranza, pouring more shots. 'Far more complex, yet far simpler than that. This force is a demon and only exists because of mankind's evil. Imagine a piece of absorbent paper sucking up dirty water and ink and all kinds of horrible stuff, well, that's what this demon does. It lives on hate and greed and pain and suffering. It loves all that. It makes it grow and as it grows it gets more powerful.'

'So this demon is inside the doll I was telling you about?' gasped Johnny.

'Could be,' Speranza continued, 'but that will only be a temporary host. No human artefact could hold a creature of this power. A human being would be destroyed instantly if it were to experience its full power. This may also explain the sudden increase in suicides. Have you noticed? Yes, you will tell me, we have always had suicides. And you are right, but this is different. Your TV show, Mr Raine, and the increase in self-death, proves the point. This demon causes mankind to lose all hope. Death is the only release. And the demon lives on the act of death. It sustains it.'

'How do you know this?' asked Shell.

'Because, my dear, I have just come face to face with it.'

There was a silence as Speranza watched Johnny carefully. Then she carried on. 'I looked at your choice of stones and your hands. The left one is your last life and the right your present. I could get something from this but not enough to explain the haunting or the possession. Let me tell you what I saw. For reasons which are not presently apparent, three individualities have visited a region where only enlightened or protected beings have been. Putting it simply, a dark angel, confined to magical sleep within another region of space-time, has been awakened. Imagine a reservoir into which has been pumped the spiritual equivalent of all mankind's evil. Imagine then that dark angel, that dakini or demon, as the reservoir and you have some idea of what you, Johnny Raine, Frank Brady and the woman known as Jordan Semiramis, have contacted.' She paused for refreshment, smacked her mobile lips and giggled. 'Now then, somehow all three of you were exposed to a zone beyond human consciousness which exists somewhere in your psyches. And without knowing it you have acted as a conduit for the demon.'

Johnny could barely contain his scepticism. 'What do you mean, the reservoir of man's evil?'

Speranza continued unperturbed. 'The demon comes from the magico-metaphysical realm, but can manifest itself. Once in a physical form it will feed on the evil it finds around it. There will be plenty to feed on around here. The demon believed it was dreaming the whole human experience, until it awoke. It is my belief it cannot tell the difference between real human evil and virtuality. It may even be able to penetrate the web as well as the human psyche. If that is the case we could be facing Armageddon. If you find the Biblical reference quaint, I suggest you access the web God-files and re-read the scripture. However, there may not be time for that. This is not an intellectual exercise. The demon is not yet fully born. It is being held in check by the spirits of the three people who awakened it. The one who guided you to the zone did so without understanding the full implications of his actions. He has paid the price.'

The silence in the caravan was as dark as night.

'The zone is like a swamp protecting the abyss; a place all of us must cross sometime and where our spirits are cleansed and purged. The ruler, if you call it that, is Ayvas, a stellar entity who is coming into power in time for the next aeon. The demon must destroy those who gave it life so that it can become fully aware. Mr Raine, why do you think Jordan has become sick? The doll created by Frank Brady is the host of the demon. It will not remain within the mannequin for long. It must destroy the three of you. Frank Brady is dead. Jordan is dying. And you will be next, Mr Raine.'

Without realizing it, Johnny had pressed his hands to his heart. The dreams, the nightmares now made a terrible kind of sense. But Speranza hadn't finished.

'How can you be sure of all this?' said Johnny.

'I'm sure you already know, Mr Raine, but let me explain it to you. Frank Brady, a man I will dearly miss, is dead. Although you say you tried to kill him, you couldn't. So who, or what, did? It was the demon, of course. The magician, Frank Brady, had served his purpose. He could be dispensed with. Next in line is the woman. She is now in terrible danger. The demon has been feeding from her but now wants more. It has tasted freedom. It has begun to recognize itself. It too is acting under a form of compulsion. When it destroys the woman there is only one part of the sacrifice left to complete.'

'It has to kill me,' said Johnny coldly.

'Precisely,' said Speranza. 'If it does it will have completed the cycle of the magical act. Think of it as the demon's entrance fee to this world. What will happen then I can only guess. I cannot think of any way in which it could be destroyed. It would need a host, but it could change hosts whenever it wished. Wherever it went, madness, destruction and death would follow.'

'So we're all finished,' moaned Shell.

'Are we, hell!' snapped Johnny passionately.

The demon must be destroyed before it reaches full power. After that, it will be impossible except by an act of incomparable magic. Weapons will be useless against it.'

'So, how must it be done?' said Johnny.

'It is at its weakest now, while it is in this host. It must be destroyed now. It has control of elements and I feel it has control of fire. Destroy the host completely and the demon will have nowhere to go. Unless it enters the woman, but I think it will try to kill her first.'

'Jordan!' Johnny gasped as the full realization of Speranza's explanation hit home.

'There is not much time,' giggled Sparanza, 'you must fly.'

Shell was already snapping herself into her body armour. Johnny took Speranza's hands in his to thank her. No words were uttered. The psychic giggled like a schoolgirl.

Johnny and Shell ran from the caravan. When they had gone, Speranza's expression changed from mirth to fear. She collapsed back on to her cushions. The effort of regression had taxed her powers to the limit. She had seen the demon, felt its awesome power and it had chilled her soul. She had sensed madness and delirium. No human could stand against it once it was free.

Chapter Twenty-two

A madness had entered into Johnny. With Shell manning the armaments he drove back across the ravaged landscape, oblivious of attack. Something was squeezing its way into his mind. It felt like a cold, clammy hand probing his psyche, searching for him, seeking him out. He had to get to Jordan, but first he had to collect the freaks Shell had promised him.

He hurtled along pot-holed streets ignoring the impact of countless shots fired from home-made weapons. He thanked his stars for the RPC. For the first time in his life he was experiencing true fear and it had turned his blood to ice.

Shell screamed directions in between bursts of fire. She looked as if she was actually enjoying it. They eventually slithered to a halt, engine running, outside the desolate building Shell called home. It was quieter here. Hurriedly Johnny swept the area with the twin searchlights, disturbing an army of rats scurrying in and out of a ruptured sewer. There was no sign of life.

'Where are they?' he yelled at Shell. 'You said they'd be here.'

'They will be. Don't worry,' she shouted back.

For what seemed an age they waited, fearing sudden attack from every direction, not wanting to remain stationary for too long.

Johnny was reeling from a piercing headache. He was fighting the psychic intrusion. All his senses told him that Speranza's fantastic story just could not be true. But he knew instinctively that it was.

Four shapes detached themselves from the shadows. From different directions they entered the light. Ix-Tab, Deep Cut, Marshmallow Heart and Mister Sister preened and primped their way towards them. Shell spoke to them through the two-way microphone while Johnny fiddled with the control which opened the rear security door.

'Welcome,' she said, 'tomorrow night you will be seen all over the world. It will be your finest hour. You will die in glory, the greatest death style ever seen. All has been arranged. Now, quickly, get into the back when the door opens.'

Johnny waited, scarcely believing it was actually going to happen. Shell's words had the required effect. Johnny felt their weight as the two Feeks and two Farooks climbed into the back. He closed the rear door and rammed his foot on the accelerator.

Around Queensboro Bridge, a wild, screaming crowd had gathered. Fights were breaking out all around them, bullets were whining and the laserjet protection system pulsed at random into the darkness killing at will. The RPC was peppered by rapid-fire machine-guns as they screeched to a halt within the laser pool. Then they moved forward, protected by a laser shield. This time no guards checked them out. They were expected. Johnny relaxed visibly as the lights of Manhattan grew closer.

Jordan opened her eyes. It was dark except for flickering lights. She was immediately filled with an irrational fear. She was sure she had been dead. Now she felt warm and comfortable. Some of her old strength had returned. She had been inhabiting that half-world between waking and sleeping but something had brought her back to consciousness. She tried to understand her fear, make sense of her surroundings. She just knew she had to get up. Hospital, that's where she was. Memories were returning with full force. The gallery. The doll. Then she remembered killing Brady. She had lashed out with all her remaining strength and he had fallen. Everything else that followed was a mixed-up dream. She remembered Johnny bending over her, his face filled with concern. And she remembered the pain.

Tentatively, she tried to sit up. Something was holding her down. Wires and cables were imprisoning her. She had to get away. Something wanted her, she could feel it in her mind. It had left her nightmare and entered the world and now it was searching for her. She was convinced it was nearby. She had to get out of here. But was she strong enough? She didn't care. Her senses were screaming at her now to run, run as fast as she could.

The medi-centre had settled down for the night. Low-level

lighting gave the corridors a shadowy appearance. Pools of pale light patterned the white walls and dark floors. In between the pools of light, the shadows were as black as pitch. The night staff went about their routine procedures like ghosts, whispering to each other, checking out sleeping patients and working on computers, updating the daily files.

Cathy Pelowski was the first to see her and she was surprised. The woman in room 77 had been brought in suffering from post-cardiac trauma. She had looked terrible, thin and weak. No one had told Cathy that the patient was up and about. Maybe she was delirious. She could see Jordan approaching, dappled by shadow and light. What on earth was she wearing? It looked like a cape of some description. She was only wearing flimsy under-wear beneath. Cathy smiled and shook her head. She shouldn't be out of bed. The staff nurse got up from her desk and walked towards Jordan. Her smile disappeared as she came closer. There was something odd about the woman. She had stopped, half in and half out of shadow. Her face looked strangely twisted somehow. The nurse could swear there was something funny about her eyes. They were glowing like red coals. She hurried towards Jordan. She was clearly unwell.

'Ms Semiramis, what are you doing out of bed? Come on, I'll take you back.'

She was standing in front of the woman when the visions hit her like nuclear missiles. Rats as big as elephants stampeded through her mind. She saw her father, lying in bed, drowning in his own blood, the empty gun still smoking, lying on the floor. She saw her own childlessness. She saw her womb twisted and festering with sores, slithering worms eating into her ovaries. Cathy Pelowski did not have time to scream. Before she could even blink she had died of fright, her face frozen into a silent scream and her hair turned pure white.

The doll moved stiffly away from the body, savouring its death pain. The demon now sensed its victim. The woman from the dream was here. She had been drained of life-force but had started to recover. She must not be allowed to do that. The demon would take great pleasure in absorbing her life and extinguishing her consciousness. That would leave only one more to find. The demon knew where that victim was. It knew it would not have to seek him out, he would come of his own accord.

A small army of security police guarded the rear entrance to Media City. Johnny was sweating with anxiety. He was desperate to get to Jordan, but he had to deliver these freaks to the studio.

He parked near the entrance. The guards had been instructed to keep a low profile. These deviants were willing participants after all. The Feeks and Farooks stepped out of the RPC and stared around them. Here they were in the Rotten Apple itself. The security guards took a step backwards when they laid eyes on them. But it was Shell, the child-monster, who caused the biggest stir.

Lloyd and other members of the production team were on hand. From an upper window, Maurice Freiberg gazed down at the scene, shaking his head. Look at those freaks, he said to himself. Have you ever seen anything like that? They were aliens. That's it. They were fucking aliens. To think they inhabited the same planet filled Freiberg with an irrational fear.

Lloyd stepped forward.

'Welcome to Media City, ladies and gentlemen,' he began.

'Well, hello media mouth,' crooned Marshmallow Heart, 'you can lick-flick my mint any time.'

Flustered, Lloyd could only stammer. 'We've prepared rooms for you. Anything you want, it's yours.'

'Anything I want, thunderfuck?' Deep Cut puckered. 'I've brought my own supply. Psychon hermdoom time. Just lead me to a sharp blade.'

Johnny didn't want to hang around. He looked at Shell.

'I've got to get going,' he said, 'you'll be safe here. When you get to a dressing room, get out of the suit and into some proper clothes. Leave the rest to me. You won't have to go back there unless you want to.'

She smiled at him. Then the entourage, led by Lloyd, entered the building. The Media City staff gazed open-mouthed at the fantastically dressed and scarred Badlanders, and the Feeks and

Farooks stared back. They had been kids at the time of the Isolation. The Badlands were the only world they knew. Johnny couldn't help thinking that, but for the lucky break of having parents who had a little money, he could have been one of them.

The media hype had been building. The suicide show had knocked the upsurge in violence off the front page. America was primed to watch the show of the decade. Middle America was still out there and regarded what had happened to New York, Los Angeles and other major cities with astonished resignation. Isolation was coming their way too as the disenfranchised masses spilled out from the cess pools of the cities and hit the road as new age settlers.

Johnny hugged Shell as she went inside. Then he ran around the corner and picked up a staff electro-turbo. Within seconds, he was speeding through Manhattan towards the medi-centre.

As he neared the building, his feeling of oppression grew until he could hardly think. His mind grew sluggish. His limbs began to feel heavy and the icy probing of his mind had increased. He felt weak by comparison to the force. What had Speranza called it? A demon! A couple of weeks ago he would have laughed at the very idea. Now he knew better. Whatever was entering his mind at will had a dark power he could not begin to fathom.

At first, everything appeared calm and normal when he entered the front door of the centre. Unusually, there was no one on reception. A neuro-net screen flickered behind the desk. Instinctively, Johnny's senses moved into red alert. He padded forward, heading for Jordan's room. He reached the first corridor crossroads and looked in every direction. Nothing. The lighting was subdued and sleepy. He carried on along corridor three. From somewhere ahead he could hear muffled breathing. Must be a patient, he reasoned. Another sound came to him. As he passed by each room he could just make out a soft moaning, as though the occupants were tossing and turning in a disturbed sleep. Still there was no sign of any staff. Johnny's skin felt clammy. There was something wrong but he couldn't put his finger on it. The soft moaning of private nightmares began to increase. Now it sounded as though every patient was experiencing the same nightmare. The moans and soft screams melded into one.

A shadow was moving ahead, just out of the light. Johnny froze, then his heart began to pound, thumping in his ears. Johnny knew he had to get Jordan out but wondered if she was in a condition to be moved.

When he saw her ahead, his heart lifted. It was Jordan. She was just standing there in the shadows, watching him. He started to run towards her.

She stretched out her arms and Johnny ran straight to her, oblivious of the rising crescendo of nightmarish screams. She was obscured in shadow and he couldn't see her properly, but no matter, she was there, that was all that counted.

Johnny was overcome with love for her then. He stretched out his arms to embrace her. He ignored the sounds around him. He didn't hear the other sound, lost in the general cacophony.

Click!

Almost in slow motion, their fingers touched. Johnny reached forward, slipping his arms around her body. She felt a little stronger, a little firmer than before. Thank God for that. Then, with a cry, he took her into his arms.

Alex Hamlisch slipped out of his hiding place in the Channel Boom Boom executive washroom and checked his camera. Then he left the room and made his way cautiously towards the studio complex. The news-vid wanted a first-blood exclusive, on hard copy and optic tape. Well, he was just the man to give it to them, gift wrapped.

The journalist ran softly to a door marked 'Studio Personnel Only' and pushed it open. Inside, he found himself standing on the ramp that ran around the studio and housed the lighting boom system. He was looking down on the set of 'All the Way'. What he saw had him drooling with anticipation. Trembling slightly, he crept forward and dropped to his knees. Then, carefully, he lay down between the metal boom-carriers, crawling forward until he was pressed up against the perimeter railing. He could see and hear everything that was going on below. This would make him a household name. But he didn't have much time. He would have to get the shots and get out in time for the morning editions and satellite schedules. The studio was throbbing with activity. Production staff were scurrying around frantically. In one corner, Maurice Freiberg was standing in the centre of a group of blue suits, all gazing without expression at the stage set. But it was what was on the stage that set Hamlisch's journalistic instincts into overdrive.

'Holy shit,' he breathed, 'I don't believe it.'

Five of the most bizarre creatures he had ever seen were standing in front of an equally bizarre contraption that looked like a cross between a scaffold and the electric chair. Lloyd and some of the other assistant producers were trying to communicate with them. They were gesticulating and explaining how the contraption worked. Hamlisch kept his finger on the button, imagining the praise and accolades he would receive when these shots hit the front page and network newstapes before the show opened. Not to mention the credits. The Feeks and Farooks began to argue amongst themselves. It was all Lloyd and his team could do to keep them from tearing each other apart. Hamlisch shivered at the prospect of what the Badlands were like if these were examples of its decadent life-forms. He felt a sudden respect for Johnny Raine who had had the guts to go in there and bring them back. Whether he could do it week after week was another question. But that would be somebody else's problem now. The network would surely send somebody else in, if things didn't escalate further. They couldn't risk their star performer any more.

Suddenly Hamlisch experienced a severe emotional charge. He had never felt anything like it in his life. Under the glare of the studio lights, the fifth freak was coming apart. Hamlisch drooled with such anticipation that his contact lenses almost steamed over. This obscene hobgoblin with the doll-face and metal talons, covered in suppurating sores, was literally cracking up.

Hamlisch could hardly keep his micro-lens focused as the most beautiful creature he had ever seen emerged like a startled moth, naked and glistening.

You could hear the entire studio draw breath, and hold it.

Hamlisch's hardened emotional arteries burst into ecstatic life as he gazed in adoration at the child-woman. For the first time ever in his life, this was it. This was love. He cursed as an embarrassed assistant threw a robe over her shoulders.

Shell looked up and smiled.

'Fuck, she's seen me,' Hamlisch murmured and he quivered with passion mixed with fear. He was hooked. He would be her slave. He would risk anything for her. He would . . .

Movement behind the stage jolted his attention back to his mission. Hamlisch watched bemused as the operations crew put the crucifix machine, as they called it, through its paces. It was awesome. It even stunned the Badland freaks into silence.

Hamlisch had seen and photographed enough. He carefully crawled away from his vantage point, then, as a precaution, took the metallized digital film out of the camera and pushed it down inside his shoe. He couldn't afford to take chances with this material. It was dynamite. As he crept back through the network of booms and lighting cables, he made a vow. Somehow, he didn't know quite how, the miracle moth would be his.

'Johnny, oh, Johnny!' Jordan collapsed into Johnny's arms. Hot tears filled his eyes as he held her close.

'Jordan, thank God you're all right. I came as fast as I could. I thought . . . I thought you might be in danger. How do you feel?'

'Honey,' she said softly, 'I'm just all the better for seeing you. I feel a bit woozy, like I've been on a long trip.'

'It's been a couple of days, no more,' Johnny told her. 'I've got to get you out of here. I can't explain now. Just trust me. There's something out there and it wants to destroy us.'

'I sensed something,'' she said. 'Something woke me up. I don't know what it was. There was nothing in the room. Just this fear.'

Click!

This time they both heard it. It was sharp and it was nearby. The moaning, meanwhile, had increased in volume. The patients were crying out. Johnny could still see no sign of any staff.

Then he saw the body. It was lying a little way along the corridor. The woman had been young but she looked prematurely old. Her face was rigid with fear, her muscles locked into a scream.

From out of the shadows across the hallway, a figure appeared. It was smiling and wearing a black cape. It moved stiffly and its joints creaked as it walked. Johnny took a step backwards as Jordan turned. She uttered a breathless scream of hopelessness.

The doll moved closer. The demon stared out from its inanimate eyes. This was wonderful. Release and freedom were almost within its grasp. The doll's eyes turned bright as amber.

The doll stretched out its arms towards them. It would take the woman first. It had already tasted her life-force. Then, the final sacrifice. It needed the man to complete the cycle.

It needed to eat his heart.

Jordan and Johnny were frozen. They held each other like children in a fairy tale facing the big bad wolf. Images began to enter their minds. They fought against them but they were too powerful.

Chapter Twenty-three

They were on the move.

In the slithering, slimy, stench-ridden darkness of the sewers they crawled in their hundreds. In their thousands. They had heard the call. They had heard the songs. They knew about the prophecy that one day all would be theirs. They would take back by fear, terror and force what had been stolen from them.

Now a new voice was calling them. It bewitched them. It was a voice of evil so pure that it transcended all human experience. And it told them their time was almost at hand. The voice was also calling their brothers above ground. They too were gathering. The time of ultimate decadence was approaching.

The army of the half-human moved inexorably along the labyrinth of sewers that connected the city under the river. They would remain undetected. When they emerged into the light of the Rotten Apple they would reclaim what was rightfully theirs. And they would taste the blood of the rich parasites that lived there.

In the dark void of the underworld their eyes gleamed. Once they had been human, but now they had lost any semblance of humanity. They emerged from the sewers as scavengers to feast on the rich pickings of the dead and dying. Like poison entering the bloodstream, they were about to erupt from the subterranean conduits all over Manhattan.

They had been infected by a new madness.

The tunnels and underground channels were filled with their rasping, stinking breath. Their claws scrabbled on the smooth, lichen-covered walls. Their fangs chattered in their jaws. They did not have far to go. The new voice that called to them was gathering strength but there was something it had to do before it reached its full power. They were in awe of the voice. It was a voice that went beyond insanity.

*

Dr Graham Williams sprinted across the tarmacked drive of the medi-centre. He was late. It was the first time he had ever been late for duty. But he was in love. He smiled at the lingering memory of recent lovemaking as he burst through the swing doors, ignoring the sparseness and the dimness of the interior. It wasn't until he was hurrying along corridor four that he heard it. The sound. The patients were moaning and crying with one voice. Then there was the darkness. The lighting level had been reduced to a bare minimum. Dr Williams wondered where the staff had got to. There was simply no one about.

A chill ran along his spine. Something was wrong, seriously wrong. He was tempted to enter one of the many doors he passed but something told him to head for administration. He had to report this to the MMA, the Manhattan Medical Authority.

He started to run. Sweat broke out on his forehead as he felt something icy yet blisteringly hot pierce his brain. Some kind of mental probe seemed to be spearing his mind. Then, with the speed and power of a steam hammer, the thought hit him hard. He wanted to die. He suddenly believed with his entire being that there was simply no point in living. Tears sprang to his eyes as he rounded a corner and collided with someone.

It was a woman. She stared at him with what seemed to be surprise. But this was no ordinary woman. Dr Williams reached out and held her arm to steady himself. As he started to mumble an apology, his brain just exploded inside his skull. Death was instantaneous. His final memory was of a pair of red eyes staring and a gaping mouth laughing.

Johnny shook himself free of his mounting delirium. He watched as the doctor in the white coat, who had suddenly appeared out of nowhere, touched the doll. The doctor's eyes widened in terror. He tried to speak but it was too late. If this was the demon at its weakest, Johnny thought, how the hell was he going to destroy it?

For a split second, the doll's attention was drawn away from Johnny and Jordan. Johnny didn't hesitate. He yanked Jordan after him and they ran and half-stumbled along the corridor as the doctor hit the floor.

Sheer fear had galvanized Jordan, weak as she was. For a

moment she had been convinced she was about to die. She heard the creature speak clearly inside her mind. Despite the terrifying power of the demon, Jordan found an icy calmness descend. It was as if the prospect of extinction had stripped away her fear of death.

Johnny and Jordan reached the reception area and headed for the swing doors. Behind them they could hear footsteps. They were stiff and artificial. And they were quick.

Johnny pulled Jordan through the doors and out into the night. In the distance they could hear the sound of a crowd cheering but it was muffled by laser fire. Outside the medi-centre everything was quiet. Everything appeared so normal.

For Johnny, as he pushed Jordan into the passenger seat of the electro-turbo, all thoughts of million-credit deals had vanished. All that mattered now was that they get out of this madhouse as quickly as they could. But still the thought nagged at him as he hit the start button. How could this thing be destroyed? Speranza had said if wasn't stopped soon, before it had destroyed the two of them, it would be unstoppable. Johnny wondered how the doll would cope with a couple of mini-nukes up its orifices. But something told him that wasn't the way. This whole business had the feeling of ritual about it. The doll, or the demon, had to go through a certain ritual before it could truly emerge into the world. Somewhere there had to be an answer. Somewhere there was a key.

Jordan screamed, 'It's behind us!'

Johnny stared into the rearview. The doll was striding across the tarmac like a demented, robotic mannequin. Johnny hammered his foot on to the accelerator and they roared away, scattering dust and leaves.

Jordan clung to his arm as they raced towards Central Park South. Johnny had no clear idea of where he was going. It was around four in the morning and there were a lot of people about. There was something disturbing about their behaviour, Johnny noticed. Until recently street crime had been negligible. Violence in its many forms could never be eradicated entirely, it was a fundamental part of the human condition. But since the Isolation and the tougher laws that came in then, Manhattan was a different place. You could walk around most neighbourhoods relatively safely and the State Police presence was subtle but effective.

Johnny could see at least half a dozen fights had broken out. There had been a couple of collisions and the drivers were screaming at each other. The flashing lights and screaming sirens of the police electro-turbos were well in evidence. It was New York like it used to be.

As Johnny swung into East 59th Street, Jordan dug her fingers into his arm and gagged. He slammed on the brakes and screeched to a halt.

A small crowd had gathered and was looking up, staring silently. A long flagpole jutted out from a hotel building some twenty feet above the street. It reached out a long way, like an upturned tooth. But there was no flag on the end of this pole. Instead, a man's body swayed gently as it hung from a rope tied to the end. The man's head lolled forward.

For a reason he could not fathom, the swinging body of the suicide victim meant something. Johnny had seen so much violence and death in the past few weeks that the actual sight of a corpse dangling from a noose above a Manhattan street hardly disturbed him. The shock of it had frightened Jordan but even she had recovered quickly. This fact worried Johnny. Was he becoming inured to death? A month ago he would have been shocked by the sight. Now, it was just another suicide. There had been a spate of them recently.

That was it!

That was the connection.

That could be the key to destroying the evil force that now haunted the city and sought to kill them both.

'Suicide. Ritual suicide!' he blurted out.

He was tired and incoherent. But he remembered Bobby Bolero's words about Guru Lennon and the prophecy that one day a force would come to liberate the land of the dead. Maybe there was a connection. A crazy idea was forming in his mind. An idea that meant he would have to go through with the show.

'Let's get out of here,' Jordan said weakly. She rested her head against his shoulder. Johnny looked at her with compassion.

How could he have forgotten what she had been through? She looked a little stronger than before, but not much. The hair loss seemed to have abated at least. He felt suddenly ashamed and filled with love for her.

He put his arm around her shoulders and spun the wheel, circling the silent, watching crowd. The hanging man dangled above them, clearly eliciting some kind of morbid fascination.

He drove with one hand on the wheel. Sleep was all he could think of now. Somewhere warm and safe, holding Jordan in his arms, lying still. But where? They couldn't go to either of their apartments. Johnny headed downtown towards the Village. There was a little hotel he knew. It would be perfect.

Half an hour later they were soaking together in a cloud of warm, soapy bubbles. Johnny watched Jordan as she stretched languorously, eyes closed, body thin and weak. She was still so beautiful. He could almost cry at the sight of her. The thought of losing her was just too much to bear.

'I love you,' he whispered to her.

She smiled. Then she said, in a small, sleepy voice, 'Love you too.'

Later they snuggled together as one body with the quilt wrapped around them tightly like a protective shell. Outside, the world could go as insane as it liked. In the distance could be heard the occasional siren. There was no need to make love. Neither of them was in the mood. Jordan was still physically thin and weak. Johnny trembled slightly as he began to relax. The tension from his hunched limbs finally began to ebb. If he prayed, he would have prayed for a warm, dreamless sleep and to awake refreshed and newborn.

Right at that moment, Commissioner Halloran was holding a bad-tempered meeting with Manhattan police chiefs, the head of the Zone Police organization and a high-level visitor from Washington. They were all dog-tired and ratty. The State Police were all for calling in a crack army helicopter warfare team. If the shit-heads from the Badlands were going to attack on all fronts it had to be treated as a major civil disturbance. The official view from Washington concurred. Manhattan might be segregated but it was still part of the United States of America. Privately, Washington wanted to make Halloran crawl. The extent of his personal power and wealth was causing a few ulcers to pop on Capitol Hill.

But even the President was apparently mesmerized by the prospect of the suicide show. He was, however, also filled with a moral outrage at the depths to which society had sunk that it would allow such a show. His dilemma was that, with the exception of the usual battery of outcries from freak-loving groups, churches, liberation movements and the like, America wanted to see someone kick some ass. The show had caught the public's imagination. So the President did nothing.

Halloran was backing the Zone Police to handle the situation. They were an expensive private army. The citizens of Manhattan expected value for the protection tax they paid. That was when the argument began to get heated. The State boys poured scorn on the loyalty of the ZeePee squad. They would crack under pressure. They would turn and run if there was any real trouble. So far there had only been skirmishes and a gradual rise in violence and suicides. The Zone Police chief was not about to take that. Halloran had to step in and separate the two of them as the ZeePee chief faced up to his State opposite number.

It was finally agreed to see what this show could do to defuse the situation. There was no doubt about it. Something was happening out there. Halloran couldn't put his finger on it but he knew. It was like an early-warning tremor before the earthquake.

In a small, dark alley off Wall Street a sound could be heard; the sound of grating metal; the sound of something heavy being moved. A sewer lid twisted and began to shift. Something was emerging from the sewer. The sewer lid was pushed to one side as though it was made of tissue paper. Something dark began to climb out, so dark that it blended with the shadows but was darker than them.

Something was breathing; deep, malodorous, rumbling breaths. Then there came the sound of teeth chattering in large jaws. That was the loudest sound of all. The darkness would conceal it. It disliked the light although it longed for sunshine and warmth. The darkness shielded its mutated form from public gaze. Like the others waiting below in the sewer, it had grown in size and strength on a diet of infected human flesh. A soft wind from the river ruffled its long, trailing hair. It moved its massive head slowly, searching for its first victim. And all the while the voice spoke to it, quelling the last remnants of humanity which remained. It was now only barely human. It listened closely to the voice. Then it began to move its massive frame out of the sewer and into the street.

The 'All the Way' set was quiet. In the darkness, the crucifix machine was an ominous shape hidden behind a black, sequinned drape. A few security guards kept watch on the studio. They lounged around casually, not expecting any trouble. Lloyd and the production staff would be in early to prepare for that evening's historic transmission. Such was the demand for tickets that queues were beginning to form even as dawn was breaking. Tonight's show would be watched by millions. The belief was that there would be another queue – of willing suicide victims from the Badlands seeking media immortality. Maurice Freiberg was keeping his options open and his private heli-jet in tip-top shape, just in case.

In some private and heavily secure rooms a floor below, a party was going on. The two Feeks and two Farooks had been separated. Ix-Tab and Deep Cut were flying – high on a shurm and rage mix – and freak-dancing to a mesmeric rock track. The room had been trashed. Splashes and trails of blood from Deep Cut's self-inflicted wounds had congealed on the walls and ceiling. The two Feeks were too stoned to sleep. They were screaming in a high falsetto, bringing each other to orgasm over and over.

It was a similar scene with the two Farooks. Marshmallow Heart was a shimmering, translucent and shivering mass of multi-coloured glutinous jelly. She posed in macho style, flexing her muscles, moving unsteadily through a bodybuilder routine. Mister Sister lay on the floor, prone and stoned, stroking her metal phallus for comfort. She hummed a little tune in a broken baritone and dreamed of hermdoom – that half-world between life and death where she would be free and immortal.

On Johnny's instructions, Shell had been given a comfortable room of her own. His protestations that she was not one of the participants in the show seemed to have worked. Unlike the others, her room was unlocked. Shell had caused the most fascination amongst the staff and security guards. The comfortable Manhattanites had never seen anything like her before. They knew that freaks roamed the streets of the Badlands but few had actually come into direct contact with any of them.

Alex Hamlisch had been busy. His story and pictures were already on the web, and millions of news-vids would carry the screamer headlines in the morning. Now, he was pursuing his own private agenda. Like a cat burglar on the prowl, he had found his way back into the studio. He had got by the initial security cordon by persuading Clark Taylor to give him a last-minute interview. Then he had slipped to the men's room and followed his earlier route. Hamlisch stopped outside Shell's door. He opened the door slowly and peered inside. What he saw made him sweat.

Shell looked up and smiled. She saw the man's eye peering through. She unclasped the body-armour suit and began to climb out. She was naked and beautiful. She smiled at the unseen reporter, then she beckoned to him. Slowly the door opened. Hamlisch looked over his shoulder nervously then came right in, closing the door behind him. He approached Shell who watched him coyly. He began to unbutton his shirt as Shell dimmed the lights.

It had been all quiet for over an hour. Fingers of golden dawn light were sliding along the East River. High in the Zone Police headquarters tower overlooking Brooklyn Bridge, Commander Shumacher leaned on the observation rail and sucked at his teeth. He stood up and brushed an imaginary piece of dirt from the shoulder of his smart, starched uniform.

'Where the fuck are they?' he remarked stiffly, making the oath sound like a military edict. Shumacher was widely regarded by his senior personnel as being something of an asshole. If he told you the world was round you'd ask for a second opinion.

His senior Zone Police officers lived in fear of an offbeat, irrational command. They knew it would come one day. Shumacher thrived on confrontation. He just wanted to kick ass. He had to be reminded, diplomatically, that the ZeePees were not the State Police or the National Guard.

Shumacher turned to the bunch of senior officers standing behind him.

'It won't be long now, gentlemen,' he barked. 'What we are experiencing is commonly known as the lull before the storm. Before dawn breaks we will be at war. Make no mistake, gentlemen. We are at war now. That is not America you see before you. That is an alien and degenerate foreign territory. Once it was part of this great nation. It will be again.

'I know, I know, we listen to the politicians and the administrators and the media men,' he spat these last words out with venom, 'who think they can stop this army of mutants from destroying everything we stand for by putting them on TV. Psycho crap! You know it and I know it. Gentlemen, your moment of glory is almost here. We are the first and last defence of Manhattan. And Manhattan is the symbol of this great nation.'

The officers regarded him stonily.

Shumacher continued. 'When they attack, gentlemen, I want us to be ready. On the bridges and on the shoreline from the north to the south of this island we will prevail. I want those fucking shurmheads destroyed once and for all. I don't want any State interference. This land is our land. This land is your land.' He paused for breath, then continued ruefully, 'I warned them. I warned them years ago to blow the bridges. Make it easier for ourselves, I said. The bridges are symbols, they said. Fuck symbols, I told those prissy assholes. What do you mean we can't go too far? They believe, gentlemen, or should I say they used to believe, that the mutant hordes would one day be reunited in the fellowship of the American spirit and come back into the fold. So the bridges must stay. They said the cost of security would be the same whether we blew the bridges or not. Crap! Who cares about cost when we have all this to protect?' he waved his arm theatrically. 'Manhattan, America's pride and joy.'

Shumacher inhaled deeply, savouring the freshness of the dawn breeze. He saluted his men, who remained ill at ease and watchful as though in the presence of a crazy.

Proudly, Shumacher marched stiffly to the elevator which would take him swiftly down to his chauffeured electro-turbo and on to an official breakfast meeting with Commissioner Halloran.

Bobby Bolero hummed a little tune as he moved slowly along the line of heavily beaten men who were hanging by their testicles from an iron girder.

It was first light as Bolero lit a cheroot with his knuckle flame. A small army of his warriors watched as he patrolled the defeated remnants of those who had sought to challenge him.

He stopped by the last dangling figure. He was crying and moaning quietly. Bolero regarded the barely recognizable human form sardonically.

'Shame on you, Petri. You need help, eh? Help, you need someone, help!' he sang the last word in a parody of a pop tune. 'Well, there's no help comin', Petri. Shame you're gonna miss the big TV show. We're all staying home tonight in front of the teevee.' He laughed at the idea. 'We're gonna have a nice teevee dinner. You'd have liked that. You and me could have been friends, Petri. But you had to go and spoil everything. We've gotta stick together, Petri. The time is here. Don't you hear it? Don't you hear the fucking call?'

Bolero shook his head in sorrow and wonderment. He placed two knuckle spikes against Petri's eyes and pushed hard. Then he twisted. Petri hardly had life enough left to scream. But scream he did.

Bolero stepped back and puffed on his cheroot. He looked over at his lieutenant – a grossly deformed hulk – and nodded.

Without a word, Bolero's army lined up behind the swaying bodies. They raised wickedly sharp machetes above their heads and went to work, hacking and stripping flesh and bone like they were on early shift at the abattoir.

As the rivulets of blood turned into a small stream flowing along the alley, Bolero grunted with satisfaction and tossed the butt of his cheroot into the warm red tide.

Johnny was drifting in the penumbric world between life and death. He was ageless here. He wanted nothing, desired nothing, felt nothing. This was, he knew in his altered state, a kind of halfway house or a staging post between one set of experiences and another. He understood without question that around him swarmed the just barely discernible remnants and echoes of his other existences. As he moved in and out of shifting levels of awareness he could feel Jordan's life-force anchoring him to his present incarnation. There was no questioning here, no cynicism, no doubt. He just was.

Only the shadow concerned him. He was being watched by something on the periphery of his heightened vision. He knew that as soon as he allowed fear to enter his awareness, the shadow would try to consume him. The shadow lived on fear and hate. Without these elements it was powerless. Still it watched and waited. The shadow had endless patience.

Jordan opened her eyes and gulped with a sudden intake of breath. She relaxed immediately she felt the comforting warmth of Johnny's body close to her, his arms wrapped around her.

Sleep had been wonderful. She felt rejuvenated. The dense fog which had enveloped her and had been absorbing her for so long had receded. But her senses were vibrating. She knew it was close by. It would come for her. She blinked in the early light, momentarily disoriented in the strange hotel bedroom. Then the memories returned. She fought back the wave of fear which threatened to engulf her once again. She would not give in to it. She would never give in.

'You OK?' Johnny grunted sleepily.

Jordan could feel the rasp of his unshaven face on her shoulder as he spoke.

'Fine,' she replied.

'Tonight's the night,' he said.

'If we live so long,' she murmured.

'I've got something to tell you,' he said. 'You might not believe it. I'm not sure I do.'

'About the doll?'

'About the doll. And about everything that's been happening.'

'I could stay here for ever,' she sighed.

He said, 'We don't have much time. You've got to listen and try to understand.'

Jordan remained silent while Johnny told her about Speranza and the regression. He told her about the demon which inhabited the doll and how it needed to fulfil a ritual magical cycle in order to be free. Once free, nothing on earth could stop it. When he had finished, she was silent for a long time.

'What did you mean when you talked about ritual last night?' she asked him.

'It's a longshot. I don't even know if I'm right. I don't know anything for certain any more. Everything seems so, I don't know, preordained. Does that sound too far-fetched?'

'I don't know. The only thing I care about is you. I'm still here, Johnny. As long as I am alive I will love you. In the end that's the only thing that doesn't sound far-fetched.'

'I've got to go through with the show. It all seems to hinge on that. It's going to come for us. We'll only have one chance,' he told her.

She turned to him and kissed him tenderly.

'But, if you're right, then it has to kill me first.'

'Only if it gets to you. I want it on TV. You might think I'm nuts but I think it just might work.' He smiled at her tenderly. 'This is where I say I love you. If I let my mind stop racing for a second it comes home to me; the whole crazy, fucked-up situation. My life has been a sham. I knew happiness but it was taken from me. Now I've been given a second chance. I'm not going to blow it. I don't want to know about fame or the media or Manhattan any more. I want out, with you. I want a life with time to think, time to live. Believe me, I'm forcing myself to go through with this.'

Before he could say any more, Jordan had taken him into her arms. His mouth searched for her pleasure zones. He savoured her skin, his tongue drifting lazily down to her warm, moist

womanhood. They made love languorously, as if there was all
the time in the world and love was all there was.

Sunlight was streaming in through the French windows. They
rested peacefully in each other's arms. Jordan glanced at the
window and saw a pigeon land on the iron balustrade of the fire
escape. The bird plucked at its feathers, then rose into the air,
squawking and flapping its wings. Johnny noticed also and
yawned.

There was a faint noise, like water dripping in another room.
Jordan was suddenly reminded of her nightmare. She shivered
at the recollection. She was relieved that she had not experienced
it last night. The noise grew louder. Now it was not water
dripping but a regular clanging sound. Like footsteps. Like
footsteps on the fire escape.

'It's outside,' she shouted at Johnny.

He was suddenly wide awake and listening. Something was
climbing up the fire escape. Something with a regular footfall
and metal feet.

In a flurry of activity they leaped out of bed and pulled on
their clothes. They were half-dressed when they saw a shadow
flickering on the net curtains.

The temperature in the room plunged. They ran for the door,
scrabbling at the handle which jammed. Johnny wrenched at it.
Jordan was rammed wide-eyed against the wall, fighting the
influx of death thoughts which were oh, so sweet.

With a scream of defiance, Johnny heaved and the door
swung open. He grabbed Jordan and half-carried her out of the
room.

There was an explosion behind them. Through the ruins of the
French window the doll stepped delicately into the room. The
plastic and metal body of the creature was rippling with waves
of energy. The sculpted photographs of Jordan which gave the
doll its realistic appearance seemed to have turned into real
flesh. The illusion was gripping. It caused Johnny to pause. The
doll moved. Johnny, fighting the onset of madness, turned and
ran. Something was driving him. Whatever force it was which
had come to his rescue he thanked with all his heart and soul.
He hustled Jordan along the corridor.

They reached the elevator. Johnny hammered the call button. Jordan was staring back, weakening by the second.

'Come on, come on!' he yelled.

Back along the corridor, the doll emerged from the bedroom. It began to walk towards them slowly. The demon was savouring the prospect of assimilating these two life-forces. Then it would be free. It could discard this man-made artefact at last. It was slowing it down with its crude construction. The demon could sense the eroticism of the mannequin. It conjured information from its unlimited memory till the face of a gaunt, haunted man shimmered in transcendental space. Hans Bellmer gazed at the world through long-dead eyes. The demon appreciated the sexual sorcery implicit in the dolls Bellmer had created. This was all part of the cycle of necromancy which had awakened it to sentience. Once the demon could transfer to another host, then and only then would its true power be revealed. If the demon had a sense of irony this would have been the moment to reveal it. It only existed by courtesy of mankind itself. Without millennia of hate and greed, the demon could not have been born in the cosmic soup of creation.

The elevator doors wheezed open. Johnny dragged Jordan inside and punched for lobby. The doll was lurching nearer. A bedroom door opened and a paunchy man with a two-day growth and a well-developed gut stepped out.

'What the fuck's all the noise about, lady?' he belched at the doll.

The doll paused and turned to the man, who leered back pugnaciously.

'I don't give a shit about women's liberation. I'm liable to belt your pretty ass up and down the hall if you don't put a sock in it.'

The doll gazed at the man. The demon was angry. It reached for the man's life-force and sucked it into itself. The man had no time to even feel pain. His eyeballs rolled around in his sockets as his body collapsed like a sail suddenly deprived of wind. This interruption gave Johnny the vital few seconds they needed. The elevator doors closed and the car began to descend. Jordan clung to Johnny, fighting waves of weakness and nausea.

Above them the demon was not to be thwarted. The doll reached out to the elevator doors and pulled them open with ease. Without pausing, it leaped into the void, hurtling down the lift shaft and landing with a loud thump on top of the car.

Inside, Johnny's bowels bubbled. It was on the roof. They only had a few floors to go. As he stared at the ceiling, the concealed escape hatch began to move. Something was pushing its way into the framework of the ceiling, buckling it like cardboard. Jordan was screaming in terror. Johnny tried to protect her but his mind was scrambling.

For what seemed an age the elevator whined slowly to a halt on the ground floor, spent several vital seconds settling into the bay, then more precious seconds waiting for the doors to open. They must have more resistance than most to the demon's infection, thought Johnny. Even so, rational thought was rapidly becoming impossible. Dreams and madness were infiltrating their minds.

The doors opened. Johnny hauled Jordan after him through a crowd of new arrivals. They barged through and ran out the front entrance. The desk clerk looked up and yelled after them.

An explosion of wood, plastic and metal heralded the arrival of the doll. For a brief second, the crowd, the desk clerk and the doll stared at each other. Then the doll moved. The crowd scattered, screaming, hands over their heads. The doll was smiling and salivating.

Chapter Twenty-four

Screamer headlines across the front page of the *Manhattan Times* and all over the laser media-web proclaimed: TV KILLING MACHINE REVEALED IN BADLANDS SUICIDE SHOW. The story was dominated by a photograph of the crucifix machine in the background with the two Feeks and two Farooks staring bleakly and unseeingly into space. The picture was riveting. It was a superb example of fly-on-the-wall photo-journalism. The story did more than hit a nerve. It sent an explosive charge right through the main artery. It took the moral high ground; it berated the US administration for inaction; it reprised the Isolation; it showed sympathy for the lost souls of the Badlands and finally came down on the side of middle America. But, the Alex Hamlisch story asked, had America become desensitized to the point where it accepted as routine the idea of murdering people live on television? Where would it end?

Hamlisch had held a mirror up to the Manhattan experiment. Was this a model for other cities to follow? Or was the State of Manhattan so self-obsessed, insular and xenophobic that it could not see that what it represented still stirred fear, loathing and real concern around the world? And yet, isolation mania was spreading. In nearly every part of the world, cities were being blockaded. The fortress society was now taking root as a bastion for the rich, the technocrats, the cybercrats and the media. A huge demographic shift was being prophesied by apocalyptic academics who warned anyone who would listen to get behind the walls now or face exclusion.

The story sold more copies of the paper and news-vids than any in history and broke all media-web records. It also guaranteed a huge viewing audience for that night's 'All the Way'.

Commissioner Halloran had succumbed to an idea dreamed up by one of his younger executives and giant TV web-screens were erected at vital points along the Manhattan shoreline, by the key bridges. The idea was to demonstrate the awesome power of the State and, at the same time, show that television was for everyone. By mid-morning the names of Ix-Tab, Deep Cut, Marshmallow Heart and Mister Sister had become part of American folklore. The news media were full of the story – some claiming to have held interviews with the Feeks and Farooks, others running in-depth features on the entire Badlands subculture, claiming inside knowledge about Feek and Farook sexual rituals. In some papers and magazines, the legendary figure of Bobby Bolero was featured, discussed and sanctified.

Beneath the streets of Manhattan an unseen army was waiting for darkness to fall.

Slowly, throughout the day, the massed ranks of the Badlands deviants had begun to assemble. A makeshift stage was being constructed by Bolero's followers from salvaged scrap. Pride of place by the stage, which faced a giant TV web-screen across Queensboro Bridge, was a wheezy old compressor. A rudimentary public address system was taking shape. Bolero was due to speak that night. These activities had not gone unnoticed by the Manhattan media. Reporters and vidi-crews battled for stories throughout the day, besieging Media City, Zone Police headquarters and the State of Manhattan administration. Others had trained sensitive directional microphones and cameras on to the Badlands, from Brooklyn up to the Bronx. Zone and State Police activity was being reinforced, especially around the North Shore bridges. Not since the Isolation itself had there been such media mayhem. Staten Island airport now saw the constant arrival of media teams from all over the world. The TV show, like the Isolation, was a world story.

Like two refugees from a war zone, Johnny and Jordan arrived at the rear entrance to Media City. Even here, crowds were gathering. The building's security guards were becoming ill-tempered and tetchy already. Johnny was unshaven and unkempt and Jordan looked barely alive. There was confusion building up at the private employees-only car park. Electro-turbos and sedans competed with mobile film and vidi-vehicles for space. Johnny kept his hand pressed on the horn. Jordan was wild-eyed and staring at the heaving mass of shouting, screaming press and public clamouring for interviews, tickets or even just a glimpse of the crucifix machine.

Johnny swerved into the exit lane. A harassed guard leaped in front of him. It took him a couple of seconds to recognize Johnny and wave him in. Johnny opened the car window.

'Thanks Herb. Is everyone here?'

'Sorry, Mr Raine. It's going crazy here. I've never seen the like of it. Yeah! Most of 'em slept here last night.'

Johnny eased the car into his parking spot and helped Jordan out. She was recovering now. Nothing that a good breakfast and an ocean of coffee would not cure. She stood stock still for a moment and Johnny looked at her.

'What's the matter?' he asked anxiously, eyes darting around the car park.

'I just want to say one thing – no two things – before we, you, get sucked into this nightmare. First is, I love you. Second is, one way or another I'm getting out of here tomorrow, whether you're with me or not.'

Johnny stared at her then took her into his arms. 'I'm not letting you go alone, believe me. I've just got to get through this day. Whatever happens, we're out of here tomorrow.'

She looked up at him and smiled. 'I feel like I'm being dragged along by an undertow. I feel like I have no control over my own actions any more. A couple of weeks ago I was moderately successful, I had a life of my own, I had you. I had a career. Now, shit, it's demons, a totally fucked-up society, freaks coming out of the woodwork, people dying everywhere, suicide machines, live suicide on television. Johnny, it's just unreal. I can't take all this. I want out and I want out with you. Promise?'

He took her in his arms and they held each other in the cool of the echoing car park.

'I promise,' he said to her, 'I promise, I promise.'

Minutes later they were eating voraciously. They drank coffee and ate some more. The third-floor staff restaurant was busy. There was an electric atmosphere everywhere in the building. Lloyd came in, looking washed out. He saw Johnny and clapped his hand to his forehead as he rushed over to the table.

'What a day,' he groaned. 'The press office is having a heart attack.' He looked at Jordan vacantly. 'Hi, I think we've met.'

She smiled at him. 'How are your special guests?'

Lloyd raised his shoulders in an expression of bewilderment.

'Well, they're still in one piece, although I can't guarantee they'll remain in that condition until transmission. Johnny, maybe you can get through to them. They're obsessed by death. It's really getting to me. It's not just a TV show any more. These creeps really do want to die. They're in love with death.'

'We're going to freshen up, Lloyd,' said Johnny, 'then I want to get Jordan settled somewhere. I want to see Stan Michaels and make some calls. Then we'll set up a meeting and I'll talk to them."

'You look like yesterday's shit,' smiled Lloyd. 'OK! Don't forget we've got the top brass here for this one. There are more VIPs and security consultants and State blue suits in the building than in the legislature.'

He looked down at Johnny wearily. 'I'll see you later then,' he said and shuffled away.

Johnny turned to Jordan. 'Come on, let's get freshened up. I'm sure we can find some clothes for you in Wardrobe.'

When they had showered and Johnny had shaved and changed in the executive washrooms, he escorted Jordan, now looking tired and thin but still elegant, up to the atrium. He introduced her to Veronica who, like all the staff at the channel, wore the haunted look of the overworked and overstressed. His PA brightened at the sight of Jordan and fussed over both of them.

'If this is going to happen every week, I'm quitting,' she told Johnny half seriously. 'It's a madhouse here.'

She brought them more coffee and Johnny put a call into accounts. He grunted with satisfaction, cradled the vidi-phone and smiled at Jordan.

'You're looking at two million credits, honey. But there isn't much time. I've got to turn those credits into currency.'

'Leave that to me,' Jordan said. 'This is where I come in. You just take care of the show. I'll need your authorization codes and private account number.'

'I'll talk to Michaels again,' Johnny said and punched up the accounts number on the vidi-phone. Briefly, he explained the situation. It was strictly irregular and breached God knows how many regulations, said Michaels. But Johnny prevailed. Jordan was his broker. He was busy. She must have access to the credits to buy currencies and make deposits. It was clear to Michaels what was going on. No one cashed in two million credits in one go unless they were pulling out. Shit, said the accountant to himself, I won't be far behind you.

Johnny kissed Jordan tenderly and headed for the production office. Jordan looked more like her old self, except that she felt like she had been vacuumed out from the inside. She set to work making calls, looking for deals. First call was the airport to book tickets to London. Then she called round the brokers and the dealers.

Johnny walked straight into a small war. The Feeks were trying to kill the Farooks and the Farooks had offered to die there and then. Johnny seemed to carry a certain amount of weight. He alone had been to their world. Somehow, he managed to calm things down. He talked them through the routine. He could hardly believe he was doing it. The point was coming home to everyone on the studio floor that this was for real. Johnny played the death style and glory card to the hilt. He appealed to their sense of style. He talked about the most famous deaths of all time. They would go down in history. And they bought it.

Shell came over to Johnny. He hardly recognized her in a simple green dress which highlighted the soft, brown texture of her skin. She smiled at him and kissed him lightly.

'Thank you,' she said.

'For what?' Johnny replied. 'I'm the one who should be thanking you.'

Shell looked off into the shadows and Johnny followed her gaze. Alex Hamlisch was lurking in the background, looking like a nervous schoolboy. He smiled and shrugged. Johnny turned to Shell.

'Good luck,' he said and walked away.

Maurice Freiberg was nervous. He puffed at a large Havana

ignoring protestations about his health. Grey faces dressed in dark suits watched from the shadows and from the observation room. Freiberg realized that this could be the end of his career if it didn't work out.

Evening was approaching. Now the crowds of mutants, deviants, hopeless and lost souls of the Badlands had gathered in their thousands. Along the shoreline and around the bridges they held their vigil, carrying burning brands and watching silently as the lights of Manhattan grew in intensity.

Bobby Bolero clambered to the top of his impromptu podium. He reached for the microphone and coughed into it. His voice bellowed tinnily out over the assembled throng. As he started to speak, his fuzzy image and distorted voice were being transmitted live across America.

'Guru Lennon lives,' screamed Bolero, 'Death style rules. There is no love, no love. The time is here. The time is now. Do you believe?'

Bolero's hazy image flickered from the dozens of screens mounted along the waterfront. The answer came from a million or more twisted throats. A sea of flickering lights stretched from Brooklyn to the South Bronx.

Bolero was in full flood. 'The spirit is calling. Do you hear it? Do you hear it? Do you hear it?'

A deafening roar answered his hoarse scream. 'Do you hear it?' yelled Bolero in a paroxysm of passion. 'Do you fucking hear it?'

The President of the United States watched with mounting fear. Then he picked up his private vidi-phone and pressed one button.

Commissioner Halloran received the call while watching his giant screen, ashen-faced in the midst of Manhattan's top brass. He wasn't given time to speak. He listened. Then he said, 'Yes sir,' and replaced the receiver.

The 'All the Way' production rehearsal had swung into action. Outside, queues stretched for two blocks as frantic Manhattanites fought to get tickets. Earlier than usual, Media City security began to let people in. The show had turned into the biggest social event of the year. Those with pre-booked tickets arrived by chauffeured limo. It was all security could do to hold back the baying crowd clamouring to get in.

Across the street a lone figure stood in the shadows, watching. The doll glared bleakly at the crowd. Within the rapidly deteriorating structure the demon was bursting with unreleased power. It knew the time was approaching. They would not escape. The demon could feel the simple life-forces underground. They were poised and ready. They hungered for flesh and they thirsted for blood. Soon, the demon projected the thought, soon you will be free.

The doll began to walk unsteadily across the street towards the rear of the building. Several security guards saw it approach. They tried to speak but they could not. The doll walked stiffly past them while they stared blindly.

Jordan left Johnny's office and stepped into the circular atrium floor. It was almost deserted. Slowly and with some effort, she started to walk towards the elevator which would take her to the production control floor. As she reached the elevator she paused, suddenly nervous and alert. Her personal antenna perceived something, something which made her swallow back a gobbet of fear as it swelled inside her.

Chapter Twenty-five

Johnny Raine bounded on stage as the familiar theme tune introduced the Saturday night blockbuster, 'All the Way'. The audience was buzzing with excitement and expectation.

Behind Johnny a heavy curtain emblazoned with the show title concealed the awesome weapon of death pictured on the front page of the *Manhattan Times*. In his production suite, Lloyd sweated profusely as he spoke in staccato whispers into a mike.

In homes all over America and in many parts of the world eyes watched in silence as Johnny Raine moved into his smooth patter.

There was silence among the flickering lights of the Badlands as a million faces, illuminated by burning torches, watched Johnny Raine's image dancing on the giant screens before them. Bobby Bolero stood atop his podium, staring at one screen, eyes filled with prophetic fervour, fists clenched and raised.

Lieutenant Mike Schroder relaxed for the first time in weeks. No crimes had been reported, other than the usual minor misdemeanours. He glanced over at the others in the precinct office glued to their media-web screens. Live suicide eh! Well, you wouldn't catch Mike Schroder watching that load of crap.

A couple of heavy squads of riot police had been despatched to Media City. There was an angry crowd outside, still trying to get in. Some people just wouldn't take no for an answer. They had to be dealt with. Gradually the crowd dispersed, spilling into bars and hotels to watch the show on TV.

Jordan had squeezed herself in at the side of the stage. From here she could see Johnny where he truly belonged, under a spotlight. He teased the audience, made them wait, reprised last week's show and talked about Dan Wilson. He was thinking of getting married again. What a guy!

Jordan was nervous. Something was ticking away in the corner of her mind like a time bomb. She felt a presence but couldn't

pin it down. But she was pleased with her performance as a
financial wheeler-dealer. Johnny's credits had been converted.
She had also emptied her own credit bank. The rate was not as
good as she had hoped but who cared? Currencies had been
deposited in London and Paris. She had ordered air tickets for
collection at Staten Island. Large credit conversions were normally reported but she had found support from Stan Michaels,
who clearly had sympathy for both of them. He knew exactly
what was going on. Because of his position in the financial
infrastructure he was able to exert some leverage on particularly
difficult State officials.

Unknown to any in the studio or to the citizens of Manhattan,
a squadron of anti-terrorist Sky Fury AK15 heli-jets was receiving
its final instructions at a base just north of Westchester. The
National Guard had been put on red alert and was standing by.

Commissioner Halloran sat hunched with the board of Channel Boom Boom watching from the observation room. He stared
at the red vidi-phone which was his direct line to Washington.
Although he was expecting the call, when the sounder bleeped
he jumped. Then he took a deep breath, composed himself and
picked up the receiver. No visual contact was made. Halloran
said little but slowly hunched a little more into his chair. Finally,
ashen faced, he replaced the receiver.

Johnny Raine lowered his voice.

'Now, ladies and gentlemen, for the first time on any television
screen you are going to witness something which may shock
you, upset you or even terrify you. I urge any of you of a nervous
disposition or anyone under medication of any kind to switch off
now!' He paused. 'Channel Boom Boom presents the ultimate
"All the Way". You are about to meet four volunteers who are
going to die. Here, on this stage, these four will voluntarily take
their own lives with wit and style. They are known in the
Badlands as Feeks and Farooks. Ladies and gentlemen, I want
you to welcome this week's suicide victims, Ix-Tab, Deep Cut,
Marshmallow Heart and Mister Sister.'

Johnny stepped aside as the Feeks pranced on stage from the
left and the Farooks from the right, heralded by a fanfare. The
audience sucked in its breath. The cameras dollied in for close-

ups. The audience stared at the grotesquely painted and scarred deviants as though they had just arrived from another world. Ix-Tab began to urinate, spraying the front row of the audience. Mister Sister stroked her metal phallus. An explosive shot rang out. The audience yelled. Many fainted, others were already leaving their seats.

'This is not just suicide, ladies and gentlemen. This act of death style is a symbol of the society we live in and of this great city of Manhattan,' Johnny continued. 'They have volunteered to meet their end on a very special piece of equipment manufactured, I must tell you, at considerable cost. But what's money when you're having fun? In a moment you will be looking at another symbol; one that is timeless and will touch your very hearts with fear. Now, the moment you've all been waiting for. Ladies and gentlemen, I want you to strap yourselves down, forget cyberspace make-believe, check out your life insurance and prepare yourselves for the true symbol of reality: I give you, the crucifix machine.'

The drapes opened and the crucifix machine was revealed to a burst of sporadic applause. But the applause died quickly, and was replaced by a stunned silence. Johnny moved fast. There was no time to waste. Deep Cut started to slice himself with a blade. Blood ran from his wounds as he posed defiantly. Ix-Tab was strangling himself with a noose as he stepped into the spotlight under the hanging electronic skullcap. He posed coquettishly as the cap snapped down and clamped on to his skull. Johnny and Lloyd were not going to allow the audience time to draw breath. Ix-Tab was hoisted, still holding his pose. Johnny yelled, 'Now!' and the crucifix machine blazed with light. Megawatts surged into Ix-Tab just as the blade snapped out of its housing. Ix-Tab disintegrated in an explosion of blood and bone. His head was left dangling from the cap. He glared at the audience defiantly before his head was released. It dropped into a chute at the base of the machine and rolled out of sight behind the stage.

The audience was in turmoil. People were already starting to leave. Deep Cut, Marshmallow Heart and Mister Sister stared at the remains of Ix-Tab. Deep Cut backed away. 'Not me, man, not that.' Still bleeding and trailing blood he turned and ran, scattering stagehands left and right. Marshmallow Heart looked at Mister Sister. They both shook their heads. Johnny was running on automatic. He had switched his rational and emotional self into neutral. He screamed at them to go for it. The world was watching. Here was their big chance. The two Farooks suddenly looked pathetically human and fragile, like two children caught with their fingers in the cookie jar. The pretence and the facade vanished. They backed away, shaking their heads.

The show was falling apart. The audience was in a dreadful state. Many had been violently sick. Others were clambering over seats in an attempt to escape. The crucifix machine waited for its next victim.

It did not have to wait long.

A scream rent the air. Johnny froze. Jordan ran on to the stage. She was panic-stricken. As she ran towards Johnny she slipped on Ix-Tab's visceral remains and crashed down into the front row of the audience. A man laid her on the ground gently. Then, as one, everybody in the audience turned to stare at the stage.

Click!

The sound sent a chill through Johnny's heart. He could feel the power emanating from stage right. Suddenly, death seemed perfectly all right. Dying was such a sweet relief.

The doll walked on to the stage. It had been almost torn apart by the forces of demonic power bursting to escape.

Somehow Johnny focused. He glanced down at Jordan's prone figure and at the audience, frozen into immobility like a still life. He heard sounds, screams, his name being called. But, before him, the demon was about to emerge at last.

The doll tottered, slipping on the coagulating blood. It stopped directly under the swaying cap of the suicide machine. Johnny knew it was now or never.

He screamed at the operator, 'Now, now!' Then he turned to the doll and screamed again. 'Die, you hell-bitch.'

The doll took a step forward and Johnny's mind was suddenly blanked out by an influx of real demonic power.

He was plunging into darkness and he screamed as he fell. Around him, clawing at him, reaching for him, were the endless dead. Cadaverous bodies, rotting with the filth of the grave, alive with bloated insects and worms, called to him. They wanted him. They yearned to consume him. Suddenly before him the gaping maw of death itself loomed. Its huge skeletal head and sightless eyes rose towards him. The mouth was open, the gullet was undulating and constricting, awaiting its latest morsel. Johnny hurtled into the throat of death, swallowed whole, suffocated by the stench and slime. He felt the gullet contract and tried to scream for the last time. He was sliding into the stomach of death itself, a writhing mass of partly consumed bodies blistered and putrefying. Here there were no names, no souls, no spirits, no identity. Here there was only pain and suffering.

The cap descended, snapping on to the doll's cranium. Automatically it yanked the doll high into the air. The demon screamed and the doll pulsed with purple light. 'I am almost born,' thought the demon. 'I must be born now, now, now.'

Jordan screamed. The studio audience was paralysed, fascinated.

Johnny heard Jordan's scream and awoke from his nightmare. He found himself writhing on the studio floor, drenched in his own sweat and vomit. Through half-seeing eyes he tried to focus. He saw the doll swaying before him. He saw the demon staring at him from the inanimate eyes of the mannequin. Pure evil emanated from those eyes.

There was an explosion. The doll erupted in a ball of fire and smoke. Its head was swinging rhythmically from side to side from the force of the electrical charge. The doll's eyes still stared at Johnny with utter malevolence. They glowed like red coals.

Jordan screamed Johnny's name. He began to crawl towards her through smoke, blood, charred bones and melted plastic.

A dense, deeply purple light shimmered around the floor of the stage. Fingers of smoke writhed across the stage like wraiths. Madness was setting in. The air was drowning in the screams of the audience as they tried to escape. Johnny could see her. Not far now. He rose to his feet and began to stagger towards her. She was lying, semi-conscious, near the front of the stage. She was about to be trampled by the mad rush of panic-stricken feet.

Then he was with her, protecting her, fighting off bodies furiously. Her arms were spread wide and her fingers were extended. Unseen by the stampeding audience, or the watching cameras, a streamer of dense smoke-like plasma slithered across towards her, seeking her. And it found her. The emanation touched one of her fingertips, caressing it gently.

Jordan screamed and her eyes shot open. Her face was distorted. It was the face of a she-devil. She hooked her fingers around Johnny's throat and started to strangle him. They lurched to their feet. Johnny wrestled with her desperately but she had suddenly become imbued with enormous strength. He tried to call her name, to calm her down, but she had become demented. Her eyes popped out of their sockets and her mouth sagged open in a broken, blubbering grin. Johnny struck out, catching her a glancing blow on the cheek. As suddenly as it entered her the madness dissipated. She crumpled to the ground, whimpering. Johnny picked her up tenderly, whispering her name. He held her tightly as they were buffeted by the animal charge of the audience.

Johnny turned and stared back at the doll's head, still spinning and swinging slowly to and fro. The machine had not released it. A shimmering curtain of dank and dense light still hung in a pall around the stage. It seemed to be pulsating with a force of its own.

Johnny didn't wait. Jordan was coming round, staring at him wide-eyed.

'Come on, let's get out of here,' he yelled.

The destruction of the doll was the signal. Like a switch being thrown, a power surge of demonic proportions swamped the Badlands.

They swarmed over the bridges, through the barriers of laserjets. Hundreds died. But they slithered and clambered up and along the bridge ramparts, killing and being killed. The bridges were awash with blood and burning flesh. Bobby Bolero led the charge over Queensboro. The sheer savagery of the attack took the ZeePees by surprise. They were firing at random but the weight of numbers pushed the army of deviants forward like a cork out of a bottle.

Beneath the streets of Manhattan the sewers were alive. The army of the unhuman emerged into the light, striated by neon, roaring with the joy of freedom at last. They attacked at random. They bounded, slithered and crawled after their victims. They did not care about death. They only desired blood and flesh. And they found plenty. These were the diseased rejects of the Badlands, surviving in the sewers and now infected with the call of the demon.

Media City had collapsed into chaos and turmoil. Johnny hustled and fought his way out to the side entrance. He was confronted by a black shape, dripping slime, teeth chattering like castanets. The beast attacked. Johnny dodged to the side, dragging Jordan with him, screaming and terrified. The beast found another victim. It sank its fangs into the stomach of a man who had slipped and fallen. His screams could be heard above the rest.

Adrenalin pumped through Johnny's veins and now Jordan too had moved into survival mode. She had found new strength from somewhere. The streets were heaving with creatures as they erupted from the bowels of the city, attacking anything that moved. They feared nothing. They enjoyed being killed as if death was a blessed release. Sirens blared, echoing and rebounding from buildings, adding to the cacophony of explosions, gunfire, screams of the dying and the near dead and the thunderous howl of laser missiles. In the near distance another wall of noise was approaching. With a chill in his heart Johnny realized what that noise was. Soon, the streets would be overrun.

From the border with the Bronx to the tip of Battery Park, Manhattan was turning into a war zone. The State Police were engaged in running battles up and down Manhattan. Explosions ripped open buildings as the gas mains started to blow. The air was filled with screaming and death. Killing was indiscriminate. Order had broken down. The administration was in a blind panic. Commissioner Halloran was stunned by the speed with which rampant chaos had overtaken the city.

Over the skyline came the Sky Fury heli-jets, plunging down, firing Lexus missiles at the bridges. Their orders were to contain the invasion and cut off reinforcements.

Johnny held Jordan tightly. He needed a weapon and a means of escape. Jordan seemed more alive now, as desperation took hold.

They ran around the back of the building, lashing out at anyone who got in the way. Fires had broken out and people were battling everywhere with the creatures of chaos.

In the streets around the bridges, the deviant army flooded in, destroying all in its path. But it was an easy target for the rapid-fire Lexus and the batteries of laser missiles ... Hundreds were mown down as the heli-jets swept along the streets as though they were mountain ravines.

There, at the back of the Media City car park, Johnny saw it. He almost wept with relief.

'Come on,' he yelled as he pulled Jordan in his wake. She needed no second bidding. They sprinted for the pock-marked and heavily scarred RPC. Johnny prayed his voice-print and password were still in operation.

They saw them attack as they neared the vehicle. There were four of them. Once they had been children. Now they were hideous hobgoblins without legs. They hauled themselves along the ground on powerful taloned hands. They were barking with hunger. Pieces of human flesh dangled from their mouths. They were encrusted with excreta, infected with parasites and riddled with pustulating sores. And they were trying to cut them off.

'Run for it,' Johnny yelled, letting go of Jordan's hand. They ran for the RPC.

'Boom, boom!' Johnny screamed. The door opened. Jordan was yards behind as Johnny reached the cockpit. He dived in, then reached back to catch Jordan's outstretched hand. A set of powerful teeth fastened on to his arm. He screamed in pain as the creature hung suspended by its jaws and began to chew. Johnny reached inside the RPC and scrabbled around for a weapon. He grabbed at the pulse pistol in desperation and in one movement brought the gun round and fired. The monster-child almost evaporated in a fountain of blood and diseased flesh.

Jordan fell into the RPC as Johnny blasted the other creatures just as they were about to launch themselves into an attack. Panting and sweating, Johnny started the powerful airturbos and they lurched into drive mode.

'You'll have to handle the guns,' Johnny told Jordan.

'I don't know how,' she cried.

'Just keep your eye on the viewfinder and your finger on the trigger. You'll get the hang of it.'

'Where are we going?'

For a second he appeared uncertain. In all the excitement he suddenly realized he had no idea what to do or where to go.

With an edge to her voice which had been missing for weeks, Jordan urged him to think of something.

'We've got to get to the airport. Head for the heliport at Washington Heights,' she yelled.

'That's impossible. I've got a better idea. Hang on.'

Johnny rammed his foot hard on the accelerator. The RPC shuddered and leaped forward in a scream of metal. Johnny hit another switch and an array of powerful headlights pierced the smoke-filled night. Outside, an elemental burst of lightning rent the sky quickly followed by a ten-megaton crash of thunder. Rain hammered down in a sudden torrential downpour.

The RPC slithered and skidded across streets soaked with rain and blood. It lurched over bodies lying dead or dismembered. Johnny aimed the vehicle downtown. Jordan had her eye glued to the night scope. The Lexus mini-rocket launchers spat fire as they swerved and shot their way through the streets.

More explosions rocked the city. Buildings burst into flames, hissing in the rain. Behind them, a black mass was approaching.

Johnny skidded into Lexington at full speed, careening off parked vehicles. Jordan was getting the hang of the sophisticated weaponry and she was proving to be a deadly accurate shot.

Shells burst around them, spraying the night with flame and smoke. Johnny gunned the RPC, mowing down anything in their way. The armoured vehicle was by now covered in the bloody remains of unrecognizable flesh and bone.

Madness was sweeping through the streets. Johnny glanced at Jordan as he swerved again, mounting the kerb.

'OK?' he shouted over the screaming noise of the airturbos.

'Never felt better,' she shouted back. Indeed she had regained much of her old spirit. She smiled at him from her thin and ravaged face. Johnny thought it was the most beautiful thing he had ever seen.

'Watch out!' she warned.

They hit the hideous creature full on. It was bear-like with a lolling head. Johnny slalomed the RPC to shake the once human beast from the front. They rammed an overturned electro-turbo, pulverizing the creature which screamed in pain and what appeared to be gratitude.

As they approached Wall Street, the streets were clearer. There were fewer warring factions here. Somewhere nearby they could just hear the sound of muffled voices barking instructions through an old-fashioned loud hailer. Jordan had to shout to make her voice heard.

'Is that thing, that demon, is it dead?'

'No way of knowing. You sure you're all right?'

'I feel free. I feel like shit, but I'm fine. Where are we going? How are we going to get to Staten Island?'

'I guess the ferry's out,' he said. 'Let's just say I know where I can lay my hands on a heli-jet.'

She stared at him. 'Can you fly one?'

'Not yet,' he laughed hoarsely.

The sky was erupting with the power of the electrical storm. There was more fighting going on as they headed down White-hall Street. Ahead, a police cordon blocked their path. Johnny could just make out a line of flashing lights.

He took a right, heading for the river. A shell exploded on the side of the RPC, spinning it round several times. Johnny fought for control. They skidded, then overturned. The RPC slithered on its side and span in a graceful arc of grinding metal, sparking like a firecracker. With a lurch, the buckled and smoking vehicle toppled over into the basement of a house. It lay jammed and steaming in the rain, belching smoke.

Johnny struggled with the emergency door control. It was wedged tight. Jordan clambered over and they both heaved with all their rapidly waning strength.

'It's no good,' she panted, 'it's jammed tight. We're trapped.'

Johnny thought frantically. 'The rear entrance. We might be able to get through. If the control still works.'

It was dark as night inside the cockpit. He scrabbled around trying to locate the right control. With a gasp his fingers stumbled on to the metal key that overrode the security locks. He turned the key.

There was a series of clicks as the interior locks opened.

Right, we've got to squeeze out through the connecting panel,' he told Jordan.

Ramming the pulse pistol into his belt, Johnny went first, feeling his way through, twisting his body in the narrow space behind him. He started to crawl back into the rear of the RPC. Jordan gasped painfully as she followed, feeling her way and keeping one hand on Johnny's ankle.

Panting and sweating with exertion, they slid into the upturned rear chamber of the security vehicle, climbing up towards the rear door. Rain was pounding like gunshots on the exterior of the RPC. And there were other noises. Johnny drew the pistol and held it in front of him as he cautiously pushed against the rear doors.

With a groan they moved. He pushed harder. By now, Jordan was at his side, weeping with weariness, frustration and rising fear.

The doors opened and Johnny poked his head warily outside.

All he could see at first was the rain and, in the distance, the flash of explosions and gunfire. Closer there were the sounds of sirens and the crackle of radio mikes.

The immediate area around the RPC was clear. But not far away, in the flickering light of a burning building, dark, twisted shapes were silhouetted. They were moving towards the crashed vehicle.

Jordan emerged from the cockpit and for a moment they both lay together, gulping air and smoke.

'Oh no, look!' Jordan cried. The shapes were getting closer. Now there were more of them, shimmering in the heat haze and spray. Johnny looked around him wildly.

'We're not far. We'll have to run for it.'

They pushed their way out of the RPC. It lurched and slipped further into the deep recess of the basement area.

One of the approaching shapes began to assume a more definite outline as it shuffled towards them through a pall of smoke, driven like a small tornado by the river breeze.

Jordan was begging Johnny to run, but he just stared at the figure as it appeared out of the smoke clouds.

The figure was a man of mid-height, moving stiffly on what looked like metal stilts. The man paused for a moment and then his face was etched in light and shadow by a flame issuing from his knuckles. It was a dark, intelligent, Latin face. It was a face Johnny remembered only too well. It was a face he could never forget and which he had screamed at in his nightmares.

Bobby Bolero clanked forward like a metal marionette. He was covered in filth, blood and slime. But he kept smiling and puffing his cheroot, and he was singing the song Brady had taught him:

'The big ship sails on the alley alley-o, the alley alley-o . . .

His hoarse voice crackled and howled.

The legs of steel cylinders and aerojet pumps sighed and clanged. Bolero held something in his hand. Johnny saw with terrifying clarity the whip-like flail, jangling with glinting blades and hooks.

'Johnny, come on,' screamed Jordan.

Johnny stared at Bolero as the memories came flooding back, drowning his frontal lobes with hate. He raised his pulse pistol and took aim. With ice-cold precision he targeted Bolero's chest as the grotesque parody of humanity whirled the flail hypnotically around his head. It whistled like a drunken banshee.

Johnny paused.

The flail began to uncurl like a steel snake. Something in the change of pitch shook Johnny into action. He fired. A hole the size of a manhole cover appeared in the centre of Bolero's chest. Through it, Johnny could just make out the rest of the group approaching. Bolero stood and grinned. The arm manipulating the flail fell to his side. Bolero's mouth opened and closed and bubbles of blood popped on his lips.

Then he fell.

Johnny and Jordan were up and running. Johnny fired. Several more shapes burst into flame, screaming with pain.

They ran down dark streets until they came to a building close to Battery Park. A phalanx of Zone Police, State Police and what looked like a squad of marines were receiving instructions. Johnny and Jordan flattened themselves to the wall of the building, crouching to avoid being picked out by the mobile searchlights that swept the area.

'What are we waiting for?' Jordan whispered hoarsely. 'Let's not stay in one place too long.'

Without replying, Johnny took her hand and they slipped down a passageway between two buildings. There was light enough to see by.

'You're telling me there's a heli-jet around here somewhere?' Jordan called to him incredulously.

'On the roof. Over there.'

He led the way to a discreet doorway. The house was large, with a small garden in front. Lights burned from several windows. The front door was swinging open. Slowly, they tiptoed inside. A crack of thunder reverberated along the nearby river carrying with it the echoes of screams and gunfire.

They were drenched and so cold they were shaking feverishly. Jordan clung to Johnny as they slowly climbed the stairs into the light.

Maurice Freiberg moved quickly around the apartment. His wife, Cora, was slumped nearby tipping a bottle of Jack Daniel's down her throat. As she sucked on the bottle, her shoulders shook with laughter. Maurice was as mad as hell. They'd just had a flaming row. Cora had said the whole Badlands invasion thing would be over by morning. All they had to do was stay put and lock the doors. Let the police and the army take care of it.

Maurice didn't see it that way. He had known this day was coming. Thank the stars he had taken precautions. His private two-seater heli-jet was parked up on the roof. He'd had the mini-hangar built specially to conceal it. Now they were getting out. He'd salted away currencies in a number of countries. Anyone in their right mind would be heading for Staten Island any way they could. Manhattan Airport had been built at the time of the Isolation. JFK and La Guardia had long since been overrun by rejects, cyberfreaks and renegades who wanted to live life on the edge. Well that was OK by him, they could stay there. With luck they would die there too.

Maurice was travelling light. He had packed a couple of suitcases and stood accusingly over Cora, who looked at him with a drunken stare, then burst out laughing.

'Are you coming or not?' he shouted at her impotently. 'I've packed a case. Now come on, let's get moving.'

'I'm not going anywhere with you,' she drooled. 'You wanna know why? OK I'll tell you. Cos on the first count, you're mad. On the second count, I'm crazy and on the third count, I hate your guts.'

'This is no time to argue, Cora. Just get your fucking ass up on to the roof.'

Cora stared at her husband defiantly and raised the bottle to her lips. She stopped abruptly and looked past him, her attention distracted.

'You're going nowhere, Maurice,' Johnny said as he and Jordan entered the room.

Freiberg whirled around.

'Johnny!'

Freiberg was staring at the pulse pistol in Johnny's hand. He began to cough. He became red-faced as the coughing got worse. He thrust his hand into his pocket. Johnny raised the pistol. Freiberg withdrew his pocket nebulizer. He put it to his mouth and nose and began to take deep breaths. Gradually the attack eased. Finally he was able to speak.

'What the hell are you doing here?'

'It's survival-of-the-fittest time. We're taking the heli-jet.'

'Like hell you are,' Freiberg snapped. His face had turned purple with rage and impotence. His veins stood out like cords. Cora found the situation intoxicatingly amusing. She giggled like a schoolgirl.

'Shut up!' her husband shouted at her.

Johnny put his free arm around Jordan's shoulders. 'There's

only room for two, Maurice. There's no need to show us the way. Don't try to stop us. I don't want to hurt you.'

Freiberg shook with rage and frustration. Suddenly he lunged at Johnny. A low-power pulse of light stopped him in his tracks and catapulted him backwards to the floor.

'Sorry, Maurice. You'll be pretty bruised later but at least you're alive.'

'Let's go, I'm freezing to death,' Jordan said urgently.

Freiberg was winded. Another coughing fit overcame him. Cora screamed with laughter. Backing away, Johnny led Jordan up the rear stairs and out on to the roof.

The two-seater craft was a cross between a small helicopter and a light aircraft. It was small, light and manoeuvrable. Its flexiglass cockpit gleamed in the subdued light of the camouflaged hangar. Twin electro-turbo jets powered her and she looked new and unused. 'Time for your first flying lesson,' said Jordan with a half-hearted attempt at humour. 'I'm scared. Suppose you can't fly this thing?'

'Got any better ideas?' Johnny said a little sharply. 'Sorry, come on, there's no time to waste. Get in.'

They clambered aboard and strapped themselves in. The hangar was little more than a hemispherical shell. By taxiing out on to the roof they would be clear of it. The storm had eased, leaving the air cleaner but carrying the tang of fire and death. Johnny fumbled with the controls. He found the console switch then stared blankly at the instrumentation. Jordan took a close look and pressed the ignition. The power pack began the familiar electro-turbo whine. Johnny experimented with the foot pedals and let out the airbrake.

'It's just like driving a car,' he said and laughed nervously. Then he glanced at Jordan. 'Well, here we go.'

Jordan had her eyes shut tight and her arms wrapped around herself. Johnny eased forward on the stick and the heli-jet rolled forward.

'So far so good,' he muttered to himself, conscious that he was sweating profusely. All the major controls were within fingertip reach. He touched a slider control and the blades began to rotate. Johnny applied pressure to his right-foot control and the whine increased. Suddenly they were off the ground, swaying and lurching uncontrollably. Jordan refused to open her eyes. Johnny increased the pressure and the heli-jet responded, accelerating and moving off into the night. Immediately they were hit by buffeting air currents. Johnny fought for control and gradually straightened out their erratic flight path. Within seconds they were over Manhattan rising at speed. Johnny pressed forward on the stick and they headed out over the island.

Jordan opened her eyes. Below them lay Manhattan, glittering like a jewel. The sky was aglow with shimmering light. From this distance it looked as if the whole of the island was ablaze. They could see pinpoints of light, the flashes of explosions and the thunder of the powerful shoreline laserjet defence beams. For a long moment, they stared at the scene, mesmerized by it, memories flooding through their minds.

Johnny was relaxed now. Flying the heli-jet was remarkably simple. Landing it might be a problem. But right now it was a problem he could handle. Warmth from the efficient heaters began to thaw them out. The cockpit began to stink of their stale, vaporous sweat.

Ahead of them lay the lights of Staten Island, with the airfield glowing like a coloured necklace. Jordan discovered the radio and their call sign. Within seconds, Manhattan air traffic control was trying to get them to turn back. Jordan told them they were coming in whether they landed at the airport or not. The controller's voice assumed a calmer tone when he realized he was dealing with amateurs. When he discovered it was Johnny Raine at the control his manner changed again. Suddenly he was helpful and full of concern. He would monitor them all the way in and talk them down when they were closer. For the moment he would stand by.

Jordan looked up at the stars. She still felt scarred inside, as though she had been through a massive internal operation. She was only now coming to terms with the events of the past weeks.

'It's awe-inspiring,' she said, smiling up at the heavens.

'What is?' he asked.

'The Purple Zone, angels, cosmic entities, everlasting life.'

'Do you believe it?'

'Oh, I don't know. I'd like to. I feel like I've just woken up from a long dream. I don't know if any of it happened: Frank Brady, the doll, the demon.' She shuddered. 'And all that other stuff about feeding on evil. It sounds like a movie script.'

'Take a look at yourself,' said Johnny. 'Believe me, you were almost at death's door. I count myself lucky to be alive. It happened all right.'

'What now? The demon has been destroyed, Manhattan is being torn apart. It all seems so final.'

'Who says the demon is dead?' said Johnny. He looked at her.

Jordan stared back at him, suddenly chilled. He looked somehow different in the semi-darkness of the cockpit. She started to say something but thought better of it. She shivered suddenly as though something icily cold had passed through her leaving only the barest trace of memory. Johnny's face flickered in the reflection of the instrument lights. He turned to her and smiled.

The crackle of the air traffic controller's voice interrupted her thoughts. With a start she realized they were almost there. The airport was spread out before them, glowing with electronic life.

Slowly and calmly the controller began to talk them down.

Two Years Later

The bearded man held his wife's arm carefully as they stepped down from Flight BA666. He smiled at her tenderly. She placed a hand on her swollen stomach. It was an instinctive gesture, protective of the unborn life inside her. She looked radiant with her dark hair cascading over her oval face. They were both casually but conservatively dressed, he in a yellow polo shirt and black jeans, she in a loose-fitting dress.

They joined the rest of the tourist group on the tarmac and walked the few hundred yards to their air-conditioned coach. The group was mixed, mainly Europeans with a sprinkling of eager Japanese. By the time she reached the coach Jordan was out of breath. She laughed. Johnny hunched his pack higher on to his shoulder and helped her up into the coach. Jordan smiled at the driver who smiled back and indicated he'd saved them a seat with extra leg-room at the front. Gratefully, they sat down.

The tour guide was young, about twenty-one or so. She moved smoothly into her routine, welcoming them all on board Apple Tours and sketching out the details of their trip.

Jordan looked out of the window. It was a warm day. She was used to the heat but she was six months pregnant and it was starting to give her some discomfort. Johnny stroked his beard and checked his camera equipment.

'Why have you brought me back here?' Jordan asked him.

'You're not worried, are you?' he said with concern.

'No, no,' she reassured him. 'I know you've got this assignment and everything, but it's just that the timing could have been a little better.'

'It's only a couple of days. Then we can take some time off if you're up to it. We're not going to have much time for travel when he's born.'

He patted her stomach.

'What do you mean, "he"?' she retorted with amused indignation.

'I just thought it would do us both good to get away. To come back, if you like.'

Jordan looked out of the window as the coach pulled away. 'Maybe,' she said.

Half an hour later they were boarding the tourist Seaport Line cruiser and catching the infectious feel of rising excitement. Johnny's assignment for the London-based *Sunday Times* was a lucrative one. After the runaway success of his first book, he had become a sought-after columnist. As the boat pulled away and began the crossing towards Manhattan, he could not help an involuntary shudder as he gazed again on that world-famous skyline.

They stood at the prow as they hit the swell of the East River. The crowd had gathered in a tight expectant knot. This is what they had come to see. This was one of the world's major tourist attractions. The guide's voice rose dramatically as they rounded the Statue of Liberty and took in their first view of the trans-formed city.

'At a cost of fifty billion dollars so far, Manhattan is being rebuilt. You can see a good deal of the renovation work going on. Construction workers now outnumber accountants in Manhattan.'

The crowd tittered. But it was not the dreaming towers and newly constructed feats of architectural majesty they had come to see. It was the other side of the river that held them enthralled and fuelled their imaginations.

Johnny was standing behind Jordan with his arms around her and his hands cradling her stomach. Her hands were entwined with his. Her hands tightened. She became rigid in his arms. He buried his face in her hair and rested his chin on her shoulder. The guide was in full flow.

'On your right, you can see the remains of what used to be the outer boroughs of New York. For years the area was known locally as the Badlands. Now, as you can see, it has been isolated. It is the world's only true urban wasteland. Nobody has set foot in there for two years. But if any of you would like to make the trip, just let me know.' She paused for the predictable response.

'It remains under official quarantine. They say that nothing lives there.'

She paused to allow the crowd to take in the scene.

An overgrown jungle confronted them. A sterile scene of urban desolation was topped by a sea of shrubs and trees and a skyline of foliage-encrusted buildings. The sheer stillness of the decaying city was unnerving. It had all the atmosphere of a long-dead civilization buried in antiquity, but it also had the awesome power of a battle scene. They were killing fields of stone, brick and iron. Johnny stared in blank amazement.

What used to be streets were avenues of rubble and vegetation. The broken city was steaming in the mid-morning sunlight. The bridges had been sealed, Johnny noted as they cruised on up past what used to be Brooklyn and Queens. Those names were now official history.

The guide droned on, explaining the Isolation, the eventual collapse of law and order and the inexplicable suicide fever which had spread like wildfire and led to the near destruction of one of the world's greatest cities.

The further they went up river the tenser Jordan became.

'I've got to get off,' she whispered urgently.

Johnny too was filled with strange feelings and misgivings.

'Do you hear them?' Jordan asked through gritted teeth. 'The voices?'

Johnny looked deep into the dark and brooding interior. It was corpse-like and dead but somehow still intimidating. Here and there, twisted shapes rose like deformed behemoths caught in a slumbering spell and held there until released.

'We call it the Dead City,' the guide carried on cheerily. 'It was utterly destroyed in the most horrific civil disturbance in American history. Now, nothing can live there. Or at least, that's what they say.'

Johnny was holding Jordan tightly. Both were frozen by an inexplicable feeling of trepidation and impending disaster. Something was in there. Something familiar. Something beyond evil. Something which had been waiting for them to return.

Click!

Jordan gave a small scream. Johnny whirled round. The Japanese tourist bowed as he took the camera away from his eye.

Jordan convulsed briefly, clutching her stomach.

'Honey, what is it, what's wrong?' Johnny took her in his arms. She was shaking, staring into his eyes.

'My baby,' she said, her voice barely a whisper. Johnny put his hands on to her stomach as their child kicked again violently.

Somehow it didn't feel right. It didn't feel like their child, their baby.

A trickle of saliva tinged with crimson ran down Jordan's chin. Johnny was holding her more tightly than ever. He was shaking. He fought against the thoughts entering his mind, refusing to accept their implications, as Jordan's stomach distended with the force of the next kick.

'No,' she begged, 'it can't be.'

The guide was wrapping up her presentation as they arrived at the new marina at Franklin Roosevelt Drive.

With their arms around each other for support, Johnny and Jordan shuffled slowly off the boat.